W9-AXC-499

The
WEDDING
GIFT

The
WEDDING
GIFT

MARLEN SUYAPA BODDEN

ST. MARTIN'S PRESS
NEW YORK

This is a work of fiction. All of the characters, organizations, and events portrayed in this novel are either products of the author's imagination or are used fictitiously.

THE WEDDING GIFT. Copyright © 2013 by Marlen Suyapa Bodden. All rights reserved. Printed in the United States of America. For information, address St. Martin's Press, 175 Fifth Avenue, New York, N.Y. 10010.

www.stmartins.com

Library of Congress Cataloging-in-Publication Data

Bodden, Marlen Suyapa.
    The wedding gift / Marlen Suyapa Bodden.—1st ed.
        p. cm
    ISBN 978-1-250-02638-5 (hardcover)
    ISBN 978-1-250-02612-5 (e-book)
    1. Fathers and daughters—Fiction. 2. Gifts—Fiction. 3. Slaves—Fiction.
    4. Slavery—Fiction. 5. Friendships—Fiction. 6. Sisters—Fiction. I. Title.
    PS3602.O32563W43 2013
    813'.6—dc23   2013013660

St. Martin's Press books may be purchased for educational, business, or promotional use. For information on bulk purchases, please contact Macmillan Corporate and Premium Sales Department at 1-800-221-7945, extension 5442, or write specialmarkets@macmillan.com.

First Edition: September 2013

10 9 8 7 6 5 4 3 2 1

Dedicated in loving memory of my parents,
MARIA BORJAS BODDEN,
who showed me the meaning of strength, and

HALL JAMES BODDEN,
who taught me how to tell a story

ACKNOWLEDGMENTS

I give special thanks to my husband, Timothy Rogers, my love and my rock. Thanks to my extended family and friends for their steadfast support and encouragement throughout the years: the Boddens, Rogers, and Lambes; Lynne Burgess, my first reader, for her eagle eye and keen insight; Mildred Berendsen, Marilyn Lambe, Sensimone Williams, Lucy Abbott, Virginia Dean, Frances Peake, Lisa Metcalf, Bettina Wilkerson, Cera Robbins, Evalyn Lee, Joshua Goldfein, Jane Bock, Amanda Moretti, and Meredith Sue Willis, my writing professor.

I also thank my agent, Victoria Sanders; Monique Patterson, my editor, for her brilliant questions and comments; Bruce Rich, for steering me in the right direction; and Eric Rayman.

Let the words of my mouth, and the meditation of my heart, be acceptable in thy sight, O Lord.

—PSALM 19:14

The
WEDDING
GIFT

SARAH CAMPBELL

I t is daytime, but the path is dark. The stench of decomposing vegetation mingles with the scent of ripe muscadine grapes. Ruby-throated hummingbirds chirr. The trunks of bald cypresses and tupelos are swollen with water, their branches laden with pitch-green moss. A cottonmouth slides by me, and then bloodhounds—I do not know how many—surround me, and my sight dims until all I can see are silver outlines of the dogs. As I twirl amid the animals, I hear their labored panting and images flood my brain of conical teeth tearing off my face. Sweat soaks through my lady's maid garment. I yell, "Help, please, somebody help me." No one answers; I wonder when the hounds are going to rip my flesh into shreds and, in an attempt to quiet my heart, I think about my life at the plantation, regretting that I came to the edge of this feral lair.

I arrived here after walking beyond the slave quarters, and I am far from Allen Hall, the residence of my master and his family, where my mother, Emmeline; my sister, Belle; and I toil. It is 1852, and I am sixteen. We belong to Cornelius Allen, Esquire, master of a 7,800-acre plantation called Allen Estates in Benton County,

Alabama, who owns more than four hundred field hands and more than two hundred other slaves who labor in the stables, the smokehouse, and the dairy as carpenters, seamstresses, gardeners, cobblers, and in other trades. Twenty-five of us work in Allen Hall. My mother manages the kitchen and a house that has a ballroom, a library, guest quarters, and family apartments. The fields where the slaves labor are continuous furrows of cotton plants with space for a field hand between each furrow, and the roads are wide enough for carts between every fifty furrows. Overseers holding rifles sit in their towers; others are on horseback with guns and whips at their sides, and there is a jail and an infirmary for the slaves in this area.

Now the palms of my hands are dry and I take slower breaths, and my vision returns. One hound is about two yards in front of me, and three dogs are farther away, at the bog's edge. Each beast is black-and-tan, with pendant ears, and weighs about one hundred fifty pounds. I step toward the swamp and the dogs snarl. I move back and they are quiet. Then I slowly back away from the swamp's edge. The dogs do not move. When I am twenty yards away, I turn. I run and I run, even though I do not hear the hounds chasing me. I run until my chest and feet hurt, and then I fall to the ground and rest.

My mother told me never to go to the swamp, but she did not say that the warning was because bloodhounds are stationed there to prevent us from escaping. In two years, I will learn, among other lessons, that slave catchers also use the dogs to catch slaves when they flee.

ONE

SARAH CAMPBELL

T his chronicle commences with the monarchs of my heart: my mother, the woman who gave me light, and my sister, to whom I clung in dire times. Both were beautiful, with delicate features and dark skin. I, however, am big-boned and, as the Alabama newspapers described me, "yellowish." Except for her yellow hair and blue eyes, I look more like my other sister, to whom I was given when she married, Clarissa Allen, the daughter of the master of the plantation and his wife, Theodora. Like Clarissa, and the man who fathered us, I am tall, have dimples, a pointy nose, and meager lips. I do not know precisely how old I was when I realized that I was a slave, but I think that I was six, the year I began helping with cooking, cleaning, and all that we had to do in the Allen household.

One morning, when we were still sleeping, someone knocked on the door of our cabin. My mother rose and wrapped herself in a shawl, telling us to do the same and to sit at the table. When she opened the door, two men were standing outside, holding lanterns and guns. I trembled, and Belle firmly held my hand.

"Why they here, Mama?"

"Shush, baby. Don't say nothing."

"Your key," one man said.

"Yes, sir," my mother said.

My eyes were sensitive to the light from their lanterns. I heard them walk everywhere, near the beds, cabinets, and in the kitchen area. One of the men had a persistent cough. Their rancid smell permeated the cabin. The lock clicked and the lid creaked when they opened the chest where my mother kept some of the money that she earned from trading baked goods, quilts, and dried cooking herbs in town.

When they were gone, my mother sat at the table and put her arm around me. She was shaking.

"Why those men come here, Mama?"

"Mr. Allen tell them to."

"But why, Mama, why?"

"Stop asking questions, Sarah. He tell them to and nobody got to tell us why or nothing else."

One afternoon, I filled two pails at the well behind the kitchen. Two boys, about my age, were there playing with clay marbles, when an overseer approached.

"What you little niggers doing?"

They did not answer him.

"You hear me, you black bastards?"

The boys continued to ignore him.

"You fucking niggers say something when I talk to you."

He used his whip to strike one boy in the arm and the other on the leg and then kicked each one, knocking him to the ground, and the boys and I screamed. I dropped my buckets, spilling water. I heard people running and my mother's voice rising above the clamor saying that she was coming to me.

She told someone to take the boys to our cabin. She kissed me and carried me home, but when she tried to put me on our bed, I grasped the sleeve of her dress.

"Sarah, baby, you going to be all right. Stay here. Let me go look after the children."

The boys were crying.

"Your mama's going to be here soon. Now let me see how bad you is hurt," she said to them. "I'm going to clean and put something on your cuts so they can heal. It's going to sting a bit, but you all is big boys and I know you going to be strong."

When the boys' mother arrived, I recognized her voice. She was one of the washerwomen for Allen Hall.

"Miss Emmeline, thank you for looking after my boys. Thank God you was there and that man didn't do no worse to them."

"You're welcome, but that's what we got to do. We got to look after each other's children, and I know you do the same for my girls. You let me know if they ain't better soon."

The washerwoman took her boys home. I felt calmer by that time, but my sight was blurred. My mother said that I should stay in bed and rest.

"Sarah, I got to get back to the kitchen so I can finish making supper. Let me wash you up first. All right, baby?"

"No, Mama. Don't leave me here by myself. What if that man is out there? And why he hit those boys?"

"Mr. Allen ain't going to like it when he hear what he did. But Sarah, listen, you always got to do what the overseers tell you. You got to obey them the same way we obey Mr. and Mrs. Allen. You understand me?"

"Yes, ma'am. But I'm scared of that man. What if he come back?"

"I'm going to be looking out for you, baby, and ain't letting you go no place by yourself until you is older. Baby, you know I can see our cabin from the kitchen, and I'll watch to make sure nobody come inside. And Belle and me going to come here to see you every so often."

That year, I began listening to the pastor who had a service in the kitchen for the Hall slaves and their families on Sunday mornings.

We did not attend church with the Allens in town because we had to prepare dinner. The field hands and tradespeople had their own house of worship on the plantation. After his sermon, the preacher spoke to us about the slave laws and our activities off the plantation.

One afternoon in the wintertime, after the Allens and their guests had their dinner, my mother took Belle and me into town to purchase goods for the Hall. An overseer met us at the gate before we left and gave the wagon driver a traveling pass.

As I had noticed when we were walking in town on prior occasions, men stopped to stare at my mother. She did not pause and looked straight ahead. That day, we went to different shops to retrieve items that the merchants had ordered from abroad for the Allens and dried cooking herbs from the Indies for my mother. At six o'clock, the driver met us at the last shop to help us with the packages.

"Johnny, I got something else to do. Please wait for us here."

Johnny gave my mother a lantern, and as we were walking toward a side road, I heard people yelling and saw them running to the square in the center of town. My mother held my hand and steered us back to the wagon. I heard someone scream, and she told me to move faster.

"Mister, please, let us go. We wasn't doing nothing wrong. We was just talking. Please don't whip us," one man said.

"Shut your mouths and take your turns on the post. You keep arguing, and you going to get more lashes."

"Please, mister, don't. I won't do it again. We was just talking."

"I hear one more thing from any of you, and you're each getting the full thirty lashes."

"Mama . . ."

"Sarah, stop. Not one word. I'll tell you what that's about later. Now we just got to get out of here."

We were silent all the way to Allen Estates. When we arrived at our cabin, my mother told me that the people I saw about to be whipped in town were being punished because they had done something that the preacher warned us about on Sundays.

"Sarah, some people in town was talking in a group. I'm only telling you this so you know not to do the same thing when you're older. If the patrollers see a group of slaves without a overseer to watch them, the patrollers can whip every one of them."

Around this time, I observed other aspects of my life and the people at Allen Hall that troubled my young head. Clarissa, the daughter of Mr. and Mrs. Allen, had a sixth year birthday celebration that began on a Thursday and ended Sunday night. There were about thirty guests, including her paternal family from Montgomery and Macon counties and neighboring planters and their families. My mother cooked all the meals and made Clarissa's cake.

When we were alone, I asked my mother about my birthday.

"You remember when I made that cake for you a little while back, and we and the others had it after supper in the kitchen, don't you?"

"But you didn't sing to me, and you didn't say it was my birthday."

"I know, baby, but it was. Mr. Allen said he wrote it down in his book where he write all the babies' birthdays."

"When is my birthday?"

"Mr. Allen said it's June 25. But you keep that just between us, all right, baby? And don't tell the other children. Not everybody know their birthdays. I know mines and Belle's because Mr. Allen's father wrote them down and Mr. Allen told me."

When the Allen relatives visited the plantation, I was not Clarissa's playmate, as I was when no one else was around, but her maid; and when she spoke to me, it was to give me orders. During one of these visits, while we were in our cabin one night and I was sitting on my mother's lap, I asked her about her family, who they were and where they might be.

"Baby, it ain't something I like to talk about, no, but I know everybody want to know where they come from. Only God know where all my kin is, if they is living or is not. They get sold, Mommy tell me, and she say it's because our people was the kind that was always making trouble for the overseers and trying to run away, and

Master Allen's father sell them off, a long time ago. Mommy tell me right before she die that it ain't no use trying to make things right on this earth. She was right, it really ain't no use. Sarah, that's why I'm always telling you that you got to obey Master and Mrs. Allen and all the overseers. If anybody make trouble and don't work or try to run, they get sold off and don't nobody got to tell us where they go and we sure ain't never going to see them again. Girl, you know I ain't got a single sister, brother, cousin, aunt, or uncle that I know where they is, nobody, nobody but you and Belle. That's all I got left on earth."

She held me closer. Belle was silent, sitting across from us at the table. I asked Mama if she knew what happened to her parents and brothers and sisters.

"Don't know about my pa, where he at, because he got sold. I remember when I was little, at night in our cabin, and Mommy and Pa think me and my brothers and sisters was sleeping, many times Mommy and Pa used to talk real soft, and Pa told Mommy he was going to run. Mommy cry and say no, because she was scared, but Pa say he was going to do it and find a way to get all of us out, he say there was people that can help him run and can help get the rest of the family out, too. Mommy, oh, my poor mother, we bury her after the overseer beat her so bad after she step in to try to keep him from beating Pa when they catch him after he ran. We bury Mommy at the graves by the fields."

My mother poured us water from the pitcher and cut us each a slice of cake. We were silent as we ate, and when we finished the cake my mother resumed telling us about our family.

"After Mommy die, Master Allen's father sold my three sisters and two brothers, who know where to, and left me to live with one of the granny women who take care of the little children of the mothers that work in the Hall. I was only about ten years old then and old Master Allen told the cook to teach me how to cook. The granny woman, Miss Thomasina, she always took good care of me, even after I was grown, but she died a few months after Belle was born."

She kissed me on the top of my head before she continued.

"If you want, on Sunday, I'll take the two of you to the graves where they bury us. I ain't been there in many years, it's hard because the last time I went was when I was pregnant with Belle and all I did was cry the rest of the day."

Later that week, my mother, assuming that the wooden cross on my grandmother's grave had disintegrated over the years, asked a carpenter to make her a cross, and she borrowed a large shovel from a gardener. That next Sunday, after the preacher read us the Bible and we made dinner, Mama, carrying the cross, took Belle, who carried the shovel, and me to the area where, I learned, the Allen slaves were buried. This was my first time at the graves for the slaves, but I was familiar with the cemetery where some of the Allens were buried, in an area enclosed with wrought-iron fences, because we passed it on our way to the fields. Their graves were marked with ornate crosses carved from stone. I was eager to know about the graves where the slaves were buried, but my curiosity was tempered by Mama's sadness. She was holding my hand tightly, and as we approached the graves, she released my hand to remove a handkerchief from her apron pocket and wipe tears from her face. I was comforted that Belle was with us because she joined me in consoling our mother, Belle by putting her arm around Mama's shoulder and I by kissing Mama's hand.

The slaves' burial ground was not a cemetery such as those one sees nowadays; it was simply open, rough land where nothing but weeds grew. We could only tell where the graves were located by the wooden crosses atop mounds of soil. We were the only ones there that day, and we dug in different places trying to find my grandmother's coffin, which, my mother said, had a carved rose, my grandmother's favorite flower. We never found a coffin with a rose. Belle and I did not cry until we found a clump of hair, which we reburied, because my mother said if that was all that remained of a person, even if we did not know whose hair it was, the Lord would want us to honor it as if it were the person's body. We said a prayer and thanked the Lord for our lives after we placed the wooden cross on top of the soil over where we buried that clump of hair.

My mother held Belle and me as we returned to Allen Hall. The sadness I felt after I learned how Mr. Allen's father treated my grandparents and our other kin in life and death made me fearful whenever our mother left Belle and me in our cabin at night. It also made me believe, for the first time, that if I asked my mother, she would agree we should leave the Allen plantation.

That year, when I was about six years old, I watched Mrs. Allen and Clarissa when they were together. When Clarissa sat on her mother's lap or embraced her, I was envious because my mother worked the entire day and most nights she was away from our cabin. I missed her when she was not with us and could not sleep until she returned, always before dawn. The mornings after she left, when her eyes met mine, she seemed ashamed, and that made me miserable.

Once, when we were having our breakfast, she seemed preoccupied. I tickled her under her chin, which normally made her laugh. This time, however, she barely smiled. I asked her why she was so sad.

"I'm just tired, is all, baby. Just tired."

I asked her why we could not go where she would not have to work so hard, and she spoke to me in a fierce voice.

"Don't you ever, ever talk about that again, and you listen to me good. Just talking like that can get us sold. You know what it mean to be sold? It mean they send us to different places, and we ain't never going to see each other again. Maybe you think just because Mrs. Allen let you play with Miss Clarissa all the time that you're just like her, but you ain't nothing like Miss Clarissa. She can say what she want. You got to watch every thing you say. And don't you forget, we is all we got."

I wanted my mother to stop going away; I was afraid that she would not come back. One night, I held on to her.

"Don't go, Mama, don't go."

She smoothed my hair.

"Say you won't go, Mama. Say you won't go."

"Sarah, I got to, baby."

I do not remember how many weeks elapsed before she finally tired of my attempts to prevent her from leaving.

"Belle's right here with you. Come on, Sarah, stop it."

She handed me over to Belle, who folded me in her long arms. I gave my mother a foul look. "I hate you, I hate you. Go, and I don't care if you never come back."

She sat on the bed and cried. I buried my face in the pillow. After some time, I heard her walk across the cabin floor and close the door behind her.

The battle between us continued, but I learned to wound her with silent reproach. One evening, after our prayers, I asked her why she had to leave us. She spoke in a gentle voice.

"Sarah, you too young for me to say what I'm about to tell you, but you need to hear it. You and Belle is smart girls. I been blessed that way. I was hoping to have this talk with you when you was grown. But in this life, we got to be older than our real years.

"I'm going to tell you something that you can't repeat to nobody, not even Miss Clarissa. You're going to have to promise me before I tell you."

"I promise. I'll be a big girl and I won't tell."

"Sarah, I go to . . . I go to . . . Mr. Allen. That's where I go at night."

"Why?"

"Because he say I got to."

"Why do you have to?"

"I already told you. We got to do everything him and Mrs. Allen, the overseers, and even Miss Clarissa say."

"Why?"

"We . . . we belong to Mr. and Mrs. Allen."

"What do you mean?"

"You know how when the preacher read us the Bible he told us stories about what happened to the Israelites, how they was in bondage and they had to do everything Pharaoh say? How when they was too tired to work, they got whipped? You remember the story about how Moses prayed to God to set the people of Israel free? And at first, Pharaoh won't let the Israelites go but then, after God put him through many trials, he had to or God was going to keep making bad things happen to him and his family and the Egyptians?"

"But why were they in bond— bondage?"

"Because most of the people ain't want to worship God. The people of Israel was in slavery for four hundred thirty years, but God told them that, if they believe in him, they was going to be free when they died. We got to believe the same thing, because if we don't, we ain't going to get through this life on earth. Whatever happen to us, Sarah, if we is ever separated, we're going to see each other again when we get to heaven. You see what I'm telling you?"

"Yes, Mama, everything, but why Mr. Allen want you to be with him?"

"Girl . . . humph. Baby, you really is too young to know that. But we're going to have that talk. We'll have that talk when you're older."

She caressed my cheek for a bit before she went to our owner. I did not tell my mother the entire truth. I did not understand most of what she told me or how we could belong to Mr. and Mrs. Allen. I did comprehend what she said about having to believe that God would reunite us after we died, and that belief helped to calm my fear every time she left us to see our master.

As I was a child, I remained resentful and provoked quarrel after quarrel. One late night, she sat, took off her shoes, and rubbed her feet. She did not change into her nightdress.

"Why you have to go to him? Stay with us, Mama."

"Sarah, stop it. I got to do everything they tell me."

I got out of bed and stamped my foot and yelled. "Why can't we go someplace else?"

She slapped me. I wiped the tears from my eyes.

"How many times do I have to tell you? Are you deaf? Maybe you ain't as smart as I think you is. I'm going to tell you one last time. If I ever hear you say that again, or if I ever hear that you say that to somebody else, I'm going to take a switch to you and beat you so bad you is every color but yellow. You hear me? Do you hear me?"

"Yes, Mama. I won't ever say that again."

"Y'all go to sleep." She pointed at me. "Get back in bed. And Sarah, you ain't putting me through this mess again."

"Yes, ma'am, I mean . . . no, ma'am."

Belle later told me why it frightened Mama when I spoke about running away. "Sarah, you need to know what Mama said happen to people who try to run. They hunt and bring them back. Then they beat them. Them that run away more than one time, they get a foot or toes cut off. The beatings always happen in front of all the slaves, even small children. They gather the slaves around so they all see. They strip the person who ran and put them in the stock with their hands screwed down and their feet tied together. Some they just sell to nigger traders. It better for us here than someplace else because we with each other and we don't work no fields."

Belle was the daughter of a blacksmith who was born in Africa and was sold when she was about a year old. When I think about Belle today, I try to remember her only when she was happy, because otherwise I am overtaken by a pain that makes me feel weak and disinterested in my daily, monotonous life. That Belle would have suffered as she did still leads me to question our Lord, and I do so because Belle was a good person who was mindful of others, especially those whose kin had been sold, as her father was, never to be seen again.

Some of my earliest memories of Belle were of how she cared for me when our mother was gone at night, and how she taught me and the little girls who lived near us and whose parents also worked at Allen Hall how to sew, knit, embroider, jump rope, and plait each other's hair. Belle would apply a poultice to the bruised skin of a child who had fallen. If Belle saw an elder who was having difficulty walking, she lent her arm to lean on. If the kin of a neighbor or friend passed away, Belle helped Mama prepare meals for the family while they were grieving.

Belle did so much for me, and for that reason I am grateful to her. When I could not sleep at night because Mama was not there, Belle would stay awake with me until Mama returned or until I could not keep my eyes open, telling me stories, some of which Mama learned from Belle's father. When I cried because I missed Mama or I was afraid that the overseers would come to our cabin with their guns and search our belongings, Belle would sit me on her lap and embrace me. When I was older, it was Belle, not my mother, who would assist me when I had a question of great consequence. As many sisters do, I suppose, Belle and I told each other about incidents in our lives that we never told our mother, not because we were afraid of what she would say, but to protect her from additional pain or suffering.

Once when our mother was away at night, Belle told me how her father and other children from his village were taken as slaves from distant lands across the ocean. Belle did not remember her father, whom she called Papa, but she frequently repeated what our mother told her about him.

"When he was a boy, Papa live in a village by a great river called the Senegal, where many birds, of all sizes and colors, fly through every year. In the dry season, the little boys always finish their chores fast so they can play by the river.

"One afternoon, the men is fishing on the other side of the village. The ladies and girls is at the market, trading. The old people and the babies is in their huts because it's too hot for them to be outside. About fifteen boys is playing by the river when they see strange men in a big boat. The men wave at the boys and sail right up to them.

"One of the men ask the boys if they want to go in the boat. A boy say no, we're too little to go fishing. The man laugh. 'We ain't fishing. We just want to show you what it be like in the ocean. Come with us. The ocean is bigger than your little river.' Well, that is the wrong thing to say to little boys because they're proud of their river, even though they're also very scared.

"The men get out the boat. A boy yell to the others and they run. Just then, some of the old people come out their huts and scream that strangers is in the village. By the time the old people reach the riverbank, the strangers have some of the boys and is chasing after others. They have guns that nobody in the village ever seen before. The old people try to stop the strangers from taking their boys, but a man point the gun and shoot. When one old man fall down with blood all over him, the village folk all stop to stare, and the strangers grab most the boys and put them in chains.

"They take the boys to the boat and start sailing away. The villagers is saying, 'Stop, stop, please, don't take our little boys.' But it ain't too long after they're sailing that Papa can't hear the people no more.

"That night, because a full moon is shining, the black ocean is made of glass. It's so cold that the boys sit close to each other to keep warm. Every now and then, they see a big fish jump up, fly through the air, and go back in the water.

"The stars is so big and bright that you think you can take one down. Papa tell one of the boys who can't stop crying to look up. He tell him they're the same stars they got back home so they can't be too far from the village.

"The next morning, they get to a island where the houses is all in pink, peach, yellow, or blue. The men take the boys off the boat. There's people walking on the sand. A boy say to them, 'Don't you see what they is doing to us? Help us.' But the people just keep looking ahead.

"Then, for the first time in their life, the boys see a man with pink skin on his face and hands. They stare at him. The men who took them pull on the chains. 'Keep moving, keep moving, you country boys,' they say.

"They get to a pink house and put them in a room that's crowded with other boys. The room stink because they don't let them wash and they only let them use the outhouse but one time a day. One thing they ain't expecting, the men who took them give them a lot of food and water. The pink house have a hole where they put you if you try to run. You have to stay in there for two days with nothing to eat or drink.

"When they been there about three weeks, they take a bunch of boys out the room. Then they take more. None of them boys come back. They take a group with Papa in it to another part of the house. Papa smell something nasty.

"When they get to another room, they tell the boys to wait outside a close door. The stink is worse. The boys outside don't hear nothing. They keep taking the boys in one at a time and none of them ever come out.

"They take Papa in the room and close the door and tell him to take his shirt off. One man is kneeling in front of a fireplace with his back to everybody. Two men put Papa on a table, face up, one man on each side of him, holding him down. One man cover Papa's mouth. Even though it's hot, Papa is shaking, like it's cold. The man who was kneeling in front of the fire get up and turn around. He's holding a steaming iron like the field hands use on sheep and cows.

"Papa try to get the men off him, but they don't let him go and they keep his mouth covered. The man holding the iron press it into his chest and Papa faint. When he come out of it, he forget where he is and look for his mama. But just the men is there. Papa look down at his chest and it look like meat that just start to cook.

"They get him up and walk him through a different door to another room where they have all the boys. All of the boys is staring at the wall looking at something that ain't there. When all the boys is branded, they take them back to the room where they put them when they first get to the island. There, the men look at the boys from time to time to see if their wounds is healing.

"After about a month since they get there, they take everybody back to the water and put them on a bigger boat than the one they bring them in. When the boat is sailing, Papa look back and stare at the island until there is no more spots of pink . . . peach . . . yellow . . . or blue."

TWO

SARAH CAMPBELL

My life, from birth, was tied to Clarissa's. I was born three months before her, and my mother was her wet nurse. We were playmates from a year old, my mother said. When I began working, at about six years old, I was allowed respite from my labor to spend time with Clarissa. There was a vegetable garden in the rear of the kitchen where we went sometimes, drawn by its pungent smells. Laughing and holding hands, we would throw ourselves facedown on a patch of herbs and breathe in the earthy smell.

One task that I liked was polishing furniture and cleaning the library. As I dusted books, I imagined that they contained paintings similar to those on the walls. I dared not open them, but I caressed their leather and linen covers. I once asked my mother what was in books. My mother put a trembling finger to her lips to signal to me to be quiet and then walked to the door of the library, which she closed.

"What's in books you don't need to know nothing about. If they catch you looking in one, they is going to punish you."

"Who is going to punish me, Mama?"

"Why you ask so many questions, girl? Mr. and Mrs. Allen, that's who going to punish you. Sarah, it's against the law to learn to read."

"What's the law?"

"A law say what you can or can't do, like looking in books. You can be whipped by a overseer, or worse, for doing that."

"But why can Mr. and Mrs. Allen read books?"

"Sarah, it's only a law for us not to read."

"Why?"

"Sarah, you ask too many questions. Stop . . . right . . . now, let's just finish cleaning in here."

"Is it against the law for Miss Clarissa to read?"

"Sarah . . . it ain't no law about Miss Clarissa reading. Enough. You just finish dusting the low shelves. "

Clarissa and I played in the nursery, where there were numerous books, all with colorful covers; small tables and chairs; a writing board; a map on the wall; and a globe. When we were there, Mrs. Allen or my mother periodically came to see us. One afternoon, when Clarissa and I were alone, I pointed at a book and asked her if it was a toy.

"No, that's a book. You know, for reading."

"What's reading?"

"Well, there are words and you . . . I don't know, but my papa, mama, and my brothers read, and I'll learn how when Mama gives me lessons. She says every lady must know how to read and write and learn her numbers."

Clarissa lost interest in the topic, and we dressed her dolls. Another day, I asked her to open a book.

"I like this one," she said. "Mama reads it to me a lot. I think it's called something like *Little Goody Two Shoes.*"

We looked at the pictures.

"What's it about?"

"Uuumm. Let's see, there's a little orphan girl who was very poor. She only had one shoe until a nice gentleman gave her two.

Then she was a nice person and taught little children. In the end, she was happy because she married a rich man."

I wished that I could read what was written beneath the pictures.

"Miss Clarissa, can you please show me more books?"

She selected one from a shelf. "All these are called nursery rhymes," she said.

"What's a rhyme?"

"It's when words sound the same. I can't really explain it."

"Miss Clarissa, I wish that you could read the rhymes to me. Do they sound pretty, like somebody singing a song?"

One day, Mrs. Allen stayed in the nursery and told stories from *Aesop's Fables* and read a book about strange animals, one of which was called a quagga and looked like a horse with black and white stripes. After that, whenever Mrs. Allen came to see us, Clarissa asked her to read. It made me so gleeful to hear the tales that I sometimes clapped in appreciation, which made Mrs. Allen smile. Once, when my mother went there, she did not move for several minutes when she saw Mrs. Allen reading to us. The expression on her face was a mixture of shock and fear; eventually, she asked Mrs. Allen if there was anything she could do for her or Clarissa.

"No, Emmeline, I will be here with the girls, you may return to preparing supper."

Clarissa and I were outside the kitchen jumping rope when two girls, daughters of Hall maids, asked if they could play with us. We took turns jumping and holding the rope. When we were tired, Belle took Clarissa back to Allen Hall, and I went to help my mother in the kitchen. I was washing string beans when she asked me to go to her vegetable garden and pull more onions. Two boys who were walking by teased me. "Sarah is a yellow belly. Sarah is a yellow belly."

That night, I told my mother what the boys said. "What did they mean by saying that, Mama?"

"It's just because you is lighter-skinned, baby. That's all. They didn't mean nothing by it, they was just being boys."

"But, Mama, why is my skin a different color than yours and Belle's?"

"It just is, Sarah. Don't you see, nobody's the same skin color like everybody else?"

"Miss Clarissa is the same color as Mr. and Mrs. Allen."

"That's just how God made them, Sarah. They get to look like each other, but we all look different."

From when I was about six to eight years old, my time was mainly spent working with my mother and Belle at Allen Hall and in the kitchen, which was a separate building from the Hall. Those years, I continued to play with Clarissa in the nursery and Mrs. Allen often read aloud to us. When Clarissa turned eight, Mrs. Allen began teaching Clarissa lessons in arithmetics, reading, writing, history, geography, and painting watercolors, and I was not allowed to be in the nursery when Clarissa was having her lessons.

Around the same time that Clarissa began her lessons, Mama showed me her herbs and flowers and taught me their names. She pointed out the ones that could be poisonous and showed me where in our cabin she stored the dried herbs.

"Sarah, I'm going to teach you, like I did Belle, how to take care of yourself when you get sick. If it's something serious, Mrs. Allen can call for a doctor from town for us, but by the time they go get somebody, it can be too late. And sometimes these doctors don't really know what they're doing, or maybe they just don't care when it come to us. Now, listen. What I'm going to teach you is just between us, you understand? Don't ever talk to nobody about this."

"Why, Mama?"

"Because we're not supposed to know about some of these herbs because some of them is . . . poison."

She pulled down six containers and told me the name of each herb and to smell each one. Then she told me to close my eyes, and I had to identify each herb by smell alone. When I had learned the herbs, she taught me how to prepare infusions.

"Bloodroot we use to clear out our chests when we catch colds in the wintertime. But bloodroot can be poison. The reason why it took you so long to learn it was because it don't smell like nothing. Now, it's strong so you just use a little bit at a time. That way, the person don't taste it. One thing you can do is mix it in a drink.

"Thorn apple is the flower you said was pretty. Some people call it devil's apple. It's poison, too, but good for pain and sickness of the chest, like when a person can't breathe right."

That day, Mama showed me how to prepare those six herbs, but her lessons continued for years, until she was confident that I could prepare twelve herbs without her assistance.

I enjoyed everything Mama taught me, but was envious of Clarissa's studies; I cared much more about her lessons than I did about her pretty frocks and ribbons. As I worked in the kitchen, I could not stop thinking about finding a way to join her in the classroom; yet it was Clarissa herself, whose parents indulged her every desire because she was their only girl, who provided an opportunity. One day, when I was in her rooms, Clarissa told me that her mother had praised her because of how quickly she was learning, but she said that she missed playing with me. Knowing that I was being mischievous, I decided to make use of her loneliness, because she was the only girl in her family and the only child at home, as her two older brothers were away studying at academies.

"Maybe I can be with you in your lessons, like when we played and Mrs. Allen read to us," I said.

She laughed. "You can't, that was different, because that was just playing and my mother said we can play together, but when we're older and I'm a married lady I'll need to know how to read and write and do my numbers. My mother said that all young ladies must have lessons, but she didn't say maids need to have them."

About a month later, she told me that she was bored. "Don't you want to play with my dolls?"

"My mama says that I have to do whatever you say, Miss Clarissa."

Then we played with her dolls and her new dollhouse, but I only pretended to be interested, and she noticed.

"Don't you like playing with me anymore?"

I shrugged. "Like my mama said, I have to do whatever you tell me to do, Miss Clarissa."

Clarissa slapped me, and I cried. She pointed her finger at me, close to my face.

"You're just jealous because I didn't ask my mother to let you sit with me when I have my lessons. I told you. You can't have lessons because you're my maid. Now go away. I don't want to look at your dirty, stupid face."

I was hurt, but I did not tell anyone, not even Belle, that Clarissa had hit me because I was firm in my plan to sit in her lessons and I was confident that it was possible to do so because Mrs. Allen previously allowed me to play in the nursery and even permitted me to stay there when she read aloud to Clarissa. My scheme was certain to come to fruition because I knew that not only was Clarissa lonely for a playmate, but also that she would summon me to play at every waking moment. It was Clarissa's weakness for silly pleasures, without thinking or caring about the repercussions of her conduct or how her actions affected other people, and her parents' indulgence of her selfishness, that would result in catastrophic events when we were older.

One day, as I was polishing furniture in her rooms, she was playing with her dolls and her dog, King.

"Sarah, if you play with me like before, I'll ask Mama if you can be in the nursery while I have my lessons."

I grinned.

We played one of our favorite games, chasing each other hopping on one foot. We played other games, some of which we had begun playing when we were two or three years old. Clarissa kept her promise and insisted that her mother allow me to sit in the nursery while she taught her.

King would sit next to us for a few minutes but soon lost interest in his role as a student and wandered away to lick and scratch. I sat still, listening to every word. When Mrs. Allen called Clarissa to write on the board, I observed how she wrote and was attentive to Mrs. Allen's corrections. Mrs. Allen said that I could return whenever I wanted to and that she would speak to my mother about excusing me from work. Many months after I began sitting in on Clarissa's lessons, Mrs. Allen asked her to spell the word "temperature."

"T-e-m-p-e-r-a-t-u-r-e," I said.

Clarissa was quiet. Mrs. Allen said nothing at first but quickly closed the door and handed me a primer. She spoke to me in a gentle voice.

"Can you spell, Sarah?"

"Yes, yes, ma'am."

"Can you read?"

"Yes, ma'am."

"Read the first sentence," she told me.

I read it out loud.

"Here is the chalk. Write the sentence."

I wrote it, but not so well. Mrs. Allen's face became flushed. She whispered, "Girls, it is very, very important that you do not tell anyone—including Mr. Allen, Emmeline, Belle, nobody—that Sarah has learned to read and write. If you do, you will never again be permitted to play together or to have lessons together. Do you understand?"

"Yes, ma'am," we answered in unison.

Mrs. Allen stared at me, but I was not frightened because she was not angry. I could not believe that I had learned to read and write and she did not say she would stop teaching me.

The next day, when I joined Clarissa for her lessons, Mrs. Allen locked the door.

"Girls, I will teach Sarah, but you will both have to promise me again that you will not tell anyone that she has learned to read and write. Sarah, you cannot even tell Emmeline or your sister. If you tell anyone else, terrible things will happen to Sarah, her mother, and sister. They will have to leave Allen Estates. Clarissa, you will never again see Sarah. Do you both understand?"

"Yes, ma'am," I said.

"Yes, Mama. We understand. We won't tell anyone. We promise," Clarissa said. Clarissa and I were both solemn.

Our lessons continued. Those were wonderful days for me because I was transported to a world that I never knew existed. Both Clarissa and I made significant progress in our first two years of lessons. We learned arithmetic as well as our letters, and Mrs. Allen, who was a talented teacher and enjoyed sharing her comprehensive knowledge, at a time when women were not permitted to attend university, surprised us with paints, brushes, and special paper and showed us how to create watercolors.

At the time, it did not come to my mind what an extraordinary blessing it was that Mrs. Allen was taking a tremendous risk by teaching me to read and write. I did appreciate Mrs. Allen's kindness to me. When I eventually learned, at an early age, that my mother was not the only woman whom Mr. Allen treated badly, I felt sad for Mrs. Allen.

As a lady's maid, I was expected to immediately be at my mistress's side when she called for me or rang a bell. She did not, however, expect me to listen to conversations or witness events to which I was not invited. When I was eight years old and became Clarissa's maid, I asked Bessie, Mrs. Allen's maid, why Mrs. Allen cried frequently, and she said that Mr. Allen did not treat his wife properly. I told my mother what Bessie said.

"Why she tell you that? Good God. Bessie know better. You're too young to be hearing them things, and if Mr. Allen knew you been told, I don't even want to think about what he'd do."

"But Mrs. Allen was crying, Mama. I was sad for her."

"I know, baby. It make me feel sad, too. Lord know she ain't got no reason to be good to you, but she is. But Bessie and me, we try to help her. Sarah, you ain't said nothing to Clarissa about this, right?" Then she looked at me as if she was reading my mind. "Sarah, you did tell Clarissa, didn't you?"

"Mama, we were in the nursery when Mrs. Allen started crying.

Then Clarissa sat on her lap and wiped her tears with a handkerchief. She stopped crying after that and read to us."

When I was not in the nursery during Clarissa's lessons, I was assigned to Bessie, who was teaching me how to be a proper lady's maid, and when I was eleven years old, I began cleaning Mr. Allen's office. I closed the door when I was there to dust the shelves behind the door. While working in his office, mindful that Mrs. Allen had cautioned Clarissa and me not to tell anyone I had learned to read and write and of my mother's warning that I could be whipped or worse if I was caught simply looking in a book, I inspected the papers and writing tools on Mr. Allen's desk. One day, I was elated to read a document that granted traveling passage to slaves and I realized it likely was similar to the one that the overseer gave Johnny, who usually took us to town in a cart, before we were allowed to leave through the main plantation gate. For the next few days after I read the pass I found myself skipping everywhere and constantly smiling whenever I thought about the pass until my mother asked me whether I wanted to share my secret with her and Belle.

"No ma'am," I said as I rubbed my belly, "I don't have a secret, but that peach cobbler you made just for us on Sunday was so good I'd sure like some mo'."

Mama and Belle laughed, and Mama shook her head.

"Girl, you really is silly, I know that ain't the reason why you're happy, but that's all right, you can keep your little things to yourself, so long as they is just little things," Mama said. She pinched my cheek and kissed me.

After that incident I decided to stop smiling and showing my joy because I did not want anyone to guess what I planned to do—to learn to write a pass by copying the one Mr. Allen had written. I was afraid, but just thinking about my scheme made me ecstatic. While I was too young to know precisely how I could use this knowledge, it was evident that with a pass written by Mr. Allen a slave could leave the plantation. It occurred to me, in my inexperienced way, that perhaps my mother and Belle were fearful of running away because they did not understand how easy it was to do, and now that I knew how to write a pass, in Mr. Allen's handwriting, I could write one for the three of us. What I did not realize until I was older was that escaping from Allen Estates was not the chief obstacle to gaining freedom—it was maintaining that freedom after escaping.

The next time I cleaned Mr. Allen's office, my heart pulsed rapidly and my hands shook, as I summoned the courage to copy a pass. It was difficult to do because the pen repeatedly slipped from my trembling fingers and I stopped each time I heard someone speaking in the hallway, fearing they might enter the office. I used a blank sheet of paper from the stationery drawer and practiced Mr. Allen's handwriting until I could see no difference between his and mine. I tore my copy into small pieces and later threw them down the hole in the outhouse. Proud of my accomplishment and no longer fearing that someone would learn what I had done, I resumed my outward displays of joy by kissing and embracing my mother and Belle while they were working, until they tired of me and laughingly pushed me away.

I still remember the pass I copied:

This traveling pass is granted to the following slaves, all of whom are owned by Cornelius F. Allen, Esq., of Allen Estates Plantation, Benton County. The driver of the cart is Johnny, who is about 5 feet and 10 inches high, of a black complexion, and well made. Johnny bears a brand of Allen Estates on his chest. Missy, about 5 feet and 2 inches high, of a black complexion with a small, thin face, is a seamstress who will purchase cloth at Russell & Strong's. Sammy is a mulatto with bright complexion, about 6 feet high, who is taking leather goods to be sold at Fielding's. Should any of these slaves be found outside the Benton County seat, or anywhere within Benton County at night, a reward of $300 each will be paid for their return to their owner.

In my twelfth year, my mother was still going to Mr. Allen at night, but I became used to her absences. Belle did not tell me as many stories as she did when I was younger, but she continued to teach me how to knit and I was slowly working on shawls for her and my mother. Belle and I entertained ourselves by discussing the events of the day.

"Do you remember that time I was crying because those boys were calling me 'yellow belly' and Mama said they didn't mean anything by it?"

"Yes."

"Well, the other day, these girls were calling me the same thing, and they didn't want to jump rope with Miss Clarissa and me. Today Miss Clarissa wasn't around, and they still didn't want to jump rope with me. When I asked them why, they said that I should jump rope with my sister, Pinky. What did they mean by that?"

Belle was silent for a moment, then said, "I think Mama should tell you."

"She didn't answer my questions about such things before, so why do you think she would now?"

"Well, you older now."

"What difference does that make?"

"Mama said you was going to ask something like that one day, and she said I should say I didn't know. But I don't want to lie to you. When she ain't here, it just you and me, and I want to keep it like we always tell the other the truth."

"Belle, I know the truth. I knew it from last year when Miss Clarissa's cousins came to visit from Montgomery, and when they left she couldn't wait to tell me where they said babies come from. So then I put that together with where Mama told us she goes at night, to Mr. Allen. I just want to hear somebody say that I'm right."

"Why, Sarah, why you care if he's your father?"

"I just want to know, like you know who your father was, I just

want to know for sure who mine is. It's not like I like Mr. Allen. I
hate him and how he treats us and makes Mama go to him and she
has to leave us alone at night."

"Well, what do you know, Sarah?"

"I know that . . . well, you're always talking about 'my papa,'
and I look more like Miss Clarissa than I look like you and Mama,
and Mama is always with Mr. Allen. Anybody, even those other
children, can figure out that Mr. Allen is my father."

Belle looked sad.

"I'm sorry, Sarah . . . I'm sorry. I wish it not like that. I really
wish you and me had the same father. But I couldn't love you no
more than I do. You my real sister. And don't listen when those children tell you anything about Miss Clarissa, she ain't no sister to you."

Belle did not have to tell me that Clarissa was not a sister to me;
Clarissa was not at all like Belle, who loved me and took care of me. I
was then old enough to know that I was Clarissa's maid, and she was
my owner. I am not sure what I felt for Clarissa, certainly not affection, but she had made it possible for me to learn to read and write,
the keys to whether I would one day obtain freedom for my mother,
sister, and myself.

I did not sleep well that night and awoke before my mother returned.

"Baby, what you doing up?" she asked when she came in. I was
sitting at the table and Belle was in bed.

"I was waiting for you."

"Shush. You going to wake Belle."

"I'm awake, Mama," Belle said.

"So why is everybody awake? Let's get a couple of hours more of
sleep before we got to go back to the kitchen." Mama began to
change into her night clothes.

"Mama, I told Belle that I know about Mr. Allen."

Mama stopped in the middle of what she was doing, and sat next
to me, but did not respond.

"I told her that I know about him, Mama."

"Sarah . . . I just wanted to protect you, baby. Didn't want you to know because I ain't want you to tell Miss Clarissa and then she was going to tell Mrs. Allen. This is serious, baby. Most times these ladies get so mad when the masters have children with us that they hurt the master's children with one of us or tell master to sell the children."

I jumped from the chair and hugged Mama. I felt like crying.

"Mama, you don't think Mrs. Allen wants Mr. Allen to sell me, do you?"

"No, baby, no, you don't need to worry about that. Mr. Allen promise me that ain't going to happen and beside, Mrs. Allen know that Miss Clarissa likes playing with you and—I did some things, grown-up women things, to help Mrs. Allen and I don't think she mad at me for having you after that." She patted my back. I was reassured because she said she had helped Mrs. Allen with something important and also I thought of how well Mrs. Allen had treated me, at a great risk to herself, by teaching me how to read and write and learn my numbers.

"But, Sarah, even though everybody know that he's your father because you look just like him and Miss Clarissa, in case Miss Clarissa ain't figured it out, don't tell her, Sarah. She may get mad at her father for what he did by having a child with me."

"What about Mr. Allen? Does he know?"

She pushed me away, almost angrily, and looked at me.

"What about him? Of course he know, but that don't mean one bit of difference in your life, you hear me? So don't think that anything is going to change. For us, it don't matter who our father is, only our mother." We were quiet for a moment.

"Mama? Mama, I have something else to ask you about, about something, something you just said." I needed to ask her a question, but was afraid of the answer.

"Sarah, please, girl, you got to stop with this. Now you know all there is to know, I just told you, Mr. Allen being your father ain't going to change a single thing about your life or mine. Since you was born, you was treated the same as Belle, and he sure ain't her father."

I summoned the courage to ask my question and put my arms back around her waist. She rubbed my back as I spoke. "No, Mama, no, that's not what I was going to ask you about. I mean, it has something to do with it . . . something else. How come— How come you didn't have more babies with Mr. Allen?"

"Girl, you is too grown for your age. I really don't know what I'm going to do with you when you really is a grown woman. Since I know you, how you is when you get a bee in your bonnet, how you don't let it go, there is . . . well. So how did you figure out Mr. Allen is your father, anyway?"

"Miss Clarissa's cousins told her and she told me where babies come from and you told me where you go at night, to be with him at the Hall."

"Like I said, you is too grown. I guess I should be having this talk with you soon anyhow, but not tonight, because you is still too young to know some things, some things that if Mr. Allen knew about them could get us punished or sold. Some things we do to, well, this is something some of us been doing for a long time back that we learn from our mothers and other older women. But you don't need to know about that now and I said too much already, don't you repeat nothing of what I just told you, you hear me? And I hope you never need to know about it because I pray one day you going to be with a man you like and not with . . . somebody who . . . some man who . . . make you be with him." I thought about what she said for a moment and felt a jolt of sorrow.

"So . . . Mama? Did you do whatever bad thing it is grown women do to try not to have babies to . . . try not to have me?"

Her eyes became swollen with tears and she held me closer and kissed my face, my ears, and the top of my head.

"Girl, no, no, you're my sweet baby girl and I love you and Belle just the same. Didn't you hear me? It don't matter who your father is, you is mine, all mine, and no law and no piece of paper could make you less mine, I carried you and took care of you from before you was even born. I keep telling you, Belle and you is all I got in this world, you two the only reason why I got any happiness at all. I live for you and I do whatever I do so we can always be together. I would give my very life for you and Belle, you hear me? My very life."

After a while my mother and I went to Belle. Mama used her handkerchief to wipe the tears from all our faces and then smiled. She put her hands together and looked up at the ceiling.

"Just one night, one night, Lord, one night is all I ask so I can come home and get a good night's sleep and not have Sarah asking me questions and making us cry."

My mother's words made us smile and also caused me to want to continue to learn from Mrs. Allen and her books about the world outside Allen Estates and of other people who did not live in this place.

The next year, when Clarissa and I were thirteen years of age, my mother said that Mrs. Allen told her I could no longer sit with Clarissa during her lessons. She said I had too much work to keep me busy and that Clarissa would soon be getting a tutor. My chest tightened and my limbs felt weak. I had been able to bear my life and to dream about freedom for my mother, Belle, and me only because of those lessons. After that, my only solace was to hide books wrapped in clean rags in my cleaning bucket. At night, when my mother left us and Belle had fallen asleep, I read at the table by candlelight.

Clarissa's tutor, Mrs. Ellsworth, arrived about a month after I stopped attending lessons. She was Clarissa's chaperone as well, and Clarissa was allowed to increase her visits to other plantations without her parents. As Clarissa's maid, I accompanied them on all travels. Around the time Clarissa began her studies with the tutor, my life changed in another way. I asked my mother to stop going to Mr. Allen and, to my surprise, she agreed.

"Listen, girls. I want you to know that all this time I've been asking Mr. Allen to free us, or at least you two, but he won't. He said it's for our own good. While we belong to him, he said, he can take care of us, and we won't need nothing. That's why I stopped going to him."

Belle and I embraced her. It made us happy that she was with us at night, and during the day, while we worked in the kitchen. My mother now laughed at the stories that the other slaves told.

One afternoon, about a month after my mother stopped going to Mr. Allen, I was in Clarissa's rooms settling her in after we had just returned from a visit the previous night to a neighboring plantation, and she asked me for tea. As I was near the kitchen, I recognized my mother's wailing. I ran in and saw her crouched on the floor and surrounded by maids. I rushed to her, my heart pounding, and held her for a moment, then I put my hands on her shoulders and made her look at me.

"They took Belle! They took Belle! They took my baby girl!" was all she said.

"What? What do you mean? Mama, where is Belle, Mama, answer me, please, who took Belle?"

She did not answer, and tears covered her cheeks. Her face was as if made of stone. I wiped away her tears with my handkerchief and then spoke to the person closest to me.

"What happened to Belle?"

"Uh . . . uh . . . two men come in the kitchen and say, which one of you is Belle, and Belle say she was, then they walk to her and me and Jonah, we step in front of Belle, then they say you niggers step aside, they had guns, I'm sorry, they push me and . . . they took Belle and left with her. Miss Emmeline ain't here then, when they took Belle, she was getting linen from the washroom."

"What two men, were they from here? Who were they? How long ago?"

"Late this morning, they ain't from around here. Miss Emmeline been crying all day."

"Is Mr. Allen in the house?"

"No, he ain't been here since yesterday."

At that moment, I forced myself to think, but not about myself, Mama, or anyone else, only of Belle, that she was in danger, and that I needed to find out where those men had taken her so I could tell my mother to beg Mr. Allen to make them return her to us. I felt no fear, no anger, no sadness, no emotion at all, I did not even wonder why Belle had been taken, all I thought about at the time was my resolve to find my sister and keep our family together. I ran out the door and, although I knew that Belle was gone, I was still thinking that somehow I would see her with the men who took her away from us. I proceeded to the main gate, which was guarded by four overseers. One, a pink-faced man holding a rifle, told me to go back to the Hall. He poked me on my arm with the rifle and then, with a fist, punched me in the abdomen and knocked me to the ground. I rubbed the area where he hurt me and I yelled at him.

"Where's my sister, where's my sister, tell me, now, what did you do with my sister?"

He grunted and did not answer, and another man came over.

"Get up. Bitch, I said . . . get up," the second man said.

I did not move and stared at them.

"You tell me where my sister is. Where is she, where did they take her?"

"You ain't got no right to be asking no questions, bitch, and we ain't got to tell you nothing. I said, get up, and if you don't, I'll make you, you sorry, yellow bitch."

I did not obey him, and he pulled my head covering off, grabbed me by the hair, wrapped it around his fist, and dragged me several feet. I kept my body stiff and I did not cry. They threw me on the back of the wagon and took me back to the kitchen. I sat next to my mother on the floor. We stayed that way, holding each other, silently, until the two Hall overseers arrived. One of them grabbed her by the arms, jerked her to her feet, and slammed her against the wall. He pointed at her.

"Ain't you got no cooking and cleaning to do? You get back to work or you may be missing your other slut, too."

He released her, and my mother, with no expression on her face, went to the water pail, washed her hands, and gave instructions to the others to help prepare supper. One of the overseers spoke to me.

"What you looking at? Go see after Miss Clarissa. And I came to tell all y'all something Mr. Allen say: Don't tell Mrs. Allen or Miss Clarissa what happened today or the same thing going to happen to each of you."

I rose and began making tea for Clarissa.

"Ain't you heard me? Go see after Miss Clarissa."

"I'm making her her tea."

He looked at my mother. "You better not make no more trouble. Mr. Allen going to hear about you not working all day."

He left, and I arranged the tea on a tray when it was ready and took it to Clarissa, who at first frowned when she saw me but then, as she focused on my hair, her eyes narrowed.

"What happened to you? Your face is red and sweaty, and where is your head covering? And your hair . . . it's disheveled. Huh . . . I've never seen your hair. Why . . . it's long, and it's not like the other Negroes' hair. Were you running or something? Are you crying? Sit down, there, on the chair. What happened?"

I tried to control my voice to make it sound as it normally did but I am sure that it was deeper, as it always was, and still is now, when I am angry or sad.

"I can't say."

"Why?"

There were tears in my eyes, but I forced myself not to cry in front of Clarissa or I would not have been able to keep from telling her what had happened to Belle. I knew that I could not disobey the overseer by telling Clarissa the truth; my mother had warned me many times to always obey overseers, and I also knew that his threat was not an empty one. If I told Clarissa what had happened to

Belle and Mr. Allen had found out, he probably would have sold both my mother and me or at least one of us and then there would have been no opportunity to be reunited with Belle.

"Well, I'm just sad, is all, because I can't have lessons with you."

Clarissa laughed.

"Sarah, you're crying about that now? That happened a long time ago. Anyway, I've been lending you my lesson books as soon as I'm finished with them. Lessons are so boring and you should be glad that you stopped going to them. Why don't you go to your cabin and tidy yourself? Heavens, one would have thought that someone had died."

That night, as soon as my mother and I were in our cabin, she told me why Belle had been taken from us. Her eyes were red. "He warned me something was going to happen if I stopped going to him, but I ain't think he do this, no, not after he promise me he'd never separate me from my child. But I can see I was foolish."

She was quiet for several minutes. When she spoke again, it was the most I had heard her say in a while.

"My mama told me it's so hard when they take your boy. She said you think you going to die from the pain. When they sold my brothers and sisters, Mama and me think we never go on. But like Mama said, it's much harder when they take your girl. Belle's father said to me, 'If they sell me, I'm going to take care of myself. But not our girl. Do what you got to to keep them from selling her.'

"When they take your man or your son you know he's going to get beat. But they ain't going to do to your man or your boy what they going to do to your girl." She rocked back and forth for a few minutes.

"After you was born, I kept going to him, not just because he told me to but because I thought, 'It going to keep my girls with me.' But then, he said he wasn't going to free us and you was so sad when Mrs. Allen said you had to stop going to lessons with Miss Clarissa."

For the first time since I saw her in the kitchen after they took

Belle, she looked me in the eye and did not look sad and I could tell that it was because she had devised a plan to get Belle back to us. That is how I remember my mother: someone who was courageous, even when her worst fear, having her child sold, had become a reality.

"Sarah, from now on, you know you can't be sad when I leave you at night. You understand me? But it's going to be worse for me this time because I hate him more than I hated him before."

She put her arm around me and told me to close my eyes. We knelt.

"Lord, I don't know the right way to pray, and I know that a sinner like me got no right asking you for nothing. But, Lord, please keep my girl safe.

"Lord, wherever she is, please don't let them hurt her. Lord, bring her back and don't punish her for my sins. And, Lord, please keep Sarah safe with me. Lord, thank you. Amen."

We then held each other, held each other until we fell asleep a few hours before we had to rise for work the next day.

Belle's absence affected all the house servants. Everyone loved her because she was kind and had a serene demeanor, but there was another reason they were sad: her sale enacted their worst fear, being separated from their families. The day after they took Belle, my mother told me to go to the fields and ask Miss Mary, the midwife to the slaves, to bring her herbs for curing fever. She had delivered Belle and me, and we thought of her as our aunt. She was so successful at her work that she never lost a baby or a mother. She began caring for a slave woman immediately after she was known to be expecting and attended to her for at least two weeks after giving birth. Because she knew so many of the women among us and sometimes helped with pregnancies on other plantations, Miss Mary was privy to information from all corners of the plantation and beyond. When Miss Mary arrived in the kitchen that afternoon, she and my mother and I went to our cabin to speak. As we sat at the table, my mother and Miss Mary had their hands folded. Mama's shoulders were slumped, and I was leaning forward, hoping that Miss Mary knew something about where Belle had been taken.

"Mr. Allen sold Belle and two others. I'm sorry, I don't know where to, I couldn't find out nothing else," Miss Mary said. I sat back, disappointed.

"But somebody must know something. Didn't nobody say they had to drive the girls to some other plantation? What about the other girls' families? Did they say something?" Mama was frowning.

"No, Miss Emmeline. I'm sorry. I talked to everybody I trust and who know about these things. I ain't heard nothing."

"Miss Mary, please, when Mr. Allen hire you out to other plantations, please ask if anybody know if Belle got sold there."

Miss Mary patted Mama's hand. "You ain't even have to ask. I already started telling people at the fields and the coachmen when they get hired out or go deliver goods to other plantations to try to find out where they sent her and the other girls. But like I told them, we all got to be very careful about what we say and who we ask. Even you two. You all know we can't ask no questions about Mr. Allen's decisions."

"Yes, you're right, and we understand that you doing the best you can. Thank you so much, Miss Mary." Mama put her hand on Miss Mary's shoulder.

"You know you ain't got to thank me. Your girls is like my own, I ain't going to give up until we find out where she is. All right, I'll come back to see you if I hear something and you go down by the fields to see me if you find something out. You all take care of yourselves, and both of you all remember to be careful who you ask questions, you hear?"

"I baked a cake and a pie for you to take back to your family, Miss Mary," I said.

"Come here and give me a hug, my sugar darling."

For about a month after Belle was sold, I felt no desire to do anything but sleep and read. My mother had to shake me to wake every morning, and she had to force me to eat. Although I performed my work, I might not notice that a pot had boiled over or that I had made no progress in rubbing the English wax into the grain of the wood. I was lonely without Belle, and Clarissa and I, now too old to play childish games, simply were mistress and maid. My thoughts always were of Belle. Why Belle? Why not me? I was the one who always wanted to flee. I was the one who barely hid an escalating rage against Mr. Allen. I wished I knew where they had taken my sister. But even if I did know where they had taken her, what could I do? I could do nothing to rescue her.

Belle and my mother had warned me. *If you run, they will hunt you. They will find you and bring you back. Everyone who runs is caught. When they bring you back, they beat you. If you run again, they cut you before they sell you.*

What of my mother? She now had just one child. If I ran away to find Belle, it was unlikely that I would find her, and my dear mother would be alone. I had to have faith in Mama that she would get Belle back. After all these many years she had managed to keep the three of us together. These were my thoughts all my waking hours.

My mother went back to Mr. Allen after Belle was sold, which meant that I could read in our cabin. One night I was reading Mr. Wordsworth's poetry and came across a sonnet unlike his other works. It was about a man named Toussaint L'Ouverture. This poem sang to me about my life.

TO TOUSSAINT L'OUVERTURE

TOUSSAINT, the most unhappy of men!
Whether the whistling Rustic tend his plough
Within thy hearing, or thy head be now
Pillowed in some deep dungeon's earless den;
O miserable Chieftain! where and when
Wilt thou find patience? Yet die not; do thou

Wear rather in thy bonds a cheerful brow:
Though fallen thyself, never to rise again,
Live, and take comfort. Thou hast left behind
Powers that will work for thee; air, earth, and skies;
There's not a breathing of the common wind

That will forget thee; thou hast great allies;
Thy friends are exultations, agonies,
And love, and man's unconquerable mind.

Who was this Toussaint L'Ouverture? How could I learn more about him? Why was he "in some deep dungeon's earless den"? I would have to search for answers the next day when I was laboring in the library. I returned to the first pages of the book where I read that certain sonnets in this collection, including the one about Toussaint L'Ouverture, were published in London's *Morning Post* in 1803.

The next morning, I looked in the library but could find no reference to Toussaint L'Ouverture or the *Morning Post*. I realized that there were never newspapers in the library, although I sometimes saw Mr. and Mrs. Allen reading them in the parlor. I did not know where they put them after reading them. That night, before she left, I asked my mother what happened to the newspapers after the Allens read them. She replied in a whisper.

"What did I tell you? Don't ask me or nobody else about books or newspapers or nothing like that. And the overseer complain that you spend too much time cleaning that library. I know why that is because I know you is smart, but I ain't going to talk about it, about what happened when you was sitting in with Miss Clarissa in her lessons. Sarah, please. You're scaring me, and I already got enough worries with Belle and don't need to worry about you."

The next day, after my mother made tea, I asked her if she wanted me to take it to the Allens on the verandah. When I finished serving, Mrs. Allen complimented me.

"Sarah, you set such a lovely tea service. Tell your mother that the pastries were delicious."

"Thank you, ma'am. I'll be back to clear everything. Is there anything else that I can bring, ma'am?"

"Not for me. Mr. Allen? Clarissa?"

"Tell her to bring me a glass of brandy. This tea business is for ladies," Mr. Allen said from behind his newspaper.

I curtsied. "Yes, sir. Yes, ma'am."

When I got to the kitchen, my mother sent me to get the overseer to unlock the cabinet where the spirits were stored. When he gave her a bottle of brandy, she poured some in a glass and I took it on a tray to Mr. Allen. I cleared the table and hovered until they were done with tea. When they went to the parlor, I cleaned the verandah and put the newspapers under rags in my bucket, which I left in the washroom near our cabin where we kept mops, brooms, and other housekeeping items. I decided that going forward I would keep my books there, too, and that night, I waited until my mother had been gone for a while before I went to read the newspapers, one of which was published in Anniston and the other in Mobile. Both reported on local events and contained numerous advertisements about slaves, their sale, and purchase, and the recovery of those who had escaped. *The Anniston Journal* contained an editorial about "fire-eating Abolitionists." The writer urged representatives in Congress to resist calls by Northern "speech makers" who sought to abolish slavery. The *Mobile Gazette* warned readers that Northern abolitionists were luring their slaves and helping them escape to the North.

The following day, when we were working in the kitchen, an overseer asked my mother what she had done with the newspapers that Mr. and Mrs. Allen left in the verandah. My mother folded her hands, which was her custom when she wanted to keep them from trembling.

"Sir . . . I . . . ," my mother said. I did not want Mama to take the blame for what I had done.

"Sir, I cleaned the verandah yesterday," I said. "I put the newspapers in the bucket and forgot them there. They're in the washroom. I'll go get them."

"Why didn't you tell her that I collect the newspapers and dispose of them?"

"I'm so sorry, sir. I forgot. It won't happen again," my mother said.

"It better not. What you standing there for? Go get the papers."

For the next few weeks, our lives resumed their normal patterns. I helped with cleaning, cooking, and taking care of Clarissa. She and I had begun menstruating that year, which we had known was going to happen eventually because Belle told me and Clarissa's older cousins told her about that delicate subject. Clarissa and I talked about it, laughing nervously as all other girls do, I suppose, but the change in our bodies only reinforced my low station in life. Bessie showed me how to cut new bleeding cloths for Clarissa every month; and although Clarissa and I both suffered from severe pain during menstruation, when she was having hers, I slept on a cot in an area by her bedroom, rising to get her a hot water bottle and tea to calm her pain.

Mama and I went to the slave quarters about once a week to see Miss Mary. Along the way, I almost could not bear to look at the toiling men, women, and children. Even during harvest, the sun was so hot that I felt weak, but the field hands never looked up. They just pulled and pulled at the cotton plants. On every visit to Miss Mary after Belle was sold, my mother asked her if she had heard anything about her and the other girls. The answer did not vary.

"No, Miss Emmeline. I'm sorry. I ask everybody that I can. When somebody come back here who been hired out to another plantation, I ask them if they got new girls over there. But nobody know nothing or they ain't talking. But I'm going to keep asking. And, Miss Emmeline, know the Lord is keeping Belle safe by the power of His hand, and you remember what the Bible say: Be strong and of good courage; be not afraid, for the Lord thy God is with you wherever you go."

At night, I continued to read and study Clarissa's lesson books. One day, my mother told me that Mrs. Allen had received a letter telling her that her father was sick, and that Mrs. Allen and Clarissa were going to Georgia for a month. She also surprised me by telling me that she and I were accompanying Mr. Allen to Mobile.

THREE

SARAH CAMPBELL

W e boarded the *Coosa Belle* in Talladega. Mr. Allen stayed in his private compartment on the boiler deck leve while my mother, Eddie—Mr. Allen's body servant—and I stayed on the main deck. We found space to put our pallets down to sleep between cotton bales, but the first night, fumes made my stomach ill. I did not rest well, which I did not mind because, when I did, I dreamed of Belle, that she was in danger. I was glad that, while we were on the boat, my mother was with me and Mr. Allen did not summon her to his berth.

The next morning, Eddie left the deck early to get Mr. Allen's breakfast. When he returned, it was time for the main deck passengers to eat, and we got plates of food from the cook in the pantry. Eddie told us that Mr. Allen had changed his mind and that we were stopping at Montgomery, the new capital, on the way to Mobile rather than upon our return. My mother did not like Montgomery at all.

"Sarah, maybe you don't remember it too good because you was real little the last time we was there, but the worst thing is the slave market. They have people sitting on benches out in the open just waiting for somebody to buy them. And everybody walk around acting like nothing is strange about it. And Montgomery got too much going on, anyway, too many people and too many buildings, and painted ladies dipping snuff."

When we stopped, my mother was relieved that we were only there for about four hours, long enough for cotton to be loaded onto the boat. A coach took us to a hotel, where we waited for Mr. Allen in the servants' quarters while he spoke to a merchant. Montgomery was as my mother described it, populous and frenzied, but I admired the new statehouse. When we went back to the boat, all the cotton and other cargo had been loaded, but Eddie told us that Mr. Allen had made arrangements with the captain to wait for his return before departing.

On board the boat, one could observe the main purpose of river travel, the transport of cotton bales, which even took place at night, when everything was illuminated by torches. Most planters built their own warehouses on the landings, some several stories high and over a hundred yards long, to keep their cotton until it was ready to be loaded onto steamers. They constructed slides made of planks on landings where the bluffs were steep. Using iron hooks, slaves loaded bales from the warehouses onto the slides and pushed them. Everyone had to be careful, even those of us on board, because the bales gathered speed as they descended and ended their journey on the main deck. The landing in the town of Claiborne had the longest loading slide on the Alabama River because the bluffs were high above the river's edge. Passengers and crew members who disembarked had to climb a four-hundred-foot wooden staircase to reach the top.

We anchored at Mobile Point in the lower bay, where slaves transferred the cotton bales from the steamboats to oceangoing ships that my mother said were bound for New York and England. When we were on the wharf, my mother put her arm around me and held me close. Sheriffs were putting chains on about forty Negroes whose papers were not satisfactory. My mother said that they were taking them to a jail nearby until a judge could confirm that their traveling passes or manumission papers were authentic.

"How does the judge do that?"

"He write a letter to the person's master or to the court in the county where the Negro say they're from, but that can take over a month and they have to stay in jail the whole time."

"What if the judge doesn't get an answer?"

"They belong to the county here and the sheriff can sell them at a auction."

A wagon was waiting for us; Mr. Allen had departed in a carriage. We had lodgings at a hotel in a busy part of the town, and when we arrived, I helped my mother and Eddie unpack Mr. Allen's luggage before we went to the servants' quarters. The hotel had an area in the kitchen where slaves traveling with their masters could eat. That evening after supper, my mother told me that she was going to Mr. Allen.

"Lock the door and use the chain. Don't let nobody in, I don't care who they say they is."

She returned just before dawn and slept for a few hours. That morning, Eddie told us that Mr. Allen wanted him to escort us around town and that the hotel had made a wagon available. I was at first excited about seeing Mobile because it was a large town, larger than Talladega, but then I felt guilty that I had temporarily not thought about Belle. Eddie and my mother had been to Mobile many times and wanted to show me different places, and my excitement returned. When we reached Royal Street between St. Louis and St. Anthony streets, where the slave market was located, a patroller stopped us.

"Where's your pass?" Eddie showed it to him. "Y'all don't forget curfew time here is six o'clock. The warning bell go off at five thirty."

"Yes, sir," Eddie said.

"That goes for y'all too."

"Yes, sir," my mother and I said at once.

I saw advertisements for slaves from the Carolinas and Virginia posted on buildings, but there was no auction at the slave market that day. We passed a three-story brick building that looked like a jail where people were looking through windows secured with iron bars. Eddie took us past the business district and to the home of a woman, Miss Adeline. My mother said Miss Adeline was born at Allen Estates and lived there until she was sold to a family in Mobile at the age of sixteen. The woman's new master had freed her and her children some years later.

"Emmeline, it's good to see you, and this is your baby girl. Eddie, how you been? And where's Belle?"

My mother, sobbing, fell into Miss Adeline's embrace. She tried to comfort Mama but could not get my mother to speak.

"Master Allen sold Belle, and Miss Emmeline's trying to find out where he sent her, if he sold her down here," Eddie said.

"I don't get out much these days. I just be here during the day looking after my grandchildren. When my sons reach home tonight from working, I'll talk to them and see what I can find out. I'll let you all know tomorrow."

She stood close to my mother and whispered, but I still heard what she had to say. "Emmeline, listen. You got to find a way to get him to at least free Sarah. I told you last time you was here that you need to get him to free both the girls."

"I tried, but he won't."

"Do he know all this time you still looking for where he sent Belle's father?"

"Yes. He told me that . . . He said that one reason he sold Belle was because I was looking for her father. So I ain't looking for him no more. Now I just got to find my child."

"So why don't he buy her back?"

"He said he may do that, if I act right."

"What do that mean?"

"Meaning if I do everything he tell me to do and if I stop thinking about Belle's father. But I can't wait. I been begging him to bring her back to me, but all he say is he don't want to hear it and if I keep talking about Belle he ain't never buying her back. But I can't stop worrying about my baby. I got to at least find out where she is and get word to her that I'm going to do everything I can to get her back."

That night at the hotel, during supper, Eddie told my mother that Mr. Allen was going to the theater and that she should go to his rooms at two in the morning. The next day we returned to Miss Adeline's home, and she said that her sons were still making inquiries of people who were hired out to work on the largest plantations outside of Mobile. She told us to get a pass from Mr. Allen to attend Sunday services at her family's place of worship, the First Baptist Church–Crichton, where my mother could ask the pastor and parishioners if they had heard about any slaves sold to local plantations from Allen Estates. Then she asked my mother to speak with her in the next room, just the two of them.

When we returned to our room that evening, I asked my mother what Miss Adeline said to her.

"It's best you don't know what she said, baby."

"Mama, if it had to do with Belle, I want to know. Please, Mama."

"This don't really have to do with Belle directly. It's just about some people that maybe can help us." My mother was quiet then, but before I could ask her again, she said, "All right, I'll tell you, but promise me you won't say nothing to nobody. This is serious, Sarah. It's one of them things that can get people killed."

"Yes, ma'am. I promise I won't tell."

"The pastor and some of the members of the church we're going to, Miss Adeline's church, work at the port like Miss Adeline's sons, and they know the captains from the ships. A few of the captains is God-fearing people from England who don't believe in slavery, and they try to get slaves to the free states. They know people here who belong to churches in the North and in the South, and they know things about what's going on in different plantations. So they might of heard about Belle and the girls."

"What's a free state?"

"Places where they don't have slaves."

"Like where?"

"Up north."

"You said that when you went north with Mr. Allen, to New York, they didn't have plantations, like here."

"Yes, but they still have slavery. Like if you was a slave from another state, you could go there with your master and still be a slave there. If you was a slave who ran from another state, slave catchers could go there and take you back to slavery. I was afraid when we was there. We wasn't allowed to leave the hotel by ourselves because catchers could just grab you off the street and sell you out the state, even if you was free."

"Mama, when the good people help slaves to escape, how do the slaves know that they'll really end up free?"

"You can ask that about anybody who get help to run. We don't know, Sarah, we don't know where people really end up. But some people think that it's worth it to take the chance."

"Did Miss Adeline say how many people they helped to escape?"

"No, and Sarah, not a word of this to her or anyone else when we get to the church, all right?"

That Saturday, Eddie told us during the morning meal that Mr. Allen wanted us to accompany him to the slave market. As we neared Royal Street, we saw shackled men, women, and children bound to each other as armed men took them to the auction block. We stood in the first row next to Mr. Allen and his agent. The auctioneer brought forward two tall young men wearing pants but no shirts. They looked straight ahead, at a distant point beyond the people in front of them. The auctioneer pointed to their chests and told them to turn. They had no lash marks or scars.

"As you can see, these seventeen-year-old bucks are obedient. They are healthy, strong, and in their prime. They make excellent field hands. How much do I hear for the pair?"

Men called out amounts of money until the auctioneer was

satisfied that the sum was the highest it would go. More slaves were brought out in lots, sometimes as many as six at a time. When a group of four young women, also partially naked, walked to the front of the block, the auctioneer pointed at their breasts with a stick. He also told them to turn and show their backs, which bore no scars.

"Anybody want to come up and knead their stomachs? Each one can give you ten to twelve future field hands."

I was thankful that no one touched them. Mr. Allen asked my mother what she thought of the four slaves as house servants, but her answer was barely audible. Her eyes filled with tears.

"Speak louder, Emmeline. I cannot hear you."

"Yes, sir, they would be good servants in the house."

The auction continued, and Mr. Allen or the agent asked my mother her opinion of the suitability of women slaves for different work. The auction ended when all the slaves were sold, about six hundred in total. After Mr. Allen had bought twenty field hands and the girls, we returned to the hotel.

My mother did not go to Mr. Allen that night, and we stayed up late. To keep herself from crying, my mother told me my favorite stories, many of which she had heard from her mother. One was about a woman named Lela whose husband had died, leaving her alone with a young daughter. The woman picked fruit and flowers and bartered them with her neighbors for meat and milk. One summer day, Lela was looking for berries by the river, finding not a single one, when she heard hissing. She saw an enormous blue-and-green snake wrapped around the trunk of a tree. The greedy reptile was moving its head from side to side.

"Mr. Snake, you are eating all the berries. How am I ever to have any to barter with my neighbors so that my daughter and I can eat?"

Snake ignored Lela as he slid down. She wanted to run away, but she had no food left at home. Snake lifted his head and spoke to Lela.

"What would you give me in exchange for some berries? Would you give me your daughter?"

"Yes, I'll give you my daughter for a basket full of fruit."

Snake nodded, and Lela filled her basket until it was overflowing. As she walked home, she began to feel guilty and decided to take a roundabout way so that Snake would not know where she lived. She kept looking back but did not see him. She did not notice, however, that she had torn her skirt and that a piece of fabric remained on the thorn of a bush. She waded through a part of the river that was deep, hoping that there were no crocodiles in the water. She did not know that one of her berries had fallen and was floating behind her. She left the river and continued walking along the bank. She tripped on a stone and did not realize that some beads had come loose from her ankle bracelet. At last, seeing no sign of Snake, Lela arrived home. She went in and embraced her daughter. Lela knew that she had to tell her the truth.

"My darling daughter, I'm so sorry. I made the worst mistake of my life. I am so ashamed."

"Mother, what is it? What did you do?"

Lela cried. She shook her head. Finally she told her daughter what she had done. "I . . . I . . . I have done a terrible thing. I promised you to Snake. But I'm not going to give you to him."

Meanwhile, Snake had been following Lela, first finding the piece of fabric that was on the thorn, then the berry that had fallen from her basket into the river, and finally the beads that had dropped on the ground from her ankle bracelet. When Snake arrived at Lela's door, he hissed and slipped in. Lela jumped from the stool where she was repairing the tear in her skirt and stood in front of her daughter.

"I did not mean what I said to you, Mr. Snake. I made a mistake. You can have your fruit back. Look, we barely touched it. No, I will not give her to you. I will not."

Lela's daughter was a brave girl. "Mother, you taught me since I was little to keep my promises. Snake gave you a full basket of berries. I am Snake's now."

Lela's daughter stepped away from her mother, who tried to hold her back, and went to Snake. She touched his scaly skin. She got him a gourd of warm milk and made a bed for him in a reed basket. That night, Lela awoke when she heard gentle voices. There, sitting next to her daughter was a handsome young man in colorful robes. Her daughter was making him a bead necklace. Lela jumped from her bed and looked into the basket where Snake had curled up to sleep. There was only a long blue-green skin. Lela took the skin and threw it in the fire. Then the young chief spoke.

"At last, as it was foretold many generations ago, the spell has been broken by a wise young girl who pitied me and a foolish old woman who burned my skin."

The young chief married Lela's daughter at a wedding celebration attended by all the villagers who lived along the river's banks.

We went to Miss Adeline's church that Sunday. The majority of the members were freedmen. Miss Adeline was sitting near the front in a pew with her family, and they had saved seats for us. Service had not begun but the choir was singing. I do not remember the sermon that day, probably because I spent my time looking at the parishioners, who were better dressed than any of us at Allen Estates, including four young men who were dressed in merchant sailors' uniforms similar to ones I had seen at the wharf.

When the services concluded, Miss Adeline introduced us to the pastor and some of the church elders in the pastor's office. "Brothers and sisters, this is Miss Emmeline, her daughter Sarah, and Mr. Eddie. They're from the Allen plantation up in Benton County. Miss Emmeline needs to ask you all something."

The elders welcomed us to their church.

My mother said, "Thank you all for having us here. We come down here because my girl . . . well, my master sold my girl and two others, and I'm just asking if anybody heard of any girls getting sold around here from up Benton County way. Since Mr. Allen got a brother down here that own a plantation, I was thinking maybe he sold her to his brother."

"No, Miss Emmeline, I ain't heard nothing," one of the men said.

"Me neither," the pastor said. "But why don't we do this? Brother Samuel is working right now at Mr. Charles Allen's place, and he'll be there for another two weeks or so. When he comes back, we can ask him if he knows anything."

"Oh . . . but we're leaving tomorrow."

"Miss Emmeline, we really wish we could help you. Maybe what we can do is, if anybody we know goes up to Benton County, we can send word if we hear something about your daughter. I really wish there was something more we could do for you, but we will continue to pray that the Lord delivers us from this wickedness soon."

"Yes, pastor. Thank you."

We returned to the hotel as dejected as we were when we arrived in Mobile. The next day, the male slaves Mr. Allen bought at the auction were on the steamboat that we boarded to go back to the plantation. They placed them in an area with slaves who had been purchased by other planters. The girls Mr. Allen bought were not among this lot. I asked my mother where they were, and she said that he had given them to his brother. Eddie saw me staring at the young men.

"They come a long way, from Virginia, the Carolinas, and Maryland. It's all right, Sarah. Don't cry. Like the pastor said, one day the Lord's going to deliver us from this evil."

Mrs. Allen and Clarissa were still in Georgia when we returned to Allen Estates, but we had just as much work to do because Mr. Allen continued to entertain planters and their wives. Since Clarissa was not at home, my mother told me to help the others serve food. The week that we returned from Mobile, Mr. Allen had special guests, a gentleman and his wife from England, whom my mother said he had met in London. They were touring the States and had already been to Boston, New York, and Philadelphia. The work and the exotic guests were a welcome diversion from always thinking about Belle.

When someone used a term with which he was not familiar, the English gentleman asked what it meant and wrote it in his journal, which he had at all times, even at meals. He expressed surprise that the servants were clean and well dressed, and his wife visited the kitchen and complimented my mother on her cooking. Mr. Allen took them to the fields, and at supper one evening they commented about the efficiency of the plantation, noting that the slaves appeared healthy and well fed. They said that their visit was not at all what they had expected based upon reports by Northerners.

About two weeks after we returned from Mobile, my mother told me when she returned to the cabin in the morning that Belle was coming home.

"Mama, do you really think it's true?"

"Yes. Mr. Allen said so."

I could not believe that Belle was coming home, but just the possibility made me delirious. I jumped out of bed. My mama and I were both smiling for the first time since Mr. Allen had sold Belle.

"When, Mama? When do you think she'll be home?"

"I don't know exactly when, but she'll be coming home soon. The good Lord answered our prayers, and we need to give him thanks."

We knelt. "Lord, we thank you. Lord, you listened to the prayers of a poor, ignorant wretch and you softened Mr. Allen's heart and you're bringing her back. Lord, I know I did wrong before by not praying to you more before they took my child. But I know better now, Lord. Amen."

About two weeks later, we were preparing dinner when we heard people outside the kitchen. We went outside, and there was Belle with a swollen belly and wearing a filthy tattered dress. Belle did not look like my sister. The Belle who had returned had a scar on her upper lip, dry gray skin, and her hair had been cut short like a man's. This Belle kept her head down. My mother and I led her to our cabin. She sat at the table and we offered her something to eat and drink, but she took little.

"Just sleep, Mama. I just need some sleep," she said.

My mother told me to go back to the kitchen to help finish cooking the meal, even though I wanted to stay.

"You're going to spend time with her come nighttime."

When we finished cooking and the Allens were eating, my mother came to the kitchen and told us that Belle was asleep. At our suppertime, we returned to our cabin, and I saw that she had cleaned Belle up some and put her in a nightdress. Belle was silent throughout our meal. I could not stop staring at her rough elbows and hands. Afterward, my mother rubbed her shoulders and back, and I put my ear to Belle's stomach, hoping to hear the baby. That was when Belle cried. My mother embraced her.

"Shush, my sugar. Shush, my baby. Shush."

I wanted to know what had happened to Belle, but I realized that whatever it was, she was not prepared to tell the tale. After supper, at my mother's direction, I pumped pails from the well and took them back to our cabin, where I heated the water and put it in the tub. As we washed her, we could see scars, welts, and scabs on her back, arms, legs, and some even on her belly. We oiled her hair and my mother braided it into neat plaits. When she fell asleep that night, I asked my mother what had happened to Belle.

"She's all right. She's back with us now. That's all that matters."

My mother, with Miss Mary's help, prepared special herbs for Belle during the final months of her pregnancy. Her appearance improved and her hair grew longer than before she was sold. Mrs. Allen gave my mother permission to decrease the amount of Belle's work after Miss Mary said that Belle was having twins.

Belle gave birth in our cabin, with Miss Mary helping my mother deliver the babies. My task was to make sure that there was sufficient hot water. When Emmie was born, my mother wiped her face and put her on Belle's chest, but Belle looked away.

"Come on, sugar. Look at your baby. Hold her."

Belle did not respond. My mother wrapped Emmie in a cloth and held her. She rubbed her back until Emmie began screaming and turned red.

"Here comes the next one," Miss Mary said.

When Ruby was born, Miss Mary did not try to give her to

Belle. The babies had fair skin and they looked more like me than they did Belle or my mother.

"Belle, sugar, I know what you're going through, but you got to—"

Belle frowned and raised her voice.

"Do you, Mama? Do you know what I'm going through?"

Tears slipped down my mother's face.

"I'm sorry, Mama, Miss Mary, and Sarah, I didn't mean to get so mad." Belle's voice now was soft.

"You ain't got nothing to be sorry about, baby."

"Yes, I do, Mama. You all are just trying to help me."

My mother asked Miss Mary to hold Emmie and she and I stepped outside.

"Sarah, go right now, run, and ask to see Mr. Davis. Say Belle had the babies but she ain't making milk yet, but don't tell him she ain't letting the babies suckle. Ask him to send for Edwina down by the washhouse and tell her we need her help."

I followed my mother's instructions. Edwina, with her newborn baby, arrived within the hour.

"Edwina, it's taking Belle time to suckle her babies. You mind helping us out until she ready?"

"Miss Emmeline, you know I'll do anything I can for you and your girls, and now your grandbabies, after all you done for me and my husband."

As Edwina settled her infant on a bed, my mother told me that she and I had to go to prepare the next meal. Miss Mary turned her attention to Belle, and Edwina sat in the rocking chair to nurse Emmie and Ruby. On the way to the kitchen, I asked my mother why Belle had rejected her babies.

"She don't feel ready to be a mother, must be because of what happened to her at Master Reynolds's. Miss Mary seen this many times before. Mothers who don't let their babies suckle happen a lot more often than you realize around here, especially in the fields. But Miss Mary know what she's doing. She know what to say to these new mothers to get them to take to their own babies. And there is something you can do. I want you to talk to Belle about what happened to her when they took her. I tried, but she won't tell me."

After supper was served at Allen Hall, we wrapped enough food for everyone at home. Emmie and Ruby were asleep, Miss Mary was knitting, Edwina was nursing her baby, and Belle was still in bed, looking outside through the open shutters at a cardinal that was perched on the branch of a crab apple tree. My mother made us tea, and everyone but Belle had supper. When we had eaten, my mother asked Miss Mary and Edwina if they would accompany her to the kitchen, where she had to prepare food for the next day. They took all the babies, and I stayed with Belle and persuaded her to eat.

"Belle, what are you thinking about? Why don't you like your babies?"

She did not reply.

"Belle, won't you speak to me? Please? We're worried about you."

"Look, I'm going to be fine. Just fine. As for the babies, I ain't got no say in what happen to them anyway. Mr. Allen will do what he want with them."

"Belle, please don't say that. You don't mean it, do you?"

"Yes, I do."

Miss Mary and Edwina returned about two hours later, and they said that my mother needed me in the kitchen. I went there and told her what Belle said. She closed her eyes.

"Dear Lord, please take her pain away so she can love her babies. I can't take care of them and do my work, Lord, and he will sell them if she don't want them."

The next day, we left Belle with Miss Mary. We made a nursery out of a room off the kitchen where we kept the three babies. My mother and I took turns looking in on Belle and taking her and Miss Mary food. The first time Belle saw her daughters that day was when we returned to the cabin late that night. Edwina had already nursed her own child, and as she was about to nurse Emmie and Ruby, Belle said that she could try feeding one of them. No one said anything. Miss Mary gave her Ruby, the baby wearing a brace-let that my mother made from a green piece of yarn. When Ruby began suckling, Belle smiled. Emmie began crying and my mother put her in Belle's arms. We watched Belle with her girls until they were calm. Miss Mary and Edwina spent the night and left after breakfast the next morning, Miss Mary declaring that Belle had sufficient practice now to care for her daughters. Belle never did say why she changed her mind about her girls, but since she did, Mama and I did not see a need to ask her the reason.

My mother obtained permission from Mr. Allen for Belle to rest for a month after giving birth. The girls were two weeks old when Mr. Davis, the overseer, arrived with gifts from Mr. and Mrs. Allen: a large bolt of cloth with a floral pattern, two piglets for our pen, a pig ready for slaughter, six large jars of honey, and two sacks each of flour, sugar, and rice. When Belle returned to work, a woman who cared for the small children of the other Hall servants also looked after Emmie and Ruby.

One night, when my mother was with Mr. Allen, Belle told me what happened to her when she was sold. It did not occur to me to ask her why she finally wanted to recount her horrific experience; I have concluded, with the benefit of time to reflect on the matter, that she needed to explain to someone, and she chose me, as we were as close as sisters could be, that she had at first rejected her daughters because of who their father may have been.

"I know that one day I'm going to forget most of what they did. I know that because I have to forget. Since the day they took me from here, I ain't been able to sleep straight through one night. You know how after I go to sleep I cry and wake you? Sometimes it's because, in my sleep, I think I'm back there. Sarah, I ain't never go-ing to forget that little girl and how she screamed. Not as long as I live. Sometimes, when I wake you and you see me with my hands covering my ears, it's because I'm dreaming that I'm back at that place, in the cabin where they put us, me and the other girls from here, when we first got to Master Reynolds's plantation. In my dreams, I'm trying to make the little girl stop screaming, but sometimes it's me that's screaming, too, and I want to make us both stop."

"What little girl, Belle? What happened to her?"

"Sarah, you can't tell Mama any of this, you hear? I don't want her to feel worse than she already feel. They took me and two other girls, field hands, to Master Reynolds's plantation. They was about your age. One was tall and looked a lot like you. Her name was Billie, but the other girl, Sippie, was a skinny thing. She looked like she was ten or maybe twelve. Two overseers from Master Reynolds's took us from here. One of them just wanted to do what they told him to do, to take us to Master Reynolds's plantation. But the other one kept staring at us, especially at Sippie.

"We went in a wagon. They had some food and pots, and me and the girls had to cook. We slept outside, in blankets on the ground. All of us girls put the blankets next to each other so we could be close, and we put Sippie between us. If any of us had to get up at night, we always went together. We was on the road for about a week. When we got to Master Reynolds's, the overseers took us to a cabin. It had three beds and cooking wares and a chimney, and they give us food to cook. They left us alone for two days. Then a overseer took new clothes for me and Billie and told us to bathe and change. We did like we was told. That night, when the sun was setting, a overseer and two young gentlemen show up. The overseer took Sippie outside and closed the door behind him.

"Me and Billie tried to fight them off, and they look surprised, like they wasn't expecting us to fight back, but like they was glad that we did. When he pushed himself inside me, it hurt more than the beating. He said, 'Oh, a virgin. It's tighter than a drum.' Then I just give up fighting him and cried, pretending like he wasn't doing it to me, but to somebody else. He smelled like wood and earth and it made me want to throw up. When he stopped, he just stayed there, didn't get up right away. I looked over at Billie. The other man was still going at her. She was quiet, just staring, didn't even look like she blinking.

"They switched places. The second one had a different smell, like spices or something. But this time, me and Billie didn't fight, because we knew it wasn't no use. I heard Sippie scream. I tried to push him off me then, and Billie tried to do the same with the other one. But they didn't let us up. They just hit us again. Sippie kept screaming, and the more she screamed, the harder the one on top of me kept pushing it in.

"When they was done with us and left, me and Billie put on our dresses and ran out. We saw Sippie curled up by a tree. We took her inside and clean her up and put her on the bed that ain't had our blood on it. I told Billie to take off the sheets on the other beds and put the blankets on them. I took a lantern and went outside to the garden in back of the cabin and I found St. Charles's wort and brewed it. All of us drunk the tea when it was cool. Then I dipped a clean cloth in it and put the cloth between Sippie's legs, hoping it was going to help her with the pain.

"They left us alone in the cabin for the next day and then they told us it was time to get to work. They took us in a wagon to the fields. They told me and Billie to get off the wagon. I asked what about the little girl? They said, 'This ain't got nothing to do with you. Who you think you is? Master?' I went for Sippie, but one of the men pushed me away. She wasn't crying or saying nothing.

"That first day in the fields, me and Billie worked with a gang watering the cotton plants and loading weeds onto wagons that the other hands picked. By the end of the first day, my hands was bleeding because there was sharp twigs on the weeds.

"That night, a overseer took us back to the cabin and there was new clothes waiting for us. He told us to wash up good this time, that the young master and his friend complained that we stink. 'And clean up this cabin, too. There's new sheets for the beds. And don't get no ideas. We're watching you.'

"The next day, the two men went back to the cabin and took turns with us again. When the second one was on me, his smell made my food come up my throat, but I held it. 'What's wrong with you, bitch? Answer me,' he said.

"I opened my mouth and the vomit came out. He slapped me. 'Go clean yourself, you nasty whore.'

"I went to the water pitcher, and he went to the bed where the other one was on top of Billie. He . . . said, 'Put her on top.' He put Billie on top and then the other one pushed inside her from behind. Billie yelled like she wasn't going to make it through the pain, so with all the strength I had, I kicked him off her. That's when they beat us again, so bad that they busted my lip, and my eyes was swole shut, poor Billie, her face was all black and blue and her arms and legs was all bruised, too.

"After they left, we was too weak to do nothing and no way tea was going to help us at all. We just stayed there until they came to get us the next morning. We was beat so bad they told us we didn't have to go to the field that day and they went for a doctor. He cleaned the cuts and put bandages on us. They had a house servant come stay with us for two days.

"Then they came to get Billie. She tried not to go with them, said she wanted to stay with me. They said, 'Come with us nice and quiet. You'll be all right.' They took Billie and . . . I never seen her again. They put me in another cabin that was in the slave quarters. I was by myself and I didn't see nobody at night. I didn't want to go out even though I could hear other people outside. At first, they put me in the fields working on the trash gang. It was real hot out there in the sun, and one of the other field hands told me to get a hat from the overseer.

"I was on the trash gang for about three months when my monthly bleeding stopped three months in a row. I started feeling sick, and one day I fainted right there on the field. They took me to my cabin and got the midwife. She asked me if I had missed my monthly. I said no, that I just finished it the day before. She said maybe I wasn't eating right. She asked the overseer to give me more food and to let me rest one day. She said she was going to come see me again, but I should send for her if I felt worse."

"Why didn't you tell her that you had missed your monthly?"

"I was trying to remember what plants Mama told me can bring your bleeding down. That night after I talked to the midwife, I went to the garden but I couldn't find none. And Mama told me never to talk about those herbs to nobody because we're not supposed to know about them, so I couldn't ask the midwife. They let me rest one day, and then I went back to the trash gang for two weeks. Then it was harvest time and they made me pick cotton. They had me and the other hands at the fields at five thirty in the morning. The driver gave me a sack with a strap to put over my shoulder and pins to put up my skirt so the hem wouldn't be on the dirt. Even though here we have to do it when we wash and polish floors, I didn't want to pin up my skirt because it show my legs, but I was afraid of getting hit by the overseer if I didn't do like he say.

"Sarah, I hope you never know what it's like to pick cotton. The bristles on the plants was sharp like knives, so I kept getting cut. My back hurt because I had to bend over to pick the cotton from the bolls and then put it in the sack. But the cotton kept getting stuck in the opening of the sack, so I had to shake the sack to make the cotton go down. They let us stop for twenty minutes to eat a biscuit and bacon or ham about noon. They had a boy coming round with water for the pickers. Then we went back to work until the sun go down.

"One day, I got dizzy and fell again. They took me to the cabin and they had the midwife look at me. She said that I was having a baby. She gave me herbs to make tea. I ask her if she knew what happened to the two girls who came with me and if she knew anybody at Allen Estates.

"'No, baby. I'm sorry. I don't know what happened to them girls, and the Allen place is a long way from here. They don't hire me out that far. This is three years now that master let his son do that. Don't talk about this to nobody. Master Reynolds's youngest son go to a college up north, I hear, and his friends come down to visit. The last two years two friends come down and Master Reynolds tell the overseers to get girls, the best-looking ones, so young master and his friends have a good time before they have to go back to school. This year only one friend come down. But this time, hurting you all like that, I bet it's going to stop.'

"From that day, they start to treat me better. A driver give me a hen for eggs and chicks to raise, and they give me more food than I was getting before. They said I only had to pick cotton from the morning to late afternoon. That was my life, until Mama got Mr. Allen to buy me back."

I did not shed a single tear when Belle was speaking because I wanted her to know that I was listening carefully to what she was saying about the terror she had been forced to endure. I embraced her when she finished, and we both were silent for a moment. I was angry, but calm, as I thought about and began to form my plan to punish Mr. Allen for the savage attack on my sister and the other girls and to free my family from this pit.

"Belle, you and Mama keep telling me that I shouldn't talk about running away, so this is the last time I'm going to say this. I will not only get back at Mr. Allen for what he did to you and those girls, and for everything he has done to all of us, but I'm going to get us out of here. I don't know how or when I'm going to do it, but I will find a way."

Belle shook her head, but this time she said nothing in response.

FOUR

THEODORA ALLEN

F rom the day I first breathed air, as she often told me, I was the center of my mother's life. Her objectives were to envelop me in harmony and protect me from odiousness. She taught me how to paint watercolors before I learned to read, and I began music lessons at the age of five. She allowed me out-of-doors only in the early evening, when there was no danger of ruining my fair complexion.

I had my own maid, Bessie, when I was ten years old. Bessie was twelve when she came to live with us, and before she became my servant, she worked in the fields with her parents and siblings. Bessie told me that she missed her family because she only saw them from Saturday afternoon through Monday morning. I told Mother and she asked Papa if he could build a cabin for them closer to our home. Papa agreed, and Bessie and her family were grateful.

Mother called those who worked for us "servants," and she told me that I should treat them well. She did not use harsh language with them and delegated their discipline to Papa. From an early age, Mother advised me on the principles of household management.

"The lady's responsibility is to teach servants how to perform their labor, and that is why I will show you how to cook, clean, sew, iron, polish silver, and how to receive and entertain guests, as well as other domestic arts."

Papa sometimes took me to our farm, where I watched about fifty hands—men, women, and children—working the fields. I did not know that our servants and field hands were in bondage until I was about thirteen years old, when my cousin Eliza told me that she had seen an auction in Atlanta. Eliza did not know much more than that the servants were slaves and that her father had complained about the exorbitant prices he paid for them.

When I was sixteen, Mother persuaded Papa, who was a professor at the University of Georgia at Athens, to tutor me at home at the same level as his students. Papa gave me courses in advanced mathematics, science, literature, and the history of the European continent. He hired a music master and a painter and encouraged me to practice writing letters.

"When you marry, your husband will have to leave you for lengthy periods of time to travel for business. You will feel less lonely if you write him about events involving your family and home."

Papa laughed when I told him that I had aspirations of being a writer and that, when my husband was away, I would write books.

"No, no, dear. Gentlemen do not find lady novelists feminine. But you should keep a journal that I shall read. Speaking of your future husband . . ."

"Papa, no. I'm too young for marriage."

"You are not. Your mother was sixteen when we married."

That year, because Mother was so concerned I would not marry, Papa introduced six or seven gentlemen to me, even before my formal presentation, none of whom I could tolerate. Papa was patient with my rejection of these gentlemen, but Mother worried that no one would meet my approval. One evening at supper, she reminded me that gentlewomen who did not marry and have families had no rank or distinction in society.

"It doesn't matter to me. I'll live here with you and Papa and write my novel, which I shall send to publishers in New York and London."

Mother lost her color, and Papa counseled me against teasing her.

"Theodora, mind that your mother does not literally push you to the altar."

"It was in jest, Mother. I will get a bow and arrow and hunt for a husband with your degree of earnestness."

Papa wrote to acquaintances in Alabama and received a response from Mr. Cornelius Allen, well known for being the eldest son of an established family. My parents were joyous when he demonstrated an interest in me. Papa said that Mr. Allen must have heard about my legendary blue eyes and porcelain skin. Mr. Allen began courting me the evening of my presentation. He was elegant and, more important, engaging because he told me about his travels to the Northern states, the European continent, and the Western Territories.

Mother prepared me for what to expect on my wedding night. She said that Mr. Allen would visit me in my bedchamber until I was with child, and thereafter only to conceive more children. Mother said that a true gentleman used servants to satisfy his vulgar needs. Based upon Eliza's description of her first night with her husband, I was glad when Mother told me that intimacy with Mr. Allen would be minimal.

Our wedding was glorious. Papa gave me Dottie, my seamstress, and he told me that Bessie would now be mine as well. They were not substitutes for my parents, but I knew that their familiar faces would comfort me in my marital home. We spent our honey-month at the Allen home in Orange Beach. The eagerness that I felt when we consummated our marriage surprised me. I believed that I would not be able to endure a man's hardness, but his fiery play was sublime, and my longing for our coupling did not abate when he took me to my new home.

I met Emmeline the day I arrived at Allen Hall, when the over-

seers gathered the household servants in the parlor to present them
to me and I noticed her because I had never seen a Negress who was
so handsome. The servants, who that day were wearing different
well-tailored uniforms, depending on the type of work they did,
curtsied and bowed. They were silent until the chief Hall overseer
presented them to me, and each expressed, in an apparently well-
rehearsed way, that he was happy to be able to serve me. None of
the servants looked me in the eye, not even when he greeted me,
and all kept their heads bowed during the introductions. My husband later said that Emmeline had become the chief housekeeper
when his parents left the plantation to live in Montgomery and he
remained as master of the estate. During my first week, my husband took me to his office, where he regularly conferred with the
chief plantation and Hall overseers, to explain to me my duties as
mistress of the house. There, he reviewed the Hall's accounts and
record books with me, showed me how to order goods and pay
merchants' bills of expenditures, and told me about my other duties
as mistress of Allen Hall.

"You do not have to teach Emmeline anything because she is a
superb housekeeper and cook. You are to meet with the Hall overseers and Emmeline at least once a day to give them orders and to
hear their reports on all household matters.

"The tasks of disciplining servants and preventing them from
stealing fall to the overseers, who are responsible for regularly
counting the silverware and other valuable items, and for keeping
food and spirits locked away. You will have to watch the overseers
to ensure that they are doing their job," he said.

"I am thankful that I will not have to discipline servants, Mr.
Allen. In fact, may I request that the overseers do not mete out punishment in or near our home? It seems altogether disagreeable."

"If any of the household servants need correction, they are taken
to the whipping post near the fields. If they do not improve their
conduct after the first time they are whipped, they are sent to work as
field hands. If they commit further infractions, they are sold. You

will find that our servants are well behaved and rarely need chastisement."

In my second week at Allen Estates, my husband took me on a tour of his domain, the plantation. It took us over an hour to reach the outpost of the fields from our home. We went to the slave quarters, which were arranged in a grid pattern of one-room log cabins, about forty rows deep and twenty rows wide. The carriage stopped in front of an old woman and six small children dressed in long shirts or dresses made from Negro cloth. They were sitting on the steps outside a cabin. When we got out of the carriage, the old woman greeted us and told the children to bow and curtsy.

"Children, Auntie Cissy, this is my bride and your mistress. I am certain that you will obey her as you do me. Well, what do you think of her? Is she not a beauty?"

The children giggled.

"Yes, Master Allen. She real pretty," Auntie Cissy said.

A boy asked my husband if he had sweets. My husband patted his head. "Sam, is that all you think about? Have you behaved well?"

"Yes, sir, master."

"Auntie Cissy, has Sam been a good boy?"

"Yes, sir, Master Allen."

The other young ones were quiet.

"Auntie Cissy, what about the other children, have they been obedient?"

"Yes, sir, Master Allen. All them been good."

"Well, then they all deserve treats."

He took candies from his pocket and distributed them.

"Auntie Cissy, are you feeling better?"

"Yes, sir, Master Allen. Thank you kindly, sir."

"How is your daughter? She is due to give birth soon, is that correct?"

"Yes, sir. She feeling good and she ready to have them babies next month. Thank you, sir."

I asked my husband if we could look inside a cabin. He and the overseer directed me to one nearby that was about sixteen by eighteen feet with a fireplace down the middle for cooking. The overseer opened two wooden shutters so that I could see that it was clean and that the slaves had cooking wares and proper furniture. A cabinet held clothing that the family had for special occasions and to attend church on Sundays. In the coach on the way back to Allen Hall, I thanked my husband for the tour.

"What you saw were the results of my father's many years of labor. I learned from him and from trade journals on plantation management that slaves are more likely to be productive and not try to escape if one treats them well.

"I do not rely on overseers' reports about the well-being of my people. I visit cabins randomly to see for myself that they are clean. Filthy cabins incubate disease that can lead to prolonged illness or death. While we still get a few imports through Mobile, because of the 1808 international ban on importing slaves, we must rely on raising our own. That is why I encourage my people to marry and have children, as it is the best way to cheaply increase the number of field hands.

"I provide them with everything they need: physicians, preachers, clothing, shoes, and sufficient food. They rest from Saturday afternoon to Monday morning. My father taught me to involve myself in every aspect of my slaves' lives. I pay for their weddings and funerals and build cabins for the newly married. I maintain records of all births and deaths, and only I name newborns.

"I permit the slaves who are obedient to keep gardens, where they grow vegetables, and to raise chickens and hogs. I even trade with them, the goods that they raise for whatever they might need beyond those supplies."

Allen Estates was an isolated and rural area, and I realized that I had to find ways to keep myself, and later my children, entertained. Three weeks after my arrival, we had a supper for the planters and their wives who lived in and near Benton County. My husband invited only those who owned a minimum of fifty slaves, but at that, our neighbors were an uneducated and provincial lot. The women spoke only about domestic matters, and some were illiterate and had never been beyond the county line. When I told my husband that I would have nothing to do when he was away, he said that, if I wanted to, I could travel with him.

One of the neighbors, Mrs. Faith Tutwiler, was unlike the other planters' wives. She had attended a young ladies' academy in Montgomery, where she was raised. It was Mrs. Tutwiler, whose husband owned over one hundred slaves, who taught me how to thrive as the mistress of a plantation. I learned from her that certain chores, such as giving slaves their Christmas presents, should not be entrusted to overseers and that the mistress's main duty with regard to the household servants was to be their advocate with the master.

As Mrs. Tutwiler said, all the household servants, except for Emmeline, soon learned that they could lodge complaints or make requests of Mr. Allen by asking to speak with me. Most complaints concerned the overseers. The servants protested disciplinary measures and, as they saw it, excessive labor. I investigated all charges and sometimes agreed with the servants.

In my first month at Allen Estates, I performed an inventory of the 1,500-square-foot library and dedicated myself to converting it into a respectable collection. My husband purchased mahogany from Honduras, and I had the carpenters, all expert furniture makers, build shelves and reading tables. I ordered books and subscriptions to magazines and newspapers, including the *Daily National Intelligencer*, from J. S. Kellogg & Co., a bookseller in Mobile.

In September, I suspected that I was with child, three months after my marriage. My husband summoned a physician recommended by Mrs. Tutwiler. Dr. Robert Atlas arrived that evening and examined me in the presence of Bessie.

"When you're dressed, Mrs. Allen, I'll speak with you and Mr. Allen to tell you my conclusion."

When he was gone, Bessie helped me to dress and I went to the parlor. My husband and Dr. Atlas were laughing and drinking brandy.

"Darling, Dr. Atlas has informed me that you are with child. Why are you crying? I thought you would be happy."

"Mr. Allen, I assure you that this is normal for a gentlewoman in her condition. There will be many moments like this, when Mrs. Allen will cry for no apparent reason. Everyone must be patient and do nothing to agitate her."

My husband asked Dr. Atlas what else needed to be done for me during my pregnancy.

"Because ladies are delicate, they have to abandon all outdoor activities, including gardening. Mrs. Allen may ride in the carriage, but she must take afternoon naps. I'll examine her once a month until her sixth month, when I'll see her once a week. If you'd like, I'm available to be in residence in the final month of pregnancy."

"Yes, those arrangements are suitable."

When Dr. Atlas departed, my husband consented to my request to invite my parents to Allen Estates. I told Bessie and Dottie that they were going to be aunties. They were thrilled and, being mothers, had many words of advice. That month, I did not feel at all ill. My parents wrote that they would arrive in early November. From the day that Dr. Atlas confirmed my pregnancy, I saw my husband only at supper because he stopped visiting me at night. At the end of September, I asked him when we were alone why he no longer came to our bedroom.

"Dr. Atlas told me that it would be dangerous and that we can't be together until you have recovered from the baby's birth."

"But I'm not ill. I feel wonderful, in fact."

"Theodora, I'll not jeopardize our child. We have to have faith in Dr. Atlas's knowledge and experience."

"But . . . it will be a long time until we can—"

Cornelius stamped his foot and pointed.

"Why are you questioning what I just said? I said no. That's my decision and there's nothing more to discuss."

I was shocked at how he spoke to me, but I thought that he reacted the way he did because of his concern. I agreed that the physician probably knew what was best for the child. I did not tell Cornelius that I wanted to be with him even more than before my pregnancy. I spent my nights alone with my books and my journal, and my days were monotonous. I told an overseer to find two boys to help me in the garden.

One afternoon shortly thereafter, as I was sitting on a bench instructing the boys, a servant gave me a letter from Papa. I read it again and again, not believing what it said. How could Mother be dead? She was in excellent health when I was married. I sent for my husband, who was in the fields, and when he arrived, I showed him the letter.

"Darling, I'm very sorry. This is shocking."

I did not reply.

"Dear, you must accept that your mother has passed on. Why don't I take you upstairs so that you can rest?"

"No, I have things to finish in the garden."

"No, you'll not work in the garden. Theodora, you have to acknowledge what happened."

"Dottie and I still have so much sewing to do."

"Theodora . . . stop it. Come with me or I'll have to carry you. You know that this is harvest and I have to return to the fields. I cannot stay with you all afternoon."

"No, please, don't leave me alone. Please stay with me. I can't be alone right now."

"I'll stay with you for a while, but I have to make sure that the cotton harvesting remains on schedule to meet shipment dates."

We went to the bedroom and he stayed with me for about an hour, and then he left me in the care of Bessie and Dottie. I felt unsettled at not having seen Mother buried. That night, I awoke with abdominal pain and I was perspiring heavily. My forehead and throat were hot. I rang the bell for Bessie. I told her to go to the overseer's house and to tell him to send for Dr. Atlas, who arrived in the early morning.

"Mrs. Allen, you have a high fever."

"What can be done?"

"Now, now, do not trouble yourself. I have attended hundreds of gentlewomen in your condition, and my practices always resolve the matter. Please stand. Your maid should stand next to you in the event that you feel weak during the procedure."

"What procedure?"

He did not answer me and withdrew an instrument from his waistcoat pocket.

"Answer me at once. What are you going to do?"

"Madam, please do not exert yourself. This is normal practice. I will perform venesection to cure your fever and the pressure in your uterus."

I was afraid and wanted to call my husband, but he had returned late from the fields and I did not want to disturb his sleep. I stood. Dr. Atlas told Bessie to help me remove my nightdress. He then tied the part of my arm above my elbow with a tight cloth. He told me the small, pointed instrument that he had taken from his waistcoat pocket was a thumb lancet.

"Do not move at all as I begin the procedure. If you do, the blade can cut a tendon or sever an artery. Most ladies look away at this point, madam."

I closed my eyes. The pain caused by the blade entering my arm was not as severe as I expected, and I opened my eyes, watching as the doctor caught the spurting blood in a small bowl.

"I believe that I have drawn sufficient blood. You should return to bed and sleep, and you will feel better when you awake. I will stay on the premises to examine you later today."

I followed his instructions, but when I awoke, I did not feel better. He said that he needed to let more blood until the fever subsided. He performed the procedure once more that day and three times more over the next two days. I felt weak. He prescribed more bed rest.

Papa wrote that he, my aunt Lucretia, and my cousin Eliza were on their way to see me and would get to Allen Estates the following week. I was happy when they arrived, although Papa was thinner and looked tired. He kissed me on the forehead and smoothed back loose strands of my hair. I did not cry until I embraced my aunt because for the first time, I noticed that she and my Mother had identical hairlines and cheekbones. When the servants settled my father and aunt in their rooms, Eliza and I retreated to my apartment.

"Eliza, my husband has abandoned our bed, and . . . I miss him."

"My dear Theo, when a lady is expecting, especially with her first child, it is appropriate, and even advised by doctors, that her husband should not visit the marital bed. You will find that, as your pregnancy progresses, you will be grateful to be alone."

"Perhaps you are right. Oh, Eliza, thank you so much for coming to see me. My dear family is a tremendous comfort."

My family took carriage rides to the fields and to neighboring plantations. When we were at home, Papa and I played chess, we read, and I continued to write in my journal. My aunt and cousin helped Dottie and me with sewing and knitting. We generally saw my husband at supper, as he was consumed by the work of preparing shipments.

Late one night, I awoke with pain in my abdomen. I called Bessie, who hurried in and lit candles. When we lifted the linens and saw that blood had soaked through my nightdress and the sheets, I told her to call my aunt, who brought Eliza. Bessie roused Dottie. They all assured me that this was common during a first pregnancy and that it was not always a sign that something was wrong. Aunt Lucretia told Bessie to run to one of the overseers' houses and tell him to send someone to town to get the doctor. I got out of bed so that Dottie could change the linens, and Aunt Lucretia and Eliza helped me to wash up and change my clothing.

"Auntie, has Mr. Allen been notified?"

"No, dear. Perhaps we should ask your papa to do so?"

"No, I will go to him."

"No, Theodora. You must stay in bed."

"No, I feel better and the bleeding has stopped. I want to be with my husband."

They did not attempt to stop me. I took a candle and went to my husband's apartment. I opened the door to his bedroom. The windows were open and the moon illuminated two nude figures, as still and as perfect as statues.

FIVE

THEODORA ALLEN

heir clothes, the blanket, and a pillow were scattered on the floor. An empty bottle of wine and two glasses were on a table. I could not stop staring at them; his open hand was on the small of her back and his face rested on her shoulder. My husband and Emmeline awoke when I could not hold in a cry. When she realized that I was there, Emmeline pulled the linens over their nude bodies, sat up, gripped the sheet close, and bowed her head. My husband did not lift his head from the pillow and pushed the sheet aside to display his nakedness. He used his fingers to comb his long untied hair away from his face and then spoke to me calmly.

"Theodora, return to your room . . . now. I'll see you there shortly," my husband said.

I did not move and closed my eyes, thinking that perhaps I was imagining what I had seen and that when I opened them again Emmeline would not be there. After a few seconds, however, I opened my eyes when he spoke again, his voice now stern.

"I said . . . leave . . . now."

He sat up and stared at me, as if he thought I had done something interesting by not obeying his command. My mind told me to flee, but my feet would not move. He smiled, perhaps amused. All this time, Emmeline was quiet and kept her head bowed. I covered my face with my hands so he would not see my tears. He laughed.

"Do you really want me to get out of this bed, as I am, and return you to your room?"

When I stayed and did not answer, his merriment instantly transformed itself into fury and, after swinging his feet and planting them on the floor, he pointed at me.

"You'd better leave this moment, or I'll get out of this bed and escort you out."

I managed to walk and went to my bedroom, where I dismissed Dottie and sent her for Aunt Lucretia and Eliza. When they arrived I told them what had transpired. Auntie embraced me and made the same comforting noises that Mother had when I was a child and something had caused me pain. Eliza wiped the tears from my face.

"My sweet, Mr. Allen is only with her to protect you and your child," my aunt said.

I said that I wanted to be alone.

"Are you certain, dear?"

I got in bed and closed my eyes. An hour later, I heard footsteps and my husband entered.

"Theodora, darling, look at me."

I ignored him.

"Darling, I regret not having said this to you earlier. My mother lost two children before they were born. I do not want the same to happen to you. I promise you that, when we have our baby and you are healthy, I will return to you."

I did not reply.

"Theodora, you are acting like a child, not like the mistress of a plantation. Please, I beg of you, answer me. Tell me that you know that I'm only doing this for you."

I cried and he held me. He smelled of soap and cologne.

"I was going to your rooms to tell you that I felt pain in my abdomen and that I was bleeding," I said.

"What? Did anyone send for Dr. Atlas?"

"I have sent the overseers instructions to bring the doctor."

There was a knock on the door. It was Bessie, who said that Davis had left for town to get Dr. Atlas. My husband dismissed her and told her to sleep on a cot in the adjacent room in the event that I needed her during the night. He closed the door.

"I'll sleep with you until Dr. Atlas arrives," he said.

He got in the bed with me.

"When you are able to travel after the baby is born, we can ask your family to stay with him, and I will take you to Charleston and New York."

I pushed him away from me. "Do you really think that because you promise me a journey that I am going to condone what you are doing, that I actually believe that you are with her for my benefit?"

"Theodora, I'm the master here, not you or anyone else. I decide what is best for you and everyone on this estate. You'll keep these insubordinate thoughts to yourself. If you cannot abide by my rules, when my son is born, you will leave him here and return to your family."

I was silent. He put his hand on my shoulder and applied pressure.

"Do you understand me?"

"Yes, I do."

The physician arrived early in the morning, and my husband went to his apartment. Dr. Atlas, with Bessie present, performed an examination.

"Ma'am, I'll speak with you and Mr. Allen when you are ready."

"No, you will not. You will speak to me first. What is your finding?"

"Mr. Allen instructed me to speak to him first . . ."

"I don't care what he has said to you. If you do not tell me your conclusion now, I'll have you dismissed, and we will retain a physician from Montgomery or Talladega."

"Mrs. Allen, it appears that all is normal. However, I prescribe bed rest. If Mr. Allen concurs, I will establish residence until I am assured that you are well."

The doctor's daily examinations made me uncomfortable, but I believed that he knew what he was doing. One day, during my afternoon nap, I felt a pain stronger than the prior time and called Bessie to run for the doctor. By the time he arrived, I had expelled two thick clots of blood. He ordered Bessie to get hot water and cloths and to tell the overseer to send for my husband, who was in the fields. Dr. Atlas said that there was nothing he could do because he had to wait for the bleeding to end before he could examine me. Cornelius came to see me that evening.

"I am worried about you. What may I do for you, darling?"

At my request, he read Keats to me until I went to sleep. When I awoke in the morning, I realized that he had stayed with me. The bleeding did not end until the next day, and when it did, I closed my eyes and said a brief prayer. Then I summoned Dr. Atlas.

"It is obvious that I have lost my child. Do you confirm that?"

"Yes, I do, Mrs. Allen."

"Why did you not tell me before?"

"I wanted to be certain by examining you first."

"Or perhaps you wanted to remain on retainer."

"Madam, that's not true. I'm only concerned about your well-being."

"I don't believe you, but, whatever the matter is, that is all that I require from you. Your services are no longer needed. Please take your leave and speak to my husband about your compensation."

"Mrs. Allen, you are in the midst of a grave event and you are not thinking clearly. . . ."

"My mind is functioning well, and I will not engage in further discourse with you. Good day."

"Mrs. Allen, perhaps—"

"I said that you are dismissed, Dr. Atlas."

When he had departed, Bessie asked if she should call for my husband.

"No. Not at this time. Mr. Allen is in the fields, and I do not want him to be disturbed. Bessie, do the field hands and servants trust Mary, the midwife?"

"Yes, ma'am. They say she never lose no babies or mothers."

"Without telling anyone else, I want you to go to the fields and tell Mary that I need to see her. Do not tell anyone else that you are going to get her. If an overseer asks, say that we need remedies for one of the servants. Dottie can stay here with me."

"Yes, ma'am. But, ma'am, can I say something?"

"Of course."

"Ma'am, Miss . . . uh . . . Emmeline . . . everybody say she know a lot about women's troubles. Miss . . . uh . . . Mary teach her all about medicines and such. Since it's going to be some time before I can come back with Miss Mary, maybe you can talk to Miss Emmeline."

At first, when Bessie said I should speak with Emmeline about my predicament, I felt a spark of anger because I presumed everyone at Allen Hall knew about my husband and Emmeline and that Bessie was betraying me by advising me to seek assistance from her, but I had known Bessie since childhood and she was always loyal and knew me at least as well as my family. I also thought of my mother and her guidance about how ladies were supposed to conduct themselves if they wanted to conform to the rules of polite society. My mother cautioned me that I had to have a family, and that meant having children, or I would fail in my most important duty as a wife. If I did not want my husband to legally dissolve our marriage, I had to have children. The pain that I endured whenever I pictured my husband in bed with Emmeline was nothing compared to the agony I felt when I thought of Papa's misery and shame if my husband petitioned the court to divorce me. I therefore decided to accept Bessie's counsel and disregard my husband's illicit conduct with Emmeline.

"Yes, Bessie, that's good thinking. Dottie can call Emmeline, and you go to the fields to bring Mary."

The door to my bedroom was open when Dottie arrived with Emmeline. Emmeline was wearing her usual chief housekeeper's uniform, a long solid navy dress with a white collar and long cuffed sleeves, and her head was wrapped in matching cloth. Both servants stood before me, Emmeline with her hands clasped, at the foot of the bed, and neither one, as was expected of them, looked at my face. "Emmeline, Bessie told me that you know about women's problems and that Mary, the midwife, has taught you about herbal remedies. Is that true?"

"Yes, ma'am, she did teach me some things, ma'am."

"I have lost my child. Dr. Atlas recommended I take tansy to expel the rest of the blood. What do you think?"

"Ma'am, I can't say I know nowhere as much as the doctor or Miss Mary, and I don't want to go against what he tell you."

"I'm asking you to do so."

"Yes, ma'am, tansy is too strong. And it make your stomach sick so you don't want to eat. And Miss Mary teach me that the most important thing a lady that lost her baby need to do is eat right and that's because those ladies lose so much blood. Eating right help them get their strength back."

"Is there something else you think I should take?"

"Yes, ma'am, you can take a tea of black and blue cohosh."

"Why?"

"Ma'am, they is going to make you push out the rest of the blood and make your womb strong again. But you need to take these teas, day and night, for seven days. And ma'am, you can take ginger tea, too, to calm your stomach and make you want to eat. After the seven days, you take some other teas to make your womb strong again, like raspberry leaf, blue vervain, dandelion root, and rose hips."

I had heard of all the herbs that Emmeline recommended from Mother and other women in my family, because we used them for different ailments when we did not see the need to consult a physician. If Emmeline had mentioned any herb with which I was not familiar, I certainly would not have taken it.

"Where do I get those herbs?"

"Ma'am. I got them, dried."

"I would like those teas, then, Emmeline."

"Yes, ma'am. I'll make them now."

"Thank you, Emmeline."

She curtsied and left, and Dottie helped me to wash and changed the bed linens. Emmeline returned with the teas, and now neither one of us was as uncomfortable as she was earlier. I drank the herbs as soon as they cooled, and she said that she would visit me periodically. I asked Dottie to call Eliza and my aunt, and when they arrived and Dottie was gone from the room, I related to them what I had done and about my conversation with Emmeline.

"Angel, do you really believe that taking advice from her was wise?"

"I have heard from two of the planters' wives that the midwives are rather knowledgeable about these matters. Bessie confirmed that the midwife here taught Emmeline about these remedies. When she is here, I will ask her to confirm Emmeline's advice."

Aunt Lucretia and Eliza stayed with me, and Bessie returned with Mary about two hours later.

"How many babies do you assist in delivering?" I asked her.

"Sometimes three a day, ma'am."

"How long have you been a midwife and how did you learn your trade?"

"Ma'am, they told me we been midwives from way back. My grandmother and my mother was the ones that teach me."

"I understand that you are very valuable to us, that you have never lost a baby or a mother."

"No, ma'am, not one."

I told Mary what Emmeline recommended, and she said that Emmeline's suggestions were the right ones.

"Mary, I am going to speak to my husband about having you assist me the next time I am pregnant."

"Yes, ma'am. If you and Mr. Allen want me, I'm happy to do it.

But, ma'am, since Miss Emmeline is here by you, I think that she can help you out, too."

"That is what we will do, then. I will rely on both of you."

I was bedridden but not bored, because Eliza, Papa, my aunt, and sometimes my husband took turns sitting in my room and reading to me. Papa gave me pencil drawing lessons, which I found challenging. My family stayed with me for another month to make certain I had recuperated. Bessie was no longer treating me like an invalid, and after my family was gone, my husband asked me if I was well enough to accompany him to Mobile, Charleston, and New York.

"We have shipped most of the cotton from this year's harvest, but I must go to those cities to negotiate prices for next year and to attend to other matters," he said.

"How long will the voyage last?"

"About three months."

"Will I be able to take Bessie?"

"Certainly. We're also taking my body servant and Emmeline."

I knew better than to ask him why we needed to take Emmeline and was certain that, even if I declined to go, he would still take her. Even though I had chosen to seek Emmeline's assistance with regard to my health, I was still resentful because of his betrayal and their immoral conduct.

"Yes, I would like to join you."

"Good. Emmeline and Eddie have made this journey with me and they know everything that we have to do to prepare. My secretary has made transportation and lodging arrangements. You and Bessie must be ready to depart by the middle of next month."

Bessie and Dottie packed my luggage over the next two weeks. My husband instructed me to write my measurements, as well as Bessie's, Emmeline's, and Belle's, whom I learned Emmeline would not leave behind, and his secretary sent the information to a tailor in New York. Cornelius said that winter clothing for all of us would be waiting at the hotel when we arrived and that we would purchase goods and other clothing that we needed in Mobile and Charleston. We departed on a cold and cloudy November morning, in the largest carriage drawn by a team of Cleveland bays. Bessie settled me in my seat and covered me with a fur lap robe. She sat in front with the coachman and Eddie, and Emmeline and Belle followed in another carriage that was loaded with our baggage. Overseers had left the plantation at daybreak, in wagons loaded with small quantities of cotton bales, mainly as samples for the New York market. The majority of the harvest had been shipped to England and France weeks prior, via the Tennessee and Mississippi Rivers and then through New Orleans.

The carriage took us to my husband's landing on the Coosa River by Talladega, which, because it was after harvest, was crowded, chaotic, and noisy, as overseers watched slaves from different plantations load cotton bales onto steamboats. The ground was muddy, and I was glad to be wearing boots for travel. My husband and I boarded the boiler deck level of the *General Brown,* and our servants took their places on the main deck below us. I was afraid of steamboats because the newspapers carried reports of accidents such as fires, falling trees, running into shoals, and boilers exploding. Bessie accommodated me in my berth, and Eddie helped my husband in his, which was adjacent to mine.

I stayed in my compartment most of the time, as I did not care for the loud men in the saloon, some of whom were itinerant gamblers. The men in the saloon smoked, played cards, chewed snuff, and spit into buckets. My husband, however, enjoyed boat travel because he met other planters on board, and they spoke mainly about cotton and slave prices. I entertained myself by reading and watching the scenes when we stopped at the landings. Slaves even loaded cotton at night, by torchlight.

The journey was slow because we stopped at every planter's landing to receive cotton. It took us six days to get from Talladega to Montgomery, where we rested for a night at the home of my parents-in-law and arrived in Mobile ten days later, on a bright and balmy day so unlike the cold weather at home. We stayed at a hotel that was convenient to the business district so that my husband could meet with factors from Northern firms that provided marketing services for cotton and with representatives of the Bank of Mobile. We spent Christmas with my husband's acquaintances and departed for Charleston the twenty-eighth day of December. On New Year's Day, we dined on seafood, of course, and the captain and his mariners entertained us by playing music.

I had imagined that Charleston would be slightly larger than Mobile, but I was not at all prepared for what I saw when we disembarked. There were so many Negroes in Charleston that it seemed they were the predominant people. I moved close to my husband, and he put his arm around me as we walked to the carriage. Mr. Peabody, my husband's associate at the Second Bank of the United States, was waiting to escort us to the Charleston home of Mr. and Mrs. Ezekiel Heywood, our hosts. On the way, I commented to Mr. Peabody that I was surprised to see that there were so many Negroes in town.

"Yes, ma'am. There are about three times as many of them as there are of us, but you need not be troubled. You will see that we have armed city guards everywhere."

I noticed houses of worship that I had not seen anywhere else, and Mr. Peabody explained that the city was home to Papists, who had built a Roman Catholic church, and Hebrews, who worshipped in their synagogue.

Mrs. Heywood planned activities for me during the day while the gentlemen transacted commercial matters. The morning after we arrived, she took me to a garden and nursery at King and Meeting Streets. We returned to her home that afternoon for tea. She advised me to rest for the remainder of the day because the social season was frenetic, as all the planters were in the city with their families and everyone hosted dinners and balls. When we did not attend dances during our visit to Charleston, we went to concerts or the theater. Saturday afternoons we attended horse races and the gentlemen played golf at Harleston's Green. One afternoon I visited the Orphan House with Mrs. Heywood, where we donated food and clothing for unfortunate children.

Instead of resting in the bedroom at the Heywood home afterward, I decided to read in the library, which was next to the parlor. I fell asleep on a settee and awoke when I heard my husband, Mr. Heywood, Mr. Peabody, and another gentleman speaking in the parlor.

"Mr. Heath wrote that he and his partners are prepared to invest fifty percent in the venture if we agree to the other half," said Mr. Peabody.

"I'm not certain that I'm willing to risk so much without a written agreement," my husband said.

"I relayed your apprehension to him, but he said that we cannot put this in writing because the authorities can prosecute anyone who is caught participating in such an endeavor, which, in fact, is a capital crime, punishable by death. He said that, when you arrive in New York, you and he will meet with the captain to give him his deposit. The two of you and Mr. DeWolf will then use the balance of the funds to jointly purchase the ship. Every term of the contract must be oral, but I know that Mr. Heath and his partners are trustworthy because I have conducted a number of these transactions with them," said Mr. Peabody.

"I have as well, and I know them to be honorable," said Mr. Heywood.

"Well then, let's proceed with the arrangements," my husband replied.

We left Charleston after three weeks, arriving in New York late one morning at the Fulton Street piers, which were crowded with ships and boats. Men were loading and unloading crates of goods, and others were peddling wares of all kinds. When we stepped off the gangway, a gentleman, Mr. Merritt, and his two servants were there to greet us. The servants handed us coats, hats, and gloves. Bessie helped me with mine and Eddie assisted my husband. We stepped into a carriage that was waiting for us on Water Street, which could not move until the coachman dug soil out from under the wheels. Once we were traveling, I noticed a pretty boy with pink cheeks chasing a piglet, and there were beggars stationed at various points on the streets, holding their filthy hands out to the people in the carriages. A man standing in front of a butcher block on Fulton Street was throwing entrails and fish heads into a bucket as a dirty child filled a bowl with the discarded viscera. Chickens picked at the mud.

We passed Pearl Street, which was muddy and full of fishmongers, sailors, and numerous people of different provenances. We crossed smaller roads until we reached a marvel that did not exist in either Mobile or Charleston, a street that was paved and more than one hundred feet wide. There were bricked footpaths on either side of Broadway and unlit lamps, which Mr. Merritt said functioned with gas. Broadway had shops wherever one looked: booksellers, print and music shops, jewelers and silversmiths, carriage makers, coffeehouses, and hatters. The carriage took us to the City Hotel, which had elegant stores on the ground level, and we were escorted to an apartment on the second floor. The hotelier spoke to my husband and me in the sitting room as Bessie put away my belongings.

"Please do not allow your servants to leave the hotel without your supervision; it is not safe. If you need anything but don't wish to go out, our staff will send someone to fetch what you desire. The reason for this precaution is that there has been an increase in the kidnapping of Negroes for resale in the Western Territories and elsewhere."

We did not question his advice. He took his leave and another employee returned to escort Bessie to the servants' quarters. I asked my husband why his luggage had not arrived.

"I have leased a separate apartment on another floor. Eddie is there now unpacking."

That afternoon, my husband left to attend to his business and told me to rest after dinner. "We will have supper at the home of

Mr. and Mrs. DeWolf, where you will meet ladies who will show you the city during our stay here."

The next day, Mrs. DeWolf and her friends took me to see St. Paul's Chapel and Trinity Church and the adjoining cemeteries. They showed me parks filled with elms, willows, and poplars, the gravel walks adorned with shrubs. In the evenings, our husbands joined us for dancing at our hotel.

New York had more than twenty newspapers, weekly and monthly magazines, a public library at Nassau Street, and public reading rooms. I felt as if in heaven, there was so much to read. Mrs. DeWolf took me to lectures on moral philosophy and botany, and I purchased books for my library. I could not help but stare at the foreigners, who seemed to be everywhere, speaking among themselves in various tongues. New York was also noisy, mainly because there were constant fires and the engines created a cacophony of sound.

One afternoon not long after our arrival, I went downstairs to the ground level of the hotel to get the *New York Evening Post* and other newspapers. As I was walking to the staircase, a well-dressed lady with hair arranged in the Continental fashion approached me.

"Good afternoon, madam. I am Mrs. Oldwick of Boston, Massachusetts."

"How do you do? I am Mrs. Allen."

"How do you do, Mrs. Allen? I noticed that you purchased reading materials. Please accept this complimentary newspaper. In it, you will note a session of the American Anti-Slavery Society, which will be held at four o'clock tomorrow afternoon at 83 Pearl Street. I invite you to the meeting, and I hope to see you there."

She handed me the newspaper, which was folded, and quickly walked toward the front door of the hotel. An employee of the hotel was standing by the staircase, watching us. When she was gone, he spoke to me.

"Mrs. Allen, is everything all right?"

"Yes, why do you ask?"

"I thought that woman was disturbing you."

I told him that she was merely being friendly, and he went on his way. When I returned to my rooms, I opened the folded newspaper, *The Liberator,* and saw a pamphlet inside called the "Narrative of James Ezekiels, an American Slave, Who Was for Several Years a Driver on a Cotton Plantation in Alabama." I read the newspaper and the pamphlet in one sitting.

When Bessie knocked on my door to help me dress for supper, I put the writings in luggage containing the books that I had bought in Charleston and New York. I let Bessie in, and we selected my clothing for the evening. She had already ordered hot water, and when it arrived, she readied my bath. I could not stop thinking about everything that I had read; so these were the firebrands who sought to abolish slavery about whom my husband and the other planters in Alabama, Georgia, and South Carolina complained. They evidently had never been to our plantations. The planters that I knew cared for their field hands and servants and disciplined them only when they refused to work or tried to escape.

It was nonsense to suggest that the slaves should be freed because they would not be able to care for themselves. The publishers of the pamphlet claimed that one of James Ezekiels's brothers could read and write, but I had never known of a Negro who could do so, although I knew that Northerners published books that they claimed were written by Negroes. Papa, however, taught me when I was younger that there was scientific evidence that the race of the slaves had limited mental faculties and that their brains were smaller than our own. Even President Thomas Jefferson said in his *Notes on the State of Virginia* that Negroes had inferior minds. The narrative that Mrs. Oldwick gave me related tales of the vicious treatment of field hands by an overseer who supposedly had bloodhounds tear a boy into pieces and had whipped pregnant women, one of whom had died after the beating and another thereafter delivered a dead infant.

I did not seriously think of attending the meeting of the Anti-Slavery Society, but I was curious about it, and Mrs. Oldwick seemed like a polite, educated lady. I thought that it would be fascinating to speak with her, to engage in frank conversation about the reality of slaves' lives on a plantation. I could tell her that her understanding of slavery was incorrect and could give her examples of how well our servants and field hands were treated.

"You all right, Mrs. Allen?"

"Yes, Bessie. Thank you. I just have a few things on my mind."

When I was dressed, my husband came to my room to take me to supper and dismissed Bessie.

"Where is the newspaper that that lady gave you?"

"How do you know about that?"

"That's not your concern. Where is it?"

"I burned it in the fireplace."

"Did you read it?"

"In part. It was rubbish."

"Good. That woman will not be permitted in the hotel again. She is an incendiary. What did she say to you?"

"She told me to read the newspaper."

"Should you see her anywhere again, you are not to speak to her. Some of these Northerners are confused and refuse to acknowledge that our cotton is the foundation of the economy. They will try to win some of us to their side, but we will not let that happen, will we? And . . . what is that? Why are you reading the *Evening Post*?"

When he questioned what I was reading, I became angry and, for the first time, I decided to advocate for myself, not only because he had disregarded his matrimonial vows and kept a concubine, whom he even brought on our travels, but also because he forbade me to read, when reading harms no one. "Why should I not?"

"Because its editor is that liberal abolitionist William Cullen Bryant."

"He is a poet, and a well-respected one."

"It is not his poetry that concerns me. Do you not know that he calls for the destruction of the Southern states?"

"Perhaps that is an exaggeration."

"What did you just say to me?" Cornelius grabbed my arm and twisted it until I cried out, and I tried to pull away from him but he tightened his grip. His brows were furrowed and his face was so close to mine that I could smell whiskey in his breath.

"Don't ever speak to me that way again. Do you hear me? And the next time I chastise you, I won't entertain any questions from you."

"You're hurting me. Stop." No one had ever caused me such injury; I was raised in a home where my parents were gentle with me and each other. I was not only shocked by his assault but ashamed that anyone would treat me in this manner. He yelled at me.

"I'll do worse to you if you ever show me disrespect again. And listen to me when I try to teach you something. You'll not read that nonsense again and I'd better not even hear that you have bought a copy of this paper." He threw it in the fireplace.

That Friday evening, we went by boat to the country home of Mr. and Mrs. Heath, which was located in the northeastern part of the island. On Saturday afternoon, I was reading in the parlor after walking in the woods with Mrs. Heath when my husband, Mr. Heath, Mr. DeWolf, and two other gentlemen arrived from riding. Before they went into the library across the hallway, they presented to me a man who was a merchant captain from Maine. They did not close the door of the library, and I could hear their entire conversation.

"We will have to fund the remaining twenty-five percent ourselves, as the bank is not willing to risk more than their present twenty-five percent."

"But I was told in Charleston that we could count on the bank here for fifty percent," my husband said.

"Mr. Allen, perhaps a solution would be to get an investor. I can make an introduction to a gentleman who may be interested in joining this venture," the captain said.

"No, it would be too dangerous to involve more people in this transaction. While prosecutions under the piracy laws are rare, international trafficking in slaves is a capital crime, after all," Mr. Heath said.

"Then we have no other recourse but to fund the remaining twenty-five percent ourselves. I can contribute an additional ten percent," my husband said.

"I will put in another ten," Mr. DeWolf said.

"And I will add the remaining five. Well then, the lawyers will create a second set of documents on Monday with different names for the captain and crew in the event naval officers board the ship on its return voyage. Captain, how much longer until the ship is completed and you can assemble your staff?"

"I believe in two more weeks."

"I cannot stay in New York that long because we have to begin planting the cotton seedlings shortly after I arrive home," my husband said.

"You don't have to be here for these transactions. Once the contract is fully agreed to by all the parties, you may leave. We have your order for one hundred children and fifty adults to be delivered to Mobile."

We remained in New York for five more days, during which time my husband instructed me to purchase Negro cloth and other items in bulk that were not available to us in the South. We then sailed back and retraced our steps through Charleston and Mobile. I looked forward to being home because my husband had promised me that, as soon as we arrived, we would conceive another child, which made me look forward to the future, when I would have children and no longer feel alone in my marital home.

SIX

THEODORA ALLEN

⸎

The years after we returned from New York were marked by my husband's increasingly erratic behavior, often tied to his excessive consumption of spirits and wine, and the births of my three children: Paul, Robert, and Clarissa. The Lord provided me Mary, the slaves' midwife, and Emmeline to safely deliver them, and I never used a physician for any of my pregnancies after the miscarriage.

After our travels to the North, my husband and I entered into an unspoken truce. I never again visited his bedroom, and he spent more time with me in our private quarters. I devoted my time to raising my children and fulfilling my responsibilities as the lady of the household and rarely traveled with my husband outside of Alabama and Georgia. Cornelius exhibited the same mercurial heat of mind as he did in New York when he confronted me about the abolitionist woman, but his fury, which seemed to be connected to reports in the newspapers that the Northern abolitionists were becoming more vocal in Washington in their opposition to slavery, was not constant, and years elapsed without him mistreating me. His abuse was chiefly verbal, but if he had been drinking spirits even more than usual, he sometimes struck me on the body or twisted my arm, as he had done in New York. I told no one about his barbarity because I was ashamed, but also because a man, as head of the family, is expected to censure and discipline his children and his wife. I did not even tell Mrs. Tutwiler because I feared she would tell her husband and he would tell Cornelius, who without a doubt would have savagely compounded my punishment. I also knew that I could never elect to leave him. He would not have allowed me to take my children, and I could never leave them with him even though he never mistreated them in any way—that is, until years later.

I began tutoring my sons when each was six years old, but when Paul was twelve and Robert ten, my husband, over my objection, sent them to Wilton's Academy for Young Gentlemen in Georgia. They attended university at Athens after Wilton's. Paul married a Georgia beauty, and he stayed in that state, working as a banker. Two years later, Robert married a young lady from Charleston, and he moved there, also to work in banking.

I learned that Emmeline was expecting one morning when I went to the kitchen to discuss supper with her and saw her belly. I was uneasy and my heart beat rapidly, thinking that she was likely carrying my husband's child. As was the custom among the servants, she did not look at me when I spoke to her. I forced myself to say something pleasant, and I am not sure why I said what I did.

"Emmeline, you must be so happy to be expecting."

There was silence in the kitchen for several seconds, but it seemed like minutes.

"Yes, ma'am."

I departed after we made arrangements, embarrassed by everyone's and my own discomfort. I did not see Sarah until she was about a few months old, when Emmeline was working in her herbal garden. Sarah, who had light brown hair, was strapped to her mother's back. When Emmeline realized that I was there, she stood and bowed her head. Sarah was smiling, and I noticed that she had dimples like my husband and Clarissa. The anger and jealousy that

I felt years ago, when I found Cornelius and Emmeline in bed, returned, and I had to compose myself to remember why I had sought out Emmeline.

"Good morning, Mrs. Allen. Anything I can do for you, ma'am?"

"Yes, we will have two more guests for supper this evening."

After speaking with her, I almost ran to my husband, who was working in his office with a bookkeeper, and opened the door without knocking.

"Yes, Theodora. How may I assist you?"

"May I speak with you privately?"

"Is it a pressing matter? We are rather preoccupied, as you can see."

"Yes, it is."

He dismissed Clark.

"I thought that you were no longer with Emmeline."

It is only now that I can acknowledge that I never believed he had stopped summoning Emmeline to his apartment, even though he was spending most nights with me beginning in the years after we returned from our travels to the North. The truth was that when I saw Sarah for the first time I simply wanted to confront him about what he had done and I had been too cowardly to say anything to him about Emmeline before I saw Sarah that day.

He stared at me and tapped his pen on the paper, splattering ink and obscuring the numbers on the page. "Theodora, you misrepresented your reason for being here. You said that it was an urgent matter."

"I just learned today that you fathered a child with a servant. How is that not a pressing concern?"

"I have shipments to account for that are going to Europe and the Northeast, I have an entire plantation to manage, and you think that women's concerns are important? And really, you have known about Emmeline for . . . how many years? And I never told you that I was no longer with her. Enough. Kindly depart and tell Clark to return. Did you not hear me? You are dismissed."

We had twelve guests that evening, including Mr. and Mrs.

Tutwiler. Mrs. Tutwiler was my dearest friend by this time, and she and Mr. Tutwiler sometimes stayed with me whenever my husband traveled. I told her, when we had a moment alone in my garden, that my husband had fathered a child with Emmeline.

"My dear, these men are such rascals, and I fear that their decadence will be the ruin of us all. But what can we do? We can ask them to change their ways for the sake of their immortal souls, and we may appeal to their sense of duty, but don't you believe that a male is innately a different being than a woman? We do not have their uncontrollable urges, after all. We are most interested in pursuing what is beautiful and ethereal, not what is physical and coarse. Dear Theo, your husband isn't the only one; Mr. Tutwiler, by my count, has at least eight children, with field hands, no less. But if you add eight to the balance sheet at the prices they fetch at auction, when you reflect upon it, it is a benefit to us, is it not?"

"I suppose I do have a rather romantic view of marriage and that it should be between one man and one woman. But I suppose those unions exist only between the pages of fanciful novels written by ladies."

My bitter conclusion that harmonious marriages only existed in romantic novels was one that I had reached only after many years of my husband's betrayal, but I did not share these thoughts with Mrs. Tutwiler, who thought it a blessing that her husband kept concubines and had children with them.

"Theodora, don't dwell on these matters. Your daughter is your companion. Teach her all you know so that she becomes a young lady of virtue and grace."

I accepted Mrs. Tutwiler's advice and devoted myself to my daughter. Bessie selected a girl to help me care for her. Clarissa was a sensitive child, and I found that, from infancy, she was happy if Sarah was with her. I told Emmeline to allow Sarah to play in the nursery. When the girls began walking, I permitted them to run on the grass in my garden and Emmeline let them play in the yard outside the kitchen. When Clarissa was weaned at the age of two, we spent almost all our time together, and I stopped traveling with my husband.

The girl who minded the children taught them the same games that my cousin Eliza and I played when we were children: hide-and-seek, stealing bases, and jumping rope. At Christmas, my husband and I gave special gifts to all the house servants in addition to the annual gifts of bolts of cloth, shoes, pork, and sacks of rice, sugar, and other foods. We gave Sarah new toys every year because Clarissa enjoyed dressing her dolls with her little companion.

I taught Clarissa to care for those less fortunate. When she was six years old, I took her along when I delivered food and other necessities to the families of the overseers who worked on our plantation. She accompanied my husband and me to the slave quarters at Christmas when we gave the field hands their new clothing and shoes and hams. I thought that she would be frightened of going there, but she helped us hand out sweets to the children. When Clarissa and Sarah turned eight, I told Bessie to begin teaching Sarah to be Clarissa's maid, and I began giving lessons to Clarissa.

From the first week, she repeatedly complained that Sarah was not with her, and we made no progress. We spent only three hours a day on lessons, and yet Clarissa fidgeted until I dismissed her. She found Sarah wherever she was helping her mother or Bessie and took her to the yard or to Clarissa's room to play. My husband asked me at supper how Clarissa was doing in her learning.

"Not well at all, I'm afraid. She does not pay attention and prefers to play with her maid."

"Papa, lessons are so boring. Why can't I play with Sarah instead?"

"Because, young missy, you will be the lady of your own home one day, and thus you will need to know how to read and write and do figures. All ladies and gentlemen must have an education. You will mind your mother and pay attention when she is teaching you, or I will join you as your schoolmaster. That, I am sure, you would not enjoy."

"No, Papa. Please don't come to my lessons. That would be twice as boring. Papa, why can't Sarah come to lessons? Mama, you let her stay when you read to us."

My husband and I looked at each other. He answered her. "Sarah does not need to know how to read and write to be your maid, dear."

"But it's just to keep me company, Papa."

We thought that Clarissa had abandoned her notion of having Sarah join her in the nursery for lessons, but she raised the subject again when I was teaching her. I was so exasperated with her that I threatened to tell her father that she was being disobedient.

"I don't care if you tell him. I'm not doing lessons unless Sarah is with me."

I spoke with my husband, and he granted permission for Sarah to be with Clarissa during her lessons. "But, Theodora, you are only to teach Clarissa. Is that clear? Under no circumstance are you to try to teach Sarah to read or write. It is unlawful, and I am sure that you understand why it is dangerous for any slave to become literate."

"Do you believe it's possible that she can learn?"

"I do not, but there are reports from the North that some Negroes can. I believe it is abolitionist nonsense, but one can never be too cautious."

I knew that I needed to do something to make Clarissa pay attention to her studies. Oddly, I was curious about whether Negroes could learn to read and write and I told Emmeline and Bessie to excuse Sarah from her duties. Emmeline unexpectedly spoke her mind.

"Ma'am, please, can I say something?"

"Yes, of course, Emmeline."

"Thank you, ma'am. Ma'am, I need Sarah to help me with the cleaning, and Bessie's teaching her to be Miss Clarissa's maid, so it's best, I think, that she go on with her work, ma'am, if you please."

"Lessons are only in the morning. My husband and I have already discussed the matter, and this is what we both wish."

"Thank you, ma'am."

With Sarah in attendance, Clarissa made significance progress. She learned to read so well that she read all the books in the nursery to Sarah and me. In all the years of lessons, Sarah missed a class only when there was much work to do, usually because we were having a large number of guests.

When Clarissa was thirteen, my husband and I agreed that I had taught her as much as I could and he retained a tutor, Mrs. Ellsworth, for her. I informed Emmeline that Sarah would no longer attend lessons with Clarissa. Clarissa did not complain because she had learned that, to be a proper lady, she had to be educated. In addition to her academic studies, the tutor taught her how to play the violin and piano. Clarissa's skills in painting watercolors also improved.

The year Clarissa turned sixteen, she showed an interest in making social calls to the young ladies who lived in neighboring plantations and went with me when I visited with Mrs. Tutwiler, who had a girl and two sons near Clarissa's age. I asked my husband to obtain a seamstress for Clarissa because she needed more dresses for the balls and parties that we held at home and those we attended in Talladega, Montgomery, and, in the winter season, Mobile. We permitted Clarissa to make social calls with Sarah and Isaac, the foreman of the stables, who that year also became Clarissa's coachman, as her chaperones. We held Clarissa's presentation at her grandparents' home in Montgomery. Clarissa had to add a second page to her dance card, as my husband had invited planters and their families from Georgia, the Carolinas, Virginia, and Louisiana. That night, after the ball, we and our families stayed up late asking Clarissa which young men she favored. She refused to tell us and laughed as we mentioned young men with whom she had danced more than once.

That year, my husband said that it was time for Clarissa to learn how to shoot.

"Papa, I don't need to go hunting."

"You don't need to learn how to shoot for hunting. Now that you are a young lady and will travel farther without me to visit your suitors' families, I would rest better if you knew how to handle a gun."

"That's a dreadful idea. Why don't you send an overseer to accompany me?"

"I don't trust overseers to protect you and your mother from the slaves. Besides, you don't only need to know how to use a gun to travel. You need to know how to shoot so that when I travel you can protect yourself, and when you marry and your husband travels and you stay home, you will be able to protect yourself as well. Your mother knows how to shoot."

"Yes, Papa taught me when I was sixteen. At least twice a year, your father takes me hunting for practice, and I am glad that I know how to use a gun. Clarissa, we keep a gun in the small trunk that we carry in each carriage. Do not divulge that information to anyone. By the way, your tutor knows how to use a gun."

My husband took Clarissa to an area not far from the fields and, over the course of a week, taught her how to shoot. He said that she was so good that she hit targets while riding on horseback.

We held a ball or an evening party at least once a month so that Clarissa could spend more time with the young gentlemen of the largest neighboring plantations. When she and I went to Montgomery to visit her grandparents, Clarissa became infatuated with a young gentleman there, Mr. Evans, who was educated in the North and in England. He was home learning how to manage his father's plantation. I warned Clarissa that she was too young to become attached to one suitor, but she did not mind me. She spent a week at the young man's home while I stayed with my parents-in-law. I had persuaded Mrs. Tutwiler to join me in Montgomery, and we attended ladies' teas in the reading room of Miss Whitefield's Young Ladies' Academy, where a poetess from Charleston was in residence. After we returned home, Clarissa continued her parties and making social calls to other plantations with Sarah and Isaac. One day, my husband received a letter from Mr. Jebediah Cromwell of Talladega seeking the introduction of his son, Mr. Julius Cromwell, to Clarissa.

"Theodora, he's about fifteen years older than Clarissa. He unfortunately did not complete his education. He was at West Point but was sent home under some circumstance or the other."

"Why is he not married?"

"He was, but his wife died in an accident. He was teaching her how to shoot, a task her father apparently neglected, and she died from a wound they say was self-inflicted."

"Oh no. I don't want to have him presented to Clarissa, not with his history."

"But he was cleared after an inquest. Other people who were present, including her brothers, testified that her death was an accident and corroborated his version of the facts. Besides, there was no motive for any wrongdoing. She was, by all accounts, a beauty, and they had been married less than a year. She was expecting their child."

"How long ago was this?"

"About eight years ago. Now his father wants him to remarry."

"But Clarissa has so many suitable suitors, and she is quite taken with Mr. Evans."

"None of her suitors are like this one. The father's wealth is almost as great as mine, and the younger Cromwell's mother is from an equally prosperous shipping family from South Carolina. I want Clarissa to meet him. Let's invite the Cromwells to spend a few days with us. Plan a ball and other entertainment for them. I will write him. How much time do you need for Clarissa's clothing? And she can wear the jewels that my mother gave her."

"She has plenty of dresses from this season that we ordered from New York."

"No, have Davis order new dresses from Mobile or New Orleans, wherever you can get them the quickest. Let's say that we will invite them for the end of November."

When I told Clarissa about Julius Cromwell, she asked his age and refused to meet him.

"Sweetness, your father made the decision that Mr. Cromwell will be presented to you. If you do not find him agreeable, your father will weigh that in his deliberations as regards whether you will marry him."

"I don't care. Why can't I continue to see gentlemen who are younger than he is? Good Lord, he is old enough to be my father."

"Clarissa. Never use the Lord's name in vain and avoid employing hyperbole."

"I'm sorry, Mama. I'll say a special prayer and ask the Lord's forgiveness. As for my exaggeration, you will have to punish me. But Mama, please ask Papa to reconsider his decision."

"I will ask your father nothing; his decision is made. We have to order your dresses and shoes."

"Why didn't you say that I would get new dresses?"

"You silly girl. What am I going to do with you?"

The day the Cromwells arrived, I told Mrs. Ellsworth to keep Clarissa occupied with her studies and to take dinner with her in the former nursery, which I had converted into a lesson room. That evening, when I went to Clarissa's room, she said that she was not going to meet Mr. Cromwell. I ordered her to get ready for supper and told Sarah to rub lavender lotion on Clarissa's face to remove the puffiness and redness caused by her crying. I threatened Clarissa with a visit from her father. When she was dressed, I went to her room and helped her put on the jewelry that her grandmother had given her. Bessie arranged a sapphire and diamond diadem in Clarissa's hair. When we arrived at the parlor, where everyone was having champagne and cordials before supper, they stopped speaking to stare at her. Mr. Julius Cromwell looked much younger than his age and had maintained his fair hair.

"You are much more beautiful in person than I was told," he said to her.

We allowed Clarissa and Julius to spend time together. I sat them next to each other at supper, and he entertained her with stories about his travels. The following week Clarissa visited the Cromwells. Sarah and Isaac served as her chaperones, as Mrs. Ellsworth had to visit her family in Montgomery. Clarissa wrote my husband and me from Talladega that they were staying for another week. My husband was pleased and said that we should discuss a wedding date with the Cromwells immediately after Clarissa's eighteenth birthday. While Clarissa was away, she received a letter from Mr. Evans, the suitor from Montgomery. When she returned home, we spoke to her about her betrothal to Julius but did not give her Mr. Evans's letter.

"Mama, Papa, I don't want to pledge to be married. As much as I enjoyed spending time with Mr. Cromwell, I prefer Mr. Evans. In fact, I'd like to visit him."

"You are trying our patience. You are not going to Montgomery, and you do not have my permission to continue to entertain Mr. Evans's attentions," my husband said.

Clarissa cried and balled her fists, just as she did when she was a little girl and we denied a request. Mr. Cromwell wrote her once a week, and she wrote him in return, but she did not tell us what they said to each other. She did not speak again about Mr. Evans, but when we went to see my parents-in-law for the holidays, Clarissa saw the young man at the constant round of balls and parties. She promised us that he was not a serious contender for her affections. Julius came to see us, and my husband consented to his request for permission to marry our daughter.

"I suppose that I'll be ready to be a married lady in two years," Clarissa said.

I sensed that she thought of two years' time as being far into the future. She continued to visit Julius in Talladega and her grandparents in Montgomery.

One evening we were alone in her room and I was brushing her hair before she went to bed.

"Mama, do you think it's peculiar that Mr. Cromwell's first wife shot herself?"

"How do you know about that?"

"David Tutwiler told his sister and me."

"Yes, it did give me pause when I heard that."

"Why didn't you tell me?"

"Because I did not want to prejudice you against him, and your father is satisfied with the explanation of the circumstances. He said that there was an inquest, an investigation by the court, and that witnesses testified it was an accident."

"But when Papa taught me to shoot, the first thing he showed me was how to hold the gun and keep the safety on."

"Perhaps Mr. Cromwell was not as good an instructor as your father."

"But he went to West Point."

"Darling, that was not the first shooting accident that ever occurred. And your father says he was told that Mr. Cromwell loved his first wife. But you have spent a substantial amount of time with him. Does he give you reason to feel uncomfortable?"

"Well . . . no. I can't explain it, but sometimes he seems a bit, how shall I say it, unsettled?"

SEVEN

SARAH CAMPBELL

One afternoon in January of 1853, the year I was seven-teen, I was alone in the kitchen drying cooking herbs to be stored in the pantry when I heard a horse come to a stop. I went outside to investigate and saw a tall stranger wearing a coachman's navy blue uniform trimmed with gold braiding. For-getting my manners, I stared at the beautiful man standing before me, who was taller than I and had curly golden hair and gray eyes. He removed his hat, and I saw his dimples when he smiled at me.

"Morning, ma'am. My name is Isaac, and I'm a new coachman here. Just started last Monday. Might you be Miss Sarah? Can I trouble you for a glass of water? I'm sorry, Miss Sarah. I didn't in-tend to startle you," he said, when I did not answer.

I shook myself out of my daydream. "How do you know me?"

"Miss Emmeline. I saw her in front of the Hall, and she said to ask you for something cool to drink."

"Please come in and I will get you that water, or would you like sweet tea and peach cobbler?"

"Sweet tea and peach cobbler sounds good, Miss Sarah."

Using Mrs. Allen's crystal, silver, and china, I prepared two glasses of tea and two dessert plates. I joined him at the table, and we laughed when we spoke at the same time. I had started to ask him how he liked his new position, and he began to speak as I asked.

"Your eyes shine like light when you laugh," he said.

Emboldened by his flattery and curious about why he spoke so well, I asked him when he had arrived and where he lived before Allen Estates.

"I was born and lived not too far from Mobile, on a plantation owned by Mr. Allen's brother, Master Charles Allen. Master Charles was good to me, and he hired an Englishman when I was a bitty boy of eleven to teach me about horses. By the time I was eighteen, I was the foreman of all his stables. Master Charles used to hire me out to other plantations to teach the coachmen how to ride and take care of their horses. I used to go to Florida, Mississippi, and Georgia, working at different plantations, and he let me keep some of the money I earned."

"Did he let you go by yourself?"

"Yes, he always gave me a pass, and I only rode by day. I came here because Mr. Allen told Master Charles that he needed a foreman to look after his stables."

I kept my hands in my lap because I did not want him to see them shaking. I could think of nothing to say, but I kept thinking that he knew the land and the roads beyond Allen Estates. We were silent for a time.

"I need to get back to the stables. Can I call on you again, Miss Sarah?"

"Yes," I said, perhaps with too much enthusiasm.

That evening, as we were preparing supper, my mother teased me about Isaac.

"Why don't you take your young man a basket and have supper with him at the other kitchen?"

"Mama, please. He is not my young man."

My mother laughed. "Go on, Belle and me will finish up."

When supper was ready, I prepared plates with enough food for

Isaac and me. My mother gave me a large covered jar of tea and two glasses, and I arranged everything in a basket. I tidied myself in our cabin and asked my mother if I could remove the cloth from my head.

"No, not yet, baby. In time. Just put on the head cover with the pretty flowers on it. You look real nice with it."

Isaac was not there when I arrived at the kitchen and meal room for the slaves who worked in trades and in the stables. One of the cooks sent a young boy for Isaac. When he walked in, he looked even more exquisite than I recalled.

"My mother sent you supper."

"Thank you, Miss Sarah."

I arranged the food. Soon other slaves began arriving and sat around us at the long table. The men looked at us and smiled. I did not mind. I asked Isaac what he had done that day, whether he had traveled. He said that he had only driven to the neighboring Greystone Plantation to help with two horses that were sick. One had a broken foreleg and had to be put down. Everyone ate quickly because we had to return to work after supper. Isaac said that he would be awake all night, tending to one of the animals in the stables. He said that he would call on me the next day. I returned to Allen Hall after eating with him because I had to ready Clarissa's bath.

That night, I could not concentrate on my reading of Mr. Wordsworth's poetry about the English countryside. My only thoughts were about Isaac, who did not look like the other slaves. The skin on his hands was smooth and his fingernails were clean. Isaac's coachman's uniforms were made of the finest fabrics and his boots from calf's leather. My mind was troubled, perhaps because part of my interest in Isaac was the possibility of fleeing with him from Allen Estates. Exhausted by my thoughts, I closed my book, hid it in the washroom, and went to our cabin to sleep.

The next afternoon, as I was cleaning the kitchen after dinner, Isaac came to see me. "Is there any tea and peach cobbler for a tired coachman?"

I set the drinks and cobbler on the table. We spent some moments together, not speaking, just enjoying the sweets.

"What are you thinking about?" he asked me.

"Oh, nothing. Well, just all those times that you traveled by yourself. Did you ever think of not going back?"

His reaction was frightening. He looked around the kitchen as if there were someone in hiding. "No, never. Look, maybe it's because you're so young, but I figured Miss Emmeline had taught you better. You can't talk about these things. And no, I have a good life. I saved money from when I was at Master Charles's. When he sold me to Mr. Allen it was so Mr. Allen was going to hire me out and let me keep some of the money. I plan to buy my freedom someday. If I have a wife and children when that day comes, of course I'll buy them, too. If I tried to do it any other way, I could get hurt and sent to work in the fields. Sarah, don't be so trusting. Don't ever say such things to someone you just met. They could tell Mr. Allen what you asked about."

I began to cry, but he smiled at me and told me that we should forget about it and never mention the conversation again. He finished his pie and returned to the stables. I did not see him for almost a month after that day because he did not come around, and we were occupied with preparing for Mrs. Allen's family from Georgia. I learned from my mother that Mr. Allen had hired out Isaac to the Greystone Plantation. She told me when he returned and said that I should go to see him after we had our midday meal. At the stables, I saw Isaac grooming a horse, a tremendous animal, but Isaac was gentle with it, and the great beast seemed to enjoy being brushed.

"I was going to come to see you, but I've been training some boys Mr. Allen just bought before he hires me out again, this time to Georgia."

Isaac must have noticed my disappointment.

"That's all right, baby girl. I'm putting aside money for us."

I smiled. "Come by for supper before you get sent out again."

"I will."

I almost skipped back to Allen Hall. There was a commotion when I stepped in the kitchen. My mother ordered me to put on an apron and help with the cooking before I went upstairs to help Clarissa dress for supper. She told me that the Allens had a visitor, a gentleman who was courting Clarissa. When my mother dismissed me, I went to the Hall and found Clarissa sitting on her bed, crying. Her mother stood in front of her.

"Puppet, your father has granted Mr. Cromwell permission to marry you. The decision is final."

"I don't care, and I told you already, I don't like Mr. Cromwell. He's an old man. I won't go to supper. I won't."

"Clarissa, stop behaving like a child. You must do what is expected of you as a lady. It is time to plan your marriage. You cannot spend the rest of your life going to dances and visiting different gentlemen."

"I don't care. I won't marry him."

"Darling, when you are married, you will not be far and you will visit with us, as we will visit with you. And, I am sure, Puppet, your papa will allow you to have Sarah as your maid."

That was how I learned what my future was to be, and my only thought was that my dreams of escaping were those of a fool. My absurd notions of running away or being bought into freedom by Isaac were exposed for what they were, empty plans made by a girl in bondage.

"Sarah, are you crying?"

I did not answer.

"Answer me when I speak to you," Mrs. Allen said.

"No, no, ma'am. I'm sorry, ma'am."

"Sarah, you are not being a good little maid to Clarissa. I will have to tell Emmeline to speak with you. Prepare Clarissa's bath and get her ready for supper."

She left the room, and I remained standing, unable to move.

"Sarah, why can't you be like Bessie? Mama has an obedient

maid who came with her all the way from Georgia, but you cry when you hear that you'll be living with me when I marry. If you don't want to come with me, I'll ask Papa to give me another maid and to send you to work in the fields."

I helped Clarissa bathe and dress and consoled myself with the thought that perhaps, after all, this turn in my life would provide a way to escape. When Clarissa returned to her rooms after supper, I was preparing her for bed, and she seemed happy. She said that everyone had told her that she was beautiful and that she had changed her mind about Mr. Cromwell, a planter in Talladega from a family that had been prosperous for many generations. The Cromwells, said Clarissa, were almost as wealthy as the Allens.

"His father owns a shipbuilding yard in Mobile and trades in goods with other nations."

"What about Mr. Evans?"

"I will continue to visit him when I go to Montgomery to see Grandmamma and Grandpapa. But Papa would never let me marry Mr. Evans because his father only owns about fifty slaves and his plantation is small."

I could not stop thinking about this change in my life. I did not want to live away from my mother and Belle, and I wondered what would happen to Isaac and me. If I was expected to couple with Isaac as my mother had indicated, would he also be sold or given to Julius Cromwell? I hoped that my mother would have answers to my questions, and in the morning I asked her what was going to happen to Isaac and me.

"Baby, I don't know. You think Mr. Allen tell me what he's going to do? But he did say that I should get you married to Isaac."

"When were you going to tell me, Mama?"

"I wanted to see what you thought about him."

"But Mama, is Mr. Allen going to let Isaac go with me when Clarissa gets married?"

"Miss Clarissa, Sarah."

"Yes, ma'am."

"I think so, baby. That's why he said to get you married to him. And he want you and Belle to be settled down. But I need you to help me with Belle. She don't want to listen to me, and Mr. Allen said to get her with a abroad man. She said that she never want to have nothing to do with no man again, not like I blame my baby, after what she's been through. Mr. Allen said he talked to Mr. Atkins, and Mr. Atkins is going to hire out one of his blacksmiths to come here so Belle and him can get to know each other. That was the best I could do."

"What if Belle doesn't like him?"

"Mr. Allen said he'd try one more time and get Mr. Atkins to send somebody else, but Mr. Allen said that'd be it. He said the only other thing she can do is go down to where the field hands be and find a man there. He said that's because it's been two years since she had the girls and it's time to have some sons."

"Poor Belle. I'm sure that you tried to get him to change his mind."

"No, I didn't, really. I got to be careful about what I say to him, especially when it got to do with saying when any of his slaves should have babies."

When I spoke to Belle, she was resigned about having to get an abroad man.

"Sarah, it ain't no secret that Mr. Allen want us all to have babies. At least Mama got him to agree that I can see if I like the man first, and if I don't, I can say no and try meeting another one."

The blacksmith, Zeke, arrived the following week, and he escorted Belle to a gathering at the slave quarters on a Saturday night. Belle invited him to meals at the kitchen after that, and he met her girls. He remained at Allen Estates for a month. When he left, Belle told my mother that she consented to him as her abroad man. My mother relayed the information to Mr. Allen, who ordered the Hall overseers to build a cabin equipped with furnishings for Belle and her daughters. Once Belle was in her own cabin, Zeke returned, and they established a pattern whereby he, as an abroad man, spent

Saturdays and Sundays with her and returned to the Atkins plantation Monday mornings. The girls stayed with Mama and me at night
when Zeke was with Belle.

Two months after Zeke became Belle's abroad husband, my
mother made arrangements for my marriage to Isaac. She obtained
permission from Mr. Allen to have a celebration in the meal room
where Isaac and the other skilled slaves ate. He consented and agreed
to pay all the costs. Dottie, Mrs. Allen's seamstress, made my wedding dress. My mother and the rest of us who worked in the Allen
kitchen cooked and baked the morning of my wedding. Some cooks
from the other kitchens were brought in to help, as the Allens'
meals for the day also had to be prepared.

Mr. Allen permitted Bessie, Dottie, most of the Hall servants,
and Miss Mary and her family to attend. My mother said that I did
not have to wrap my hair. She made two braids intertwined with
blue stars from her garden and tied them in a knot on top. Her smile
told me that I made an acceptable bride.

There was no ceremony because the preacher was not allowed
to marry us as our marriages were not lawful. After we ate, Isaac
and I went to his—now our—cabin. I was anxious about the night,
but when Isaac kissed me, I forgot my worries. When he undid my
braids, the flowers fell on the floor. Then he helped me with the
buttons in the back of my frock. While he was undressing himself,
I turned my gaze away at first, but then I saw that his body was as
beautiful as his face. He lay next to me, kissing my lips, my neck,
and each inch of my skin. When he was inside me, I could not separate the pain from the exquisite sweetness that spread through my
body.

With the exception of our nighttime coupling, our lives continued their routine of working from dawn until late evening. As any
new bride, I wanted to make our cabin pretty. Mrs. Allen ordered
the seamstresses to sew linens for us and the furniture makers to
build a table, chairs, cabinets, and a new bed. I planted vegetables in
the little garden. Soon I had made a home for my husband and me.

My monthly bleeding ended when Isaac and I had been married for two months. When I realized that I was expecting, Isaac had been hired out to a plantation and would be away for another week. I spent the night crying. In the morning, when I went to the kitchen, my mother asked why my eyes were swollen.

"Because I miss Isaac."

She seemed satisfied with my answer. At the end of the day, I asked my mother and Belle if Belle could sleep in my cabin that night because I did not want to be alone.

"Yes, and Emmie and Ruby can stay with me. I don't have to go to Mr. Allen," my mother said.

As soon as we were in my home, I told Belle that my bleeding had not come down. "Belle, I lied to Mama. I think I'm going to have a baby, and I don't want to because if I do, I can't ever run away."

Belle took my hand and spoke firmly to me.

"Sarah, you're a grown, married woman now, but you're still talking like a child about running away. I thought you was happy with Isaac. So why do you want to run?"

"I am happy with him, but I'm not happy here. It's not like anything has changed just because I got married. We still live in fear that Mr. Allen is going to do something to us, that he's going to get tired of Mama and sell us all. Did you ever think about that, Belle? What if he decided to sell . . . No, I can't even say it. But really, what if he gets tired of Mama? What's going to happen to all of us?"

"Sarah, what's going to happen is going to happen. Ain't nothing we can do about it. Yes, I do think about it, all the time, but all we can do is be obedient and pray that he won't do something like what he did to me again. And anyway, even if you ain't got no baby, you can't run. Look at what happened to my own papa. Look at what happened to me. You can't run, Sarah, that's just a dream. And anyway, if you try to take the baby out, you could die."

"What? What do you mean take the baby out?"

"Nothing, never mind. I'm just talking foolishness."

"Belle, what did you mean take the baby out? Tell me."

She did not answer.

"Tell me . . . Belle."

"All right, but don't say this to nobody. When they had me at Master Reynolds's, they said a field hand died when she got another girl to help her try to take her baby out."

"But what do you mean, take the baby out?"

"They told me they put a knitting needle or something like that inside that made her bleed and that made the baby come out."

"That sounds like it would hurt too much. I couldn't do that. The only thing I can do is . . . never mind."

"The only thing you could do is what, Sarah?"

"Kill myself. I won't spend the rest of my life like this."

"Sarah, don't even talk like that."

"Why not, because it's a crime for slaves to talk about killing themselves? If you think about it, Belle, that's the only power we have over Mr. Allen, and that's why it's a crime. If I want to kill myself, I'll go ahead and do it because it's my life, not Mr. Allen's."

"Sarah, I don't know what Mama and me do without you. Please don't say that again, please. We love you so much. Baby girl, promise me that you won't do that."

"All right, I promise. Besides, I don't think I'd have the courage to do it anyway. And it's a sin. I wouldn't see you, Mama, and the girls in heaven. But I need to do something."

"This is what I'll do. I'll go by the field tomorrow and see Miss Mary. I know she ain't going to say nothing to nobody if I ask her if there's something she can give somebody to bring down the bleeding. Sarah, you do know that, if Mr. Allen find out anybody is asking for something like that, they could be beaten and sold? But Miss Mary, she won't say nothing because she's like our own auntie, that's what she is."

The next day, Belle whispered to me, even though we were alone, that Miss Mary had given her four herbs, three of which she already knew. I knew that Belle did not want us to be overheard because I remembered Mama's admonition when she was teaching me about herbs that we were not supposed to know about because some were poisonous. Belle opened the shutters and looked outside to ensure that no one was nearby who could hear us. A boy was whistling as he walked on the path in front of our cabin, but then turned and went in another direction. Belle closed the shutters and said that Miss Mary taught her about the fourth herb and gave her instructions for preparation of all four together. Belle had placed the herbs at the bottom of a basket and covered them with a cloth. On top of them, she had placed ordinary cooking herbs that Miss Mary had sent to our mother, whom we told that I still needed Belle's company that night.

"You all go ahead. Mr. Allen ain't back yet," Mama said.

That evening, after our work was done, we went to my cabin. We lit a fire, and Belle brewed separate teas from the three herbs: goldenseal, pennyroyal, and cotton root bark. The fourth herb, blue cohosh, she placed in a jar and poured rum on it that I kept in the kitchen for cooking. She covered the jar and hid it amongst my cooking wares. The blue cohosh, said Belle, had to sit until the next evening. Once the teas had cooled, I drank each, grimacing as bitterness stung my mouth and throat. I felt nothing afterward, other than a horrible taste that lingered on my tongue.

The following morning, we learned that Mr. Allen had returned to Allen Estates. Mr. Davis, one of the Hall overseers, told my mother to go to the Hall that night. Belle said that we had to continue with the remedies for the next two nights and that she would not be able to sleep in my cabin because she needed to care for her girls. She told me to take the herbs, including the jar with the blue cohosh, and sleep in her cabin.

The next two days, I still felt nothing and my days were uneventful, but the third evening, while we were cleaning the kitchen, I felt jabbing pains in my abdomen. I told my mother and Belle that I had to go to the outhouse. There, I looked but there was no blood on my undergarments. I returned to the kitchen and continued my work. As I was washing a pot, I felt a stab of pain so strong that I tumbled to the floor. My mother and Belle helped me to my mother's cabin. I told them that I felt something on my legs and lifted my dress. Blood had soaked through my undergarments and had flowed past my knees. The sharp pain in my abdomen intensified. My mother asked me why my bleeding was so heavy and whether I had missed my last monthly.

"Yes, ma'am. It didn't come down last month."

I tried not to cry as the pain worsened, though the bleeding seemed to ebb. My mother sat next to me on the bed, periodically feeling my forehead and throat. She asked Belle to make me camphor tea. After a while, my mother felt my forehead again and told Belle to ask Mr. Davis to find someone to take her to the slave quarters to bring back Miss Mary.

"Tell her what happened and that the bleeding stopped, but the pain is still bad and she got a fever."

Belle left and my mother tried to comfort me. The ache throbbed, and I screamed every so often when I thought I could not stand the pain a moment longer. Belle returned with Miss Mary, who brought a carpenter's satchel. She felt my forehead and throat.

"She's burning up. I got to give her something for the fever."

"Can you give her something to make all the blood come down?"

Miss Mary looked at Belle and me. "I thought you sent Belle down to me the other day. I gave her herbs to bring down the bleeding, but I thought it was for her. If I give Sarah more now, that could kill her, like poison."

"But if it don't all come out, she's going die. What's still left in her is going to rot inside. Please, do what you got to do to take it all out."

"I can't do that here. She's going to scream too much from the pain, and I'm going to need the girls who help me with these things. We're going to have to take her over to a cabin that I use in the fields. If Mr. Davis ask, we got to tell him she's sick but for me to take care of her she's going to have to come with me because I got to look after some girls who about to have their babies. Get her ready and let's go. Bring all them clean rags, more if you can find any."

They helped me to a wagon, and a slave took Miss Mary, my mother, and me to the slave quarters. I felt a torturous pain every time the cart's wheels rolled over a small stone. They led us to a well-maintained cabin where, I later learned, the field hands gave birth. Miss Mary left us there and returned about thirty minutes later with three other bondswomen. My mother helped them to remove my clothing, and someone brought me a cup of whiskey and told me to drink. I almost choked on the liquid, but after the first cup, they made me drink another. I became lightheaded. Someone put a rag that had been soaked in tea in my mouth. Miss Mary told me to suck on the rag and to bite down on it because it would ease the pain. As soon as I sucked the tea out of the rag, they gave me another one. After I was done with the second rag, I was floating above everyone. I heard Miss Mary speaking, giving orders to my mother and the other women.

"All right, Miss Emmeline and Cissy going to hold her down by the shoulders and waist. Diana and Fanny, you all know what to do, hold her down by the knees and feet. She's going to ask you to let go, but you can't. If she move, the needle can go right through her."

Fear overtook me and I began pleading. "Please, no. Just let me go. Don't stick a needle in me. Let me go. Let me go, please. Let me go."

They did not release me but placed a folded cloth under my buttocks and spread my legs wide.

"Sarah, Miss Mary's about to put a knitting needle inside you. Don't move, Sarah. You can't move at all, you hear me?"

"Mama, make her stop. Don't let her, please. I beg you—don't let her. I changed my mind. I don't want to do this."

"Shush, my darling. It's going be over soon. She's got to do it, Sarah. If that blood stay inside you, you going to die."

When the tip of the needle reached my insides, my body tried to jerk, but the women held me down. The rag fell from my mouth, and I screamed so loudly that I was sure they could hear me all the way at Allen Hall. I had never felt a pain so intense. I momentarily lost consciousness when Miss Mary began moving the needle inside me in a circular motion. When I regained my senses, I could not speak, not even to plead for mercy. I could not cry because I had no tears left in me.

When Miss Mary finally withdrew the needle, her hand was covered in blood. After wiping me, she asked for another rag soaked in tea, which she folded into the shape of a tube and inserted inside me. Someone wiped me with cool cloths and dressed me in a long blouse. Miss Mary told Cissy, Diana, and Fanny that they could leave. My mother thanked them for helping us. Throughout the night, I vomited various times, and my mother brought me ginger and cinnamon teas to ease the nausea.

In the early morning, before dawn, one of the slaves took us back to my mother's cabin. Belle brought us food and stayed with me so that my mother could return to the Hall to work. Belle and my mother took turns caring for me for the next several days. My mother explained my absence to the Hall overseer by saying that I had a fever. Belle assumed my duties as Clarissa's maid. When I was strong enough to return to Allen Hall, I still felt quite a bit of pain and continued to bleed, heavily at times.

I resumed my duties caring for Clarissa, who claimed that she wanted to marry Mr. Cromwell and chattered about gowns, shoes, and gloves. Her incessant chatter made me want to slap her, as she had done to me when we were children. She had not matured much since then; she continued to do whatever she wanted and to spend all her time pursuing pleasure, at dances and dinners and anywhere she knew young men would be present.

When Isaac was home, the week after my ordeal, I told him that I had lost a baby. He did not ask me any questions and said only that I should not be concerned, as we would have one the next time. He also said that the overseer at the stables had informed him that he was going to be Clarissa's new coachman in addition to being the foreman at the stables for Allen Hall.

Isaac's first journey with Clarissa and me was to her grandparents in Montgomery. The day we arrived, Clarissa, who was staying by herself in the guest quarters, told me that she would not need me in the evenings and made arrangements for Isaac and me to sleep in a cabin near the servants' homes. Isaac said that I should not wait for him that first night, as one of the horses was sick and he was going to care for it until late.

We remained in Montgomery longer than I expected, about three weeks. During the day, Clarissa made social calls. I was alone at night because Isaac said that the horses were tired from so much travel and that he had to be with them to make sure that they were comfortable and rested. I borrowed books from Clarissa's grandparents' collection and read because Isaac never returned from the stables before four in the morning.

By permitting Clarissa to travel to Montgomery and Macon County with Isaac and me as chaperones, Mr. and Mrs. Allen misjudged my ability to anticipate and prevent Clarissa's impetuous disregard of the moral edicts to which she was bound.

EIGHT

THEODORA ALLEN

My father died the year Clarissa was sixteen. My husband had taken Emmeline and Sarah to Mobile and refused to accompany us to Athens to see my ailing father. I assisted my father's wife and the physician, but there was nothing to be done. Had it not been for my daughter, I would have felt completely alone when he died. I did not have time to mourn because his death affected Clarissa more than I had expected, which I should have foreseen, as they had begun corresponding when she learned how to read and write. At first, I helped her with her letters, but as she grew, she did not share with me what they wrote to each other.

The year my father died was the year I lost the final vestige of jealousy regarding Emmeline and my husband. I had believed that she had gone to his bed willingly, but when Bessie told me that he sold Belle, I felt nothing but pity for Emmeline, who thereafter became meek, even anxious in his presence. If she served us tea, her hands shook as she passed a cup and saucer. When Belle returned, she and Belle both seemed fragile, while Sarah became stronger and, I am sure, developed a deep hatred for Cornelius.

When Mr. Cromwell began courting Clarissa, I told her that we needed to sort her childhood possessions, some to put in a trunk for her children and others to give to the servants. We set a rainy day aside to revisit her early years, only the two of us. We found the letters that Papa had written her, and she said that she wanted to keep them all. I read them that evening and was surprised to learn that Clarissa was more perceptive than I knew. In one letter, written when Clarissa was twelve, he revealed her worries about my husband.

Dearest Clarissa, my favorite granddaughter:

I send you greetings and trust that you are applying yourself to your studies every day. This is the time to develop a thirst for a lifelong love of learning.

Always remember that you are your parents' greatest treasure and that your father loves you, despite his frequent absences. He has to leave you and your mother because his commercial interests are burdensome and complex. Do not trouble yourself about your mother, because she has an intellect that is the match of any gentleman. She entertains herself with her literature and writing in her journal, which, I understand, you have no interest in undertaking. Please, dear, pay heed to your mother. Writing is a joy and offers a refuge from the troubles of the world.

You similarly should not worry about your father. It is unfortunate that the young gentlemen of today do not practice moderation in all things. I have seen lives destroyed by the excessive consumption of alcoholic beverages, but I believe that your father will recuperate from his illness if he completes his physician's prescribed course of treatment.

My sweet pea, it concerns me that you believe that you overheard your father speaking to your mother in an uncivil tone and that you think that he struck her. That cannot possibly be the case, for your mother has never mentioned this to me, and your father is too much of a gentleman to ever hurt a lady.

I had never mentioned any of these incidents to my father, and I told him that my husband's illnesses were caused by exhaustion. It was a relief that he did not believe what Clarissa told him. Had he known that my husband had been hitting me since Clarissa was an infant, he would have been distressed and blamed himself for encouraging me to marry. The first time that my husband struck me was after I confronted him about fathering Sarah. He went to my bedroom when Bessie was helping me to prepare for supper and dismissed her. I could smell the whiskey on his breath and his face was red.

"Do not ever again interrupt me when I am working."

"But Cornelius—"

"Mr. Allen—"

"I only wanted to—"

"I said, address me as Mr. Allen." Then he slapped me and broke the lining of my mouth. I tasted iron, but I did not cry. For a moment, I believed that I was asleep and having a bad dream.

"And never question me again. I am the master here and will do as I please."

After that, he did not always hit or kick me when he was angry. Sometimes he pushed me against the wall and applied pressure to my throat. Afterward, he either was complimentary or tormented me with his words.

"Theodora, you really ought not to wear that color, as it makes you look longer in the tooth," he enjoyed saying.

Worse than the physical pain, however, were his threats for some perceived infraction. When he made such comments in Clarissa's presence when she was younger, she cried, which made him angry. He once threatened to strike her because she put her arms around me and kissed my cheek.

One year, at least twice a month, he went to my bedroom and forced me in a way that I cannot even describe. I did not know that anyone, especially a gentleman, committed such acts. When he was angry, I learned to ask Bessie to sleep in my bedroom when I feared that he was going to visit me after supper. As he aged, perhaps because of the whiskey and brandy that were his daily staples, his skin became sallow, his eyes sunken and surrounded by dark circles, and he became thinner. Eddie, his body servant, had to help him to his bedroom most evenings. I was thankful for those nights because he did not disturb me.

When Sarah married the coachman, my husband ordered that I dismiss Mrs. Ellsworth.

"Clarissa has been sufficiently educated, and Sarah can now be her chaperone with Isaac as Clarissa's coachman."

"Mr. Allen, do you believe Sarah will be a satisfactory chaperone, given that she and Clarissa are the same age?"

"If I did not think so, I would not have made the decision. And I want you to arrange for a betrothal ball to take place in two months."

Clarissa was not excited about the ball and had no interest in participating in the preparations; she spent weeks in Montgomery visiting with her grandparents. My husband's family from Montgomery and his brother, Charles, and his wife, Emily, from Mobile attended the dance. Emily and I had an opportunity to speak privately in my sitting room upstairs the day of the dance and she brought me news of Mobile society and the ladies I had met during our visits there throughout the years.

"Dear Theo, I was surprised to hear that our former coachman married your housekeeper's daughter."

"Why do you say that?"

"Oh, I beg your pardon. I thought you knew that Isaac and Sarah are first cousins."

Initially, I was surprised to learn that Isaac and Sarah were cousins and then it made sense because they resembled not only each other but also Clarissa. It was interesting that Cornelius had not objected to Sarah and Isaac's wedding, knowing his and his family's aversion to consanguinity in marriage, which was why, he said, his father had urged him to seek a bride outside Alabama.

"No, I didn't know that. How exactly are they cousins?"

"My husband had a . . . concubine, a mulatto wench, and she was

Isaac's mother. After Isaac was born, I found out about her and told my husband to sell her, and he did, but he insisted on keeping Isaac on the plantation. Please don't tell Cornelius this because he may not know that Isaac is his brother's son."

"No, I surely won't, but I have a feeling that he does know, but doesn't care, given that they are slaves. Whatever the situation, I don't discuss such matters with Cornelius; he . . . would be . . . angry if I mentioned it. I only confronted him about Sarah once and, as you can imagine, he was very angry. Tell me, was it just the one . . . mistress who was a . . . slave, or has Charles had others?"

"I wish I could say that it had just been that one, but our plantation isn't nearly as large as yours, so one hears things."

"But were any of the . . . servants . . . that is, did your husband ever conduct himself . . . inappropriately under your own roof?"

"I don't know. I have always chosen our house servants, and never pretty ones, from among the field hands or at auctions that I attend with my husband."

"My husband told me when we were married that I was never to concern myself with obtaining servants, but even if that had been one of my responsibilities, it would not have changed my predicament, as Emmeline was here before me."

Emily bowed her head and stared at the floor as she spoke. "I'm sorry, Theo, but we're not the only ones to suffer this way, you know. It's just that it's not something we're supposed to complain about."

I did not reply to Emily because there really was nothing to say about matters over which she and I had no authority. In an attempt to change our melancholic mood, I asked her if she wanted to go downstairs and enjoy the party, to which she agreed.

Clarissa was uncharacteristically quiet at her betrothal ball. It was late afternoon, and some seventy of the two hundred guests were enjoying the festivities in my gardens before supper. The others were indoors, where they were spared the sun's still harsh rays. I was sitting not too far from Clarissa and Julius, who were surrounded by perhaps twenty people. Everyone was drinking

Emmeline's special punch or wine that my husband had imported from France. A string quartet was playing on the verandah. The young children, Clarissa's nieces and nephews, were playing at some game or the other involving tormenting the carp that I kept in ceramic Chinese bowls throughout the gardens.

The group surrounding Julius and Clarissa was completely focused on him and paid her no attention, even though she was magnificent in an Alençon lace gown. Julius was a formidable figure, and he delighted the guests with tales. The scar on Julius's face, which appeared faint when he was indoors, was striking. Sunlight accentuated the smooth skin that had been created by the healing of the wound. One woman asked Julius if that was the scar from his infamous duel. At first he appeared to be disturbed by her question, but then he smiled, touched his face, and said that he had earned it when he vanquished a scoundrel who had challenged him to a swordfight. While I had never heard the story, some guests were apparently familiar with this account.

"I was on leave from West Point when a fellow whom I had known since childhood alleged that I had insulted his reputation and challenged me to a duel. He sliced my face, but I put my sword straight through his heart. Of course, I was not invited back to West Point after the incident, but my father was not disappointed, as he needed me at home to preside over his commercial concerns."

While Julius was speaking, I kept my eyes on Clarissa. She shivered when he said that he had murdered a man. I wanted to put my arms around my darling, but I did not want to draw attention to her discomfort. My cousin Eliza's daughter, also apparently noticing Clarissa's distress, whispered something that made her a bit more cheery. Julius looked at Clarissa in a way that chilled me, and suddenly, instead of feeling blissful because of my daughter's engagement to be married, I felt inexplicably guilty. Should I have fought my husband about his decision to agree to her marriage to Julius Cromwell?

After the ball, Clarissa did not spend much time at home. With

Sarah as her chaperone and Isaac as her coachman, she regularly visited her friends in neighboring plantations, her grandparents in Montgomery, and Mr. Cromwell in Talladega. My husband said that it was appropriate that she visited her intended without one of us present, as he was living at his parents' home until his new house was completed. With Clarissa gone, I was alone most of the time. My husband did not disturb me in the evenings, which he spent with Emmeline.

I received a letter with devastating news of my dear cousin Eliza, who had been ill with fever for two weeks, and I told my husband that I had to go to Georgia to be by her side, to which he did not object. Clarissa was in Montgomery at the time, and I wrote her about the developments. When I arrived at Eliza's bedside, I held her, even though the physician said that I should not get too close. When her husband, Abraham, was not in the room, the physician said that her recovery was not likely.

Abraham's family loved Eliza, and his brother, Kenneth, whom I had met at Eliza's wedding but had not seen since I was in New York, had come to be with her. Back then, he had been recently widowed and had moved to New York with his children to teach at the university. He had dined with us one night, but it was not a pleasant experience because my husband was boorish. When in New York, I never thought of Kenneth with romantic notions, even though I was drawn to his elegant appearance and interest in literary matters, because I was a recent bride and still loved my husband, even after finding him in bed with Emmeline. By the time I saw Kenneth again when Eliza was ill, any caring emotions for Cornelius had ceased. My hatred for him, in fact, is something that I only now acknowledge because I never thought about my own happiness.

"He does not speak about anything other than poetry and novels," my husband had said when we returned to the hotel in New York after dinner with Kenneth.

I told him that Kenneth had invited me to a literary salon to hear a poet who was visiting from London.

"You are not attending. It is unseemly that you should accept an invitation to be seen alone with a widower."

"But . . ."

"You are not going, and I will entertain no discussion about it."

"I will ask someone to take him a note that I . . ."

"No, you will not. I will inform him of my decision."

Twenty years later, Kenneth was still a professor in New York and had not remarried. He was now a poet of some renown. We spoke after we left Eliza's bedside.

"And you, Mrs. Allen, are you still writing?"

"I keep a journal, but I would not call it writing."

"Of course it is. Did you bring it?"

"Yes, I carry it everywhere."

"Excellent. If you oblige me, I'll read some of my poems, and you can read selections from your work."

"I would enjoy your poetry very much, but my humble journal is not worthy of being read."

"Nonsense. Please, Mrs. Allen, nothing would give me greater pleasure than to hear you read to me."

We spent the next five days either with Eliza's husband and children or reading to each other in the parlor. On the fifth night we were there, Eliza asked Kenneth to read her his poetry. No one in the household slept that night. My dear Eliza passed in the early hours of the morning, but I am comforted that, while she drew her final breath, she experienced beauty in the form of Kenneth's finely crafted words.

I was relieved to find when I arrived home that my husband had gone to Mobile. Three weeks after my return, I received a letter from Kenneth. He had written a new poem and dedicated it to me. I wrote him and thanked him for the lovely gift, but I asked him not to write me again, as my husband would not find it appropriate.

The next time that Mrs. Tutwiler visited, I showed her Kenneth's poem and told her that I had asked him not to write me again.

She asked me, evidently confused, why I had done so. "But why, Theodora? There's is nothing untoward about the letter or poem." I told her about the incident in New York twenty years ago. "Perhaps that was just a newlywed husband's jealousy?"

"No, I don't think so."

"Does Mr. Allen . . . open your correspondence?"

"Yes." I was so ashamed to admit that my husband treated me as if I were a child.

"Mr. Tutwiler doesn't see the mail when it comes in; I sort it and distribute it to my husband and the children and I keep mine. Why don't you tell the professor to send your letters to me at my home?"

"You're such a dear friend. But what if your husband learned about it?"

"He wouldn't find out, but if he did, he would think that the professor was writing to me and he would laugh at the thought that a gentleman was sending me poetry."

I thus imposed on my friend to receive Kenneth's letters to me, and I am glad that I did so, because I do not believe I would have withstood the forthcoming events without Kenneth's wise counsel and reminders that, despite the ugliness of life, one can find succor in beauty.

When Clarissa was betrothed, I told her it was unseemly that she was traveling so frequently and that she needed to stay home to assist me with her wedding arrangements.

"Mama, please. Why do we have to do so much now? The wedding is almost two years from now."

"It may seem as if it is far in the future, but I assure you it is not, and you have been spending too much time away from home. Does your intended know about your constant visits to Montgomery? Also, I believe your father would be displeased to know the true reason for your visits there. I want your word that the next time you go to Montgomery you will not see Mr. Evans."

"But, Mama, I don't go to Montgomery to see Mr. Evans."

"Do not lie to me, Clarissa."

"All right. I'm sorry. I won't go as far as Montgomery. May I still see my friends close to home?"

"Yes, Puppet, but limit your visits to about every two months."

"Mama, please. I won't be going far. Oh, and, Mama, Aunt Martha wrote Papa that I never visit her."

"You may certainly visit your aunt as often as you wish."

Clarissa did indeed stay home more after this conversation and assisted with her trousseau, but she was gone at least once a week. My husband said that he was glad that Clarissa was visiting his widowed sister, who lived by herself in a large house in Macon County. One afternoon, Clarissa and I were reading in the parlor after dinner when she suddenly turned pale. She tossed her book aside and ran from the room with her hand covering her mouth. I followed her upstairs and found her retching into a chamber pot. When she was finished, I asked her whether something she had eaten made her sick. She answered me quickly, and her shoulders relaxed, almost as if relieved I had asked her that question.

"Yes, I think the meat wasn't fresh. Don't you?"

"No, I don't feel at all ill. Are you better?"

Clarissa did not have a sensitive stomach, and I was concerned that perhaps she had a serious ailment.

"Yes, I do feel a little better, thank you, Mama."

I rang the bell for Sarah and told her to see Emmeline about something for Clarissa's stomach. Sarah brought her ginger tea. Clarissa drank it and slept until supper. She ate well that evening but retired early because she was fatigued. Her nausea continued for several days.

"Puppet, shall we summon the doctor?"

"No, Mama. I'll be better soon."

She was not improved, however, and I called for the physician, who examined her and pronounced her fit and prescribed bed rest. By the next day, she was well, but did not resume her normal activities. She did not speak about visiting anyone and was content to read in the garden or on the verandah.

She visited me in my chambers one evening, her face still drained of color, as I was dressing for supper, and she dismissed my maid. "Bessie, I need to speak with Mama, alone." When Bessie was gone, Clarissa told me the reason for her visit.

"Mama, I want to tell you something, I . . . want to . . . marry Julius . . . now."

"Why, darling, why the sudden change of heart? Didn't you vehemently tell your father and me that you were glad to have a lengthy engagement?"

"That was before I knew about all those boring wedding preparations. Really, Mama, do I need so many clothes? I'm so tired just thinking about all the parties and all the guests that we have to receive who want to tell me how happy they are for me."

"But before you wanted nothing to do with Mr. Cromwell and all you wanted to do was to make social calls of your own and go to parties."

"I know, but . . ." She sobbed, bowing her head, then covered her face with her hands.

"Clarissa, my darling, why are you crying? Look at me, Clarissa, look at me, darling."

She shook her head and refused to uncover her face. I sat next to her on the long seat and held her, rubbing her back. She continued to cry.

"I'm sorry, Mama, I'm so sorry."

"What are you sorry about? Clarissa, answer me, why are you sorry? Puppet, tell me what you're thinking."

She removed her hands from her face. I stood and lifted her chin to try to get her to look at me, but she closed her eyes.

"Clarissa, there's nothing that you can't tell me. Really, Puppet, you can tell me anything."

"All right, Mama, I'll tell you what happened. He, he . . . forced me, Mama. He forced himself on me."

I tried to understand what she had just said to me, that a man, perhaps Julius or Mr. Evans, had violated her, but no, how could that be? Clarissa never went anywhere alone, she always traveled with a chaperone, first her tutor and now with Sarah and the coachman, Isaac. My heart beat quickly, and my cheeks burned.

"What? What do you mean? Clarissa, what are you telling me?" I grasped her shoulders and applied pressure. "Look at me and tell me . . . now, exactly what you mean."

"About . . . three months ago, when I visited him, he made me . . . When we went riding . . . there was no one else there. We stopped and got off the horses. He put a blanket on the ground, and I thought we were only going to sit and talk."

I could not believe what she was telling me. "Was this Mr. Evans?"

"No, no, not him, it was Jul— Him, that man Papa is forcing me to marry."

"Clarissa, are you certain?"

"What do you mean, am I certain? How could you ask me that?"

"My darling, Puppet, I'm so very sorry, it's just that this is a serious accusation."

"What do you mean accusation, that's what he did to me, he pushed me down and he forced my legs open . . . he forced himself in me."

I sat next to her and held her close while she began to cry again and then I suddenly realized why she now wanted to quickly marry Julius.

"Oh . . . and that is why . . . oh my dear Lord, that is why you were sick. Dear Lord, what are we going to do? We must tell your fa—"

"No, no, Mama, we can't tell him, he'll be angry, and you know what he'll say, he'll say it was my fault. Everyone always says that about girls who are expecting when they marry, they never say it was the man's fault, that he forced her."

"Clarissa, your father would never hurt you, and he would believe you, I promise."

"How can you say that after what he's done to you?"

"What do you mean by that?"

"Oh Mama, I've heard the mean things he's said to you and when he's been really drunk how he hits you."

"Sweetheart, I'm sorry that you had to hear those things, I wish you had spoken to me about them earlier, but . . . but we have a much bigger problem on our hands now. Clarissa, your father loves you, and I'm confident that he wouldn't treat you the same way. Clarissa, he would never hurt you, and when he's angry at me it's only when . . . he drinks too much. I know he'll take your side, I'm sure of that."

"Well, I'm not sure of that. Please, Mama, let's just tell him that I'm ready to be a married lady."

"Darling, he will not believe you. You should abandon that line of thinking. After all, I didn't believe you when you said the only reason you wanted to marry now was because you were bored with going to parties, and your father is more intelligent than I am. Besides, you did initially tell him that you did not want to marry Mr. Cromwell. And we'll tell him together; I won't make you face him alone." I kissed her. "You're his pet and he has never denied you anything. And, after all, he did consent to your visits to Mr. Cromwell."

"That's true, Mama, I hope he remembers that."

"All right, Puppet. We'll tell him after supper. And not a word to anyone."

Clarissa and I made an effort to appear as if nothing unusual had occurred. Cornelius had a bottle of wine by himself at supper and brandy after we dined.

"Mr. Allen, Clarissa and I want to speak with you privately."

"Certainly. What do my favorite ladies have to discuss? Details of the wedding, that you need more frocks and hats?"

We went to Clarissa's sitting room. She and I sat on the sofa, and Cornelius sat in a chair opposite us, tapping his foot. I held Clarissa's hand. Cornelius was the first to speak.

"Who is going to say something?"

I took a deep breath. "Mr. Allen, something . . . horrible happened to . . . Clarissa."

"What?"

"About three months ago—"

"Not when, what?"

"She was visiting Mr. Cromwell and—"

"And what happened? Say it."

"He violated her."

He leaned forward and spoke loudly, unconcerned that a servant may have been listening.

"What do you mean by 'he violated her'?"

"He forced himself upon her. They were riding, just the two of them."

His eyes narrowed as he looked at me and then at Clarissa. He stood and walked toward us, grabbed Clarissa by the arms, and pulled her from the sofa. I stood and reached to try to get him to release her, but he pushed me away as he screamed at her.

"You little bitch. You couldn't keep your legs closed until you were married? Dear God. Jesus Christ. What am I supposed to do now?"

I could not believe that my husband was calling his own daughter such a vile name, but I was more worried that his treatment would not end just with his use of coarse language. I tried again to get him to release her, but he pushed me so hard that I fell and remained on the floor.

"Papa. . . ."

"Be quiet, let me think. And stop crying, you're irritating me, you selfish bitch."

He dropped her and she fell back onto the sofa. I stood and went to the sofa and sat next to her, holding her hand.

"You selfish slut, I'm not even close to finalizing the business arrangements with his father." He paced and was silent for a moment. "Before you went riding, you told him that you couldn't ride alone with him, correct?"

"I didn't want to go riding. I preferred to stay in the garden where we were having tea with his parents."

"Good. So, his parents were present when he asked you to go riding, and they didn't say you shouldn't ride alone with him? Very good. But listen carefully to what I'm saying: you told him that you couldn't ride alone with him, without a chaperone."

"No, Papa. I didn't actually say that."

"Listen to me, you whore. Why would you ride alone with a man who was not your husband? He forced you, you say? It seems to me as if you threw yourself upon him."

"No, Papa. That's not—"

"Don't you contradict what I say." He stood in front of her and closed his hand on her throat. She tried to scream, but he applied more pressure. Tears fell down her face. I tried to pull his arm away, but he pushed me off with his other hand. He released Clarissa and struck me in the abdomen. I bent over and fell to my knees. Clarissa was crying with her head in her hands.

"Stand up."

She did not obey him.

"When I order you to do something, you do it."

He struck her. Then he spoke again, but as if to himself. "I will invite them here. I will make my dowry terms much more favorable, and we will have to appeal to the mother as well as the father. I will say that the wedding should be held sooner. Oh dear God. You're expecting, aren't you? That is why you told your mother. You wouldn't have said anything otherwise. You conniving bitch!" He looked at me.

"This is all because you failed to properly raise her." He slapped me. "You two will speak to the mother separately. I expect a lot of tears from you. Do not say that he forced her, but that he 'took her honor' and that the only way to restore it is for them to be married immediately."

He departed, and I rang the bell for Sarah to help me with Clarissa. We took off her clothes. Her throat was red and mottled. I told Sarah to ask Emmeline for something to help Clarissa.

The remedy was successful. I stayed with her until she fell asleep and returned to my rooms. Bessie was sitting on her cot.

"Ma'am, everything all right?"

"Yes, Bessie. Thank you."

As she was helping me undress, she touched the areas where he had hurt me. "The skin ain't broke no place this time, ma'am. Can I get you something from Miss Emmeline?"

"No, Bessie. That's not necessary. Just light more candles and lamps in here and you can sleep in the adjoining room."

Bessie folded her cot and left, and I read and wrote in my journal. There was no thought of rest because I assumed that he was going to arrive at any moment.

NINE

SARAH CAMPBELL

A s I was turning down Clarissa's bed I heard everything that transpired that night when Mrs. Allen and Clarissa told Mr. Allen that the wedding needed to be held earlier. I wanted to go to my family to tell them that we did not have two more years together, as we expected, but I could not go just then. Mrs. Allen told me that I could not leave Clarissa alone. If she woke and I was not there, Mrs. Allen would know about my absence. I had to wait until morning to leave. I was asleep when I heard Bessie.

"Sarah, get up. Sarah, Master want you to wake up Miss Clarissa and get her ready for dinner."

I rubbed my eyes and stretched. "Dinner? I can't believe I slept so late."

"Sarah, come on. You ain't got time to act like you the missus. Master Allen himself told me to tell you get Miss Clarissa up."

I remembered the events of the previous night. "Is my mother in the kitchen?"

"I don't know. I ain't been over there. Mrs. Allen just woke up, and I got to get back to her. Get up."

"Yes, yes. I'm up. But, Bessie, I need to speak to my mother."

"Talk to her when you go get water for Miss Clarissa to wash. And tell Miss Emmeline to make tea for Mrs. Allen and Miss Clarissa."

Clarissa was awake. The windows were open and she was staring outside.

"Miss Clarissa, your father wants to see you at dinner. There's some water in the pitcher. Why don't you begin washing? I'll go downstairs and get you hot water and some tea. Let me look at you."

She unbuttoned her nightdress. Her throat was now red and blue.

"I'll bring you something with a high collar."

She did not answer me. She rose and went to wash.

I found my mother and Belle in the kitchen. "Mama, I need some tea and hot water for Mrs. Allen and Miss Clarissa, and, Mama, I need to speak with you, now. Have you seen Isaac?"

"Calm down, girl. There's plenty of hot water. Make the tea. Isaac is gone since about three in the morning. I fixed him food to take with him. Master Allen sent him to Talladega. Baby, I know everything. Now go on, take care of Miss Clarissa. We're going to talk later."

When the Allens were having dinner, my mother, Belle, and I went to my mother's cabin. As soon as we were inside, I started crying.

"Why are you crying, Sarah? Mama, why is she crying?" asked Belle.

My mother put her arm around me. "Miss Clarissa is getting married next month," she said.

"Why?"

"You don't need to know that. It better if you don't know," my mother said.

"Oh, no . . . that mean that Sarah and Isaac is leaving us."

"Yes, and five more from the Hall, but not you and me. But they're only going to Talladega. Sarah, look at me. You won't be that far, and you know Miss Clarissa is going to be coming back to visit all the time and you'll come with her."

I embraced Mama and rested my cheek on her shoulder.

"But I've never been away from you, Mama, and I don't want to leave Belle and the children."

Belle was crying now. "Mama, there ain't no way out of it, is there? Sarah's got to go with Miss Clarissa, right?"

"Yes, you know that's why they picked Sarah to be her maid, so one day when Miss Clarissa get married she didn't have to go to her husband's house by herself. Sarah, Mr. Allen's not going to break you and Isaac up. At least you're going to be with your husband."

My mother could not say anything to console me, and I wanted to tell her and Belle that Clarissa claimed Mr. Cromwell violated her. I thought about that day when we were in Talladega. I had been sitting in the garden, out of view of the Cromwells and Clarissa, in the event that she needed something from her guest room.

"What a perfect day for a ride. This is the type of day that Papa and I take our horses and go as far as the hills," Clarissa said.

"It is indeed a lovely day, not too warm but not too cool. If my gout were not flaring, I would say that I would join you," Mrs. Cromwell said.

"Well, Mr. Cromwell, shall you and I ride?"

"Yes, that is a splendid idea. You don't need to go far, Julius. Show Miss Allen the plantation."

"Yes, Mother. I can do that."

Clarissa called me, and we went upstairs. "The blue riding costume and the matching hat, Sarah, and there's no need for you and Isaac to follow me in the carriage. Mr. Cromwell and I will ride alone."

When she returned from her ride that day, the sun had begun to set, and she wanted to rest before supper. I went to the kitchen for hot water so she could wash and helped her out of her clothing when I returned. Her face was flushed. When I was brushing her hair, I had to remove a few leaves of dried grass.

"Miss Clarissa, why do you have grass in your hair?"

"Oh, can you believe it? I fell off the horse."

"You? You've been riding since you were how old, five?"

"Well, this was not my Coty—this mare was spirited."

"Are you all right?"

"Absolutely, I feel wonderful."

The morning after Mrs. Allen and Clarissa spoke to Mr. Allen about Clarissa's marriage, Mrs. Allen summoned my mother, Belle, and me to Mrs. Allen's rooms, where she, Clarissa, Bessie, and Dottie were waiting.

"Our dear bride-to-be has decided that she does not want to wait two years to be a married lady. She will be married early next month. The festivities, by necessity, will not be as elaborate as we initially planned. We will need everyone's effort to ensure that the wedding is lovely, and Mr. Allen expects that we will all work hard. Dottie is going to alter my wedding dress to fit Clarissa, but she will need your assistance in that task."

From that day until Clarissa was married, in addition to our normal responsibilities, we did nothing else but prepare for her wedding. Mr. Allen brought in ten field hands to assist, but as they knew nothing about housework, they were of more help to the gardeners and yard people.

My mother and I did our best not to burden Belle because she had recently given birth to my nephew, Edward. Belle's life had changed in another momentous way because my mother had persuaded Mr. Allen to purchase Belle's abroad man, Zeke, who was now living with Belle in her cabin. I was thrilled that my sister was happy. While she still drifted into her own dark world of the past sometimes, growing quiet, sullen even, she often laughed now as she did before she was sold. Zeke was a good father to Emmie and Ruby, which was a relief to my mother.

When Isaac returned from Talladega, I spoke to him about the recent events. "Did anyone tell you why you had to go to Talladega?"

"No, the overseer just told me to take Mr. Allen's best horse and come back here as fast as I could, so I figure it's something important."

"Mr. Allen wants Clarissa to be married next month, and the letter you took was an invitation to the Cromwells to come here on Friday."

Isaac raised his voice. "Why? Why do they want her to get married so soon? I thought she wasn't getting married for two years or something."

I lowered my voice, even though we were in our cabin and the door and shutters were closed. "Don't speak so loudly, Isaac, and you can't tell anyone what I'm about to say, and I mean it. Mama doesn't even want Belle to know. Clarissa is expecting."

"What? Who said that? Was it Miss Clarissa? I don't believe it. Miss Clarissa, expecting? Sarah, who told you that?"

"I was in the room next to Clarissa's bedroom when she and Mrs. Allen told Mr. Allen."

"Are you sure that's what they said?"

"Yes, I know what I heard. That's why they sent for the Cromwells. They're going to offer them more money and slaves, including us, for her dowry, so he marries her next month now that she's expecting his baby."

"Miss Clarissa said the baby is Mr. Cromwell's? After all the time she spent with Mr. Evans in Montgomery? And what did Mr. Allen say? Did he believe Clarissa when she said the baby is Mr. Cromwell's? Was he upset? Was Mrs. Allen mad? What did she say?"

"Why are you excited, anyway?"

"I'm not excited. I just want to know what's going to happen to us, that's all. I don't want them to separate us as soon as she's married. I thought you and me was going to have more time together."

"Well, Mr. Allen told my mother that you're going to Talladega with us, that he's not going to separate us. Anyway, yes, they did believe her, probably because she told her parents that it was against her will, but that's not what I think. When we were in Talladega, Clarissa asked Mr. Cromwell to take her riding and said you and I shouldn't follow them in the carriage. And when she came back, she was happy and said that she felt 'wonderful,' and oh, there were dried leaves in her hair."

I could not suppress a giggle, and I knew that I was being mean.

"Sarah, you think this is funny?"

"Yes, don't you think it's funny, that she told her parents that Mr. Cromwell forced her after all the time she spent with Mr. Evans in Montgomery?"

"No, it ain't funny because . . . uh, what if he don't send me to Talladega with you after all? You sure Mr. Allen told your mother he's going to let me go to Talladega, too, that he ain't going to separate us?"

"You don't need to worry about that. No, that's the only good thing about all of this, that we'll be together in Talladega."

The next week my mother and I went into town for our weekly errands. Johnny, our usual driver, did not take us. When we had been to all the merchants who ordered goods from abroad for the Allens, my mother took a lantern and told the driver that we had something else to do. She asked him to wait for us by the square. She and I walked down an unlit path and arrived at a shop with a sign on the door that said "Adams' Bespoke Tailors." My mother knocked and a well-dressed man invited us in.

"Good evening, Miss Emmeline. Is this Sarah? Welcome."

"Sarah, this is Mr. Adams."

I must have appeared confused.

"Yes, Sarah, this is my business."

He closed the shutters and locked the door and we went to an area in the rear of the shop, where he showed us a dress.

"What do you think?"

"It's pretty, Mr. Adams."

He wrapped it in heavy paper and tied it with a string. My mother paid him.

"Sarah, it's a pleasure to meet you. I'm certain that you're curious

about me. I have been a tailor since I began learning at my father's
knee when I was six years old. Our master permitted my father to
sew clothing for the gentlemen and ladies in the vicinity and to keep
a portion of his earnings. My father worked seven days a week, for
his master and for himself, and eventually, he saved enough to buy
his freedom. He opened this shop and earned money to buy my
mother and me. The three of us worked to buy my four younger
brothers and sisters. A schoolteacher who was a member of our
church taught me how to read and write.

"Now, you cannot repeat anything that I am going to tell you,
Sarah, not even to your husband or sister, not at this time. Please
remember that, if you tell anyone any part of what we discuss today, all our lives could be at risk.

"The pastor of my church, the First Methodist Church, is the
Reverend Townsend, a young man who was educated in a divinity
school in the North. His life has been threatened because he once
preached from the pulpit that all men should be free, even though
he never said publicly that slavery should be abolished. When away
from the pulpit, however, that is another matter. For years, since the
current preacher's father was alive, a group of church members have
been trying to help bondsmen flee. Miss Emmeline's husband was
one of the first people we assisted. It's sad, because all have been
caught and returned to slavery. But we have not abandoned our mis-
sion. You are here because your mother sent us word that Miss Allen is going to be married early next month and not in two years, as
we expected."

"Why is that important to you and how did my mother notify
you, Mr. Adams?"

"It is better that you do not know how we found out, but as you
know, slaves leave plantations for legitimate reasons. Now, the Cromwell plantation in Talladega has long been of interest to us. It is
known to be the most brutal of any in these parts. The overseers
there rule with impunity and have even killed slaves. As a result,

slaves are more likely to attempt to escape from there than from other plantations. When your mother learned that you and your husband are going to Talladega with your mistress, she asked me to speak with you.

"Your mother's first concern is your well-being. Mr. Cromwell, the son, is known as a decadent gentleman who has no purpose in life other than to pursue . . . physical pleasures. He has a particular fondness for mulatto girls. Now, your husband, I understand, is a coachman, and knows many regions in a number of states. You and he could benefit from our assistance. If your new master seeks to make you his . . . well, to force you into an arrangement against your will, you and your husband may summon the courage to avail yourselves of an opportunity to escape, should it arise. However, if you decide that you do not want to attempt such a drastic and perilous measure, you could be of assistance to us by being our eyes and ears and relaying information to us."

I looked at my mother. She seemed worried.

"Sir, it has always been my dream to escape, but what about my mother and sister and her family? Could you help them, too?"

My mother held and squeezed my hand before she spoke.

"Sarah, you know we couldn't run away. I'm too old and . . . scared, and Belle has those children. But if one of my children got away, Lord, I'd be happy. And Sarah, if any of us could do it, it's you," my mother said.

My mother's confidence in me had the opposite effect of making me feel afraid and not at all courageous about escaping.

"I don't know, Mr. Adams, it's . . ." I stopped speaking because I was embarrassed that my voice was quivering. Perhaps I was hoping that my mother or Mr. Adams would tell me to change my mind and not to run, but they were silent and looked at me to continue.

"It's one thing to dream about escaping and to tell yourself that you would be one of the brave ones to run the second you had the chance and not get caught and brought back, but it's another thing to actually do it. Yes, when you're dreaming it's always easy to be strong and see yourself overcoming whatever challenge you face and to only think about the good things that are going to happen. And, well, there's something else that I think about every time I think of running, I . . . I . . . I would never see my family again," I said.

"Sarah, I understand the difficulty and danger of making such an attempt, but some slaves would rather surrender their lives than continue to live in captivity. You'll have to ask yourself, if the opportunity presents itself, which group you fit into."

"That is true. At least I don't have to make the decision now."

"Miss Emmeline, may I speak alone with Sarah?"

My mother moved to the front of the shop, and Mr. Adams whispered, "Sarah, do you know how to read and write?"

"Sir?"

"Sarah, I can tell by the way you speak that you have had book learning. I will not reveal your answer to anyone, not even your mother."

"Yes, sir, I do; and I know my numbers, too."

"This is welcome news. You will be of even greater help to us . . . and to yourself. When you get to Talladega, someone will make himself known to you."

We went to my mother. "Miss Emmeline, we should conclude so that you will be on your way before the curfew bell in the square rings. Sarah, we may not have another opportunity to see each other again before you leave. Godspeed, and may the Lord keep you."

Mr. Adams shook our hands, and we joined the driver at the meeting place. In the wagon, my mother told me that she needed to speak with me in her cabin after supper. When we arrived at the main gate in Allen Estates, an overseer asked us why it had taken us so long to return.

"Sir, they said they had to do something else and they left me waiting by myself at the square," the driver said.

"Oh, what else did you have to do?"

My mother pointed at the package from Mr. Adams. "Sir, we had to go to the tailor. He made my daughter a dress to take to Talladega."

I went to my mother's cabin after supper. We sat at the table next to each other and held hands.

"Mama, I was thinking about everything that Mr. Adams said, but when I think about all the things that could go wrong, I don't feel as brave as I used to. And, Mama, I would never see you and Belle and the children again."

My mother put her arm around me.

"Baby, listen. It's not like something is going to happen right now. It ain't like we know you is really going to get the chance. But, Sarah, I mean it. If one day you do get the chance, I want you to take it. Look, even if you couldn't make it to the North, you can go to some big place where they have more of us that is free than here. When I went to New York with Mr. Allen, I talked to some people who was free and worked at the hotel. I didn't find out too much, people is always afraid of talking, but they did say there's people up there trying to end slavery. And, Sarah, I've been saving money for you from the things I make and sell in town. I got it in the lockbox. The dress we got from Mr. Adams is for you. Listen, I'm going to sew pockets above the hem inside the dress—Mr. Adams told me to do this—and I'm going to put money in the pockets. Don't wear the dress until you need to. If anybody ask you about it, say I made it for you to wear for something special."

"Oh, Mama. I love you so much; I'm so glad Mr. Adams said you should do that." We hugged each other.

"I love you too, baby. But listen, there's something else very important I need to talk to you about. I finally got Mr. Allen to . . . to say he's going to free Belle, the children, and me when he dies."

"Really, Mama? Really?" I jumped up and smiled and then kissed her.

"Yes, baby. That's what he said. He said he change the papers with the lawyer. But baby, this is why I want you to run if you can. He said . . . he said . . ." She could not finish her sentence and shook her head, then breathed deeply before resuming.

"He said that he can't free you because you is about to belong to Mr. Cromwell."

"Oh, Mama, I care more about you, Belle, and the children than about myself, and if it's true that he's going to free you all, then I wouldn't be so sad about leaving you. I just hope that Mr. Allen was telling you the truth about changing the papers. Oh, and Mama, what about Zeke? Did he say anything about freeing him?"

"No, and you can't say nothing to Belle. I ain't talked to her about it yet."

"Mama, do you think Mr. Allen would write it down for you? So when he dies, you and Belle can show the paper to prove it's true?"

"I don't think so, baby. I think he might say I didn't trust him if I asked him that."

"But you don't."

We both laughed. "No, I don't, but I try not to show it."

"Mama, if he's serious about freeing you, he'll put it down on a piece of paper. You can show the paper to Mr. Adams to read it to you to make sure that's what it really says."

"But what if it don't say he's going to free us? I can't tell him I got somebody to read it to me."

"That's true, but wouldn't you rather know if he's telling the truth?"

"All right. I'll do it, but I'm going to have to find the right time, maybe after the wedding."

"No, Mama. Now, before the wedding. I want us to take the paper to Mr. Adams before I go to Talladega."

"Oh, Sarah."

"Please, Mama. Do it for me and for Belle. You'll feel better telling her if it's true, and, Mama, you can tell her where to find the paper if, God forbid, something happens to you before he dies. And you can tell him that it's not him you don't trust, but Mrs. Allen. You can say, what if, after he dies, she tries to change the papers to say he didn't free you?"

"I'll ask him, but I can't promise you I can make him do it."

About a week later, Mama asked me to go to her cabin. She closed the shutters and locked the door. She lifted the hem of a dress that was hanging in the cabinet and gently took out a piece of paper from a pocket. My heart beat fast and my lungs tightened. She handed the paper to me.

"What do it say?"

"Ma'am?"

"Read it to me and stop your foolishness, girl. Just because I ain't got book learning don't mean I'm feebleminded. Read it to me."

"Yes, ma'am."

To All to Whom These Presents May Come:

I, Cornelius Francis Allen, Esquire, being of sound mind and body, hereby set my seal and declare that it is my wish that, upon my death, in accordance with the codicil to my last will and testament, executed by me on the 23rd day of December 1853, my slaves Emmeline Allen and Belle Allen, and all of Belle Allen's present and future issue, shall be freed.

My mother and I said nothing for several minutes.

"Give me back the paper. I'm going to put it back in the pocket of that dress, and I'm going to tell Belle where it is."

"Mama, I can't believe it, but it's there, in writing. I wish he had freed you now, but I know that we should be grateful for this, at least. Mama, how did you know I learned to . . . ?"

"Shush, girl, I knew from when you was sitting with Miss Clarissa in her lessons, as smart as you is, I knew you was going to learn, even better than her. You know it's against the law, what she done in teaching you, and I hope I can pay her back one day. Don't talk about it. Isaac don't know, do he?"

"No, ma'am. He's afraid of doing anything that would get him in any kind of trouble. I don't think he'll want to run if we get the opportunity. I may have to go alone."

TEN

THEODORA ALLEN

T he night we confessed to my husband that Clarissa was expecting, I was afraid that he was going to continue his punishment, and I told Sarah that she must not leave Clarissa's bedroom. Emmeline's remedy calmed my daughter, who was trembling after her father struck and choked her, and I stayed with her until she went to sleep. Then I read and wrote in my journal until four in the morning. When he did not appear, I rested.

"Wake up, darling. Do you intend to sleep the entire day?" My husband was smiling and smelled of shaving cream. I looked at him without answering, and he gently brushed the hair away from my face before he bent down and kissed me on the cheek. The sun through the window indicated that I had slept quite late. He stood while holding my hand. I still said nothing.

"Bessie, come help your mistress to rise," he said.

My maid entered and curtsied. "Afternoon, Mr. Allen. Afternoon, ma'am."

He grinned at her and pointed to her maid's dress, which looked like all her other maid's dresses.

"Bessie, wherever did you get that lovely frock?"

"Sir?"

"Run, Bessie, and tell Sarah to make her mistress rise and shine, and she is to tell her mistress to give God thanks for a beautiful day and that I expect to see her at dinner. Then return here to attend to my darling wife."

Bessie was probably as perplexed as I but did a better job at hiding her puzzlement.

"Yes, sir."

Bessie left me in the presence of my husband, who apparently had undergone some type of metamorphosis that reminded me of a cheerful lunatic I saw being pursued by police officers when we were in New York, who was said by bystanders to have escaped from Bellevue Hospital's ward for the insane.

I was wary of Cornelius and afraid that he would suddenly revert to how he was the night before, using vile language or striking me.

"Theodora, my one and only love, I trust you slept well and that you'll forgive me for my conduct last night. You do know that you and Clarissa are my dearest possessions. Don't pout, sweetheart. It does not become you.

"I've written to Mr. Cromwell, the elder, and sent Isaac to deliver the letter. He should arrive in Talladega by tonight. I've invited them to be here this Friday, which will provide us an opportunity to ensure that our version of the incident is consistent. I've thought about what we'll say to them. We'll admit that she is expecting, and I'll offer them, in addition to the previously agreed sum, Isaac and six house servants, including Sarah. In addition, I'll give them twenty field hands, but only upon the birth of the child and Julius's written acknowledgment to me that the child is his."

His plot did not seem logical. "If he is so wealthy, why would he be so easily seduced by your offer?"

"Because, on the open market, he could get $2,000 for Isaac, $1,500 for Sarah, $1,000 each for the five house servants, and $800 for each of the twenty field hands, and $24,500 is not a sum of money at which anyone would scoff. And would they want it to be known that Julius refused to marry Clarissa after ruining her?"

"I don't know what we'll do if you are not correct."

"Then you have an incentive to ensure that you and Clarissa put on your best performances, don't you?"

Isaac returned from Talladega with a letter from the elder Mr. Cromwell, stating that he, his wife, and son accepted Cornelius's invitation and that they would be at Allen Estates by Friday evening. My husband told me to speak to Emmeline and impress upon her that all domestic arrangements had to be flawless.

"And I want Sarah to be one of the servers at all the meals and teas."

When I told Clarissa that the Cromwells were coming, she was not at all perturbed. "Puppet, I am glad that you are tranquil."

"I'll do what I have to do to ensure that my child is born in wedlock."

"Your father wants to discuss with us tonight what we will say to Mrs. Cromwell."

"But we already spoke about this."

"I know, darling, but he wants to be certain that the three of us state one version of the plan. Clarissa, do you understand that this is probably the most important argument you will ever make in your life?"

"Yes, Mama, I do."

After supper, during which my husband drank only one glass of wine, we went to the library.

"You'll confess to the mother that you are expecting. You will cry and tell her you know that you and Julius acted imprudently, but that it was a foolish mistake by two young people in love. Theodora, you will say that you want your grandchild to be born in wedlock and that he should not be penalized for his parents' error.

"Mrs. Cromwell will not likely become involved in the financial aspect of the marriage, but if she does ask you, tell her that I am prepared to be very generous, that I will give her son six house servants and a highly valued coachman. Additionally, upon the birth of my grandson, I will give to Julius twenty young field hands." He paused when he saw the look on his daughter's face. "Yes, Clarissa?"

"Papa, what if . . . they don't agree?"

"The most difficult part was getting them here quickly. Mr. Cromwell, the elder, wants to expand his plantation, for which he needs more field hands, and his shipping concerns in Mobile, for which he needs more capital. I expect that he will ask for money and more than twenty field hands, and I am prepared to grant him both. You do not need to know the details, but he and I have been involved in negotiations whereby I will invest in his shipping enterprises. I know that he needs my capital because my agents have inspected his ledgers and concluded that the shipping company is not performing as well as he claims."

The Cromwells arrived late Friday night. On Saturday afternoon, after dinner, the gentlemen went to my husband's office and the ladies to the library. I folded my hands in my lap, as they were shaking, because I was uncomfortable about having to begin the conversation.

"Mrs. Cromwell, this is extremely difficult for me, as a mother . . ."

"Yes, Mrs. Allen?"

"Sometimes our children do not conduct themselves in ways that are consistent with their upbringing. Clarissa and your son, they . . ."

"Mama, please, permit me to . . . Mrs. Cromwell, what Mama is trying to say is that . . ." Clarissa closed her eyes and dabbed them with her handkerchief.

"What is it, dear?"

"I'm so ashamed, Mrs. Cromwell. Julius . . . he . . . he took my honor." Clarissa now cried and put her head down.

"Oh dear. Are you saying that you and my son . . . ?"

"We were both at fault, Mrs. Cromwell. I should have insisted on not riding alone with him. But please, please do not punish your future grandson because of what Julius and I did. Please, Mrs. Cromwell."

"Oh . . . you are expecting? So that is why we were invited here, to consent to a much earlier wedding date."

"Yes, Mrs. Cromwell," I said.

"Come here, you little angel. Of course I agree. I would never permit my grandson to be born out of wedlock."

Mrs. Cromwell kissed Clarissa then, and they embraced.

"I am so relieved, Mrs. Cromwell. Clarissa, it is a blessing that you will have Mrs. Cromwell as your mother-in-law."

"Thank you, Mrs. Allen. You are gracious. Let us pray that the gentlemen will arrive at the same conclusion."

We spoke at length about the wedding and agreed that there would be no honey-month, given that Clarissa was expecting. Mrs. Cromwell reminded us that the new home would not be completed until the following year and that Julius and Clarissa would initially have to live with his parents. Mr. Cromwell, Julius, and Cornelius, who were all smiling, joined us in the library. My husband embraced Clarissa and me.

"Ladies, all is well with us, and with you?"

"Yes, with us, too," I said.

"Then you may go forward with wedding arrangements, for early next month. Gentlemen, join me in the parlor for a well-deserved brandy."

The wedding ceremony was held on a Saturday afternoon at our church. Early the next morning, the servants loaded two carriages with Clarissa's possessions. I promised my darling that her father and I had already spoken with Mrs. Cromwell about visiting them in two months, and that we certainly planned to be there for the baby's birth.

The month following Clarissa's wedding, my sister-in-law wrote that her father was gravely ill and my husband and I traveled to Montgomery. I notified Clarissa, and she wrote to me there:

Dear Mama:

Every night, before I fall asleep, I make a pact with myself that, in the morning, as Papa taught me, I will "rise and shine" and "seize the day." But, after Sarah brings me breakfast and I eat, I cannot leave my bed. She warns me that it is not good for the baby if I do not stretch my limbs, but I do not go outside. Sarah wakes me to dress in the evening, and that is the first time of the day that I venture outside my bedroom. At supper, the gentlemen report on their activities, and the women listen. Afterward, I go upstairs to the bedroom. My husband sometimes joins me later. Whether I am asleep or not when he arrives, he does to me what he wants. Sarah says that you should visit soon, as only you will be able to make me change my newly acquired slothful ways.

I told my husband about Clarissa's letter.

"Write her and tell her to stop behaving like a moronic child."

"I would like to see her soon."

"No. Stop coddling her. We will visit her when we are able."

My father-in-law passed away, and we stayed in Montgomery after the funeral to dispose of estate issues and to comfort my mother-in-law. When we returned home after a month, I asked my husband if we could go to Talladega, but he said that we had been away from the plantation for too long and there was much to be done. Clarissa wrote again, briefly stating that she had lost her appetite and some days did not even rise for supper. I told her father what she said.

"Well, damn it, tell her to eat. Has she lost all common sense?"

I wrote Clarissa pleading with her to eat and to take care of herself, but she did not reply. Emmeline and Bessie came to me one afternoon when I did not rise from my own bed.

"Ma'am, we're sorry if you was sleeping and we woke you, but we thought maybe you was sick and need something."

"No, I am not ill, but thank you, Bessie."

"Ma'am, I beg your pardon, but I need to ask you if you heard anything about Miss Clarissa and my Sarah," Emmeline said.

I turned on my other side to look at them. "No, I have not received a letter from Clarissa in quite some time, and I don't know what to do. I believe, based upon her last letter, that Sarah is well, but not Clarissa."

"Ma'am, can't you go to Talladega?"

"No, Mr. Allen says that now is not a good time to leave home."

That night my husband came to my bedroom. "I understand that you want to go to Talladega to see your daughter."

"Yes. Yes, I do."

"I don't believe that it is necessary, but since you have taken to your bed, the servants are worried about you. The coachman will take you in my carriage tomorrow. Bessie and Emmeline may go with you."

"Thank you. Thank you. I am truly concerned about Clarissa."

"I am certain that she is well and simply wants you to rush to her side."

When we arrived at the Cromwell home, a servant sent for Mrs. Cromwell.

"Mrs. Allen, what a surprise. We did not know you were coming."

"Clarissa has not replied to my letters, and my husband and I decided that I should immediately come to see her. I apologize, but I was not able to write in advance. I pray that you understand that this is an unusual circumstance."

"Mrs. Allen, you are welcome here at any time."

"Thank you. Please direct me to my daughter."

"Please have some refreshments first and your servants may go to their quarters."

"No, thank you. I need to see Clarissa straightaway and my servants will accompany me."

"Yes, yes, of course. I will show you to her chambers. My husband and son are not here. They are traveling."

My dear Clarissa was asleep in a dark room. I asked Bessie to open the draperies. Clarissa's hair was dirty and her skin jaundiced. Her belly stuck out of her thin frame.

"Mrs. Cromwell, where is Sarah?"

"She is in the kitchen."

"Why is she there? As Clarissa's maid, her responsibility is to be with her mistress at all times to care for her."

"That is a decision my husband has made. I will send someone for her." She departed.

"Clarissa, dearest, your mother is here. Please, Puppet, please open your eyes."

Her eyelids fluttered. I touched her cheek and she awoke.

"Mama. Mama. Are you really here, Mama? I've called for you many times, but . . . how silly of me. You couldn't hear me."

"Puppet, Emmeline and Bessie are here, too."

I continued to reassure Clarissa that I would take care of her.

Sarah arrived and embraced her mother.

"Sarah, what has happened to Clarissa?"

"Ma'am, I asked Mrs. Cromwell to write you a letter saying that Miss Clarissa was sick, but she wouldn't do it. I would have asked her again, but she told me that if I ever spoke to her again in that manner she would tell her son to put me in my place. And she said there was nothing wrong with Miss Clarissa."

"Dear God, why are they mistreating my child? Sarah, did they call a physician for her?"

"Yes, ma'am. He comes two times a week."

"Are you present when he examines her?"

"No, ma'am, not anymore, only in the beginning when he first started coming. Now, they don't even let me see her much. They told me that I had to help in the kitchen and only look after Miss Clarissa in the morning and at night. And they said that I was going to get whipped if I didn't stop asking to go to my mistress."

"Did they hurt you, baby?" Emmeline asked.

"No, Mama. They didn't."

Emmeline asked Sarah what Clarissa had been eating. "Mama, I try to do the best I can to get her to eat porridge in the morning and meat at night, but I think she only eats when I feed her, ma'am."

"Do you know if the doctor bled her?"

"Oh yes, Mama. I saw him do it, and, ma'am, look."

Sarah lifted the sleeves of Clarissa's nightdress. Clarissa's forearms were blue and swollen. I wiped the tears from my eyes. "Emmeline. . . ."

She nodded and approached Clarissa. "Miss Clarissa, please wake up. Miss Clarissa?"

"Is that Emmeline? Where is Mama?"

"Bessie, please go see if you can find somebody to bring a tea service with three pots and some very hot boiled water. And I'm going to need some clean linen cloths," Emmeline said.

"Miss Clarissa, I'm going to need you to try to stay awake, all right, just until I ask you a few things. Can you understand me, Miss Clarissa?"

"Yes, Emmeline. Emmeline, having you here is like I'm back at home. . . ."

"Miss Clarissa, the doctor took blood from your arms, right?"

"Papa. Where is Papa? Is he here?" She closed her eyes and went to sleep.

"Sarah, do you know if the doctor gave her laudanum?"

"Yes, Mama, he did. He gives it to her every time he comes."

"How do you know that?"

"I have to clean up after him."

"All right, Sarah. I have some other questions for you. Try to remember back to when Miss Clarissa first got sick. Did she have any bleeding?"

"Yes, Mama. She called me in the middle of the night. She was screaming."

"Was it a lot of blood, like during your monthly, when it's heavy?"

"No, Mama. It wasn't that heavy."

"Did it get on the bed linen?"

"No, ma'am. It was only on her undergarments."

"Did she say if her belly hurt, too?"

"Yes, ma'am."

"And her back, did she say if it hurt?"

"Yes, ma'am, that, too."

Bessie returned with the tea service and linen cloths. Emmeline withdrew three dried herbs from her baggage and allowed them to steep in the pots for about ten minutes. She strained the teas and poured them in cups.

"All right, we're all going to help to wake Miss Clarissa and sit her up so she can start drinking the teas. Sarah, so you know what to do after we go back home, the teas I made are ginger root to make her stomach feel better and make her want to eat, red raspberry to make her strong, and alfalfa to stop the bleeding. Before it gets dark outside, Sarah, me and you is going to look for dandelion root that you will boil for Miss Clarissa to eat, or at least to drink mixed with beef broth. She's going to feel better, too, because she won't be getting bled or taking laudanum."

When Clarissa had finished drinking the ginger tea, we let her rest. In the meantime, Emmeline asked for more hot water, which she used to brew calendula to make poultices to heal the wounds and ease the pain on Clarissa's arms caused by the physician's bleeding. We followed Emmeline's instructions, and the third day after our arrival, Clarissa was markedly improved. Her cheeks were rosy and she spent more time awake. Sarah and Bessie helped Clarissa bathe and washed her hair. The afternoon of the fourth day, the physician arrived, and Mrs. Cromwell took him to Clarissa's bedroom. I was in the adjoining room with Bessie. Emmeline was with Clarissa, and Sarah was in the kitchen.

"Ma'am, the doctor is here," Emmeline alerted me.

I went to Clarissa's bedroom.

"Ma'am, you are looking very well," he was saying to Clarissa.

Mrs. Cromwell presented the physician to me.

"Yes, Dr. Walker, my daughter is much improved because she is eating and taking tonics that my servant has prepared for her, and she is feeling much better because you have not recently bled her and given her laudanum. Because of your mistreatment of my daughter, your services are no longer needed."

"Mrs. Allen," said Mrs. Cromwell, "Dr. Walker is the physician for all the ladies in Talladega County and has safely delivered all their babies, including my grandchildren."

"Thank you. I am certain we will rely on Dr. Walker for the delivery, if he agrees that he will stop bleeding my daughter and giving her laudanum."

"Mrs. Allen, these are standard medical practices."

"They are not effective for my daughter. You will not bleed her or give her laudanum again. Is that understood?"

"Yes, Mrs. Allen."

"When I return to my home, Sarah, my daughter's maid who lives here with her, will see to all her needs. This is Sarah's mother, Emmeline. She has learned midwifery and, in fact, assisted the physician who delivered my children. Emmeline has taught Sarah how to care for women who are expecting. You will be available, then, to deliver the child? Or shall I request a physician in Benton County to attend to my daughter?"

"I will be available for the delivery."

"Thank you, Dr. Walker."

"Should I examine Mrs. Cromwell today?"

"That will not be necessary."

We remained in Talladega for three weeks, until Clarissa was able to take short walks in the garden. She and I joined Mrs. Cromwell and her guests at supper several times. The Cromwell gentlemen returned from their travels two days before we departed for home. The evening before we left, Mrs. Cromwell asked to speak with me privately.

"My husband asked me to discuss a delicate matter with you. He believes that a gentleman should not have this conversation with a lady. I told him that you objected that Sarah works in the kitchen. He said that I should explain to you that he had to send four of the servants that your husband gave to my son to the fields. He asked whether you and your husband would consider giving my son an advance on the twenty field hands that are promised to him upon the birth of the child."

"Mrs. Cromwell, my husband does not involve me in any aspect of his financial matters. As mistress of my household, my only concerns are domestic."

"I see. Well, this is a domestic concern. How shall I say this? Mrs. Allen, I have a sister who married into a family in Montgomery. Perhaps you know them? The Andersons? My sister informed me that, months ago, while my son was courting Clarissa, she frequently visited another young gentleman in Montgomery."

"Clarissa's paternal extended family lives in Montgomery, and that is who she was visiting. Your sister should not have repeated such a baseless allegation."

Mrs. Cromwell widened her eyes and lifted an eyebrow.

"Mrs. Allen, one cannot characterize this knowledge as baseless when your daughter was expecting a child on her wedding day. And please understand that I am not trying to be callous."

"That may not have been your intent, but it is the result."

"I apologize to you. But you do understand my son's predicament? He will be expected to acknowledge a child that may not be his."

"Mrs. Cromwell, you may tell your husband and son this: Your son did not merely take my daughter's honor but forced her to surrender it. No amount of unsubstantiated claims concerning my daughter's visits to her grandparents will negate your son's unlawful conduct. You may also tell them that my husband read law at the University of Virginia and has informed me that, once a child is born in wedlock, he is presumed to be legitimate and the child of the mother's husband. The only reason my husband consented to the financial arrangement whereby your son will receive twenty field hands is because he did not want you and your family to spread lies about our daughter and destroy our name, but if that is what you nevertheless plan to do, I am certain that my husband will retract his offer."

"No, no, Mrs. Allen, I assure you that this conversation is only between us. I will tell my husband your reply immediately. Please wait for me here. I won't be long."

She returned in about five minutes. "My husband apologizes for our misunderstanding. He did not know that Clarissa was visiting her grandparents when she went to Montgomery. Please, let us forget this conversation, shall we? There is no need for Mr. Allen to hear of this, do you think?"

There was a knowing, but silent, acquiescence.

ELEVEN

SARAH CAMPBELL

Our cabin on the Cromwell plantation was near the stables and smelled like horse manure. There was no garden. Isaac replaced a piece of wood that was missing from the shutters, and he put more nails on the walls so that we could hang our clothes. Isaac's first uniform belonged to a prior coachman. The length of the trousers fit Isaac, but the other man apparently was wider and heavier. I asked the overseer whether a carpenter could make repairs in my cabin and build us furniture, but he said that he could not spare someone until Mr. Cromwell's house was completed. When we had been in Talladega about a week, I asked him for maid's uniforms, but he said I would not need those, as I was going to spend most of the time in the kitchen.

"Sir, I beg your pardon, but I'm Mrs. Clarissa Cromwell's maid."

"I got instructions from Mrs. Cromwell, the mistress of this household, that, starting this coming Monday, you'll work in the kitchen during the day. You can attend to Mrs. Clarissa in the morning and evening."

"But I also have to clean Mr. and Mrs. Julius Cromwell's quarters and do their washing and ironing."

"And? You still got to do them things, too."

I found Clarissa in the garden, sitting on a bench, alone.

"Miss Clarissa, I need to speak with you."

"We may speak here. Just keep your voice low."

I told her what the overseer said.

"Tell him to come here immediately."

"But he may be angry at me for telling you."

"Nonsense, he's just an overseer."

"Miss Clarissa, I know how these overseers are."

"I'll speak with Mrs. Cromwell. Go ahead upstairs and wait for me in my bedroom."

I was dusting when she returned. She stamped her foot and threw her hat on a chair and spoke loudly.

"How dare she? How dare that woman speak to me that way? Who is she and who is her husband, with his little plantation?"

"What did she say?"

"I'm writing Papa and Mama a letter, right now."

She sat at her desk and began writing, then paused while she spoke to me. "She said that, because her husband sent four of the house servants that Papa gave them to the fields, you're needed in the kitchen. She said that it was her husband's decision, which she cannot overrule. I'm telling you, this will not stand. That is not how my parents raised me. I need a maid who will devote all of her time to me. And I will tell Papa that they have you washing and ironing for Julius and that Isaac is no longer my coachman but his." She continued writing and finished the letter. "Here, tell the overseer to send this letter home."

There were only four servants who worked in the kitchen, including me, whereas at the Allen house, there were ten. At the Allen house, once I became Clarissa's maid, I only helped Mama when there were guests, but here, I would only be able to attend to Clarissa between many other tasks. Isaac's life also changed because there were fewer stable hands helping him than at Allen Estates. He was gone more often and told me that he drove Julius to town, where Julius spent a week at a time with his mistress. He cautioned me not to repeat that information to anyone, as Julius warned him that he expected not to hear anything about it from Clarissa.

"I'm glad that his attention is elsewhere," I said.

"What do you mean by that?"

"He's not looking for a woman here."

The only benefit to working as much as I did was that I had no time to be bored, and I would have been, as there was no library in the house. There was a Bible in Clarissa's bedroom, and she brought newspapers to her room for me.

"These people are an ignorant and uneducated lot. I'll ask Mama to send me books, or our brains may rot."

"Miss Clarissa, is there a place in town where they order books?"

"That's a good idea. I'll ask Mrs. Cromwell."

Mrs. Cromwell told Clarissa that they could go to the general store, where the proprietor could order goods for her from Mobile and New Orleans. I was not able to accompany them because I had to work in the kitchen. When I saw Clarissa that evening, she had no kind words to say about her expedition with her mother-in-law.

"The so-called general store is a smelly hole, and the filthy owner, who scratched himself, said that he had never had a request for 'things to read.' I never imagined that there was a more back-woods town than ours. Dear God, what have I done? Sarah, I hope you'll forgive me."

"Forgive you?"

"For bringing us to this godforsaken place to live among these wretched people."

Several weeks passed, and when Clarissa did not receive a re-sponse from her father, she wrote him again. She said to me that, in the interim, I had no choice but to continue working as I had been ordered. The overseer told me one day to go to the cobbler in town to get Mr. Cromwell's new riding boots and to take his other boots for repair. I met the wagon driver by the stables. We left the planta-tion without being stopped. I asked him if he had a pass.

"We don't need a pass because the patrollers in town know us. So long as we leave town before the curfew bell ring, we're all right."

The cobbler's shop was busy, and I waited my turn to speak to the man as he assisted other customers.

"Are you new in town?"

"Yes, sir. I'm the lady's maid for the new Mrs. Cromwell."

"Where did you live before coming here?"

"At Allen Estates in Benton County."

The man then showed me the new boots and wrapped them in brown paper, which he tied with a string. As he took the boots from me that needed to be repaired, he lowered his voice. "These will be done next week, Thursday. That's a nice quiet day here. My master, Mr. Stephens, he's not here Thursdays to Saturdays. Make sure you come get these yourself, all right, Miss . . ."

"Sarah."

"I'll be here. My name is Daniel."

The following Wednesday evening, Clarissa told me to sleep in her room because her husband was not at home and she was not feeling well. Early Thursday morning, she woke me because she was bleeding and in pain. I lit lamps, and when we lifted her nightdress, we saw blood on her undergarments.

"Do you want me to go to Mrs. Cromwell and ask that she send for the doctor?"

"No, no. Is there anything that you can give me?"

"I don't know too much about stopping bleeding. That's why I think someone should send for the doctor."

"No, Mama warned me about those doctors."

"All right. We can try alfalfa tea."

After I helped her to wash and change her clothing, she drank the remedy and we went back to sleep. When she awoke, she said that her back hurt but that the bleeding had stopped. I told her that I had to go to the cobbler's for Mr. Cromwell's boots.

"No, you can't go. I need you here with me. I'll tell his mother to tell the overseer to send someone else. What is it? You seem disappointed that you can't go to get his boots."

"No, that's not true. I don't care who collects the master's boots."

Clarissa complained of back and abdominal pain and stayed in bed. The bleeding returned, and this time it was heavier and the pain more severe. She agreed that Mrs. Cromwell should send for a physician. When he arrived, he ordered me to stay in the room in the event he needed me to fetch anything for him.

"How far along are you, Mrs. Cromwell?"

Clarissa looked at me. "Well, about . . . um . . . four months."

"Would you say more than four?"

"No, I would not. I was married four months ago. Four."

"Mrs. Cromwell, then we must consider that you are carrying twins, because your abdomen appears about seven months. . . ."

"Dr. Walker, I will say this to you once again, and I expect no more discussion about it with me or with anyone else: I am four months along."

"Yes, ma'am."

"What can you do to end the bleeding?"

"The accepted practice for ladies in your condition is to divert the blood. Thus, I will bleed you from your arm."

"That is the only remedy?"

"Yes. It takes time, but it does successfully end abnormal bleeding."

"Is there anything that you prescribe for the pain?"

"Yes, I can immediately end your pain with laudanum. I will not prescribe it on a daily basis because of your condition, but I will give you enough to last you until I return."

I was present the first time that he bled Clarissa and gave her laudanum. When she began to resist his treatment, he told me to hold her down.

"Doctor, she doesn't want you to bleed her."

"What is this impertinence? Do not speak to me unless I speak to you first. Go call Mrs. Cromwell. Now."

When Mrs. Cromwell arrived in Clarissa's room, Dr. Walker told her that I did not obey his commands and that he did not want me present. She told me to go to the kitchen.

"I will speak with the overseer about your discipline," she said.

"I want Sarah here. She is my maid, not yours," Clarissa said.

"Clarissa, dear, Dr. Walker is simply trying to make you better. Your maid is interfering with your treatment."

"He is not treating me. He's cutting my arm."

"Can you give her anything to make her less irritable?" she asked Dr. Walker.

"What are you still doing here, idiot? Leave now," the doctor said to me.

I went to the kitchen and stayed there until the overseer arrived and castigated me in front of the other slaves.

"Mrs. Cromwell told me to discipline you for your conduct this morning."

"But I was only attending to my mistress."

"Don't interrupt me. And here, she's not your mistress. Mrs. Cromwell wanted me to give you ten lashes, but she decided to wait for Mr. Cromwell's return for what he thinks is the right punishment."

I was afraid.

"Mr. Pinnock, I'm sorry for what I did, and I won't do it again."

"Oh, I know that."

Mr. Cromwell must have decided not to have me whipped or else they forgot about my infraction, for upon his return, I was not called to stand before him. The following week, when I was working in the kitchen, Mrs. Cromwell's maid told me to go to Clarissa. As I approached her bedroom, I heard familiar voices and ran into the room. My sweet mother was there with Mrs. Allen and Bessie. I curtsied to Mrs. Allen and embraced my mother and Bessie.

"Ma'am, did you get Miss Clarissa's letters?"

"We received only two letters. How many did she send?"

"Ma'am, she wrote you five letters since we've been here," I told Mrs. Allen.

"I will discuss that with Mrs. Cromwell later, but first, we have to care for Clarissa."

It was a joy to have my mother with me, even though it was under difficult circumstances. I told my mother and Mrs. Allen everything that had transpired regarding Clarissa's illness before their arrival. After a few days of my mother's care, Clarissa was greatly improved. They stayed with us for three weeks. Clarissa and I cried and pleaded with them to stay longer, but Mr. Allen had written that they were to return to Benton County.

"Clarissa, dear, Emmeline, Bessie, and I will return for the baby's birth," Mrs. Allen said.

"Mama, why can't you stay until the baby is born? What if something happens and you're not here?"

"Dear, Sarah will be here with you. Emmeline has taught her how to care for you."

"You'll see, baby; we'll be back soon. Don't cry," my mother said to me.

I walked with them to the carriage and watched until they passed out of the plantation gate. The following week, the overseer gave me a list and told me to go to the smokehouse to get meats for the cook. When I arrived, I gave the overseer there the list, and he told a slave the quantities of each meat to load on the wagon. The slave told me to follow him into the smokehouse, where there was a low fire on the dirt floor and meats dangling from the rafters. He gave me a ham to carry, and he put the rest of the meats in a wheelbarrow. We were alone at the wagon as we loaded the goods.

"Miss, you're Sarah, right?"

"Yes, I am. How do you know about me?"

"Daniel, the cobbler in town, he need to talk to you."

"Pardon me?"

"We ain't got much time. The cobbler sent word that you was in his shop last month, and he was expecting you to go back. Can you go back to see him?"

"No, I can't. My mistress is sick, and I can only go to town if I go with her or they tell me to do something there."

"All right. I'll get word to him that you can't go to him, and he'll find another way to talk to you."

I continued to care for Clarissa in the morning and at night. Her health deteriorated again because, contrary to Mrs. Allen's orders, Dr. Walker visited her two times a week to bleed her and give her laudanum. When she was lucid, I tried to get Clarissa to write her mother, asking her to come see her again, but she said that there was no purpose in doing so because she believed no one was actually sending the letters. During the day, I worked in the kitchen and in Clarissa and Julius's quarters. Julius was gone most of the time, and when he was home, he slept in his own rooms. I did not see Isaac much because he drove Julius's carriage, and I had to stay with Clarissa at night.

Mrs. Cromwell's maid, carrying a basket of her mistress's garments, came to see me one afternoon when I was washing clothes. "We can talk. Ain't nobody else around. But we got to talk fast before somebody come by. My husband belong to the Wilkes Plantation, and he come to stay with me Saturday and Sunday. He's a blacksmith in town and he know Daniel, the cobbler."

She put down the basket and stepped outside the washroom. "I was looking to see if anybody had come around. Daniel sent word that he need your help. Master Wilkes is taking slaves to auction next week, and two of them want to run."

"Why does he think I can help?"

"I really don't know. But, Sarah, I think that one of the slaves Master Wilkes is going to sell is my husband. He's worth a lot of money because he's a blacksmith."

"I'm so sorry, Grace. If there's any way that I can help, I will; but really, they don't let me go anywhere and they watch me all the time. Now that Miss Clarissa is sick, I can't even go to town at all."

"I don't know how they think you can help, but my husband said

Daniel want you to ask for permission to go to the fields this Saturday night. When you get there, somebody's going to give you a package that only you can open. Open it when you is alone. You don't have to ask for nobody, they'll find you."

Clarissa was alert that evening because Dr. Walker had not been to see her in three days.

"Miss Clarissa, do you think you can give me permission to go down to the fields Saturday evening? You know, back home, Saturday and Sundays were our nights when we didn't have to work, but I haven't had any rest since we've been here."

"Yes, Sarah, of course. Dr. Walker is coming Saturday afternoon. I'm sure that I'll be asleep from the laudanum all night anyway."

"Would you speak to Mrs. Cromwell?"

"Yes. Make sure you ask her to come see me today."

Mrs. Cromwell consented to the request. That Saturday evening, Isaac was gone with Julius, and I went to the fields in a wagon with seven other slaves. As we neared the quarters, I heard singing and clapping. When we arrived, the area, much like the Allen Estates slave quarters on a Saturday, but on a smaller scale, was transformed from its normal appearance. The slaves had created a festive marketplace where they sold or traded goods that they had made or grown. I regretted that I did not take money because a woman was selling colorful quilts, and other people were selling preserved fruit, honey, pies, cakes, baskets, hats, flowers, eggs, and even shoes.

Kate, one of the house servants, stayed with me as we walked. A woman gave me sweet tea, which made me think of Isaac, and when it was dark, Kate took me to meet her family, who were gathered at her grandmother's cabin. The children were playing, and the sight of them caused me to miss my family even more than usual. Kate's mother gave me food and more sweet tea.

"What's wrong, darling? You don't like tea?"

"Yes, ma'am, I like tea just fine. It's just that, the first time I met my husband, that's what I gave him, sweet tea and peach cobbler."

"I bet you did."

I realized that I had not laughed since we arrived at the Cromwell plantation. They lit lanterns, and we gathered in a circle around Miss Patience, Kate's grandmother. She told us stories, most of which I had heard from my mother and other women at Allen Estates. When it was late, the man who worked at the smokehouse arrived. He was holding a package.

"Miss Sarah, my wife met you at the market. She said you was admiring some of her fruit. Here's a jar of her strawberry jam."

"Oh, but, I didn't bring . . ."

"No, this is a gift. Maybe next time you come you can buy something."

"Please thank her for me, and the next time I will bring money to buy some things from the market."

We stayed until about midnight, and then Kate and I met the others from the house and the man who drove us at his family's cabin. When I arrived at my cabin, I locked the door and opened the package, which was wrapped in brown paper and tied at the top with a string. There were stones instead of jam in the bottle. An unsigned letter in a blank envelope that was wrapped around the bottle read:

To Bearer:

> *You are asked to prepare a traveling pass in the names and descriptions of slaves which you will obtain from the slave in the washroom. Use a pen and ink from the house. Make the pass tomorrow, put it in the envelope, wrap it around the same bottle, and then cover the bottle. Someone will retrieve the package the next evening.*

The blank envelope also enclosed a sheet of Mr. Wilkes's letterhead. I was afraid but also excited.

I rose before dawn Sunday morning and went to the kitchen to start the fire. When the cook arrived, I had drawn water from the well and made tea.

"Why you up so early?"

"I was at the fields last night, and I want to see Miss Clarissa to make sure that she's all right."

I went to the house, and the night watchman let me enter. I put the tea service on a table next to Clarissa's bed. She was asleep. There were two pens on the desk in her room and bottles of ink in the drawer. It was not likely that anyone would know if these items were missing because I was the only one who polished and dusted the desk. It was not difficult to fit the pen in my pocket, but the ink was visible. I went to the broom cabinet and took my pail to Clarissa's room. I put the pen and ink under my cleaning rags and took my bucket to my cabin. On the way, the only people I saw were two children going to the well. Once I was inside, I hid the pen and ink in the rice that I kept in a jar. Then I returned to Clarissa, who was still sleeping. I went to the kitchen, and as I was cooking ham, Grace entered and greeted everyone. She stood next to me to speak, but there were too many people within hearing distance.

"Miss Georgianna, Grace's stomach is sick. Could someone else finish the ham while we go to my cabin to get her something?" I asked.

"Sure, sure. Go ahead," the cook said.

When we were in the cabin, Grace told me the names and descriptions of the two men.

"Grace, I need to ask you something. If your husband runs, won't it be the same as if he's sold? You'll never see him again."

"I know, I know, and it's killing me, but if they sell him, it could be to a worse place. They're selling a lot of people for new plantations out west. If he run and make it, he'll be free. He's a good man. He said he's going to put money away, and that the same people who is helping him could help me and the children to try to get out when the children is older. I know it's just a dream, Sarah. I know."

"I will help in any way I can."

"Thank you, Sarah. I know I'm not supposed to ask, and I

won't, but whatever it is you're doing for us, I know that you're taking a chance."

"You're welcome. I hope one day someone will do the same for me."

That evening, after we finished making supper and I helped Clarissa to eat, the cook gave me permission to go to my cabin. I wrote the pass, using the language that I had memorized years before, and signed it as Mr. Wilkes. My only concern was that all of Mr. Allen's passes had wax seals and this one would not. I put the pass under the bed to let it dry while I had my meal, and I put the pen and ink under the rags in the bucket. I completed the instructions for wrapping the pass in the package and sat down to rest. I fell asleep with my head on the table and awoke when there was a knock on the door. It was Kate. I let her in.

"How was the jam?"

"It was delicious."

"The wagon driver is taking me to the quarters tonight. I'll sleep there and come back early in the morning with meat from the smokehouse for tomorrow's meals. If you want, I can take the empty bottle back and bring you more jam."

Two days later, I was in the kitchen when two patrollers arrived. One asked the cook which one of us was Sarah. She pointed at me.

"You, come with us."

"Sir?"

"Are you Sarah?"

"Yes, sir."

"Then come with us. Now."

I followed them, keeping my hands in my pockets so that they could not see them shake. We stopped next to their wagon.

"Why was Grace in your cabin?"

"Sir?"

"Don't play dumb. Somebody seen you talking to her in the washroom and whispering to her in the kitchen, and then the two of you went to your cabin. What was you talking about and why did you go to your cabin?"

"Sir, she, well, my mother taught me about remedies for women's troubles and Grace asked me if I had any. I gave her some when we went to my cabin."

"Why you talk so good?"

"Sir, my mistress and I are the same age. We played together when we were children and I have been her maid since I was eight years old."

"Did Grace ever ask you to do anything for her husband?"

"Sir? No, I don't even know her husband. Who is he?"

"We ain't here to answer your questions. Now go back to the kitchen. If we ever hear that you been in any trouble again, it's off to the whipping post and jail for you. We'll let Mr. Cromwell decide what to do with you after that. You're going to learn how we handle niggers, even yellow ones, here. You understand?"

"Yes, sir, I do. Thank you, sir."

When I returned, no one spoke to me. That evening, I told Clarissa what happened.

"I don't like the idea of patrollers speaking to you without my permission. I'll ask that decayed strumpet why they questioned you. Tell her maid that I request an audience with her mistress."

Mrs. Cromwell arrived after supper, and Clarissa dismissed me. I stood outside the room until she departed, and then I reentered.

"She said that her maid's abroad husband who lived on the Wilkes Plantation escaped. They think that Grace, with help from slaves here, helped him escape."

"Did he escape?"

"Well, that's why I don't know why there is a fuss. Mr. Wilkes retained slave catchers, and they brought him and another slave who ran with him back within a day."

"What makes them think that someone from here helped them?"

"This is the interesting part. The crone said that every year about six slaves escape from here, and they think that someone here helps them write passes. Sarah? You were not involved, were you?"

"Miss Clarissa, how could you think that? I don't know most of the people here or in any other plantation in Talladega. I don't leave this place. And why would I risk my life for people I don't even know?"

"Sarah, if anyone ever asks you to help them in something like that, you must be certain that you do not. Papa told me about these things, including about fraudulent passes, and this is not the first time it has been tried. Whenever a slave escapes, the owner hires slave catchers immediately and places advertisements in the newspapers, and if a slave presents a pass, the slave catchers know it was not written by the slave's master. And don't tell anyone that you know how to read and write, because you could implicate my mother and me."

"No, ma'am. I would never tell anyone that. I know it's against the law."

I saw Isaac the following evening. I did not have to be with Clarissa for several hours because she said she was well enough to have supper with the Cromwells.

"Somebody told me that patrollers was here today, and they talked to you about those slaves who tried to run. Why did they talk to you? You didn't have nothing to do with it, did you?"

"No, of course not. Why did you think I did?"

"Because you like to talk about running away. If you had a hand in this, stop it. You could get us both in trouble. And don't listen to these fools around here. You got to be a idiot to think you can escape. Ain't they never heard of patrollers and militias?"

"Maybe some people think it's worth the risk. Not every single slave is caught, you know."

"Every slave that runs thinks he the one that's going to get away."

"But some do escape, don't you know that?"

"Name one that you know."

"My mother told me that when she went to New York, there were freedmen there who had escaped."

"How long ago was that?"

"Well, before I was born."

"That's your answer, right there. The laws keep getting harder and harder against us, making it tougher to escape. Now how many people do you know bought themselves and their families out of slavery? That's right, a lot more than those who escaped."

TWELVE

THEODORA ALLEN

T he return journey from the Cromwell plantation in Talladega to Allen Estates was uneventful, until we crossed the boundary into Benton County. Blue patches of sky were being overrun by cobalt clouds, and when we passed the Tutwiler property, the wind accelerated, blowing dust around us. Lightning hit a tree and sawed off one of its limbs. The sound of thunder made me jump in my seat. The front left horse halted, causing the other five to drag the carriage to the right and we veered off the road until the coachman pulled the reins and we stopped. He descended from his seat and tried to calm the animals. Bessie and Emmeline came to my assistance.

"You all right, ma'am?"

"Yes, I am well. Thank you."

The coachman inspected the wheels of the carriage and shook his head.

"Ma'am, one of the wheels hit a rock. Ma'am, I'm going to need you to get out; please, ma'am, so I can try to fix it."

Bessie and Emmeline helped me down from the coach. I put on

my hat and lowered the veil to prevent particles of grit from getting into my eyes. My servants covered their faces with their shawls.

"Ma'am, I don't think I can fix it, and the horses is scared from the lightning and thunder. And it's going to rain real hard, soon. Ma'am, I think I should take one of the horses and go get some help. Ma'am, should I go home or try to find somebody closer?"

"You should go home and come back with my carriage. Tell an overseer to send someone with you who can fix the wheel."

The coachman covered the horses with leather blankets and their heads with fly masks before departing. I told Bessie and Emmeline to come into the carriage with me. At first, they hesitated.

"Come in, come in. It's too dusty outside, and it will begin to rain soon." When the coachman had been gone about ten minutes, drizzle turned into torrent. "Let us pray," I said.

I thought that we would have to wait only about three hours, but the coachman and a blacksmith did not arrive until more than six hours had elapsed.

"We're sorry, ma'am, but the rain's coming down harder closer to home. They say it's been raining since yesterday without stopping."

"Did you see Master Allen?"

"No, ma'am. They say he's been at the fields most of the time since the weather's been so bad."

It was still raining when we arrived home. There was no sentry posted at the front gate or at the house. Bessie and I waited in the carriage while Emmeline went inside. She returned with the overseer, who said that just he and Belle were at Allen Hall, as Mr. Allen had ordered all the other house servants to help in the fields.

"Ma'am, I stayed behind to wait for you, but I'm going down there to help to try save the cotton plants."

"Is there any hope?"

"Well, ma'am, we've been putting tarpaulin over the shrubs and draining water from the roots. Mr. Allen said that when it stop raining and the sun come out, they'll dry out. Ma'am, Mr. Allen said that Bessie and Emmeline are to stay with you. He'll be back late."

The overseer left for the fields. Bessie served me supper and helped me to bed. I fell asleep quickly, and when I awoke, I thought that it was still night. I called Bessie, who said that it was afternoon. She opened the draperies. It was still raining.

"Did Mr. Allen come home?"

"Yes, ma'am. He slept for a few hours, had breakfast, and went back to the fields."

"Who else is here?"

"Just you, me, and Miss Emmeline and Belle, ma'am."

I spent a quiet day reading and writing, and when I went to bed that night, I told Bessie to wake me when my husband arrived. Around eleven o'clock, Bessie said that he was having supper. I told her to ask him to see me before he went to bed. He did not appear, and I went to sleep.

The next day was identical to the prior, except that after supper I waited for him in the parlor. When I heard the front door open, I went to the foyer. Emmeline was there to help him out of his wet outer clothing and handed him a jacket. His eyes were sunken and he needed to shave.

"Theodora, how are you, darling?"

"Mr. Allen, I am well, but how are you?"

"It appears that we may lose much of the crop. The plants, which are still young, are already showing signs of water damage. How is Clarissa?"

"She is better, but there is something else I wish to discuss with you privately."

"Certainly. I will go upstairs to see you after I eat something."

"Shall I sit with you at the table?"

"No, Theodora. I promise I will speak with you afterward."

He arrived as I was fighting sleep.

"Yes, Theodora. What did you want to say?"

"Mrs . . . . Cromwell, she . . . well at first, she said that, just before we left Talla—"

"Theodora. I am exhausted. Speak."

"Mrs. Cromwell at first asked that you give them twenty field hands now instead of waiting until the child is born. She said that it was because they heard a rumor that Clarissa was courted by Mr. Evans in Montgomery at the same time as she was courted by her son."

"What did you tell that numskull?"

"That Clarissa was visiting her grandparents in Montgomery, not Mr. Evans, and that you said that the law presumes a child to be of his mother's husband."

"Well done, Theodora. You do listen to me, after all. What did the ugly dunce say in return?"

"She spoke with her husband and then gave me their apologies. She asked that I not speak of it to you."

"Let us hope that this is the end of that nonsense."

"How do you think we will fare with the crops?"

"Unless it stops raining soon, harvest will be ruined. We may have lost thousands of cotton bales these past three days."

It rained for two more weeks, not a downpour as before but steadily, and then a cold mist supplanted the precipitation. The skies remained gray, and I stayed indoors with the fireplaces lit and saw more of my husband, who by then was spending only a few hours a day in the fields. He was quiet at dinner and supper, and with no guests, we had nothing to say. Each night, after eating only a small amount of food, he drank a bottle of wine by himself and at least two glasses of brandy. One evening he did not come downstairs. I asked a servant where Emmeline was, and he said that she was in the kitchen. I went upstairs and found my husband at his desk, his head on a pile of papers. I woke him.

"Let me help you to your bedroom."

He rubbed his eyes. "No, I have a letter to complete and other work to finish regarding my appointment of the new circuit court judge by the end of this month."

"Why is that always your responsibility? Is there no one else who could handle that matter? It would be better if you rested and finished it tomorrow."

"No, Theodora, I cannot. The state judiciary committee depends on me, as the planter with the largest landholdings and plantation in the county, to appoint the judge and prosecutor on a timely basis. Tell Emmeline I will have my supper later. You go ahead and eat."

When I had dined, I returned to his office. He was asleep again with his head on the desk, but this time he was holding a glass of brandy. I woke him again, but he did not resist this time as I took him to his room and helped him to bed.

"Mrs. Allen, do you make it a habit of undressing helpless men?"

I did not answer him. He went to sleep. The next day, when my husband did not appear for the midday meal, I went upstairs. I found him in his bedroom, alone. He was unclothed under the linen and his face was drawn.

"You're not well?"

"It depends on how you define 'well.'"

"Will the loss of the cotton be devastating?"

"Theodora, Theodora, do not worry about my financial situation. We will still be able to purchase your pretty frocks."

"That was not what I was thinking about. I was asking because your health has deteriorated since the storms began."

"Thank you, dear. Well, let us see. It's not just the lost cotton but the lower cotton prices in Europe and the Northern states and the increase in slave prices. I intended to invest in a new plantation in Texas as well as in Cromwell's shipping business, and now I may not have sufficient capital to participate in either venture. So you see, I am in a bind. Oh, yes, in addition, I promised twenty slaves to Cromwell to prevent my grandson from being born a bastard." He closed his eyes.

"I am so sorry about all of this. I will leave you to your rest," I said.

"No, sit here with me for a moment. Speak to me. I have not heard an intelligent voice in quite some time."

"I am thinking of Clarissa and of going back for the baby's birth. I'm also wondering about the Tutwilers. Should we visit them?"

"I've thought of doing that. Perhaps there is sunshine where they live. Some days, I think of leaving this place. They say the Indies are beautiful, that the rains there are delightful, and that they even have a fanciful name for them: tropical storms. What do you say, Theodora, shall we board a ship in Mobile and go to Barbados or Jamaica?"

We laughed.

"Theodora, the boys say that the roads are still muddy. We should wait until the sun returns to travel."

I stayed with him until he slept. That afternoon, I found a book in my library that I had purchased when we went to Charleston. It depicted scenes of Barbados, the ancestral home of the South Carolinians, and I painted a watercolor for my husband. When I presented it to him later, he was pleased.

"This is what I saw in my mind, dear Theodora, azure skies and palm trees. Thank you."

I enjoyed a temporary respite from Cornelius's capricious nature and regretted that he could not always be as he was that day.

A few days later, Thad, a servant, interrupted our breakfast to say that there were gentlemen waiting to speak to us, and he gave my husband one of their calling cards. We went to the parlor.

"Gentlemen, welcome to our home. Thad, go to the kitchen and return with coffee and tea for everyone. Mr. Fitzhugh, perhaps you care to speak on behalf of our neighbors? Does Mrs. Allen need to be present?"

"Yes, Mr. Allen, I will speak. And, yes, Mrs. Allen should be present because this is a situation that concerns our families. Mr. and Mrs. Allen, two of my slaves escaped yesterday, and they have not been caught."

"Before we say anything else, let's go where we may close the door and speak privately," my husband said.

He told another servant to tell Thad not to disturb us when he returned. We continued the conversation once we were in the drawing room.

"Who has been after them?" my husband asked.

"Two of the most successful catchers with the Pinckney and Jenkins firm, but as you know, if we don't find them within a day, the likelihood is that they'll move beyond our grasp and someone else may find and keep them."

"Was there an event that precipitated their running away?"

"One of my overseers disciplined a slave two weeks ago, but he went too far and killed him. One of the escaped slaves was due for a whipping for theft, and apparently he ran to avoid his punishment."

"Was not the overseer who killed the slave the same one who was almost prosecuted for murder?"

"Yes, and that's another reason why we are here. As you know, sir, we successfully argued against any prosecution because it was not murder, as one cannot murder property. But first, may we discuss the issue of the escaped slaves?"

"Of course. Please proceed."

"Pinckney and Jenkins has information that the Methodist church in town may have helped the slaves to escape, in tandem with a free nigger. . . ."

"Mr. Fitzhugh, do not use coarse language in my presence," I said.

"My apologies, ma'am. The free Negro in town is a tailor who belongs to that church, and we believe he is working with other church members to steal our property."

"Do you have any evidence of this activity?"

"No, sir, we don't, but we have paid Pinckney and Jenkins to post people in the church who pretend to be new members and to watch the ni— Negro. We realize that you have your own searchers, patrollers, and slave catchers, but we ask that you join us in paying Pinckney and Jenkins to provide this service until we apprehend these lawbreakers."

"Permit me to add," another planter said, "that Pinckney and

Jenkins believe that this church is affiliated with abolitionists, as the former and current ministers, father and son, were educated in a divinity school in the North. I think we should find a way to close the church."

"That is a serious allegation," my husband said. "Yes, I will absolutely participate in this endeavor, but only if we find evidence that the church is engaging in illegal activity should we consider disbanding it, encouraging its members to join other places to worship and its minister to find another flock elsewhere. As to the tailor, if we find any proof of his participation, he should be told to go to another town. If he refuses to do so, we can threaten to commence proceedings in court to revoke his freedman's status."

"Thank you, Mr. Allen. The other matter concerns your appointment of the circuit court judge and prosecutor. We cannot have a prosecutor who does not respect our property rights. The prosecutor should not have arrested my overseer. We ask that, when you appoint the incoming judge and prosecutor, they take an oath that they believe that the rule of law should not extend to our treatment of slaves when they are inside our property lines."

"I am in absolute agreement with you. I will suggest to you, however, that with regard to the discipline of slaves, we should similarly instruct our overseers and slave drivers to have respect for our property. Thank you, gentlemen, for promptly notifying me about these concerns. I will send for Pinckney and Jenkins and speak with them concerning my involvement in the resolution of these problems."

Dark skies during the day and constant cold at all times spent us, and another week elapsed where we did not leave home. I was in the parlor reading by the fireplace late one afternoon when I heard my husband's heavy steps upstairs in his office. I heard him slam the door and go downstairs. His hands were trembling, and his face was red. He pointed at me.

"Come upstairs. Right now. Now, I said. Hurry."

I followed him to his office.

"This can't be. It can't be. They are lying," he said.

"What has happened? Who is lying?"

He pointed to his desk. "This . . . is . . . all your doing."

"What? What have I done?"

"Read the damned letter."

I sat down because I was afraid of fainting as I read and reread the first paragraph.

8 June 1854

Dear Mr. Allen:

    By the time you receive this letter, your daughter and your bastard grandson will be on their way to you. I am returning her because she gave birth today to a son who is not mine.

"It cannot be. Why do they hate my child, why are they making up this awful lie about her? My darling girl must be in a lot of pain after the birth, and yet they forced her to travel when she should be confined to her bed. It can't be. I agree with you. He's lying. Of course he is. They just want more field hands. How could they be so greedy?"

I looked at Cornelius, who was silently staring outside the window, and I was trying to guess what he was thinking, fearing that he had changed his mind and now believed Julius's allegation that the child was not his.

"You do agree that they're lying, don't you? That's what you just said, didn't you?"

He slowly turned his head and stared at me.

"You haven't read the next paragraph, where he says why the child can't be his, have you? Read it."

I looked down at the letter and twice read the second paragraph. I began wailing. I let the letter fall from my hand to the floor, and Cornelius picked it up, before leaving the room. He slammed the

door behind him, and then I heard his footsteps on the staircase going downstairs. I stayed in his office, rocking myself, praying that it
was all a bad dream, that Julius had not written a letter accusing our
daughter of having committed such a disgraceful act. After about
an hour I rose and went to my bedroom where, fully clothed, I fell
asleep.

THIRTEEN

SARAH CAMPBELL

The cook, other Cromwell slaves, and I were in the kitchen making supper, several days after I had written the pass for the Wilkes slaves, when the overseer arrived to tell me that, commencing the next morning at nine o'clock, I had to take Mr. Julius Cromwell's morning tea to his apartment.

"But sir, I . . ."

"Be careful what you say, or I'll report to Mr. Cromwell that you questioned his authority."

When I told Clarissa, I was surprised by what she said.

"Sarah, just obey them. There is no use arguing. Anyway, it's only another tray that you have to carry in the morning."

Isaac's statements that evening similarly disappointed me.

"Sarah, why do you think you shouldn't have to do whatever they tell you to do? What's wrong with you? Are you trying to get a whipping?"

"It's just that I don't want to be alone with him in his bedroom."

"He has that woman in town, and he's not interested in you that way."

"I hope that's true, Isaac. I really do."

The next morning, I knocked on Julius's bedroom door.

"Enter. Put the tray on the table. Please pour a cup of tea and bring it to me."

He was sitting in a chair by a window, wearing a robe over his sleeping garments. I handed him the tea and stood in front of him with my head bowed, waiting to be dismissed. He smiled at me and spoke gently.

"Look at me, Sarah. Yes, as I thought. Other than the fact that yours are brown and hers are blue, you have similar eyes. Quite lovely. Your hair, what does it look like? Why do you always have it covered with a dreadful scullery maid's rag? Well? I don't suppose you'd like to remove that cloth so that I can see your hair?"

"No, sir."

"Why not?

"I never take my head covering off, sir."

"Not even for your husband?"

I did not reply and bowed my head again, looking at the floor, with my hands clasped in front of me so he would not see them tremble. I was apprehensive about being alone with him in his apart-ment, knowing what Isaac had said about the Negro mistress he had in town, but I would have been uneasy in such a situation with any man, even if I had not known about the Negress, because of what happened to Belle when she was sold.

"Look at me, Sarah." He laughed, which made me even more uncomfortable. "You look even prettier when you blush and I can see your dimples. You are shy, aren't you? So unlike your sister. All right, Sarah, you may leave. Until tomorrow."

I was surprised that he mentioned that Clarissa and I were sis-ters, as it was not a topic anyone had openly acknowledged, other than the children who had teased me when I was younger, but it was evident that Clarissa and I were related by blood, as we did have a strong resemblance to each other.

I had never been so grateful to leave the presence of any of my masters or mistresses as I was that day. Relief, however, turned into dread that night as I thought about what he would say or do the next morning. I wanted to tell someone, but I knew that there was no sympathetic ear.

For the next two weeks, each morning was similar to the first. He made comments about my appearance and asked me when he was going to have the pleasure of seeing me without my head covering. I stood before him, saying little, as he sat holding his cup of tea. As time passed, I became less frightened of him. That is, until the morning his language changed.

"How long are you going to continue this pretense of being a shy little girl, when you're a married woman? Answer me; I've had enough of your silence."

I lowered my head and stared at the floor. He stood and lifted my chin, and his touch startled me. He told me again to look at him, and I obeyed.

"Sarah, I'll never force you to do anything, but you know that I could, that forcing you is within my purview. If you consent to what I am going to propose, you will no longer have to be Clarissa's maid, and you won't have to work in the kitchen, as your responsibility will be to care for me." Still holding my chin in place, he took my hand and I tried to pull it back, but he held it firmly as he turned it over.

"Look at your hands. You're ruining them. Let me tell you something, when the new house is completed, my apartments will be on the opposite side of Clarissa's and you won't have to worry about ever seeing her. And you'll have all the pretty dresses you want."

I frowned, thinking about how Mr. Allen also had his own apartments where my mother could be with him without Mrs. Allen knowing that she was there.

"What is it? Are you worried about Isaac? I can keep him busy by hiring him out, you know. What do you say, Sarah? All right, I don't have to have your answer today. Promise me you'll give me your reply soon. Sarah?"

"Yes, sir."

He asked me the next morning whether I had made a decision.

"Sir, I can't do what you asked me. I just can't."

"It's Isaac that you're worried about, isn't it? I'll give you more time to think about it. You'll see. There would be so many advantages to accepting my proposal. Remember, your work will increase once Clarissa has the baby. By the way, you're not expecting, are you?"

"Sir?"

"Never mind. That's not important at this juncture, but it's something else you should consider, the fate of your children when you bear them. I could free you and your children, you know. I see that sparked an interest. Very well. Yes, Sarah, that's something I could easily do. What do you say?"

"Sir, I will think about it."

Mr. Cromwell appeared to lose patience, but strangely, he also seemed amused by my refusal to tell him what he wanted to hear.

"I'll convince you that being with me would be to your best advantage."

It was nighttime, one week later, in early June. I was asleep on a cot in Clarissa's bedroom when she screamed.

"Oh, that hurt! That really hurt. Sarah, I think the baby's coming. Tell them to send for the doctor, now! Hurry!"

She managed to speak between crying and taking short breaths. I went into the adjoining room to change into a dress.

"Hurry, hurry. Oh, oh, oh . . . this hurts . . . so much."

By the time the physician arrived, Clarissa's water had broken. Her labor lasted over fourteen hours. When the baby was born, Dr. Walker suctioned his nostrils and cut the umbilical cord, and the child cried and turned pink. Dr. Walker told Jessie, the other maid assisting him, and me to wash and swaddle the infant.

"No, give him to me now," Clarissa said.

"Wash his face first, and cover her with a sheet," he said to me before he departed.

Clarissa took her son and asked for a wet cloth, which she used to clean his head and hands. "My angel. Yes, that's what you are, my angel on earth. Mama loves you." She caressed his back. "Sarah, tell my mother that his name is Theodore."

"You can tell her that yourself when she gets here, Miss Clarissa."

"Sarah, do you remember how happy we were when we were children?"

I said nothing, because the many thoughts whirling in my head after I saw Clarissa's baby were confusing, and I could not believe what I saw. I forced myself to listen to Clarissa, but wondered what was going to happen to all of us, now that she had had the baby.

"Weren't we happy when we played in the nursery and I had lessons?" I answered her, with no emotion in my voice, knowing that she was asking me that question because she was about to ask me to do something for her.

"Yes, we were happy then."

"That's how I always want you to remember me."

I suddenly was alert. "What do you mean by that, Miss Clarissa?"

"You know what I mean, Sarah, you know. Look at him. What do you think they're going to do to me and my baby, Sarah?"

"I don't think they're going to do anything . . . bad to you."

"Sarah, you know very well they're going to punish me, they'll never let me get away with this, but I won't let them hurt my baby, no. I know what I'll do, I know, I'll convince Julius to let you take the baby back home, to my mother. Please, Sarah, I know it's a lot to ask of you, but, but, will you promise me that you'll get my baby to my mother?"

I hesitated while I thought about how doing what she asked me to do could be to my advantage.

"Sarah, please, I'll do anything, I'll give you a letter asking Papa to free you if you do this for me. Will you?"

"Yes, Miss Clarissa, if you do that for me I'll do whatever I can."

There was a knock, and the door opened and Mrs. Cromwell,

Julius, and Dr. Walker entered. Mrs. Cromwell told me to hold the baby, but Clarissa refused to give him to me. Mrs. Cromwell scowled, her laugh lines looking even more pronounced than usual. Julius was frowning and said nothing, while Dr. Walker could not stand still, apparently delighted to be present at this family spectacle surrounding the birth of an illegitimate child. Mrs. Cromwell spoke roughly.

"All right, then, turn him around so we can see his face," she said.

Clarissa, whose eyes were puffy from crying, reluctantly agreed, and seeing the child's face, Mrs. Cromwell was silent for a moment, as she pursed her lips and then nodded.

"Yes, Dr. Walker, I see what you mean," Mrs. Cromwell said. She looked at the other maid and me and told us to wash Clarissa and the baby and clean the room. We persuaded Clarissa to give us the child so that we could follow Mrs. Cromwell's orders. Moments later, the overseer knocked on the door, and when I answered it, he told Jessie and me to go outside the room and spoke to us in the hallway after closing the door.

"Mrs. Cromwell said that you ain't to repeat nothing about the baby's birth to anyone, you hear me? And you ain't to allow no other servants inside this room. You hear me? And you, Sarah, Mr. Julius Cromwell want you to tidy yourself and go to his office in a hour."

He was at his desk when I arrived. He told me to sit in one of the chairs in front of the desk. I had expected him to be angry, but he was calm, as if he had more important concerns. I, however, had an aching head, thinking about what I needed to do and about what decisions the Cromwells had made or were going to make that were going to affect Isaac and me. I knew that whatever actions I was going to take entirely would depend on what the Cromwells were going to do to Clarissa and her baby and decided that Julius could provide me with intelligence of the Cromwells' plans.

"Sarah, you look as if you need to sleep. If you had accepted my proposal, you wouldn't have had to be there when that little . . . baby was born, you know. But, I'll not keep you long. You know, I care more about your future with me than I do about my past with Clarissa. Have you given thought to my proposal? Sarah? Answer me."

"Sir . . . no, sir, I haven't thought about it, I, I haven't had time, helping out with Miss Clarissa and the baby."

"That's not what I wanted to hear. I've thought of little else. All right, I will tell you something in confidence that, right now, only my parents and I know. I'm telling you this because it directly affects you. I am sending Clarissa and her son to her parents. You're not surprised, are you?"

"No, sir. I suppose not, I didn't think you would want them to stay here."

"Do you prefer to wait until she leaves to give me your answer? Sarah, why is this not an easy decision for you? Think: When she's gone, you won't have to play second fiddle to her. All right, I'll expect your answer when she leaves."

"Sir, may I ask, when are you sending her to Allen Estates?"

"I will allow her to recuperate a few days, but beginning immediately, Jessie will be her maid, and you will not have to work in the kitchen. Your only duty will be to attend to me."

"Does Miss Clarissa know your plans?"

"No, and you're not to tell her. In fact, I don't even want you to go to her room. I'll speak with her tomorrow morning."

Isaac was there when I went to our cabin.

"Clarissa had the baby." I was so exhausted that I lay on the bed with my clothes on.

"That's what they said at the stables and in the kitchen."

"Yes, Jessie and I helped the doctor."

"You ain't saying much. Why?"

"I'm really tired, and the overseer told us not to say anything about the baby's birth."

"Why not?"

"I suppose I can tell you. The doctor said that the baby looks like he was born after a nine-month pregnancy."

"Oh? He can really tell that?"

"He's a big baby, and long, too."

"Did Mr. Cromwell see the baby?"

"Yes, and his mother."

"What did they say?"

"Nothing."

I could barely keep my eyes open and went to sleep. I spent the next day cleaning Julius's apartment. He did not ask me anything about his proposal when I saw him. That evening, Isaac said that an overseer told him to prepare Clarissa's carriage. I learned the significance of the carriage the following morning, when I took Julius his tea.

"Sarah. My darling Sarah. Tell me, how much sway does Clarissa have with her father? Could she persuade him to overlook what she has done?"

"Sir, since she was a little girl, he and Mrs. Allen agreed to all her wishes."

"Yes, but do you think her father would agree to her wishes now?"

"I'm not sure."

"Is there a likelihood that he would?"

"Yes, there is a likelihood."

"What I am about to tell you, you cannot repeat. Clarissa, perhaps because of her guilty mind, thinks that I want to cause her and her son physical harm. I do not. I simply want her and that . . . bastard out of my parents' home. She begged me to let you accompany her to Allen Estates."

I kept an expressionless face.

"She said that she will ensure that you return. I told her that I have no reason to accommodate her delusions, but she said that, if I allow you to accompany her, she would prevail upon her father to give me the agreed upon number of field hands."

"Sir, I do think that she could accomplish that. Mr. Allen, as I'm sure you know, owns about four hundred field hands."

"Well then, here is what I want you to do: On the journey there, help Clarissa because she is not thinking clearly. Help her to craft a convincing story for her father. If she succeeds in getting me any number of field hands, when you return, I will free you. Of course, that means that all your children will be free. What do you think about that?"

"Sir, would you really do that?"

"Yes, my sweet Sarah, I will. I promise you."

"Thank you, sir. I will do what I can."

"All right, be prepared to leave in two days. Do come bid me good-bye before you depart."

That evening, Isaac said that the overseer told him to have the carriage and a team of four horses ready for the day after the next. "Did you hear anything else?" he asked.

"Yes, a lot. The carriage is so that an overseer and a coachman will take Clarissa, the baby, and me to Allen Estates," I said.

"What? Why are we going there so soon after the baby's birth?"

"Because Julius is denying that the baby is his."

"We're going there to stay?"

"Isaac, you're not going. Julius didn't even want me to go. He's afraid that I won't return, and well, let's sit down. I need to tell you something important. I'm not coming back."

"What do you mean? You have to. We belong to Mr. Cromwell now. Mr. Allen will have to send you back. Don't you want to come back to be with me?"

"I'm not coming back here to live my mother's life. And do you know what Mr. Allen did to my mother's husband, Belle's father? He sold him."

Isaac was silent for a few moments. "What makes you think that Mr. Allen won't send you back?"

"I'm going to run."

"Sarah, stop it, you can't . . ."

"No. You stop it. Don't tell me I can't run. I can and I will. And if I were you, I'd run, too."

"Well, since you made up your mind, why don't we run together, now?"

"No, it's easier to catch two people. It would be more difficult to blend in when we got to a town."

"But we'll never see each other again."

"Isaac, the only thing that's going to get me through all of this, and the reason I won't cry my eyes out when I run, is that I believe I'll see everybody I love in heaven one day."

"But how can I run and not get caught? Those Wilkes boys, look what happened to them."

"One was a blacksmith and the other worked on a farm. As a coachman, you know the roads as far as Georgia and Florida. And there's something I haven't told you. There's a way that I can help you escape."

"How?"

"First, you have to tell me if you're sure you want to run."

"I think I do."

"No, I need to know for sure, and I need to know now so I have time to do what I have to do."

"Yes. Yes, I will."

"I can write you a pass because I know how to read and write."

"What? I don't believe you."

"Well, then. Do what you have to do on your own."

"Sarah, really? How did you learn?"

"I can't tell you that."

"Did Miss Clarissa teach you?"

"All right, if it's so important for you to know. Mrs. Allen did."

"That explains why you talk like they do. But how good is a pass going to be? As soon as they know I'm gone, the slave catchers will know the pass isn't real."

"That's why you have to use your brains. Take a horse and go into the woods for a few days. Then, only ride the roads at night. If somebody stops you, then you show the pass. I'll make it for you tomorrow. Is there ever a time when the main gate is unguarded?"

"Not really. They leave the bloodhounds there when the patroller leaves around eleven at night."

"Do they have dogs all around the plantation?"

"No, it's too big. They only have them by the slave quarters, the fields, or the streams and swamps."

The next afternoon, when Julius was at dinner, I went to his office to clean and to use his writing materials, and that night I prepared for the journey. The following morning, the overseer went to our cabin to say that we were departing at eleven o'clock. Isaac and I said good-bye before he went to the stables. I made us breakfast, but neither of us felt like eating. When he was gone, I put on the dress that my mother had altered. I did not wrap my hair and wore it the same way I arranged Clarissa's.

When Julius saw me, he smiled. "Sarah, how beautiful you look."

"Thank you, sir. Sir, I wanted to give you my answer before leaving. I accept your proposal."

"Sarah, I'm at a loss for words. I thought I would have to wait until your return. You have made me happy."

"I also came to say good-bye and that I hope our time apart will be short."

"What made you change your mind?"

"You are right, sir. Everything will be different with her not here."

"I'm so glad about your decision. Sarah, there's something that I planned to give you when you made your decision. I will give it to you now, so that you'll think of me when you're away. Wait here."

He left the room and returned with a velvet pouch. He took out a gold necklace that was decorated with pearls and ruby stones.

"Turn around, darling." He fastened the clasp and placed the necklace inside the bodice of my dress. "Always wear it underneath your clothing so that no one will see it and it will be close to your heart."

I thanked him. Then he embraced me and kissed me on the cheek. I went to my cabin to get my baggage and then to the carriage that was waiting outside the house. Clarissa and Jessie, holding the baby wrapped in a blanket, came out. Another servant helped Clarissa walk. The overseer objected when Clarissa told me to sit inside the carriage with her and the baby.

"This is my carriage, and she is still my servant. I decide where she sits. And mind your impertinence."

The carriage could not move fast because Clarissa was in pain. I asked her at several stages whether we should stop at an inn.

"No, I want to get home."

She developed a fever toward the end of the journey and was delirious when we arrived at the main gate of Allen Estates. An overseer opened the door and helped Clarissa. When I stepped down holding the baby, he told me to give him the child.

"No, Sarah, don't. Give him to me."

She stood in front of me and tried to take him, but the overseer pushed her away. Another overseer took the baby from me, and they got into another carriage. Clarissa tried to follow them, and I tried to help her, but she was too weak to walk.

"Go after them, Sarah. Please, try to get my son back."

I ran behind the carriage as far as I could, but it went faster and faster, and I returned to Clarissa when there was no possibility of my reaching them. The two Hall overseers were helping her into a smaller carriage. I climbed onto the seat next to the coachman. Two servants were waiting for us at the front door of Allen Hall. They took Clarissa out and told me to follow them upstairs.

"Where is Mrs. Allen?" I asked.

"Somebody's going to get her."

"And do you know if my mother and Belle are here?"

"Yes, we can get someone to tell them you is here."

I settled Clarissa in her bed. Her face was hot. Mrs. Allen woke Clarissa when she arrived.

"Mama. Mama, I came to you to help me, but they took my baby. They took my angel. Do you know where they took him, Mama?"

"Sarah, where's the baby?"

I told her what had occurred.

"Dear God. Sarah, I'm going to find my husband and send for a physician. Stay here with her. Oh, and I'll send someone to get Emmeline because Clarissa is feverish."

When my mother arrived, we embraced and I whispered in her ear, "Mama, I have so much to tell you."

"I know everything, baby. We'll talk later."

"How are Belle and the children?"

"They're all right. You'll see them later. She know you're here."

She felt Clarissa's forehead and throat. "How long since she had this fever?"

"Since we got to Benton County."

Mrs. Allen returned. "Emmeline, what do you think?"

"Ma'am, we should wait until the doctor come."

"It's just a fever, though, is it not?"

"That usually mean the new mother got a infection when she had the baby."

"Isn't there something you can give her?"

"Ma'am, with a fever this high, I don't think what I give is going to do anything."

"Emmeline, try it, please. Mr. Allen refuses to send for a doctor because he says that she does not need one."

"Sarah, go to my cabin and brew catnip. Ma'am, me and Bessie can give Miss Clarissa a cold bath."

The people whom I passed on the way tried to engage me in conversation about why we were back at Allen Estates, but I hurried past them in silence. When I returned to Clarissa's room, I heard my mother, Mrs. Allen, and Bessie in the adjoining bathroom. They were putting Clarissa in the tub and speaking to her to keep her awake. When the tea was cool, Mrs. Allen gave it to her when she was still in the water. Neither the tea nor the cold bath lowered her temperature. Her lips were cracked, and the dark circles around her eyes were more pronounced than that morning.

"Ma'am, do you want to try again with Mr. Allen? She's getting hotter. Ma'am?"

"I heard you, Emmeline, but I doubt he will send for the physician."

"Ma'am, if her fever keep going up, she . . . she's going to . . ."

FOURTEEN

THEODORA ALLEN

W hen I entered his office, my husband was sitting at his desk drinking whiskey. He walked toward me. He was pale. I took a deep breath and tucked a loose strand of hair behind my ear. I prayed that he would not strike me.

"Please, I beg of you, Mr. Allen, send someone for the doctor."

"No. Have you not heard me? She has destroyed us. How will we ever show our faces anywhere? How will we ever dare leave these grounds?"

"But she's going to die. She has a high fever and is in pain and—"

"I . . . do . . . not . . . care. I do not care how much pain she is suffering. Her pain certainly does not compare to how she has ruined me, ruined my family's name. We have worked so hard to build our wealth, to build it from nothing, and now, because of her, we will be outcasts. And how do you think this will affect my sons and grandsons? This scandal has reached Mobile, Georgia, and beyond. It was your duty to mind your daughter. That was all that was expected of you, to raise your children. But you chose to bury your head in your books, in your flowers, in your music. Did you think that all you had to do was to be beautiful? Did you think for one second to keep an eye on your daughter?"

"But—"

"Do not interrupt me. You know better than to interrupt a man when he is speaking. There is no 'but.' There is nothing you can say to explain your failure to prevent your daughter from being a whore."

"We don't know that it was voluntary. . . ."

"What? Who would believe that, other than you? She intentionally misled us by making us arrange her marriage with Cromwell."

"Can you not show your own child a bit of mercy?"

"Mercy? Mercy? Who is showing me mercy? She turned me into a laughingstock. I hoped that, with her marriage, I would be able to expand my trade. Now, who will want to conduct business with me? Who will advance me capital? And worse, for generations to come, my family name will be associated with the name of your daughter, who is lower than a harlot."

"Please. . . ."

He stepped directly in front of me and clenched his fist. He smelled of alcohol.

"If you interrupt me one more time, I swear . . . I swear to you that I will beat you until you can't speak. Stop crying. It is too late. I said, stop crying. The damage has been done. If your selfish daughter dies as a result of her debauchery, so be it. I hope she rots in hell. Stop crying. Your crying makes me want to throttle you. Look at me. I said, look at me."

He took my face in his hands and squeezed. He forced me to look up. His eyes were red, and his nostrils flared.

"If your daughter dies, there will be no living reminder of her abomination."

He released his grip and stepped back. I left the room and returned to Clarissa. She was still, and her breathing was so shallow that at first I thought she had passed on.

"Emmeline, is there anyone in the fields who can help us with Clarissa?"

"Maybe Miss Mary, ma'am."

"I will send for her straightaway."

"Ma'am, maybe you should send Johnny. He will get to her cabin quick. And he should tell her to bring laudanum and all her remedies."

When Mary the midwife arrived, Clarissa was worse. Mary asked Emmeline what she had given Clarissa and suggested trying echinacea for the fever.

"I got it in a tincture, it work faster that way," she said.

We spent the rest of that day and night caring for Clarissa, giving her cool baths and wiping her brow. I tried to keep my eyes open as I sat next to the bed on a footstool, but I found myself waking up with my head on Clarissa's bed.

Sometime in the morning, before dawn, I held my girl as she died. They had to loosen my hold on her. Someone tried to lead me out of the room, but I refused to go and sat on a chair staring into the space between me and Clarissa's body. I fell into a deep sleep, and when I awoke, they had covered her with a bedsheet. I lifted it, and her eyes were closed. I kissed her cheeks.

"Bessie, tell Mr. Allen's body servant to come here, and then tell someone to summon an overseer, perhaps Davis. He is closest."

I met Eddie in the hallway.

"When Mr. Allen rises, tell him that Mrs. Cromwell passed on."

"I'm so sorry, ma'am. Miss Clarissa was a lovely child."

"Thank you, Eddie. Also tell your master that I will bury her tomorrow morning, at eleven o'clock."

I waited for the overseer in the parlor. He already knew about Clarissa's passing.

"Send someone for the Reverend Crawford this morning. I will write notes soon, to be delivered to some of the neighbors. Tell the carpenters to make a coffin and a cross today, and tell someone to dig a grave near her great-grandparents. I want hers to be under the big magnolia tree. You know the one? We will have a proper headstone made later. Oh, and I want all the Hall servants to be present at the burial."

"Ma'am, are you going to have a wake here in the parlor?"

"No, we'll leave her in her bedroom until tomorrow morning. Then they will put her in the coffin."

I wrote my sons and my husband's family in Montgomery, Macon County, and Mobile. I told Emmeline the arrangements and asked her to prepare a repast for the guests.

"Yes, ma'am. And, ma'am, do you want me to help Bessie prepare the body?"

"Oh, sweet God. I did not think of that. Thank you, Emmeline. Yes, please."

"What dress do you want her to wear? If you pick one, I can let it out at the seams because nothing she has from before may fit her."

"That is true, Emmeline. Thank you. I will go upstairs and choose everything that she should wear."

Sarah was in Clarissa's wardrobe and had already selected clothing for my approval.

"Sarah, were you crying?"

"Yes, ma'am. I was thinking it was Miss Clarissa's idea that I sit with her during her lessons. I will always be grateful to her for that. Ma'am, I just remembered that Miss Clarissa told me to tell you that she named the baby after you: Theodore."

"Thank you, Sarah. Thank you for telling me."

I went to my husband's apartment the day of the funeral, around ten in the morning. He was asleep in a chair in his bedroom, an almost empty bottle of whiskey on a table next to him. I woke him.

"What? What do you want?"

"Are you coming to Clarissa's burial?"

"Why would I do that? I hope you have not made grand arrangements."

"I invited a few of the neighbors."

"Have you no shame? Do you actually think that they will appear?"

"They do not know what happened."

He was suddenly alert.

"I had not thought of it that way. If they ask you what happened, say the child died at birth."

"No, I will not say that."

"Yes, you will, or I will bar your guests from entering my property, and I will order your daughter interred without a preacher immediately."

"You would not do such a thing. You would not have your daughter treated like an animal."

"You know that I would, and why not? That is how she behaved. So which is it going to be?"

"Yes, I will say that the child died or anything that will guarantee her a Christian burial. Are you truly not going to be present when your daughter is buried?"

"Leave me alone. Go bury that bitch by yourself."

The neighbors I invited did attend, including Mr. and Mrs. Tutwiler and their children who still lived in the area. If Mrs. Tutwiler knew what had transpired, she was kind enough not to say anything. When the guests were gone, I retreated to my apartment to read and write. The following day, I confronted my husband about my grandson.

"I will not tell you where he is. Why do you need to know? Surely you do not want to try to find him. Don't be an idiot. With him gone, that Cromwell moron has no evidence. If he had any sense, he would have kept Clarissa and the bastard."

"You have come to hate Clarissa, but I hope you will spare your other daughter. You do not intend to send her back to Julius, do you?"

"What a turn of events. You were so angry and stormed into my office to confront me when you first saw Sarah when she was still a baby."

"She was good to my daughter, and that makes her a better person than you."

He slapped me, and I left the room, not caring that my cheek was bruised or that someone might have noticed that my husband had struck me. I sent for Davis and spoke with him in the parlor.

"Who took Mrs. Cromwell's baby?"

"Ma'am, Mr. Allen told me not to tell you. I'm sorry."

"Where did they take him? I am ordering you to tell me."

"I can't, ma'am. He said if I told you he would dismiss me."

When Davis was gone, I told a servant to send for the other Hall overseer. When he arrived, his reply to my question was the same as Davis's. I found Sarah cleaning my husband's office. She was surprised to see me.

"Sarah, come with me to the library. I need to speak with you."

"Ma'am, Mr. Allen is in there."

"Really? He's reading?"

"No, ma'am. He's asleep."

"We'll speak here." I closed the door. "Sarah, do you remember anything about the men who took the baby? Were they from here? Had you ever seen them?"

"Yes, ma'am. They were overseers from the fields. I've seen them there before."

"Do you know their names?"

"No, ma'am."

"What did they look like?"

"One was tall and fat, and the other was tall but a regular size."

"If you saw them, would you recognize them?"

"Yes, ma'am. I think so."

"This afternoon, around two, I want you to accompany me to the fields, and I want you to point them out to me."

"Yes, ma'am, but I'll be up front with the coachman, so how should I tell you?"

"Tell the coachman to stop and to tell the overseers to come to the carriage to speak to me."

We had been in the carriage for about two hours when Sarah saw the men we were seeking. They were on horses. I asked their names and then posed the same questions as I had to the Hall overseers. They had the same replies.

I spent the next week in mourning. I read and wrote in my journal and took my meals in my apartment, avoiding my husband. Mrs. Tutwiler brought me letters from Kenneth and visited me twice. The following week, my son, Paul, and Eliza's husband, Abraham, who had remarried, arrived with their families from Georgia. Robert and his family arrived from Charleston five days later. I had not anticipated that I would feel joy after Clarissa's death, but I did. I played with my grandchildren and read to them in the lesson room. I joined the adults at meals and was relieved that my husband slept through dinners and was too inebriated to attend suppers. I spoke privately with my sons who, although they were still young men, had assumed their roles as fathers and bankers. They were content in Georgia and South Carolina and had no interest in living in Alabama or in being planters.

"Mother, spend time with us away from here. This place is untamed," Robert said.

"I will. I will. Being with you and your families has made me see that, despite Clarissa's passing, I can still be happy."

"Mother, I apologize for asking you this, but is it true what Papa said about Clarissa?" Paul asked.

"Yes, it is."

"It cannot be. Did you see the baby?" Paul said.

"No, I did not and, in fact, perhaps you can help me. I tried to find out where your father sent him. He would not tell me and ordered the overseers who took him not to say anything to me. Would you ask him? Perhaps he would tell you."

"But, Mother, what if it's true? Why would you want to know where the baby is? If it's true and everyone finds out about it, our family name will be ruined, and worse could happen. Not only would we be expelled from society, but the bankers we work with would shun us. Robert and I, despite being investors, could lose our positions in the banks."

"You have already spoken with your father, I see. It seems as if I am the only one who cares about Clarissa's son."

"Mother, please, think about us, too. Clarissa thought only about herself."

"I am thinking about her son, my grandson, and, whether you like it or not, your nephew."

"Mother, you really shouldn't think of him that way," Paul said.

"How else can I think of him?"

"Mother, what about us? Are you thinking of our families and your true grandchildren? What will happen to them if this becomes a scandal?"

"I only want to know where the child is and that he is well, that someone is caring for him. If I knew that, I would stop asking about him."

"I think that is a reasonable request. Robert and I will speak to Papa," Paul said.

My husband's family from Montgomery arrived that evening.

"Theodora, how is Cornelius?" my mother-in-law asked.

"Mrs. Allen, he has not been well since Clarissa passed away. He stays in his apartment and his office."

"Paul and Robert told me that Clarissa's child was born early and passed away?"

"Yes, yes, that is what happened."

"My poor dears, it is quite a heavy burden to lose one's daughter and grandson that way."

Cornelius's mother was unable to persuade him to stop drinking whiskey. When he emptied a bottle, he threatened to have the servants flogged if they did not immediately bring him another. She told Davis to send for a physician, but when he arrived, Cornelius refused to see him. He told the doctor that, if he did not leave of his own volition, he would have his slaves escort him off the premises.

I was painting on the verandah one afternoon when Eddie came to say that my husband wanted to speak with me and was waiting in his office. My mother-in-law was resting, and the young people were riding or playing in the game room. My husband seemed sober.

"I've received four letters from Cromwell. He has retained slave catchers because Isaac has escaped. He said that he wants Sarah back immediately. I wrote him that I'll return her to him if he agrees not to reveal anything publicly about what happened. We've been negotiating the terms of the agreement, and I think we're close. As soon as we finalize the contract, I'll send Sarah back to him."

"I don't want you to send Sarah back. Why don't we buy her from him?"

He laughed. "Why do you make that request? Is it that Sarah reminds you of Clarissa? Or is it that she is a better person than I am? By the way, Sarah learned more from you than how to speak properly, did she not?"

I did not answer any of his questions. "Why did you laugh when I suggested we buy her?"

"It appears that Cromwell can think of nothing else but Sarah. He refused my offer to buy her from him, and at a premium price, by the way. I even said I would give him five field hands. He threatened to commence a petition for her return in the Talladega Circuit Court. That, of course, would be the worst action he could take, as the sordid scandal would be reported in the newspapers. Thus Sarah is going back to Talladega, possibly as early as next week."

FIFTEEN

SARAH CAMPBELL

Clarissa died after her father refused to send for a doctor, in spite of my mother's and Miss Mary's efforts to save her. The day after her death, when I was in her wardrobe looking for her burial clothes, Mrs. Allen arrived, and when she noticed that I had been crying, I told her it was because I was thinking about Clarissa's kindness in insisting that I join her at her lessons. But it was much more than that; I had decided that I was going to run, and even though I had made the decision, I was still afraid of all the unknown consequences of my action. I knew that, if ever there was a time to make an attempt to escape, this was it, and that if I did not try now, I would never again have either the courage or the opportunity. I was crying also because of everything that had happened, including the circumstances of my separation from Isaac, and, most of all, I was crying because I knew that once I ran this would be the last time I would see my family, either because I would get caught and sold or I would successfully escape and not be able to return to them.

Mr. Allen did not attend the burial, and I believe that Mrs. Allen told the neighbors it was because he was ill. The truth was that, after Clarissa died, he was too drunk every day to go downstairs for his meals. Eddie took him trays from the kitchen, which he barely touched. There were full and partially empty bottles throughout his apartment, his office, and in the library, where he spent time staring at a watercolor of an island that Mrs. Allen painted.

Mrs. Allen was determined to find out where Mr. Allen sent Clarissa's baby. I went with her in a coach to the fields to look for the overseers who took the child. They told her that Mr. Allen had ordered them not to tell anyone where they left the infant. I do not think that she ever abandoned her quest to find her grandson.

I saw Belle for the first time the day before Clarissa was buried. I cried as we held each other.

"Sarah, I wish Mr. Allen wouldn't send you back, but I know you want to be with your husband."

"Belle, I'm so happy to be with you and Mama and the children."

Belle helped our mother and Bessie to dress Clarissa's body while I worked in the kitchen. My nieces had not forgotten me, and I resisted the desire to teach them the alphabet. My nephew, who looked like Belle, was too young to remember me, but he was happy to spend time with me. My mother and I were together most evenings because Mr. Allen rarely summoned her those days. When she and I were alone, I told her what happened with Julius and that I had decided to run.

"Sarah, I know I said before that you should run if the need or the chance come up, but thinking about you running scare me. Listen, Sarah, I know it's a big thing to run, so I talked to Mr. Allen about buying you from Mr. Cromwell and he said he's going to try. Let's see first if that do happen, but if it don't, you going to run, because at least somebody in our family is going to make it out of here, and it's going to be you."

"Mama, even if he does buy me from Mr. Cromwell, I'll still be a slave, and anyway, I don't think it'll happen, so yes, I'm still running."

"The only thing is, sugar, if he buy you from Mr. Cromwell

maybe he'll free you like he's going to do with me and Belle and the children."

"Even if he did, I'm not going to live like this until he dies. Mama, I'm afraid of what may happen to you and Belle and the children and even Zeke, when I run. So that's why we can't tell anybody, Mama, and I'm only telling you because I need your help or else I wouldn't have put you in danger by telling you."

I embraced her, and she patted my back.

"Mama, I won't tell you now when I'm going to run and I've thought of a way to make it look like you didn't know about it ahead of time. But it makes me sad that I won't be able to say good-bye to Belle and the children and Zeke. She can't know ahead of time, it has to be a real surprise when she finds out I ran. But you'll tell her good-bye for me, Mama, won't you? And please let her know how much I love her, and I'm so happy that she has a family."

I could not hold back the tears, and my mother held me close.

"Shush baby, shush. That's all right, you can cry now, but girl, listen to me, shush, now, when you run, you keep going and you never waste no time to cry, you hear me? Look at me."

Holding my hands, she stepped away from me so she could look into my eyes.

"When you run, you don't stop for nothing or nobody. And ain't nobody going to help you but yourself, you grown and you is smart and Mrs. Allen teaching you to read and write, well, that was all you need to get out of here. You hear me? Sarah, you need to stop crying now, because this is the most important thing I got to tell you."

She wiped my tears away with her handkerchief and smiled, and I forced myself to stop crying.

"Sarah, you already got everything you need to run, and when you run, you can't be crying because, listen . . ."

She stopped speaking for a moment.

"Sarah, you got to always be thinking about what's going on around you and what you got to do next. They're going to send patrollers and slave catchers after you, and they is going to be every place you go looking for you because two people going to want you back, real bad, Mr. Allen and Mr. Cromwell. So you got to be smarter than they is, all the time."

I paused to think about what Mama said, to let her know that I had listened to her and understood the wisdom of her advice.

"Yes, ma'am. I'll remember everything you said, I promise. Mama, there are some things I need you to do for me."

"Baby, you know I'll do anything I can for you."

"First, I need to know when Mr. Allen is going to send me back."

"All right, I'll find out."

"And can we go see Mr. Adams tomorrow?"

"I don't know, because there's been trouble in town. Some slaves escaped from the Fitzhugh plantation, and there's been more patrollers there. The last time I went to Mr. Adams, he said they is watching him and the church, so I don't think he'll be able to help you."

"I still want to try to speak to him."

"All right, but he said when I go back, make like it's to buy cloth or something, and if I'm ever there when somebody else is there, to make sure we only talk about clothes or sewing."

We went the next day, and as my mother said, there were more patrollers on the road and in town. Mr. Adams was alone.

"Miss Emmeline, Sarah, what a pleasure to see you. What may I do for you?"

"May we speak?"

"Yes, but first I have to tell you both that the patrollers paid me a visit. They said that if they find any evidence that I'm helping slaves run away, the county is going to make me move. They also threatened to close the church, but one of our members is a lawyer in town. The planters use him and his firm for their legal and business matters. I'm sure it's only his membership in our church that stays their hand at this point, but I don't know how long that will hold them off. So we must be careful."

He and I moved to the rear of the store.

"Mr. Adams, I have made the decision that we discussed before I went to Talladega. I'm running."

"Sarah, that is brave and I'm sure you reached that decision after much thought. How may I help you?"

"Is there anyone who can take me by wagon from the outskirts of Allen Estates to . . . ?"

"Don't tell me where to, the less I know the better. Yes, that is something I can arrange. Decide a date and come back to tell me as soon as possible."

"Thank you so much. Mr. Adams, I have another important request. I received a necklace as a gift from my master in Talladega. Would you take it as payment for making me two suits of men's clothing, the type that a body servant would wear for traveling with his master?"

"As you know, the fabric for those garments is fine wool, which is expensive. How much do you think the necklace is worth?"

I took off the necklace and he examined the clasp.

"It's twenty-four carat gold and the pearls and rubies appear genuine. Sarah, this is probably worth a lot more than the value of the clothing. I will make you the clothes and I will give you currency, whatever I can afford."

"Mr. Adams, that's generous of you. However, what is more important to me is that I have the suits quickly because we don't yet know when Mr. Allen is going to send me back to Talladega. That's something my mother is trying to learn."

"I will try to have them both ready within a week. Come back in four days to get the first one so that you'll at least have one in your possession. If he decides to send you back earlier than the four days, tell your mother to beg him to let her spend a few more days with you.

"Sarah, although it appears to me that you have prepared carefully for your escape, let me give you a bit of advice. You know you're going to have to do a lot of walking, correct? Make sure you wear sturdy, comfortable boots. Do you have any?"

"Yes, I do, the same ones I use to walk around the plantation."

"Good. And you know that you should only travel late at night, after the patrollers are gone."

"Yes, sir."

"Have you written your document?"

"Yes, sir. I wrote it in Talladega in the event I could not write it here."

"Well done, but you should also write a general traveling pass stating that you are free to move about during the day. There may be times when a pass would be better to use than your freedman's paper because patrollers and the militia, especially at boat landings and stagecoach depots, take a closer look at a paper that says you're free. Unfortunately, that's the sum of the limited advice I can offer you. But if anyone can succeed, it's you. Now, as I said before, I can get someone to take you in a wagon and get you as far away as possible before they realize at Allen Estates that you're gone."

When we returned to Allen Estates, I asked my mother to let me clean Mr. Allen's apartment and his office.

"Be careful, Sarah. He might be drinking more than ever, but he still see what's going on around him."

I took socks, men's undergarments, and a black hat from Mr. Allen's well-stocked wardrobe and put them under clean rags in my cleaning bucket, which I hid in the washroom near our cabin. I still needed a small blanket and two of Clarissa's dresses, but I would wait until just before I left to take them. When we went back to Mr. Adams four days later, he had completed both suits of clothing, which he had wrapped inside two separate bolts of cloth. He and I went to the rear of the shop.

"I put currency in the inner pocket of one of the jackets. But, Sarah, I have very bad news for you. I can't get someone to drive you. I'm so sorry, but they're watching us. In fact, we have reason to believe that new members in our church are working with the company that provides planters with patrollers, searchers, and slave catchers. You may have noticed a patroller who is stationed at the turn to this road. He's here to watch me, I'm sure."

"I'm sorry, too, for you and your church. Of course it will be much more difficult for me to get away, but I'll think of another way. I pray that no harm will come to you and your fellow church members."

"Amen. Also, Sarah, I don't know if you and your mother have heard, but they caught the two Fitzhugh slaves, even though they were already as far as Georgia."

"Do you know how they were caught?"

"It was similar to what happened in Talladega. The owner placed advertisements for their return and warned that they might have forged passes. That's why it's important to travel late at night, to avoid having to show your papers, at least until you're far from the plantation, where the patrollers may not know your master and where there may be no advertisements offering rewards for your capture."

"Well, Mr. Adams, this may be the last time we see each other. Thank you so much for everything you've done, sir."

"I'm merely God's vessel. Remember to seek strength from the Lord. In your darkest hours, when you'll want to surrender, look to the heavens and pray, and He will deliver you. Sarah, I wish you Godspeed."

Mr. and Mrs. Allen's families arrived about two weeks after Clarissa died. The servants now had to work as we did before Clarissa, Isaac, and I went to Talladega. Mr. Allen continued to drink excessively, and his own mother could not get him to stop. I attempted to clean Mr. Allen's office one afternoon, but he told me to leave after I knocked. I went to the library instead, where I closed the door and spent about an hour reviewing a map of Alabama. When I returned that evening to Mr. Allen's office, the door was open and he was gone. There was nothing unusual on his desk. The next two afternoons were identical to the first; he was locked in his office and told me to leave. When I returned in the evening and there was no evidence of his secretive labor, I decided to return to clean in the morning. I asked my mother whether she was going to Mr. Allen that night.

"I don't know. Eddie ain't said nothing yet. Why?"

"I can't say, but I need you to go to him and make sure he stays in his bedroom tomorrow morning."

The following day I saw Eddie, and he told me that Mr. Allen was still in bed. I went to the office and closed the door. I looked in the desk drawers and other places in the room, but I did not see any documents of interest other than pieces of burnt paper in the fireplace. That afternoon, my mother accompanied me to see Miss Mary. When we arrived at the slave quarters, I asked her to visit with Miss Mary's neighbor so that I might speak to Miss Mary alone. Miss Mary was shelling peas on her porch. She said that we could speak inside her cabin.

"Miss Mary, I need your help, and I need to know if you will keep what I say secret."

"Sarah, I know everything you've been through. Your mother came here crying when she got back from Talladega, and she told me everything. She already asked me if I can help you. You don't know everything your mother do for all of us down here, do you? She's the one that talks to Mr. Allen when us here in the fields and in the Hall need help. She's the one who asked him to let me hire myself out to make some money. That's how I bought my two oldest boys, the ones in Montgomery. So you know I'll do anything I can to help Miss Emmeline or her girls. What can I do for you, baby?"

"Miss Mary, I can't go back to Talladega. Things got worse after my mother left Talladega. Mr. Cromwell wants me back to be his . . . I can't do it."

"What about your husband?"

"Well, my mother and Belle don't know this, but he ran."

"And you want to do the same. You all going to try to meet up?"

"No, there was no way to do it because Mr. Cromwell didn't let him come back here with us."

"I'm sorry, baby."

"Thank you, Miss Mary."

"So how do you think I can help you?"

"Well, I need to get as far away as fast as possible. Do you think any of the men who take goods to other places could take me with them? I could hide in the back of a wagon."

"Sarah, yes, they can do that, but what would you do after that?"

"I've already thought about it. It's better that I don't tell you the details."

"But, Sarah, you is just a girl. Are you sure? What do Miss Emmeline say? Do she know?"

"She tried to get me to change my mind."

"But she couldn't."

"No. I'm going to do it, no matter what."

"All right, I do need to know what direction you headed to."

"South, but I want to stay east of Talladega County."

"All right. I know they're getting shipments of leather goods ready to go to different plantations and to the boat landing. I'll find out when the next ones is going south. I'll let you know when I go up to the Hall to ask how Mrs. Allen doing. I'll look for you."

"Thank you so much, Miss Mary. Do you think that the wagon will leave within a few days?"

"It's a lot of wagons, many more than one going in each direction. So you got a few days to be ready, but I'll find out the right day and let you know. Sarah, I know I ain't got to tell you this, but I will. Please be careful. And I'll be praying for you."

"Thank you, Miss Mary. It's like Belle said. You're like our auntie."

I was ironing when Miss Mary arrived one day later. No one else was in the room, but she whispered. "You got three days. There's a wagon going to a plantation in Chambers County at dawn on Thursday. That's as far as they can take you. They'll load the wagon by sundown Wednesday. You're going to need to get yourself to where the wagon is going to be, by the tannery. Early Thursday morning, before dawn, get inside the back of the wagon when it's still dark, before the overseer get there with the pass. All right, Sarah. May the Lord keep you and protect you." I hugged Miss Mary, and I realized that I would never again see her and that she truly was like an aunt to me.

It was late afternoon when I finished ironing. My mother was in the kitchen, and I asked her to find a reason to get Mr. Allen out of the office.

"Right now, Sarah? I'm cooking, and I can't go to him in the middle of the day. You know I only go to him at night, and only when he send for me."

"This one time, Mama. I need you to get him out of that office. Tell him that you need to speak to him about me, that you're worried about me. Ask him again to change his mind about sending me back. Belle and the others will finish supper. And, Mama, what I need to see is the papers he's writing. Don't give him the opportunity to put them away."

She agreed to my request. I waited until she was gone about twenty minutes, and I went to the Hall with my bucket. He was not in the office. The document that I was looking for was on his desk. As I read it, my hands were shaking. When I was finished, I left quickly because I was afraid that my mother would not be able to keep him in his apartment.

The following day, I took a small blanket from Mr. Allen's wardrobe, and I took two of Clarissa's dresses and a pair of her riding boots. I put those items in the sack that I used for collecting dirty clothing. My mother returned to Mr. Allen that night. She said he had complained that he had a headache and pain in his chest. I went to the stables and asked Mr. Allen's coachman if he had a knapsack that he could spare. I told him that I needed one for my return to Talladega.

"We got leather and canvas ones, but I don't think I can let you have a leather one."

"Oh, a canvas one is just fine. Thank you."

I hid the knapsack in the washroom.

When my mother came home Wednesday morning, she said that Mr. Allen was sicker, but that he still refused to let his family send for the doctor.

"What's wrong with him, Mama?"

"He said his head hurt so bad he can't even open his eyes. The room have to stay dark because the light make it worse, and he said that his chest hurt, too."

"Did he at least stop drinking whiskey?"

"No, his mother and Mrs. Allen tried to take his bottle away, and he wouldn't let them. He said it's the only thing dulling the pain. Mrs. Allen asked me if there's something I can give him, but I told her no, that he just got to stop drinking. His mother said, if the pain keep up, she's going to send for the doctor and tell him to give Mr. Allen laudanum."

"Did he say anything about sending me back to Talladega?"

"Yes, he said he think you'll be going back next week."

I spent most of the day Wednesday in the kitchen to be with my mother and Belle.

"Baby girl, why you look so sad? You thinking about Isaac?"

"Yes, and you and Mama and the children. When I go back, I'm going to miss you all so much. Belle, tell the children about me. Don't let them ever forget me, all right?"

"They won't forget you, Sarah, and you won't be that far. I'm sure Mr. Allen will let us go see you in Talladega, or he'll let you and Isaac come here."

My mother and I had our supper in our cabin.

"Sarah, you're sure you won't change your mind?"

"No, Mama. I can't."

"I know, baby. I know you can't go back to that. But I can't help but worry about you. And . . . I'll never see you again."

"Mama, please don't cry. And, Mama, remember what you told us when we were little? That we'll see each other again in heaven?"

"Yes, I did say that, didn't I? But it's one thing to say that to a child who is afraid of losing you and another thing to say it to yourself when you is about to lose your child. Having faith is not always easy. But you're right, I have to believe that, I really do. Still, I'm going to miss you and worry about you, baby. At least, if I knew you was going to be all right, I would feel better."

"All I can do, Mama, is promise to take care of myself, the way you told me to."

We prayed.

"All right, Sarah. I got to go. Mr. Allen's mother asked me to watch him."

"Mama, I'm going to need you to stay with him all night, all right? Don't come back here before tomorrow. And, Mama, this is important. When you get here in the morning, tell the overseer right away that I'm gone. I don't want them to think that you had anything to do with it."

"Yes, Sarah."

"Mama, before you go, there's something I need you to do. Cut my hair as short as you can. Cut it to my scalp."

"Oh, Sarah. This is it, right?"

She wanted to cry, I could tell, but she did not. She held my hair by the ends and cut it with her sewing scissors. I touched my head; the hair was just below my ears.

"No, Mama. I need it really short. You know it's going to grow fast."

She cut it until it was close to my scalp and I saw in the mirror that she had made me look like a man. She embraced me before she left, and when she was gone, I sliced and cooked bacon, made corn bread, and cut a piece of ham. I wrapped the food and took it, along with the clothing that Mr. Adams had made for me and my boots, to the washroom, where I packed all my items into the knapsack. I went back to the cabin, where I bathed and put on Clarissa's dark blue day dress and her riding boots. I wrapped my hair and waited until about two o'clock in the morning.

It was quiet, and there were no lights on in Allen Hall when I went to the washroom, where I retrieved my knapsack. It took me about two hours to walk through the woods to the tannery, because I stayed off the path. When I got to the covered wagon, I hid behind a bush nearby, to wait for the men. I could see them when they arrived. They were looking for me. When I was sure that there were just two of them, I walked to the wagon. I recognized one of them, LeRoy.

"Morning, Miss Sarah. This is Arthur. Quick, get in the back. We'll help you hide under some sacks. You going to have to stay there and be real quiet until we leave the main gate. We'll let you know when it's all right to sit on top of the sacks. You got to always be listening to us because there's patrollers on the road who want to look inside the wagon. When we see one, one of us going to say, 'Let's stop soon and eat something.' That's when you need to get back under the sacks, fast; but in the beginning, stay under until we tell you it's all right to sit up."

The filled sacks were not as heavy as I thought they would be, but they did not smell good. When the sun had come out, I heard the overseer arrive.

"Here's your pass. You boys know to get back here by Sunday at the latest. Don't do like last time, getting back here a week after you left."

The overseers at the main gate asked to see the pass and told the driver to exit. We had been riding for about thirty minutes when the wagon stopped.

"All right, boys, stop. Let me see your pass and I need to look in the back. What you all got there?"

"We're taking leather goods down to Chambers County."

"Where in Chambers?"

"The Henderson Plantation."

I was lying on my stomach with my knapsack next to me. My hands were shaking so much that I tucked them under me. The overseer did not lift any of the sacks, and the wagon was only stopped for a few seconds, but it seemed much longer. We traveled for about an hour when LeRoy told me that I could sit up and stretch. We rode that way for another hour, and then we stopped to rest. LeRoy and Arthur said they had packed enough food for the three of us and that I did not have to use my supplies. I ate by my-self in the back.

"Miss Sarah, you can go in the woods and stretch your legs. We'll stay here by the wagon."

Two more hours of traveling passed before a patroller stopped us as we neared what sounded like a town. He did not bother to look in the back and was satisfied with the pass the men presented. Each man took turns driving. On the second day, I asked where we were, and LeRoy said that we were about to cross from Randolph County into Chambers County. He agreed to tell me when we neared the plantation. There was still light when the wagon stopped. The men went to the back of the wagon and lifted the canvas, and I climbed out quickly, though my legs were stiff. At first, I was unsteady on my feet.

"This is it, Miss Sarah," LeRoy said. "Miss Mary said to leave you on the road by the woods on the other side of the plantation. Here's the rest of the food. You can keep the sack, and keep that tin cup for water. And only drink water that's moving."

"Thank you both so much, for everything. I know this was a big risk for you."

"Miss Mary is the granny woman to everybody on the planta-tion. We do whatever she tell us," Arthur said.

"Where does this road lead?"

"Into town. La Fayette," Arthur said.

"About how long will it take me to get there from here?"

"Let's see, walking, it's going to take you at least one full day," Arthur said.

"Go on ahead into the woods before somebody come along and see you. And you going to be all right, Miss Sarah. I can tell you ain't scared," LeRoy said.

If he had not said that, I believe I would have told them to take me back to Allen Estates, but those kind words encouraged me. I prayed and recited a verse as I went into the woods: "For thou will light my candle: the Lord my God will enlighten my darkness."

Deep in the forest, I turned south and continued parallel to the road for about two hours, until it became dark. For my bed, I chose a spot under a tree where the earth was covered in moss. I rested before getting food from the sack that LeRoy and Arthur gave me. The meat and biscuits were hard. I wrapped myself in the blanket because it was colder than I expected on a July night. I heard crickets singing and small animals scurrying in the bushes. I felt lonely and thought about the things that we did at home on summer nights. After we cleaned the Allen kitchen, we and the neighbors would take chairs and lanterns outside. There were always at least two peach cobblers and sweet tea for everyone to enjoy. The children played hide-and-seek and other games. Later, the adults told stories that we had heard many times before, but we never tired of them, listening as though we were hearing these tales for the first time. If my mother was with us, I begged her for one of my favorites.

Wolves howled, and I shivered as I asked, "Dear God, what have I done?" I decided to end my folly and go home in the morning. If I was so miserable just one night out of bondage, how could I possibly sustain myself for a week? A month? A lifetime? The wolves seemed to be closer then and I thought of moving, but I knew that they would find me anyway, with their keen sense of smell. Was that a snake I heard hissing? I put Clarissa's dress on the ground and lay upon it, the fabric soft on my face. The howling grew louder, and fear overtook me. I kneeled.

"Dear God, thank You for Your blessings, for waking me up today, for giving me food, and for making me safe. Please protect my family and keep them by the power of Your hand. Lord, please forgive me for my sins and for breaking Your laws. Dear Lord, I know things that I did were wicked, and I understand that You may punish me by returning me to captivity. But, Dear God, if it is Your will that I flee from bondage, please show me the way.

"Lord, You have commanded me to be strong and of good courage, to be not afraid, and, Lord, You promised that You will be with me wherever I go. Lord, I will be brave, because You made a covenant that Your angels will always be with me. In the name of our savior, Jesus Christ, Amen."

The wolves seemed closer still. I walked to a clearing in the forest canopy and lifted my face to the heavens to look at the stars. I do not think I ever saw the sky as beautiful as that night.

SIXTEEN

THEODORA ALLEN

My grandchildren and my sister-in-law, Martha, did their best not to leave me alone. I played games with the young ones and helped them paint watercolors. Martha also enjoyed reading and writing, and we spent much of our time in the library and the parlor. When I was alone, to keep myself from crying about my dear child's passing and the whereabouts of my grandson, I was comforted by thinking about Kenneth and re-reading his letters and poems that I kept hidden in a box where I stored my watercoloring supplies.

Martha and I were knitting in the parlor one evening when she asked me about my daughter.

"Theodora, what is it that no one is telling me about Clarissa's passing?"

"Your brother doesn't want anyone to know, but I will tell you because I know that you loved her like a daughter."

I told her everything, and she held me as I cried.

"Do you want me to try to talk to Cornelius? Maybe he will tell me what he did with the child."

"Yes, please. He may listen to you."

Martha had no more success than I, and Cornelius accused her of conspiring with me to ruin the family's reputation.

"Theodora, I fear for him. His mind has deteriorated, and while I was speaking with him in his office, he coughed blood. Should we send for the doctor?"

"I don't think a physician would be of assistance to Cornelius. Did you try to persuade him to stop drinking whiskey?"

"No, and Emmeline told me outside of his presence that he continues to drink at all hours. I am certain he would only grow angrier if I told him to cease drinking."

No one expected to see Cornelius at meals, and we got used to visiting with him in his apartment. He made an effort to play with the children, but confused them when he told odd stories of his boyhood. My sons and daughters-in-law stopped taking the young ones upstairs when my husband refused to groom himself. His hair became stringy and his face cadaverous.

Cornelius was in his bed when I went to see him Wednesday evening before supper, and Emmeline was sitting next to him.

"Has he had any whiskey today?"

"This morning and afternoon, ma'am. But Eddie said he took all the bottles away when Mr. Allen was coughing blood."

"Has he been up at all today?"

"No, ma'am. Eddie said he ain't want to get out of bed. I try to get him to eat something, but he's been sleeping most the time. He's still coughing up blood."

"If you would like me to, I can help you with him."

"Ma'am, you should go down to supper. I'll watch him and send for you if he get worse. And, ma'am . . ."

"Yes, Emmeline?"

"I don't think he's going to get better. Maybe you should tell your family to make sure to come see him tonight."

"Thank you, Emmeline."

Emmeline was the only one who regularly saw or sat with him at this time, but even she could not persuade him to stop drinking or to eat his food. I was relieved that he did not summon me to be with him and preferred Emmeline by his side. I thought back to the beginning of our marriage, how I wanted Cornelius to stop being with her and hoped that he would soon tire of her and want only me, which he never did. By the way she attended to him when he was dying, I suspected she might have even forgiven him for selling Belle, and despite such a cruel reaction to Emmeline's challenge to his authority, it was apparent that he had genuine affection, if not love, for her all these years. If his father had not urged him to marry, perhaps Cornelius would have treated Emmeline more like a common-law wife just as any number of other planters did.

We were in the game room after supper when Eddie came to speak to me.

"Ma'am, Miss Emmeline said to please come up, now."

Cornelius's breathing was slow and shallow.

"Emmeline, please wash his face. I'll return with the family."

We filed into his bedroom, and everyone said good-bye. My mother-in-law led a prayer. She, my sister-in-law, and I stayed with Emmeline to sit in vigil. My husband died at three on Thursday morning. Davis went to town for the undertaker. I do not know what I would have done about the plantation if my brother-in-law, Charles, had not been with us.

"This is the time when slaves think they can do whatever they want or that, with their master gone, they don't have to work. It's important that everything continues to function as if the master still walked among them," Charles said to me.

He left us at the house and went to the fields to be with the manager of the plantation and the overseers. I went to my husband's office to write death announcements. There was a pile of papers on his desk. I read the document on top that he was drafting and tore it into small pieces, which I put aside to burn in the fireplace in my bedroom that evening. I was writing a notice to the local newspaper when an overseer interrupted me.

"Ma'am, we can't find Sarah."

"Pardon me?"

"We think Sarah ran away."

"When?"

"Must been last night. When Emmeline went to her cabin this morning after Mr. Allen died, she saw Sarah was not in the cabin, and she came to tell me the last time she saw her was last night."

"Well, can she be elsewhere on the plantation?"

"Yes, ma'am. I'm going with a couple of boys to the fields to tell Mr. Allen . . . Mr. Charles, that is."

I told Bessie, who was rather cheerful under the circumstances, to tell Emmeline to see me. "And, Bessie, pretend that you're unhappy about your master's passing."

She tried not to grin but was unsuccessful. "Yes, ma'am."

When Emmeline arrived, I could tell she had been crying.

"Do you really think it's true that Sarah has run away? Perhaps she is visiting acquaintances in the quarters?" I asked her.

"Ma'am, I sure hope you're right. What would I do if my girl was gone? She's just a child. Ma'am, can I go down to the fields to look for her?"

"Sure, Emmeline, but the overseer has already gone there. But if it would make you feel better, get one of the boys to take you in a wagon."

"Thank you, ma'am."

No one could find Sarah. They let the dogs smell her clothing and searched for her in the slave quarters and in the swamps. That evening, when it became a certainty that she had indeed escaped, Charles retained the slave catchers at Pinckney & Jenkins. Mr. Pinckney interviewed me in Cornelius's office, with Charles and Davis present.

"Mrs. Allen, please accept my condolences for the tragic passing of your husband and daughter. Now, about your runaway. I want you to know that we have a ninety-nine percent rate of catching slaves. We are successful because owners provide us with valuable information. To that end, I need to ask you some questions. We know from experience that slaves steal clothing to disguise themselves and jewelry to sell to finance their escapes. Do you know if she has stolen anything at all from you or your family?"

"I do not believe that she has stolen anything of mine."

"What about your daughter's belongings?"

"I don't know. I have not been in her apartment since we buried her."

"Would you please accompany us there to see if you can tell whether anything is missing?"

We inspected Clarissa's rooms. They found two empty hangers in her wardrobe where we kept her dresses that she did not take to Talladega.

"Ma'am, do you recall what dresses were on these hangers?"

"Let me think. Yes, they were yellow. She loved those gowns."

He wrote in his book. I suppressed a smile as I remembered that Clarissa had despised yellow and never would have worn that color.

"Mrs. Allen, can you think of anything else that may be missing?"

"Now that I think of it, I do not see the matching hats and parasols."

"Anything else?"

"That would be all."

We returned to my husband's office.

"Mrs. Allen, we have a physical description of Sarah. Is there anything you can tell us about her personality or skills that would help us to describe her in advertisements and public notices?"

"Yes. She is intelligent."

"Anything else?"

"Not for your advertisements."

"Yes?"

"You will never catch her."

We buried Cornelius next to Clarissa, and the day after the funeral, the adults, except for my relatives from Georgia, who had departed that morning, met in the library at Charles's request.

"I am the executor of Cornelius's estate. It is going to take quite some time, perhaps two months, to enter the will into probate. The lawyer, Mr. Harris, will arrive tomorrow to begin reviewing financial statements with the accountant and bookkeeper. They will stay here in residence until that labor is completed, by the end of August at the latest, because I have to return to my plantation before harvest. No one is legally required to be present for the reading of the will, and I understand if you have obligations at home. But it would be appreciated if you stayed to comfort Theodora."

I asked Charles to remain after everyone else left the room.

"Dear Charles, I have a delicate matter to discuss with you. How much did Cornelius tell you about Clarissa's . . . situation?"

"Theodora, I know how difficult it is for you, but you must try to forget everything that happened with Clarissa."

"I cannot. I need to know where my grandson is. . . ."

"I believe Cornelius intentionally did not tell me that because he knew you would ask me. Really, I do not know."

"Have you read the will?"

"Not recently, but the lawyer is bringing his copy. Mine is at home and I haven't seen it since it was executed. Why do you ask?"

"I wondered whether there were any codicils referring to the child."

"I don't know whether there is anything specifically referring to the child, but, yes, I understand that there are amendments to the will."

The lawyer and accountant arrived the next morning, and Davis directed them to Cornelius's office. I spoke with the lawyer privately that evening.

"Mr. Harris, did you bring the codicil to my husband's will?"

"Yes, Mrs. Allen, of course."

"What is it about?"

"At this stage, I'm not at liberty to discuss these issues."

"Would you at least tell me whether it has to do with my daughter, Mrs. Clarissa Cromwell, and her son?"

"No. The codicil does not concern either of them."

"How does the will affect Clarissa's son?"

"I believe I've said too much already, ma'am."

"Mr. Harris, I am not only a widow but a grieving mother and grandmother."

"Mrs. Allen, I promise you I will work as quickly as I am able to settle the estate so that all your questions might be answered. I will reveal to you that there are certain bequests in the will that will anger some of the beneficiaries. My job will be to ensure that those beneficiaries do not challenge the will and seek its nullification.

"Please understand that I cannot divulge information to anyone, not even to the executor of the will. This is for the protection of the estate, in order that no one tries to waste or abscond with any of the assets. But from what I have read thus far, I believe you will be pleased with the distribution of the estate."

"I do not care about the financial aspects of the estate as they concern me. I am only concerned about Clarissa's son."

"Mrs. Allen, actually, I have a question for you about that matter. I have organized your husband's documents that were on his desk and in the drawers. When I last met with him, he said he was drafting another codicil and that he had made arrangements about his grandson. But those papers were not here. Do you know where else he kept his documents?"

"No, they would have been in this office. This is where he did his writing. But I will search for them."

I did not tell the lawyer about the document Cornelius had been drafting that I tore and burned. The lawyer's query reminded me that, during my first week at Allen Hall, when Cornelius was teaching me about managing the household, he took me to a room in his apartment where he showed me a steel coffer hidden behind a painting. He had given me a key for the lock.

I located the key and went there after speaking with Mr. Harris. Initially Cornelius had kept our jewels in the coffer, but he later had had another one installed in my apartment for that purpose, and I had forgotten about the first one. When I opened it, I saw piles of paper currency, gold coins, and a set of documents. My heart beat fast as I learned where Cornelius had sent my grandson. When I had read everything, I had to decide what to reveal about the contents of the coffer to Mr. Harris. He did say that I would be satisfied with the terms of the will, but how might the documents indicating the whereabouts of my grandson modify his conclusion? I was troubled because the lawyer had intimated that some benefi-ciaries would likely oppose the will, and I had no idea what that might mean in terms of Cornelius's specific choices. Ultimately I decided to tell Mr. Harris about the papers because I believed him when he said that he would enforce Cornelius's wishes.

I settled into a comfortable routine of playing with the children, tutoring them, sharing meals with everyone, and receiving guests. About two weeks after Cornelius's death, however, there was more surprising news: Charles informed me that slave catchers had found Isaac and taken him to Allen Estates. He was being held in the jail on the plantation.

"I read a letter from Cromwell telling Cornelius that Isaac had run. He said that Isaac stole a horse and was probably coming here to get Sarah so they could escape together. Since they brought him here, the overseers beat Isaac to try to learn Sarah's location, but he maintains that he doesn't know where she is," Charles said.

"What are you going to do? Are you sending him back to Julius?"

"I'll speak with the lawyer about it. Cromwell is more con-cerned about getting Sarah back."

"Charles, do you think we should abandon the search for Sarah?"

"No, we can't. Julius said in his letters that he's going to file a petition in court and reveal everything if we don't return her. I think that, if they don't find her soon, we'll have to tell Julius that she escaped, of course. And oh, yes, I forgot to tell you that tomor-row afternoon, after dinner, the house servants will be released to go to the fields for Isaac's public whipping."

"Why do the house servants have to go, too? Cornelius never made them."

Charles spoke slowly, even sadly, as he answered me.

"That's probably because no house slave has tried to run since Cornelius became master, but, even so, Cornelius should have made them go to all the whippings because treatises on plantation management say that all slaves, not only the field hands, have to watch the whipping of a runaway who is caught. It teaches all slaves that they have to obey our laws and that, if they try to escape, they, too, will be severely punished."

Charles discussed the future of Allen Estates with my sons and me. "As you know, I left my sons and wife to manage our plantation while I'm here, which means that I can stay until harvest begins. But I have to return home soon after that.

"Your mother has never been involved in managing the plantation. Is anyone interested in assuming Cornelius's place?"

"Well, Uncle Charles, I'm not, because I like being a banker. I really couldn't see myself as a farmer," Paul said.

"I agree. I'm not one for working the soil, surrounded by savages," Robert said.

"Theodora? Are you interested in learning how to run the plantation?"

"No, Uncle Charles, Mama couldn't do that. And we wouldn't allow her to stay here by herself."

"Theodora, Cornelius did an excellent job of teaching the overseers how to manage the plantation, and he showed you how to take care of this house. If you were interested, I could teach you to take his place."

"Charles, thank you for having such confidence in me, but the truth is, as Cornelius often said, I am more interested in the arts than in commerce. And I could not live here alone."

"Well, then, we all know what this means. You will have to sell the plantation and the house. There will be a public auction for selling the slaves and livestock."

The slave catchers arrived at Allen Estates the next day to meet with Charles and me and Charles spoke to them.

"We're sorry, but we couldn't find your slave," one of the slave catchers said.

"Do you have any idea where she might be?"

"No, sir. We thought she was going to Macon County, where you said she has friends. We watched them, but Sarah never appeared. We put up notices at places where stagecoaches leave and at boat landings."

"How far south did you look for her?"

"Our agents went as far as Montgomery. Runaways often go through Wetumpka and Montgomery because of the frequency of steamboat and coach departures, and it's easier for them to blend in because there are more people than in most other towns around there."

"Why do you think the dogs were not able to track her movements within this plantation?"

"That I don't understand, Mr. Allen. Our agents let the dogs smell her maid's dress, but the dogs couldn't match her scent on the paths. We're usually able to find out how the slave got out of the plantation, but this time, it was like she never left her mother's cabin."

We consulted with Mr. Harris, who began the conversation by asking us a question, which Charles answered.

"I assume Mr. Cromwell knows that Mr. Allen and Mrs. Cromwell have passed on?"

"Both deaths were widely reported in the newspapers throughout the Southern states. Why?"

"In his recent letters, Mr. Cromwell hinted that the petition he will file, if you do not return Sarah, is for Mrs. Cromwell's share of the estate," Mr. Harris said.

"What? How could that be? He ended the marriage by sending her back," I said.

"I'm sorry, Mrs. Allen, but legally he did not end the marriage. He could argue in court that his actions were those of a wounded husband."

"What should we do?"

"I suggest you continue your retainer with the slave catchers, and I will write Mr. Cromwell a letter telling him about Sarah and ask him to allow us to try to find her before he takes any action," Mr. Harris said.

I asked what we should do about Isaac.

"I think you should continue to hold him, at least until I receive a reply from Mr. Cromwell. Are you prepared to send Isaac to him?"

"Only if Cromwell does not file a petition," Charles said.

"Then there is no reason to send Isaac to him now."

Charles told the slave catchers to continue their search, and Mr. Harris wrote to Julius. He received a reply several days later.

"He berated Cornelius for supposedly allowing Sarah to escape. He's convinced that Sarah has met Isaac somewhere, and he has launched a search for them, even though I told Mr. Harris that you had already retained a company to look for her," Charles reported.

"Should we tell him we have Isaac?"

"That is your decision, but please hear what else he said. He said that, if Sarah is not recaptured in two weeks, he will file a petition in the Talladega Circuit Court for Sarah, Isaac, the twenty promised field hands, and Mrs. Cromwell's share of Cornelius's estate."

SEVENTEEN

SARAH CAMPBELL

The sun was hot on my face. Had I forgotten to close the shutters? Why did my mother not wake me to go to the kitchen to get Clarissa's tea? I went back to sleep, but awoke with a start when I sensed that someone was staring at me. I opened my eyes to find a family of deer, a mother and her two young ones, looking at me with mournful eyes.

"You're so pretty. Oh, don't run. . . ."

The deer disappeared into the bushes. I said my morning—no, noon—prayers, because the sun was almost in the middle of the sky. I had never slept so late, and I could not believe that I did not have to rise from my bed to do anything for anyone. I took out my food and ate it with relish even though it was stale. I folded my blanket and put it in my bag. The rest of the food and Clarissa's dress that I had worn I buried away from my sleeping site.

I surveyed my home for the next three days: blackjack oaks, shortleaf and loblolly pines, shagbark hickories, and winged elms. Not losing sight of my bed, I took my knapsack and walked until I reached a stream and used my tin cup to drink. After I washed myself, my stomach called for more food and I wandered looking for edible fruit. I ate lingonberries off the bush and picked some to take with me when I realized that I had lost the direction of the road. Dear God, how was I to find my way south? There were no familiar signs. My boots had left few marks, and following what I could make of my trail did not take me far. I explored until I found a clearing in the trees, and from there saw the peak of a mountain. I recalled that, from the area where I had slept, I could see the mountaintop as I faced in the direction of the road.

Holding my knapsack, I sat down and memorized as much as I could about my new surroundings to avoid getting lost again. Then I fell asleep under a tree by a new clearing, even though my body hurt from lying on the ground. The nocturnal creatures were active when I awoke, and I was lonely and afraid in the dark. I ate berries and listened to life in the wildwoods, then prayed and recited my favorite verses. When I thought it was about eleven o'clock, I went to the road and walked until just before dawn, and then I returned to the thicket alongside the road.

The next two days I spent in the forest. Nothing occurred on the first day, but the second almost made me want to surrender.

I was sitting in the shade, resting, when I heard two voices arguing, and they sounded like the overseers at Allen Estates. I took my belongings and crouched behind a bush, from where I could see two men, one of them obese, carrying rifles. Their backs were to me.

"We ain't never going to find nobody in here."

"Let's walk around some more. They said they saw three niggers coming in this direction. If we catch all of them, we can get a good two hundred dollars in rewards."

"I'm tired and hungry and it's hot. I say we wait for them in town."

"Come on. Let's walk around a little more, and we'll go."

"All right, but I got to piss first."

The obese one turned to relieve himself, and I thought he saw me. I stayed still because I did not want him to notice any sudden motion. He narrowed his eyes.

"Hey, you see something over there?"

"Where?"

"Straight ahead."

"Nah. I don't see nothing."

"Well, let's go over and look."

They walked toward me, and I knew that I had to risk moving or they would catch me. I crawled backward until I found a different bush to hide behind. I heard them speak as they inspected the area where I had been. They must have assumed a deer had lain under the tree where I had slept, and having found no one, they left.

The third night, before it was dark, I went toward the road. When I was near it, I hid until around midnight, and then I resumed traveling. Using moonlight to see and the North Star as my guide, I walked south until the sun was about to rise before I returned to the woodlands. I rested by a brook where I could not be seen from the road.

When the sun was out, I took off my dress and washed. Then I used one of the cloths that I had brought to wrap around my chest. I tied a tight knot in front and tucked it underneath. I put on the men's undergarments and one of my men's suits of clothing and the hat, which I smoothed and tried to shape, as it was crushed from being in the bag. I transferred some of my currency and my traveling pass from the pockets of the dress to the inside pockets of the jacket. My headscarf and dress, with the rest of the money and my freedom paper, I folded and put at the bottom of the sack. I went back to the road and walked, and after about thirty minutes, I reached La Fayette. There were people about, but not many, on horseback and in wagons and small coaches. They looked at me, but not in a hostile manner. The town had a general store, a blacksmith, a lawyer's office, a cobbler, and three or four other merchants' buildings. I went to the grocery store and spoke to the man behind the counter.

"Good morning, sir. I needs some food. I got money to pay for it."

"Sure, but you need cooked food, right?"

"Yes, sir."

"Corrine. Corrine, get out here."

A servant came out.

"Fix this boy a plate of food."

He told me to pay him in advance, and I did. Corrine took me to the kitchen, which was in the rear of the store. She thrust a piece of pork and a biscuit in my hand.

"Run. Go. He getting the sheriff. He know you a runaway."

"But I have a pass."

"He don't care. They'll put you in jail until they find out if it real. Stop talking, boy, and run."

"But how did he know?"

"Stop asking questions. You ain't got no place to stay or cook food. See that path yonder? Go on it. It going to take you to the road to Tallapoosa."

My feet seemed stuck to the ground, but after she pushed me, I ran and did not stop until there was sufficient bush to conceal me. The Negro dogs barked in the distance, but they appeared to be going in a different direction. I rested and then continued on the path for about two hours. I saw an abandoned shack near a stream and took shelter there until late that night, and then I resumed walking. Tallapoosa was not where I wanted to go, but to Macon County, where Clarissa's aunt and her freed servants, who had been hospitable to us whenever Isaac and I went there with Clarissa, lived.

My plan had been to take a stagecoach from La Fayette to Macon County and seek assistance from the servants. I wanted to stay in Macon County for a few weeks, until the slave catchers hopefully stopped looking for me. From there, I planned to avoid the city of Montgomery by going around the southern border of Montgomery County, and then head west to the Alabama River. Now I would have to go through Tallapoosa County, which was just below Talladega County and north of Montgomery County. Slave catchers from throughout the state were always in Montgomery, waiting for runaways seeking to board the steamboats.

With no other recourse, I walked on the path at night, hiding in the woods during the day, until the path merged with the main road. Whenever I came upon a body of water in the forest, I soaked my feet in it, as I had developed blisters that bled. I was so hungry that, more than once, I thought of eating worms. If I had had a gun and known how to hunt and build a fire, I would have had plenty to eat, because the forest was full of wild ducks, turkeys, and cotton-tail rabbits.

One night, as I was dreaming about my mother's cooking, I smelled roasting venison. I woke when the aroma wafted around me, and I walked a few yards following the smell. I saw smoke in the distance. I continued forward, moving from bush to bush to ensure I would not be seen, until I heard men speaking. They did not sound like slave catchers, but I wanted to be sure. Cautiously, I made my way closer until I saw two Negroes sitting on rocks by a fire. I considered approaching them, but thinking of what had happened to Belle, I was afraid of being alone in the presence of unknown men. My hunger pangs returned, and then I remembered that, thus far, those who had seen me assumed me to be a man. I tightened the binding around my chest, folded my blanket, and put it in my sack. I went near them and cleared my throat. They saw me but did not appear surprised.

"Who you?"

"Sir, I is William, William Campbell."

"Well, don't just stand there, come over here, yella fella."

I greeted them and they said that they were brothers, Henry and Oliver.

"You like the smell of our deer, don't you, William?"

"Yes, sir."

They laughed.

"What's so funny?"

"Ain't nobody ever called us 'sir' before," Oliver said.

"My mother taught me to call men older than me 'sir.'"

"You work in the house, huh?"

"Yes, sir."

"So what you doing around here?"

"Stop asking the boy questions, Oliver. All he want to know is if we going to let him have some of our food."

"Of course we is. I just want to know what a nice house nigger doing here in the middle of the woods so far away from his mama."

"Ain't none of your business, Oliver. You don't like it when nobody ask us why we not at home."

"Ain't that the truth. So what you doing here, William?"

"Sir, my master can't afford to keep me, so he told me to go find work on boats that go on the Tombigbee. I know you don't like nobody asking you why you not at home, but why is that?"

"We can tell you, William. We run away, but just for a time," Henry said.

"What do you mean, 'for a time'?"

"We going back."

"Why?"

" 'Cause we already try running for good, three times. . . ."

Both men laughed.

"Why is that funny?"

"It ain't really funny. It's sad, but if you don't laugh, you cry," Henry said.

"So what happened to you?"

"First time, right after master died, was the worst. They caught us and put us in jail until the old lady got us out," Oliver said.

"What old lady?"

"Mrs. Farrow. Master Farrow died about six years ago. So you going to let me tell you what happened, or what? So she paid the sheriff to whip us, fifty lashes each, and to take us back to her."

"But that ain't even the worst part," Henry said. "When we get home, our wives yell at us for leaving them and the children, and our mother is crying, saying that she thought she was never going to see us again."

"And the other two times?"

"By the next year, we remember how it feel so good to run and try it again, but they catch us again. That time we ain't get too far. But the sheriff didn't put us in jail or whip us. He just took us back to the old lady. Then the last time was the next year after that, and we got far, but they catch us again and take us back," Henry said.

"We seen that every time we done it, the old lady was less and less mad. She was just glad that we went back and that we never went during harvest. And we figured out to earn some money when we run by telling people Mrs. Farrow sent us to hire ourselves out. So we give the old lady some of it and our families the rest, and everybody be happy," Oliver said.

"Look like the food is ready," Henry said.

They had a small sack of salt. We ate the meat and potatoes they had roasted with our hands. It was one of the tastiest meals I had ever had. I asked them how they killed the deer.

"With a rifle. What you think?"

"Well, where did you get a rifle and how did you learn to shoot one?"

"Did anybody ever tell you you ask a lot of questions, William? It's one of master's. He the one teach us how to shoot. He said we had to help him with the hunting. We know where the old lady keep the guns, and when we want to go hunting, we just take one. She don't mind, so long as we give her half of what we kill. Why? You don't know how to shoot?"

"We're not allowed to use guns on our plantation, only master and the overseers."

"What about a knife?"

"No, only small ones for cooking. We can't have any weapons, and if they find any on us or in our cabins, we get punished."

"But you have a knife with you now, don't you?"

"Well, no."

"You in the woods with no knife? How you going to defend yourself?"

"I didn't really think I was going to need to."

"You thought you was going into the woods and you wasn't going to run into some crazy person? Oliver and me'll give you one of our knives. If somebody try to start something with you, all you got to do most times is show them the knife, and they'll leave you alone."

"What if they don't?"

"You big, fight them. Kick them where it hurt them most. You ain't got a big brother to teach you these things?"

"No, I don't. I have one more question for you," I said.

"What now?"

"Well, when you first saw me, you didn't look surprised."

"Just by saying that, I can tell you never worked no fields."

"Why?"

"When field hands is tired, they go into the woods right by the plantations where they is at, and stay there for days, sometimes weeks, and then go back. You never heard of that, huh?"

"No, it just seems to me that once you run, you should keep going."

"Well, it ain't so easy for us because most times nobody going to believe a field hand when he say he not on the plantation because his master sent him to look for work."

"So, why wasn't you surprised to see me?"

"You crazy? Every time we run we see something like ten other slaves hiding in the woods. When we in the forest and make our fire, they find us."

"Why don't the slave catchers find you?"

"They ain't coming in no woods at night. They wait until we go out, 'cause we got to sometime."

We spoke until late that night. I thanked them and told them that I had to continue to my destination.

"Oh, here's the knife, and I hope you make it, William," Oliver said.

"Thank you. Me too."

I walked away and, when I was about fifteen yards from them, I stumbled when Henry gave me some parting advice.

"Hey, William."

"Yeah?"

"If you really want people to think you a man, sit with your legs open, not crossed at the ankles."

Their laughter carried as I resumed my travels. As before, I stayed in the forest during the day and walked on the road late at night. Three days later, I arrived in Dadeville, Tallapoosa County. The town was larger than La Fayette, and more people were on the street. There was a delicious smell emanating from a public dining establishment. I went there and stood outside, waiting for someone to exit. Two children were playing in an alleyway.

"Y'all know where I can buy some food around here?"

"Yes, sir, in the kitchen back there."

A woman who was cooking invited me in. "Come in, come in. I'm Henrietta."

I introduced myself as William Campbell.

"Where you traveling from? You kind of young to be on your own, ain't you?"

"No, ma'am. I'm eighteen years old. I'm looking for work."

"Sit down. I'll get you a plate. You like ham?"

"Miss Henrietta, to be truthful, I'm so hungry right now, I'll eat anything you have."

"After you eat, you can tell me where you from 'cause I know you ain't from these parts." She smiled as I ate fast. "I hope you saved room for my cobbler."

"Yes, ma'am. I always do."

I told her that my master could not afford to keep me and had sent me to hire myself out.

"He give you traveling papers?"

"Yes, ma'am."

"Where you going now?"

"Out west. They told me there's work on the docks by the Tombigbee."

"Yes, I hear that, too, but that's hard work. You don't look like you could do heavy lifting like that."

"Ma'am, when I wasn't taking care of my master, I was working in the kitchen with my mother. You know you got to lift heavy things in here."

"True enough. So you here to get the stagecoach to Wetumpka?"

"No, ma'am. I'm trying to get to Macon County."

"There ain't no stagecoach to Macon until Friday. You ain't got no place to sleep, do you? I'm sure my master going to let you stay here. I'll get you a quilt and you can put it there, in the corner. And you can help me in the kitchen to pay for your board."

"Miss Henrietta, I do thank you very much. I have money to pay for the food, and you sure there ain't no problem with your master if I stay here?"

"None at all. I been telling him a long time I need somebody to help me. Even if you only here a few days, that's better than nothing."

"What time do the stagecoach leave for Macon?"

"I think seven thirty, but I ain't sure. Why don't you go down to where it leave from? It just down the street. Ask somebody around there."

I took my bag and asked a man who was grooming a horse, and he said that the coach left at seven in the morning on Fridays. As I was speaking to him, I saw public announcements nailed to a post. I thanked the man and crossed the road. Pretending to be looking in another direction, I read the notices. One said:

ONE HUNDRED DOLLARS REWARD, RUNAWAY, from Allen Estates, Benton County, a Negro woman, tall, about 5 feet 10 inches in height. Sarah is mulatto, handsome, intelligent, and speaks excellent English. She may be wearing a yellow dress and hat and carrying a yellow parasol that she stole from her mistress. She is likely to be going to Macon County, where she knows free Negroes who will help her in her escape.

I returned to the man who told me about the Macon coach. "Sir, can you tell me when the coach to Wetumpka be?"

"That's daily, at seven."

"Where it leave from?"

"Right over there, by that post. Young fellow, make sure you got your pass. They check them. And make sure you got full fare."

"Yes, sir, thank you. I got both."

I went back to the kitchen. "Miss Henrietta, since the coach to Macon ain't 'til Friday, I think I'll take the coach to Wetumpka, 'cause it leave tomorrow. But I can help you today and this evening, ma'am."

"You don't worry about that. You need to get going to find you some regular work."

Henrietta got me a quilt from her cabin. I put my blanket on top of it and slept well that night. The following morning, I rose at four thirty and began making breakfast for Henrietta's master and his family, who lived in the same building as the public dining room. Henrietta arrived at five thirty and thanked me for my assistance. She packed a sack of food for me.

"They stop by where there's water to drink so the coachman and Negro passengers can have their meals during the day. You'll get to Wetumpka before it get dark, and you can go right on the boat. You ever been on a boat before?"

"Yes, ma'am, plenty of times, but with my master."

I thanked Henrietta and said good-bye. There were two other Negro passengers waiting to board the coach, a man and a woman. The man who reviewed our papers reminded me of an overseer at

Allen Estates. He looked at the runaway notices on the post and at the documents that we presented. He asked me why I was going to Wetumpka.

"Sir, I is trying to get to the Tombigbee so I can look for work."

"You kind of far from Madison County."

"Yes, sir. There ain't no work up there. My master, he the one told me to try and get work over by the Tombigbee."

"All right, pay up and you can sit up front with the coachman and the others."

"Sir, can I please keep my things with me?"

"There ain't no space. You're going to have to put it in the back."

"Mr. Murray, we put our things in the back. There's room up front for the young man's things, he ain't got much," the Negro woman said.

Mr. Murray grunted, and I took my seat. I introduced myself to the coachman and the married couple, freedmen, who were going home to Pike County. They owned a tailor shop there and were in town to take the measurements of a planter's family to sew them their fall and winter clothing. Our journey was uneventful, except that the couple tried to get me to work for them.

Wetumpka seemed to have become more crowded than it was when Isaac and I were there with Clarissa the prior winter. I saw bloodhounds as I walked toward the place where they sold tickets and forced myself to stop staring at them. Twenty people, all Negroes, were waiting in front of me to buy their passages. The others were already boarding the *Tallapoosa Belle*, and, as I recalled from journeys with my mother, they did not have to pay for their fare until they were on the boat.

My legs shook as the slave catchers were near me. I tried not to look at them when they started telling all Negro women to go with them. I almost obeyed because I temporarily forgot that I was hiding my true identity. A slave catcher held my maid's uniform from the Cromwell plantation to a dog's nose. He then led the animal to the group of young women. The hound did not recognize their scents, and the catcher told the women that they could leave. The catcher and the dog walked by those of us waiting to buy our tickets, and the dog barked when it smelled something familiar. They were next to me, and the dog became excited. The catcher told me to go with him. The dog continued to bark. My legs were unsteady.

The catcher led me to the location where he had taken the women and told me to wait there. He left me to speak to another slave catcher. He pointed at me. Then I saw a public announcement about me nailed to a wall. The beginning of the description was similar to the notice in Dadeville, but this one offered a two hundred dollar reward and said that I was probably going to Montgomery to meet with my husband, Isaac, who also was a runaway. It described Isaac as being handsome with gray eyes, light-colored hair, and bright yellow skin, and it said that I had stolen a pearl and ruby necklace that I would try to sell. Both catchers returned with the dog.

"You got a pass?"

I took it out and gave it to them.

"Where you going?"

"Sir, I is trying to make my way west so I can look for work by the Tombigbee."

"How tall are you?"

"Sir?"

"Your height, what is it?"

"Sir, I . . . I can't say. Ain't nobody ever tell me how tall I is," I stammered.

They spoke with each other.

"The husband is over six feet."

"And he's older. This one is a young boy."

"All right, go ahead."

My heart pounded, and my head hurt so badly that I thought I was going to faint. It would be several minutes before my breathing returned to normal.

My ticket cost eight dollars and entitled me to sleep in any available space on the main deck among the cargo of bundles of leather, sacks of grains and dried peas, crates of candles, and stacked lumber, mainly cypress, all of which, I learned, fetched high prices. The fare was to Claiborne, along the county line between Mobile and Baldwin Counties, where the Alabama and Tombigbee Rivers merge. Immediately upon boarding, I claimed a spot, avoiding the stacks of firewood and lumber. When I was last on a boat, passengers were injured because logs rolled and hit them. The boat departed when all the upper-deck passengers were settled in their private compartments.

There were about two hundred landings on the Alabama River because the most prosperous planters had their own boat stops. The *Tallapoosa Belle* was only about one-third full with cargo, and it would receive another one-third in Montgomery and the balance on the rest of the landings before it arrived in Mobile Bay, where the goods from the steamboats would be transferred to ships going to England, France, and the Northern states. I was contemplating my next two days on the boat when a crewman approached me.

"I hear you're looking for work, boy. You want to make some money?"

"Me, sir?"

"Yes, I see you're wearing expensive clothes and we need help on the boiler deck, serving the passengers."

"Yes, sir. I can do that work. Sir, how much do it pay, sir?"

"You get one dollar a day plus free food and passage."

"Sir, I done paid my fare."

"You'll get that back with your pay at the end. You want the job or not?"

"Yes, sir, I do want it. Thank you, sir."

"All right, go upstairs and see the cook."

I said a quick prayer because I could not believe my luck; I was going to earn two dollars and travel for free, and for the first time in my life, I was going to get paid for my labor. The cook told me to clean myself before I served the passengers and asked me whether I had a clean shirt. I said that I did and he directed me to a wash-room. There, I locked the door to prevent anyone from coming in while I was undressed. Before I left, I put my manumission paper and the rest of my money in the pockets of the jacket that I was wearing.

The cook put me to work serving food and spirits and wine to the gentlemen travelers who were sitting at the tables or on the sofas in the saloon. When it was quiet on the boiler deck, the cook sent me upstairs to the hurricane deck to attend to the officers. I did not have to serve the ladies, who were at the rear of the saloon, sepa-rated by a folding door. Their maids cared for them.

When we arrived in Montgomery several hours later, the captain asked the gentlemen to retreat to their private berths because we had to clean the saloon. He told us to eat something first before we continued working. As I was wiping a table, the captain and an-other man went to speak to me.

"William, that's your name, isn't it, boy?"

"Yes, sir, Captain."

"This man needs to see your traveling paper."

I forgot in which pocket was my traveling pass and I patted the right one. I felt the wax seal of the manumission paper and gave him the traveling pass from my left.

"Where are you going?"

"Sir, I is going to Claiborne so I can look for work on boats go-ing up the Tombigbee."

"What's wrong with working on this boat?"

"Nothing, sir, but they told me I is only working here 'til I gets to Claiborne."

He shrugged, returned my paper, and left with the captain. When everyone boarded at Montgomery, we had more work to do because there were more gentlemen, and they spent most of their time in the saloon, playing cards and drinking spirits. I asked the cook why we had few additional passengers at the Selma landing, and he said it was because the town had never recovered from the bad times that started in 1837, when cotton prices fell in Alabama, and from the sickly seasons that began in 1840.

Whenever we docked at a landing, I expected slave catchers to board and question me, but they did not until we arrived at Prairie Bluff. There the captain told all Negro passengers who were not traveling with their masters to disembark and present their papers to officials. We walked up a long staircase to the landing, where I saw that these were not officials but slave catchers with bloodhounds, one of whom instructed us to separate into two groups by gender. One man had one of my maid's dresses from the Cromwell plantation, and another had one of Isaac's jackets. A dog smelled my dress and then tried to find me among the women, while the other smelled Isaac's jacket and searched for him in my group. When the hounds identified no one, the catchers released us, and we returned to the boat.

The captain asked me before we arrived at Claiborne whether I wanted to stay on until Mobile.

"Sir, thank you, but my master say he want me to find work on the Tombigbee."

"I certainly want you to obey your master, but do you think that it matters to him where you find work?"

"Yes, sir. Well, he say I can earn more money on the Tombigbee because it got one hundred more landings there."

"So that's what this is about; you want more money. I can't pay you more than one dollar a day. All right, I wish you well. Mr. Pratt will bring you your pay and refund your fare before we get to Claiborne."

The landing in the town of Claiborne had the longest slide and staircase of all. Viewed from the bluff, the river and the town, with its shops and houses, were magnificent. No one disturbed me, and I saw no slave catchers or even notices for runaway slaves. A man working by a warehouse on the landing told me where I could get a boat to take me across the river. For twenty-five cents, a ferryman, a Negro who asked me no questions, took me to the western bank of the Alabama, where I took a stagecoach to Clarke County. I boarded another ferry, also piloted by a Negro, to take me across the Tombigbee and made my way from there by coach to a desolate settlement on the northern edge of Mobile called Prichard. I was the only passenger who asked to stop there, which prompted the coachman to ask me if I meant to do so.

"Yes, sir. My master say to try earn some money at one of the plantations around here. He say they going to need extra hands come harvest time to take the cotton to the river."

"Well, you do what you want to do, but I don't know why you just don't stay on 'til we get to Mobile proper. That's where they really need men to work on the docks."

Prichard did not have any merchants or shops where I could buy food, so I went directly to the woods, where I foraged for my supper, fruits and wild greens, and went to sleep. The next morning, I searched until I found a coffee tree, from which I picked berries to use as soap. I washed my clothes and put them to dry on a bush. I stayed there until late that night, and then I packed my knapsack and resumed walking.

My hunger returned. From the road the second night, I smelled meat being smoked. I entered the woods next to a farm, where I slept until dawn. Crouched behind a bush, I observed the inhabitants, about fifteen slaves and a master and mistress, performing their tasks. I found a stone and set it aside for the evening. It appeared that the man who worked in the smokehouse did not lock the door at the end of the day. Having had only fruit for breakfast and dinner, I was glad when darkness arrived, and the slaves went to their quarters and the masters to their house. I left my knapsack under a bush by a clearing, took the stone, and went to the smokehouse. The door creaked when I opened it. I propped it with the stone to let in the moonlight and entered. It was smaller than the smokehouse at the Cromwell plantation but similar in other respects.

I took a ham off a hook and was about to cut a large piece off with the knife that Henry and Oliver gave me when I heard a dog's bark. I took the entire ham and ran, but the hound was so swift that it closed the distance between us quickly, until it was only about twenty yards behind me. The dog's barking woke the owner, who went outside and yelled to the animal to get me. When it was about ten yards from me, I dropped the ham. The dog stopped, and I ran into the woods. I heard a shot fired, which confused me, and I forgot the location of the bush under which I had left my knapsack and the jacket with my papers and money.

Now the dog was growling and coming closer. My sight darkened but did not become completely obscured. I was out of breath, and my heart was beating so fast that I had to sit. After I said a prayer, I regained my strength. My vision returned, and I searched for a clearing in the treetops. The dog was quiet, but I was certain that the owner had led it into the woods to look for me. I located a break in the canopy and crawled to search for the area where I had left my knapsack. By its labored panting, I could tell that the dog was near. Standing underneath the clearing, I flung a stone as far as I could, and the dog, barking, went to the area where the stone broke a few tree limbs before landing. I found my knapsack and put on my jacket, resolving never again to leave them anywhere, and walked, even though the path I took led away from the road.

The following morning, I found a brook, and as I was about to wash my face, I saw a Negro man and young boy, both holding rifles, walking toward me. I grabbed my jacket and knapsack.

"You don't need to run from us. You look like you need help, or at least a meal. We was just going hunting, but why don't we take you to our home? The missus will fix you something to eat."

"No, thank you, sir. I need to get going."

"Come on, we won't hurt you. I'm Josiah Green, and this is my son, Matthew."

I introduced myself.

"Where you going, William?"

"South, to Mobile."

"Well, you're in Mobile. What part you want to go to?"

"I think I'll keep that to myself, sir."

"I understand. Listen, you're away from the road, east of it. I'm a carpenter, and my boy and me, we're building a house for some people south of here. Come Monday, we're going back there to work. If you want to come with us in the wagon, we'll take you."

"That's all right, sir. I think I'll continue walking, just the same."

"All right then. We'll go on with our hunting, but if you change your mind, just go on that way. When you go out the woods, you'll see our house. Tell the missus I sent you."

When they were gone, I decided that, if they had wanted to harm me, they would have done so. I washed myself and went to their home, a pretty house, standing by a small farm. Mrs. Green was working outside with her four older children, and when I told her what her husband said, she welcomed me. She took me to her kitchen and fed me and did not ask where I was coming from or where I was going. She said that she and her family, as well as thirty other Negro families in that area, were freedmen.

"William, we have a cabin that nobody is using and you can stay there, if you want to. On Monday, my husband can take you where you want to go."

"Ma'am, thank you, but I need to get going."

"I understand, but it looks like you could use some rest and need to wash your clothes and take a proper bath."

"Yes, ma'am. I should do that. Mrs. Green, if your husband takes me to Mobile, won't somebody ask questions, like about who I am?" It had taken some effort to work up the courage, or perhaps the trust, to ask the question, but the woman's manner had put me at ease.

"We've done this before, William. We and the other freedmen get people coming through here on the way to Mobile proper. He'll find a place for you in the back of the wagon. The back is covered and you can hide under a canvas cloth. It won't be comfortable, but it'll get you where you going."

"Do you have your own church by here, ma'am?"

"Yes, all the families got the money together, and my husband built it. But you shouldn't go with us tomorrow because the sheriff keep a close eye on us. He know freedmen take care of others seeking the same thing. So if you decide to go with my husband on Monday, you shouldn't go off our property until then."

EIGHTEEN

THEODORA ALLEN

It occurred to me that I had not seen Emmeline since Cornelius's passing; my sister-in-law had assumed my household management duties while I was in mourning. Martha said that, with all the family, the lawyer, and the accountant in residence, Emmeline did not have to clean the house and should devote her time to cooking. I summoned Emmeline to my apartment. Since Sarah ran away, she was thinner, and the skin beneath her eyes was sunken.

"Emmeline, I want to tell you how sorry I am that Sarah is gone. I know it's not quite the same, but I know how you must feel. Neither of us will ever again see our girls."

"Ma'am, I do thank you for saying that. Ma'am, do you know if they're still looking for her?"

"Yes, they are, but we both know how intelligent she is. I don't think that they will ever catch her."

She bowed her head. "But if they do, ma'am, please, is there anything you can do so they won't beat her when they bring her back?"

"I can try, but I doubt they would listen to me about that.

Emmeline, I should not tell you this, but the slave catchers said that if they do not capture a slave soon after he runs away, it is not likely he will be caught. That must offer you a bit of comfort."

"Yes, ma'am, it do. I don't think I could stand watching them hurt my baby girl."

"Emmeline, there is something else I want to say to you that I was not able to tell you when Cornelius was alive. When I learned that Belle was sold, I confronted him and asked him to buy her back. His response was . . . well, we do not need to repeat those things because you know what he did to me when he was angry. He accused me of telling you to stop . . . going to him, and he said that, if I continued to interfere, that he would . . . sell you and Sarah. That is why I did not say anything to you about Belle at the time. But I want you to know how sorry I was for you, and how happy I was when Belle returned."

"Ma'am, I'm thankful that you told me this. Thank you, Mrs. Allen."

I did not tell her—and I hope it did not show—that simply speaking about Cornelius made me want to cry because in my dreams he was beating me or forcing himself upon me. When I had those dreams, I would awake to escape. It is difficult to describe the relief that I felt each time I remembered he was dead, knowing that he would never be able to hurt me again.

I made my decision to tell the lawyer that I had found the documents concerning my grandson.

"Mr. Harris, I have good news to report. First, I need to know that you will not reveal what I tell you to anyone else until the estate is settled."

"Yes, I will keep in confidence whatever you tell me."

"I remembered that my husband maintained a second coffer, and in it I found documents showing my grandson's location. How much longer do you think it will be until the assessment of the estate is completed?"

"Mrs. Allen, that is indeed good news, and I also have something favorable to report. I believe we will have finalized our work in less than two weeks. Now, may I please have the documents?"

I showed them to him.

"Well done. Was this everything in the coffer?"

"In terms of documents, yes, but I left the paper currency and gold coins that were in there. Here is the key to the coffer."

"Do you know how much currency?"

"Yes, it was $70,000."

"Mrs. Allen, I know I asked you this before, but you are sure your daughter did not have a will?"

"I am certain. I believe she would have mentioned it to me. I have her letters that she sent to us when she moved to Talladega. She was afraid of her husband, and I doubt that she would have written a will and not told us."

"These documents concerning Clarissa's son resolve the final piece of the puzzle with regard to the bequests. However, since your daughter died without a will, we will have to appoint someone as administrator of her estate. We should do that as quickly as possible, before her husband thinks of doing so. Would you like to serve in that capacity?"

"Yes, certainly."

"Good. I will draft the papers, and after you sign them, I will take them to the judge for his signature. I should take them tomorrow morning."

"What does the will say about Clarissa's share of the estate?"

"Again, Mrs. Allen, I cannot say. But you will know soon."

My grandchildren were making progress in their learning, and they reminded me of Clarissa when she was having her lessons. We were painting in the garden several days after my conversation with the lawyer regarding the whereabouts of Clarissa's son when a servant said that Mr. Harris asked to see me in the office. I told the servant to take the children inside to their mothers. Charles, my brother-in-law, was already there, but he and the lawyer had waited for me to discuss the developments.

"First, the judge signed the papers appointing Mrs. Allen as administrator of Mrs. Cromwell's estate. Secondly, I have received Mr. Cromwell's response to my letter. He has by now probably filed a petition in the Chancery Court for the Fourth District in Talladega."

"Did he say what he will allege in the petition?"

"Yes, Mrs. Allen. I will show it to you, but in summary, he says that the petition will be filed against the executor of Mr. Allen's estate, that it seeks Mrs. Cromwell's share of her father's bequests, the return of Sarah and Isaac, and the twenty field hands that Mr. Allen had promised him."

"But that is absurd. He ended the marriage and did not acknowledge the child as his," I said.

"He says that he did not end the marriage and that, this will be difficult for you to hear, he will state in the petition that, at the time of their marriage, Mrs. Cromwell was pregnant and that she fraudulently concealed that fact from him."

"That is not true. We told him and his parents that she was expecting and that is why my husband promised him the twenty field hands."

"Well, he will allege that the child was the result of illicit intercourse, and Mr. Cromwell will name the putative father. He says that, by her fraud, she forfeited all obligations on his part."

I closed my eyes and said a brief prayer. "What can we do, Mr. Harris? Is there a possibility that the petition would succeed?"

"In sending her back here, Mr. Cromwell did not legally annul the marriage, and the law holds that a husband has absolute title to property brought to the marriage by his wife. But with your permission, this is what I recommend. We should send someone to Talladega immediately with a letter from me asking Mr. Cromwell not to file the petition or, if he already has, to withdraw it on the following grounds: he will get the twenty field hands; Sarah, or her monetary value; Isaac; and Mrs. Cromwell's share of her father's estate if he publicly acknowledges that he is the father of the child.

"If he does not accept your offer, we will argue that the court should not rule in his favor on his petition on the grounds that the marriage cannot be valid for the purpose of inheriting her estate and yet not valid as regards the child's legitimacy."

We followed Mr. Harris's recommended course of action, but Julius had already filed the petition, which he refused to withdraw. The lawyer told Charles and me that, because of Julius's actions, it was wise to accelerate entry of the will into probate.

"If the bequests are distributed before the Chancery Court rules on Mr. Cromwell's petition, it will be difficult for him to obtain the grant that would go to Mrs. Cromwell's son. By the way, I have already spoken with the judge here in Benton County. As you know, Mr. Allen appointed Judge Atkins to the bench, and he has agreed that, as soon as assessment of the value of the estate is complete, he will sign the necessary documents to probate the will."

I anxiously awaited the conclusion of Mr. Harris's task, but there was nothing I could do to make him work faster. The following week, my sons, holding newspapers, interrupted a lesson on geography that I was conducting in the lesson room and asked to speak with me privately. Their faces were red. We took the children to my daughters-in-law, and my sons and I went to the library.

"Mother, do you not know what they're reporting in the newspapers?"

"No, I haven't read today's edition."

"Mother, these newspapers are from last week, from Mobile and Atlanta. We received them with the mail."

"Well, what do they say that is so disturbing?"

"Everything about this sordid, filthy scandal concerning Clarissa. The Atlanta newspaper reports that Mr. Cromwell was planning to file a petition against Papa's estate and alleged that . . . well, the paper revealed what Clarissa did."

"This is what your father feared, that it would affect you. Have you heard anything from the banks?"

"Not yet, but, Mother, you know how people are. They are

unlikely to trust us with their money if they think we come from an immoral family. What should we do?"

"Let's discuss this with your uncle. And we do not yet know that this news will have any impact on your business partnerships."

"Mother, really, you can't be so innocent. We're going to be out-casts after everyone hears about this."

"You're exaggerating. Remember that men who engage in commerce are worldly. It's possible that they will see Mr. Cromwell's petition for what it is: mere allegations."

"Mother, Clarissa did what only common women do, and the conduct that gentlemen might associate with the lower orders is not what they tolerate in a lady."

We spoke with Charles and with Mr. Harris. Neither believed that there was anything to be done. Shortly after Mr. Cromwell filed the case in court, we learned that all the details with regard to the petition had spread throughout Alabama and Georgia. We retained Mr. Harris's partner to represent the estate's interests, and he agreed with Mr. Harris's opinion that Mr. Cromwell had mounted a challenge that was difficult for him to win because he could not argue that the marriage was valid and at the same time deny paternity of the child.

Mr. Harris finally announced the conclusion of the estate's valuation, and he went to the courthouse and returned with papers signed by the judge, entering the will into probate. He asked to speak first with Charles and me, and then he wanted Emmeline, Belle, Eddie, Bessie, and Dottie to join us. When only Charles and I were present, he told us how Cornelius wanted his estate to be distributed. I asked about Isaac, and Mr. Harris said that he was still Charles's property, as Charles had never sold Isaac to Cornelius. Charles said that he had already arranged to sell Isaac out of the state. Mr. Harris sent for the servants. They were uncomfortable in our presence, but the lawyer was gentle with them. He asked them to sit. They hesitated, but I joined him in persuading them to do so.

"First, I need each one of you to promise that you will not repeat, to anyone, what I am going to tell you," he said.

They each promised.

"Mr. Cornelius Allen wrote a document, a paper, called a will, saying what he wanted to be done with his property upon his death. I will come straight to the point. Emmeline, Belle, and her children, Bessie and her children, Dottie and her children, and Eddie are free."

The eyes of each of these former slaves stared at Mr. Harris, in stunned disbelief, and no one knew what to say or do. Emmeline looked at me, seeking confirmation.

"Yes, Emmeline, it is true."

They cried, even Eddie, and tears came to my eyes, too.

"Thank God. Thank you, Mr. Allen. Thank you, Mrs. Allen. And thank you, Mr. Harris," Emmeline said.

"You don't have to thank us," I said.

"Yes, ma'am, we do. Thank you for doing what the paper said," Emmeline said.

Belle was still crying.

"Sir, what about my girl, Sarah? Did Mr. Allen say if she's free, too?"

"Yes, in fact, although it may seem somewhat confusing. Mr. Allen's will basically says that Sarah was the property of Mrs. Clarissa Cromwell, but only during Mrs. Cromwell's life. Upon her death, Sarah reverted, or went back, to Mr. Allen's estate. But Mr. Allen said in his will that, if Mrs. Cromwell died before him, Sarah would be free upon his death."

Belle whispered something to Emmeline.

"So if she didn't run . . ." Emmeline said.

"Yes, it's a shame that she did, but let us pray that Mr. Cromwell's catchers do not find her.

"Now, there is more important information that you need to know, and this may be one reason why Belle and Eddie are still unhappy. I know that Mr. Allen bought Belle's husband, Zeke, and that Eddie has a wife and children on the Barkley plantation. Now, in addition to freeing you, Mr. Allen said that you are each to get money from his estate. He gave fifteen thousand dollars to Emmeline, fifteen thousand to Eddie, fifteen thousand to Bessie, fifteen thousand to Dottie, and ten thousand to Belle. That is enough money for Belle to buy her husband from Mr. Allen's estate and for Eddie to buy his wife and children from Mr. Barkley."

Eddie was so happy that he could not stop smiling, but Belle was still sad, which Mr. Harris noticed.

"Belle, is there still something that concerns you?"

She kept her head bowed and struggled to speak.

"Go ahead, baby. Answer Mr. Harris," Emmeline said.

"Sir, what about my sister?"

"I'm sorry, Belle, but we are doing the best we can to bring her back. The truth is that, because they have not yet caught her, they probably never will and she probably is free. That should give you some comfort.

"Now, there is a recent amendment, or change, to the will that says that the five of you and your families, should you wish to purchase them, must be taken, at no expense to you, to a free territory. I have consulted with the pastor of a large congregation and two prominent lawyers with whom I studied law in Connecticut and who live in Ohio, and they agree that the prospects are good for free Negroes in a town called Xenia in that area. I understand that this is all surprising to you, but Mr. Allen and I discussed this change to the will in detail, and he was clear that it was a requirement that you must be moved to a free state."

"But, sir, how is we going to get there?"

"Mr. Allen thought of that too, Emmeline. He said that the lawyer handling his estate at his death should choose a pastor to take you there, and that the pastor was to help you find homes and employment. I have selected the Reverend Townsend, of the church that I attend, to perform this task."

"Sir, what if they find Sarah and bring her back and we're gone?"

"Sarah would be able to join you in Ohio. Now, for reasons that I cannot discuss with you, it is important that you leave here as quickly as possible. Eddie, if you want to buy your family, please tell me now, and I will speak with Mr. Barkley tomorrow to arrange the purchase; and Belle, if you wish to buy your husband, I can immediately write the papers for Zeke's purchase from Mr. Allen's estate."

They both agreed.

"Remember your promises to not discuss this with anyone. You should pack your belongings, but do so quickly and quietly, and be ready to leave Saturday night. Yes, Emmeline. Is something else worrying you?"

"Sir, I was thinking about Miss Mary, the midwife. She's been so good to me and my girls. Is there any way that I could pay to buy her freedom?"

Charles spoke for the first time. "Mr. Harris, Mary is probably one of the most valuable slaves on this plantation. And I don't think we should start giving all the slaves notions of freedom. If Cornelius wanted her to be freed, he would have provided for her in his will."

Mr. Harris said, "Emmeline, Belle, Eddie, Bessie, and Dottie, please step outside and wait in the hallway." Then he closed the door behind them.

"Mr. Allen, I understand what you're telling me, but one of the privileges of freedom is the right to buy and sell property. And since the slaves are going to be sold anyway, what difference does it make if Emmeline wants to buy Mary and free her?"

"The truth is, I want to buy her for my plantation, but I really am concerned about the effect of freeing slaves other than the ones in Cornelius's will. What ideas will be planted in the other slaves' heads?"

"You are more knowledgeable than I about plantation management, but I know that Mary bought her sons' freedom, and thus it would not be unusual if she is similarly freed. What I suggest is this: you could purchase the rest of her family that is still enslaved as a lot and take them to Mobile County with you. I'm sure Mary would move there to be close to them and would work on your plantation as a freed person."

"I can see why Cornelius put so much trust in you," Charles said.

We called the freedmen back in, and Mr. Harris told Emmeline the welcome news about Mary, but he warned her not to say anything to her yet. He said that he would handle the purchase and would draft manumission papers. He then dismissed them.

"Now to the difficult part, speaking with your sons, Mrs. Allen."

I sent a servant to call them and my sister-in-law. Mr. Harris addressed them. "The will has been entered into probate. A copy of it, and all supporting documentation, has been duly filed with the court. The valuation of the estate, after deductions for the payment of debts and smaller bequests, including the manumission of the former slaves Emmeline, Belle and her three children, Bessie and her four children, Dottie and her five children, and Eddie, costs associated with said manumission, and legal fees and costs related to the settlement of the estate, not including the proceeds of this year's harvest, is a total of one million and two hundred thousand dollars."

My sons smiled when they heard that figure.

"I will tell you how the estate is apportioned among all of you, but first you must know that one of the terms of the will is that anyone who contests any grant made by the grantor or seeks to nullify any or all parts of the will forfeits his or her grant."

No one said anything.

"One half of the estate goes to Mrs. Theodora Allen, one quarter to the estate of the late Mrs. Clarissa Cromwell, and the balance, in equal shares, to Paul Allen, Robert Allen, Mr. Charles Allen, and Mrs. Martha Laurence."

"I don't understand what you mean when you say that Clarissa's estate gets one quarter of my father's estate. Who actually gets that money?" Paul asked.

"Because she died without a will, the court has appointed your mother as the administrator of Mrs. Cromwell's estate. The money will be placed in a trust for Mrs. Cromwell's son."

"What are you saying? That money was our father's, and we are his legitimate heirs. Therefore, Clarissa's share should go to us, not to her bastard. And why do we have to share a measly one quarter of the money?"

"My duty is to enforce your father's wishes, as he specified them in his will."

"But you wrote the will."

"These were your father's wishes. I am the executor of the will. Your father, who, I remind you, studied law, made certain that the will was properly drafted and witnessed," Charles said.

"What is the date of the will? Wasn't he sick for some time before he died? How do we know he was legally capable of entering into it?"

"The will was written in 1836. There was a recent amendment, but it does not affect any of your grants," Mr. Harris said.

"Whose grants are affected?"

"The manumission of and bequests to the former slaves," Mr. Harris said.

"How recent was the amendment? Was my father already ill when he made it?"

"No, he was not. He met me in my office, and he was healthy and of sound mind."

"I can't believe he willingly freed those niggers."

"Paul, do not use vulgar language in my presence."

"I'm sorry, Mother, but I'm sure you understand why we're so angry and can't believe that Father treated us like that. Especially given that, now that everyone knows what Clarissa did, we may not even have positions at our respective banks when we return. Mr. Harris, it just occurred to me, since we don't know where Clarissa's bast— er . . . son is, how will he get the trust?"

"Mr. Harris, there's no need to discuss that now. I will tell the family the details about that matter at another time," I said.

"There is one other issue we do need to speak about. As you know, Mr. Cromwell filed a petition to try to get Mrs. Cromwell's share of Mr. Allen's estate. My partner and I do not believe he will succeed, but we want you to know that the possibility exists. If he is successful, it will only affect Mrs. Cromwell's share and no other," Mr. Harris said.

"Are you sure, Mr. Harris, that the court would find that only Clarissa's grant was affected?"

"Yes, of that I am certain, and I remind you that, if anyone tries to challenge his or any grant, by operation of the will, he will forfeit his share."

NINETEEN

SARAH CAMPBELL

Mrs. Green showed me to the washroom and told me where I could hang my clean clothes to dry, and she gave me a set of her husband's garments to wear. Mr. Adams's advice to take some of Mr. Allen's unused undergarments, which I at first had rejected, turned out to be sound.

"Mrs. Green, can I help to wash your laundry?"

"No, William. I think it's best if you help me in the kitchen. You never know when patrollers or the sheriff are riding around, looking into people's property."

I cooked for the family while they were at church on Sunday. In the middle of dinner, however, I cried.

"You're missing your family, William?"

I told them that, at home, after we made Sunday dinner for our master and his family and while others served them, my mother, Belle and her family, and I went to my mother's cabin, where we had our own meal. "I was thinking that I'll never have this with them again."

"You'll meet someone, William, and you'll have your own family. And you can raise your children the same way your mother raised you."

I packed my bag Sunday night and thanked Mrs. Green and said good-bye to her children. Mr. Green told me that I could keep the overalls, as it was an old pair and would be better for me to wear in the wagon than my own clothes. We departed at five thirty Monday morning. He gave me similar instructions to what LeRoy and Arthur had offered, except he said that he would say "get down" when he saw a patroller or militiaman.

"We always get stopped at least once in every settlement or village along the way, but the patrollers all know us and they don't bother looking at our freedom papers. Sometimes they look in the back, though, so make sure you hide yourself real good when we say 'get down.' It's another thing when we get to Mobile proper. Most the time they have patrollers, slave catchers, and sheriffs there because they know runaways go for help in the freedmen's villages and escape to the North on ships. And after they check our papers or look in the wagon, make sure you stay down until we tell you to get up."

As Mr. Green said, patrollers stopped the wagon to speak to him and looked in the back of the wagon only twice before we reached Mobile.

"All right, William, we're about to enter Mobile proper. There's going to be patrollers and sheriffs in about forty-five minutes. I'm stopping the wagon now and going to the back to give you my blanket. Wrap yourself in it and make sure you hide yourself real good. They might have dogs and the smell from my blanket should throw them off any scent they're searching for."

He told me to get down about fifteen minutes later, and I heard men's voices.

"Your papers."

I heard dogs panting. My leg began to shake and would not stop.

"What're you coming here for and how long are you staying?"

"Sir, we're building a house in the Springhill village. We'll be here until Friday afternoon, and then we go back home."

"We know them. They come down here to work all the time," someone else said.

"Just the same, we need to check their papers. Josiah, I'm going to describe two people to you and you tell me if you saw anybody matching their descriptions on the way down here. One is a mulatto woman, yellowish, tall, long hair, speaks good English; the other is a man, very tall, over six feet, bright yellow mulatto with gray eyes. Did you see anybody who looks like either one of them?"

"No, sir. I didn't."

"All right, do you want to make some money, Josiah?"

"Sir, how?"

"There are large rewards for anyone who turns in either of these two runaways, and we think they're going to Mobile. Two hundred for the woman and one hundred for the man. If you come across either of them, or if you get any information about where they may be, you go down to my office on the corner of St. Francis and Water Streets. If we catch them based upon what you tell us, you'll get the reward. Now, we need to look in the back of the wagon."

I heard them walk to the rear. I thought about my family and felt a prick of pain that I would never see them again but forced myself to pay attention to the present and remembered my mother's sound advice to always be vigilant and to think of what would be my next step. Here, I just had to stay as still as possible, despite my shaking leg. Someone opened the canvas covering and helped a dog to climb aboard. I kept my body stiff so that I would not tremble, and I hoped that the animal would not smell my fear or hear my heartbeat. The dog sniffed, and it apparently lifted something with its snout. As the animal moved around the wagon, it stepped on my arm. I stayed still and held my breath so my chest would not move. It got off me. The hound evidently was unable to identify my scent or Isaac's scent, and the patrollers ended the search and permitted us to continue. The heat from the blanket and the bundles covering me, coupled with my accelerated heart pulses and shallow breathing, almost caused me to faint. Even though the slave catchers were gone, I did not—could not—move for the longest while.

When we had traveled a little farther, Mr. Green told me to stay down because it was likely that men were posted near where we were going. After about an hour, we were stopped again. This time, it seemed as if only a slave catcher was present. He inspected the wagon and repeated the information about the rewards offered for Isaac's and my capture. The wagon slowed as we made a turn. I stayed down. Mr. Green got out of the wagon. I heard a familiar, sweet voice answer after he knocked on a door.

"Good morning, sir, how can I help you?"

"Good morning, ma'am. I'm looking for Miss Adeline."

"You found her."

"I have somebody here, in the back of my wagon. He come a long way to see you. Is it all right if he comes out?"

"Sure, if it's me he came to see."

He opened the canvas cover. We were in an alleyway. Miss Adeline did not at first recognize me, not only because I was disguised as a man but also because it had been over two years since I was at her house with my mother and Eddie.

"Good Lord, sweet Jesus. Sa— Uh, get out of there and come inside, quick. Mr. . . . . come in, and I see you got somebody else with you. Come in, everybody."

We entered her home. She was careful to not say much about my identity. Her grandchildren came in from playing on the front porch. They either did not remember me from my prior visit or did not see through my disguise. Miss Adeline gave us dinner, and after we ate, Mr. Green and his son took their leave. I thanked them and asked that they give my regards to the rest of their family. When their wagon had pulled away, Miss Adeline told me to bathe, and I agreed to tell her everything afterward.

"But, Miss Adeline, did you hear about Belle? That we got her back?"

"Thank you, Jesus. That's wonderful news. You know I never stopped praying. I want to hear everything about how her and Miss Emmeline is doing. But first, I'll get you some of my daughter's clothes to put on and a scarf to wrap your head after you bathe."

It felt good to wear a dress, even though it was too short for me, but I was surprised to find that I missed wearing trousers and not having to cross my ankles when I sat. I told Miss Adeline almost everything about my escape from Allen Estates and why I had fled.

"What trouble me is that they is looking for you all the way down here and willing to pay so much money for you. You know you can't leave the house. They have catchers and patrollers all over the place."

"But I have papers, Miss Adeline."

"What kind of papers?"

"I have a traveling pass and freedom papers."

"How you get those? Never mind. I don't need to know."

"And almost everybody believes that I'm a man. And Miss Adeline, I can't stay inside forever."

"We're going to think about what to do, baby. Did you tell Miss Emmeline this is where you was coming?"

"No, I told her as little as possible. But she cut my hair and took me to a tailor, a freedman, who made my clothes and gave me advice. Miss Adeline, can your sons help me get a job on a ship, one that's going to a free state?"

"Sarah, you can't be going on a ship full of men."

"But my mother told me about when she went up North with Mr. Allen on ships that had passengers, women and men, and cargo."

"That's true. When they come home tonight, we'll talk this out with them."

I helped Miss Adeline cook, and when supper was ready, she called the children inside. They were obviously confused but too well-mannered to ask why I was now wearing women's clothing. After we ate, they showed me their books from Sunday school, and I gave them lessons in the parlor. That evening, Miss Adeline sent one of the older children to ask her sons, Steven and Samuel, to her house. She summarized what I had told her, including how I had disguised myself and worked on a steamboat.

"We work on the docks, loading and unloading cargo, and we

know some of the captains and merchant marines. In fact, some of the sailors go to our church when they're on leave. The thing is, most of the ships is from England and their sailors is from the West Indies. I never heard of them hiring anybody from here. But you're tall, and since you got freedom papers, maybe we could get you work on the docks. That way, you can get to know some of the sailors," Steven said.

"Yes, but if they have to check my freedom paper with the court in Madison County, they'll know it's not genuine."

"That's a big problem. The same thing would happen if you tried to get on a ship."

They must have noticed my disappointment because the three of them looked at each other with concern.

"All right, we'll see what we can do. Mama, maybe we need to talk to the pastor about this."

"Could you stop by his house tonight and ask him to come over tomorrow morning?"

The next day, Miss Adeline sent the children out to play when the pastor arrived. After she explained the matter to him, he said that he had an idea but that he had to make inquiries before discussing it with us. He remembered my mother and me from our visit.

"Did you ever hear anything about your sister?"

I smiled. "Yes, sir. Master bought her back."

"Thank God. The church kept your family in our prayers, and I know that the Lord is going to answer yours."

When Steven and Samuel returned that night, Miss Adeline told them what the pastor said.

"I hope he can think of something, because today at the docks we noticed runaway notices about you and your husband. We didn't even ask if there's any work for you. One thing you can do is just stay here and wait until they give up looking for you."

I had much to ask for in my nightly prayers. The following day, the pastor reported that it would be another month before he had an answer to an inquiry that he had made. Miss Adeline assured me that she and her daughters were happy to have me there, especially because her grandchildren were enjoying their lessons with me. I asked her to purchase primers, pencils, and paper; and I kept myself busy by helping Miss Adeline with her housework and teaching the young ones.

The pastor sent word throughout the first month I spent with Miss Adeline that he had not forgotten me and encouraged me to continue to pray. One Sunday, when she returned from church, Miss Adeline asked one of her daughters, a seamstress, to take my measurements and write them on a paper, which Steven took to the pastor. No one told me the reason for this activity, and I knew better than to ask.

Early one morning, almost three months after I had arrived in Mobile, the pastor came over and asked Miss Adeline if her daughters and their children could stay at another home that day and night. I said good-bye to them as they left for Steven's house.

"Sarah, I know you want to go to a free state, but that's not a good plan, mainly because of the Fugitive Slave Act. Under that law, slave catchers from the South are allowed to go to states where slavery has been abolished and return runaways to their masters. The catchers not only bring back runaways, but sometimes they kidnap freedmen and sell them back into slavery. I think the best course, and one that I have been able to arrange, is for you to go to a British land, where slavery has been abolished. I know I've given you almost no time to consider this, but as you know, it's dangerous to reveal too much information. Based upon what I have told you, are you willing to go forward with your flight to freedom?"

I did not think for long. "Sir, yes, I am. I can't hide inside for the rest of my life. My only question is—and perhaps you can't answer it—how do I know I will be taken to freedom and not to slavery somewhere else?"

"Sarah, the reason it took me so long to make preparations for you is that I wrote a letter to a British captain of a commercial ship who is a member of a Christian denomination called the Religious

Society of Friends, or the Quakers. When we first met ten years ago, he told me that he and many Quakers believe in the abolition of slavery. Miss Adeline knows him, as he has worshipped with us. His ship was in port a month ago, and he spoke with me at the church. We made arrangements for you, which are now complete. I need to see your freedom paper."

He read it.

"The captain will need to see your freedom paper because the company that owns the ship requires that everyone on board is legitimately there. Make sure that you take it with you."

The pastor gave me a bag containing clothes and shoes and told us that Miss Adeline needed to cut my hair short to my scalp like a sailor's. He said that I should be dressed and ready to depart that midnight. He then led us in prayer and wished me Godspeed.

After supper, Miss Adeline cut my hair and I took a bath. At ten, I changed into the merchant marine's uniform and shoes that were in the bag. I transferred my papers and clean undergarments into the bag, and then Miss Adeline and I prayed. We could not keep ourselves from crying. About two hours later, we heard a hackney outside.

Miss Adeline opened the door and signaled me to go. I embraced her and thanked her and her family. I asked her, if she ever saw my mother again, to tell her everything and especially to let her know that I was well. The driver waved to Miss Adeline and beckoned me. There were two sailors inside the coach, James Carter and Anthony Eden. Anthony gave me a paper and said, with a delightful way of speaking, that I had to show it to the customs officer before I would be permitted to board the ship.

"Your name is Bradley Ebanks. The three of us will be drunken sailors. Me and James are going to act the way we normally act after a night of carousing with wenches while on leave. But you can't take that rucksack on board or they won't believe we've been in town drinking."

"I have my papers and . . ."

"Just take them and put them inside your socks, like so."

I wished I had taken the knife Henry and Oliver had given me, because I had the same misgivings I felt the night that LeRoy and Arthur left me on that road in Chambers County. It was too dark to read the paper that the sailor gave me, and I was afraid to ask what it said. To calm myself, I prayed and silently recited the paper that I had written proclaiming my freedom:

DEED OF MANUMISSION, WILLIAM CAMPBELL
To all whom it may concern: Be it known that I, Gregory Campbell, of the County of Madison, have released from slavery and manumit my Negro boy named William Campbell, being of the age of eighteen and able to work and gain sufficient livelihood. Him, the said Negro, I do declare to be henceforth free and discharged from all manner of servitude to me, my executors, or administrators forever.

We arrived at the wharf at the same time as about thirty other sailors. A clerk was standing outside a booth holding a lantern and reviewing papers that the sailors were handing to him. James and Anthony were singing a strange song about drinking rum. When it was our turn, we each gave the clerk our documents. He looked at them quickly and told us to go ahead to the gangway. The captain was waiting for us as we stepped onto the main deck. I imitated the others and saluted him.

"Give me the paper the deckhands gave you, sailor, and come with me," the captain said.

He led me to the cook-room, closed the door, and read my freedom paper.

"William Campbell, you are now in the service of the British West Indies Trading Company. You will be paid sixty pounds a month to be the chief steward of this ship. Two utility men will assist you to cook and serve meals to the officers and the deckhands. Because of your . . . situation, you will not sleep belowdecks, but here. Tomorrow morning Merchant Marine Ebanks will bring you two uniforms. You will thereafter use his uniform when you are on shore leave. You will report to me. I will speak with you in detail about our voyage tomorrow, after the evening meal. Do you have any questions now?"

"Sir, Captain, may I have my freedom paper back?"

"No, sailor. I will keep it in the coffer, where it will be safe. Now go to sleep. I take tea at six thirty in the officers' dining room, and the morning meal for everyone must be ready at eight o'clock. Your assistants will be here at five thirty to tell you how everything is done, but they are terrible cooks, so we are grateful that you are here. There are new night clothes and other garments in that bag over there. During the day, you can roll the pallet and put it in the corner. You can put your clothing in that cabinet there. Lock the door, and good night."

I lit a lantern and closed the wooden shutters. There was a straw-filled pallet on the floor, a pillow, and folded bed linens. I arranged my bed and knelt by it to say my prayers. Perhaps because it was late and the ship was rocking gently, I went to sleep fast.

The following morning, my assistants arrived promptly at five thirty. Without them, I could not have cooked three meals a day for sixty people. Bradley Ebanks arrived after the morning meal with my chief steward's uniforms. He was my height but much older than I expected. We were alone in the cook-room, and I thanked him for the use of his uniform.

"You're welcome. My nephews enjoyed the little adventure. I remember you from Mobile. You and your mother visited the church in Mobile at the same time we did."

"Uh, you remember me?"

"Yes. Well, I remember your mother. What a beautiful lady. Well, the captain is going to talk to you, and he'll explain everything. In the meantime, if there's anything I can do for you, please let me know."

As he promised, the captain came to the cook-room to speak to me that night. I admitted to him that I was afraid of spending the rest of my life in a foreign land where I did not know a soul, and that it pained me that I would never again see my family.

"Sailor, I have found that young people have the ability to thrive in new surroundings. You will never be alone because the Good Lord will always be by your side, and I trust that he will guide and comfort you as you make your way."

I stood on the deck that night before going to bed and tried to remember Mrs. Allen's astronomy lessons, but I could identify only a few constellations. Having nothing else to do, I went to the cook-room. I thought about the library at Allen Hall, and I thought how odd it was that there was nothing to read now that I no longer had to hide my literacy.

We arrived at the port of Key West the next morning. Mr. Ebanks came to the cook-room after the meal to ask me if there was anything I wanted from shore. As we were speaking, James and Anthony interrupted us.

"William, do you want us to bring you something from Key West?"

"Thank you. I was just about to ask Mr. Ebanks if he could get me a book."

"A book? From Key West? I don't think they have booksellers there, just taverns. Besides, the officers have books that you can borrow from them."

"Really, I didn't know that. Then I don't need anything from shore."

The captain had said the night before that I should not even go on the gangway to help unload or load cargo. Local governmental officers in Key West had ties to the slave states, particularly to Alabama and South Carolina, and they accused British ships of assisting runaways and so kept a close eye on them. He was concerned that someone on the wharf might request to board to inquire about my identity and ask why I did not disembark. James and Anthony assured me that there was not much to do on the island other than patronize taverns.

"But, William, look over there. There's something interesting to see. That land is an island called Cuba. Have you ever heard of it? It belongs to Spain."

"Yes, I studied it in geography lessons. I can't believe I'm actually looking at Cuba. Are we going there?"

"Oh, no. The Spaniards are even worse than the Southerners, if that's possible, and our company trades only with the former or present British colonies."

The captain left the first officer in command and told me to speak to him should I need anything. With nothing to do before it was time to prepare the midday meal for the few of us on board, I walked on the side of the deck facing away from shore, admiring the majestic ship with her four-masted rig. There I met First Officer Nathaniel Trusty, who, to my surprise, was a Negro. He was older than James and Anthony but not as old as Mr. Ebanks.

"I trust that your accommodations in the caboose are tolerable, but I'm sure you understand, given your situation, that it was the only possible solution."

"Yes, sir. And it really isn't that bad."

"Good. Please tell me if there's anything I could do for you."

"Officer Trusty, I understand there are books on board that I may borrow."

"Yes, we do maintain a small library in the officers' quarters. Why don't I take you there now?"

The collection was small but interesting. He left me there to browse, and I found material about the Religious Society of Friends. There were no novels or poetry, but there was a copy of *The Tempest*, which I thought was an odd book to have onboard, since Clarissa and I learned from Mrs. Allen that it was about a British shipwreck on the island of Bermuda. I selected that and a work by Anthony Benezet called *A Caution and Warning to Great Britain and her Colonies, in a short representation of the calamitous state of the enslaved negroes in the British Dominions*. I also took a pamphlet entitled "The Sinfulness of Colonial Slavery: Extract from a

Lecture on 'The Sinfulness of Colonial Slavery,' delivered in the Meeting-house of Dr. Pye Smith Hackney on February 7, 1833," by Robert Halley.

I began reading *The Tempest,* which Clarissa and I read and discussed in our lessons with Mrs. Allen, who had to explain to us Mr. Shakespeare's language. One day, Mrs. Allen had assigned a short essay to us on what she said was a well-known quotation from the play, parts of which I still remembered, although I did not recall the schoolgirl's analysis that I wrote. The quotation, to this day, rocks me to the core of my being.

> *These our actors,*
> *As I foretold you, were all spirits, and*
> *Are melted into air, into thin air,*
> *And, like the baseless fabric of vision,*
> *The cloud-capped towers, the gorgeous palaces,*
> *The solemn temples, the great globe itself,*
> *Yea, all which it inherit, shall dissolve*
> *And, like this insubstantial pageant faded,*
> *Leave not a rack behind. We are such stuff*
> *As dreams are made on, and our little life*
> *Is rounded with sleep.*

I forced myself to stop reading to prepare the noon meal, and after everyone had eaten, I sat on the deck, on the side not facing shore, to read more. The captain and the second officer returned in time for supper, but the deckhands did not return until after I had fallen asleep.

Someone woke me by knocking on the door. I wrapped myself in my blanket and answered. It was Nathaniel.

"The captain wants you to get dressed, quickly, and go to the library. He will explain to you what this is all about."

When I arrived there, the officers and perhaps ten deckhands, including Mr. Ebanks, were gathered around a table looking at maps.

"Chief Steward, when the second officer and I were on land, we met with officers of the United States Navy who said that they received a report of a ship near Havana, Cuba, illegally flying the flag of the United States. The ship was bound for Mobile and loaded with Africans who were kidnapped from the West African coast. We believe we are now close to that ship. The United States Navy is going to stop the slaver. If it is true that there are Africans on board, the navy is going to take them out and put them on their ship. Depending on the number of people who are being held captive, they may not all fit on the navy's ship, and we have agreed to take some on board. We have done this before, and what we found both times is that the Africans, about half of whom are children, had been living in horrible conditions.

"When we rescue them and bring them on board, we will have to give them water and food. The deckhands will assist in this effort, and we need your help as well. But enough speech for now. We have about two more hours before we meet the American ship and begin operations."

I did not understand how this was possible. The captain told me that international slave trading was abolished in 1808, but then he explained that this was an illegal smuggling operation and that it happened far more often than most people knew.

The captain told all hands to gather as many blankets as we could find, even those belonging to the officers. Our ship stopped when we were close to the American navy's. The blowers sounded their horns, and both ships intercepted the slaver, named the *Lackawanna*. American officers in rowboats were already next to the ship, which I later learned hailed from New York. We were too far to hear what the officers said, but they apparently requested and were granted permission to board. There was enough moonlight to see that the American officers were holding men on the *Lackawanna*'s main deck at gunpoint. Then deckhands from the American ship rowed to and boarded the *Lackawanna*. Fifteen minutes later, the deckhands emerged carrying children, sometimes two at a time,

or leading emaciated adults to the boats to row them to their ship. I
counted two hundred Africans, and as the captain had predicted,
about half were children. The Americans arrested the *Lackawanna*'s officers and also took them on board their ship.

The captain told us that our ship was not needed because the
Americans had accommodated all the former captives, officers, and
crew. He said that the navy was taking the Africans to a country on
the West African coast named Liberia and that the officers and crew
of the *Lackawanna* would travel with them. Eventually the officers
would be taken to New York to be tried for piracy, which, as of 1820,
was a capital crime for United States citizens.

"These laws are difficult to enforce. The *Lackawanna* was built
and financed in New York. Unfortunately the courts in the United
States and in Britain have made a mockery of the laws against international slave trading and kidnapping. It is not likely that they will
be convicted, or even prosecuted, for their crimes."

Our next port of call was Bodden Town, the capital of a small
island called Grand Cayman, 195 miles northwest of Jamaica. There,
the deckhands unloaded manufactured goods from Massachusetts
and loaded ship parts that were made in Grand Cayman. We were
not there long, but James and Anthony went to the beach and
brought me back a small turtle.

"You can keep it as a pet or you can make a delicious soup out
of it."

I named my new companion Mariner.

Our next stop was Kingston, a large town located on the south-
eastern coast of Jamaica. The captain told me, when he spoke with
me that second night on board, that I could disembark there, and
that he and the other officers would accompany me off the gangway in order that the local officials would be less likely to ask for
my papers. No one stopped me. The officers went into town, and I
joined the deckhands unloading goods from Massachusetts, Connecticut, and New York that the ship had taken on in Key West.
When that labor was completed, we loaded sugar and spices.

The captain assigned James and Anthony to show me around Kingston while on shore leave, but he told them to have me back in time to make supper, and he gave me money so that I could buy groceries for the ship. We went to the lovely and crowded Harbor Street. James was pointing out a fruit vendor when I stopped walking because my knees almost buckled.

"What's wrong?"

"It just occurred to me. This is the first time I've ever been on free soil. It's true, isn't it? Every person I see is free."

"Yes, every single one, since 1838," James said.

Tears came to my eyes. "And no one has the right to ask me for my papers?"

"No. No one," he said.

I must have embarrassed them because I stared at people, marveling that they were free. I also noticed that there were no public notices on posts or walls advertising runaways.

"William, by the way, do we still have to call you William?"

I laughed. "When did you know?"

"I thought so from the beginning," Anthony said.

"Why?"

He lowered his voice. "You're too pretty to be a man. And I knew it was true when the captain didn't let you sleep belowdecks."

"And, yes, you do have to keep calling me William. After all, he's the one employed by the British West Indies Trading Company."

We wandered around the main roads and on side paths. There were brick buildings wherever I looked. James bought us dinner at the home of a family that sold meals to sailors, and we sat underneath a tall tree in the yard in the back of their house to eat. For dessert, I tasted, for the first time, mango.

"This is the tastiest fruit I have ever had. Do they grow all over the Caribbean?"

"Yes. And not just in the Caribbean, but in Central and South America, too. If you like mango, wait until you try the other fruits that grow on our island, like guava, soursop, papaya, pineapple, and of course bananas and coconuts. The best part is that we all have these fruits on our yards. All you have to do is pick them."

"Does your island look like here?"

"In many ways, except that ours is much more beautiful and much less crowded."

We walked around town after we ate. It was quite hot, and they asked me if I wanted to go to the beach.

"Sure. I've never been."

"Not even in Mobile?"

"We went with Mr. and Mrs. . . . our . . . masters to Orange Beach, but we weren't allowed to actually go on the sand or in the water."

When we got to the beach, James and Anthony rolled up the legs of their trousers and took off their shoes and socks. They told me to do the same. I jumped because the sand was scalding, and they laughed at me. We ran to the water's edge, but at first I was afraid to put my feet in the water.

"When we get home, you can ask Grandmother Ebanks to make you a bathing costume, and we'll teach you how to swim," Anthony said.

"Me? I'd be afraid of drowning."

"That's why you have to learn first," he said.

After an hour, we went back to Harbor Street, where we bought supplies that I needed for cooking. The vendors delivered the goods to the dock by wagon, and we met them there to load them on the ship. James and Anthony returned to town to visit taverns.

When everyone was on board that night, we sailed to the next destination, my new home.

TWENTY

THEODORA ALLEN

T he week after Mr. Harris told us the terms of the will, I quietly began planning the rest of my life, and how Kenneth and I were going to spend time together, the thought of which always made me smile. Now that the estate was settled, or so I thought, I could reflect on my feelings for him. Kenneth had become dear to me, and I hoped to be able to see him soon after I moved away from Alabama. My sons did not figure in my arrangements. They were angry that Cornelius left them relatively small portions of the estate and because the scandal had ended their nascent professions. I would have helped them, but they treated me not as their mother but as someone who did not merit their respect. Cornelius had blamed me for Clarissa's transgressions, and I blamed him for my sons'. He took them from me when they were small, claiming that I was not qualified to teach them and that they needed to be taught by men. Thereafter, I saw the boys only at holidays and summertime, when we went to the lake house in Madison County. When they completed university, my husband decided that they should work in commerce. He gave them substantial sums of money and introduced them to bankers in Georgia and South Carolina.

Had Cornelius not died when he did, their older colleagues would not so easily have pushed them out of their businesses. When Paul received a letter telling him that his services were no longer needed, he waved it in my face.

"This is your fault. You always coddled her. What am I supposed to do now?"

"Darling, I . . ."

"Don't speak to me as if I were a child."

"What is it that you want from me?"

"You should share the bequest that you got from father with Robert and me."

"Why should I? Your father gave you large amounts of money to establish yourselves."

"That money is gone. Don't you know anything about business? Some investments have significant risk." He stood close and pointed at me.

"Paul, do not do that. How dare you treat me with such disrespect?"

He walked out of the room without answering me. A few days later, Robert received a similar letter from his bank. They found me in the library.

"Now neither of us can return to our professions. Since you won't share your bequest with us, we want you to join us in filing a petition in court that Clarissa's grant will go to us instead of to her bastard."

"Don't call him that. And did you hear what Mr. Harris said? If you do that, you will lose your share."

"No, we won't, because we have information about your Mr. Harris that will show his inappropriate interest in father's estate."

"That's absurd. The court has reviewed all the documents and found them all legally sound. As head of this household, I order you to abandon this scheme."

"Don't be ridiculous. A woman can't take a man's place. As the eldest son, I have assumed head of the estate."

When they left, I alerted Charles and Mr. Harris, who said that there was nothing to be done to prevent them from filing a lawsuit. Later that week, Mr. Harris informed Charles and me that the Talladega Court had rendered a decision on Mr. Cromwell's petition and gave us a summary of the proceeding.

"The judge indicated that, if Mr. Cromwell publicly acknowledged that the child was his, the court would conclude that he could inherit Mrs. Cromwell's share of her father's estate. Mr. Cromwell refused to do so. Therefore the court, in its final decision, agreed with our argument that Mr. Cromwell could not say that the marriage was valid for the purpose of inheriting Mrs. Cromwell's property but not valid for the purpose of the child's legitimacy."

Charles and I smiled, and I felt fortunate that he was by my side. Had he been anything like Cornelius, he may have allied himself with my sons and fought against me over the estate. He was so unlike his brother; Charles was gentle and kind. I was also glad that Mr. Harris was true to Cornelius's final wishes to treat me fairly in his will.

Charles and I told my sons and Martha about the outcome of the case. The next day, Paul and Robert and their families departed for Talladega, and my mother-in-law returned to Montgomery. Dear Martha stayed with me. Without her I do not think that I would have been able to say good-bye to Bessie and Dottie. The Reverend Townsend took all the freed servants and their families to Ohio, quietly, in the middle of the night, so that the other slaves would not learn of their freedom. Mr. Harris had written their manumission documents, which the judge signed and the clerk sealed. Emmeline and Belle could not permit themselves to be totally happy.

"Mrs. Allen, if you hear anything about Sarah, can you get word to us? And if they bring her back, can you please look out for her and send her to where we're going to be?"

"Emmeline, yes, of course. I want you to be reunited with her."

Early the next week, Mr. Harris shocked Charles and me with the news that Paul and Robert not only retained a lawyer in Talladega to file a petition in the Benton County Court to annul Cornelius's will but also had joined Mr. Cromwell in his petition.

"But does not that mean that they forfeit their grants?"

"Not yet. They have been quite clever. They claim that, when Mr. Allen amended his will to free Emmeline, Belle, Bessie, Dottie, and Eddie, he was not of sound mind and body and therefore did not intend to make changes to the will. The issue is that the clause stating that challenges to any term of the will results in forfeiture of the challenger's share is in the same amendment to the will as the one freeing the slaves. Further, they allege that Mrs. Allen and I exerted undue influence upon Mr. Allen and forced him to make that final amendment," Mr. Harris said.

"Why would they say that about you, Mr. Harris?"

"Some of the planters have accused my church of helping slaves to escape, and they maintain that the church has ties to Northern abolitionists."

"Do you?" Charles asked.

"I was educated in the North and perhaps that is why they think so."

I continued my preparations to move, knowing that, even if I obtained only one quarter of the estate, I could accomplish what I wanted for my grandson and myself with $300,000. Charles retained a real property agent for me in New Orleans, who was also responsible for hiring household servants on my behalf. I chose the furniture that I wanted to take and gave the rest to Martha and Charles. The contents of the library and the lesson room I shared with no one, as I would expand my collection in my new home and give the children's books to my grandson. My only regret about leaving Alabama was that my dear child was buried there.

The judge of the court in Benton County decided my sons' and Mr. Cromwell's case in two weeks. Mr. Harris brought Charles, Martha, and me a copy of the decision, which was short. Mr. Harris explained the legal jargon.

"The judge said that the petitioners, Paul, Robert, and

Mr. Cromwell, were too late in bringing their lawsuit because the will had already been entered into probate and distributions had been made. He also ordered that Paul and Robert have forfeited their bequests. Thus, Mrs. Allen maintains her one-half share of the estate, one quarter of the estate goes to Mrs. Cromwell's son, and the remaining quarter goes to Mr. Charles Allen and Mrs. Laurence, in equal shares."

We thanked Mr. Harris for his work. He promised to continue to assist us until the property was liquidated. When he left us to return to his business office, I told Charles and Martha that I had no desire to see my sons.

"I did not tell you how they behaved toward me. I feared that, at one point, they were going to strike me. I never again want to be afraid in my own home. Now that they will receive nothing from the estate, they must be even angrier. I want them barred from here."

"I'm so sorry, Theodora," Charles said, "and I wish you had told me earlier. I'll speak with Davis right now. They won't be permitted to enter the property."

The servants were packing my china, crystal, silver, books, and paintings, but they needed my assistance in numbering the crates and trunks. While I was engaged in this mindless labor, I realized that I had not heard from Mrs. Tutwiler in a while, nor had I received social calls from the neighboring planters' wives. I wrote Mrs. Tutwiler a letter, which I sent the following morning, asking her when would be a convenient time to visit, and I instructed the coachman to wait for a reply. When he returned, Davis told me that Mrs. Tutwiler declined to respond.

"That's peculiar. Do you trust that the coachman accurately conveyed what she said?"

"Ma'am, I think so. He's usually reliable."

"I cannot imagine why she would say such a thing. I am going to pay her a visit tomorrow morning. Please tell the coachman to have the carriage, my husband's, ready at eleven o'clock."

"Ma'am, your sons took that carriage to Talladega."

"Who gave them permission to do so?"

"I don't know, ma'am."

"All right. I will go in mine."

When Charles arrived from the fields that evening, I told him what my sons had done. He said that he had assumed they would return the carriage on their way back to their homes.

"I suppose now we will have to permit them on the property," I said.

When I arrived at the main gate of the Tutwiler plantation, a guard told the coachman that Mrs. Tutwiler was not receiving visitors.

"Proceed to the house," I told the coachman.

A servant opened the carriage door and escorted me to the parlor. About thirty minutes later, Mr. Tutwiler appeared holding several envelopes.

"Mrs. Allen, how are you?"

"Greetings, Mr. Tutwiler. Is Mrs. Tutwiler not well?"

"Mrs. Allen, I believe I owe it to you to be frank. I cannot permit my wife to be associated with you. Your daughter's conduct was reprehensible, and my own daughters' reputations would be sullied should my wife continue to have social intercourse with you. I am sure that you understand. And, Mrs. Allen, here are your letters. Please inform your paramour to stop writing you here."

"Mr. Tutwiler, I bid you good-bye."

I held my tears until I was inside the carriage, and I waited until I was home to read Kenneth's three letters. He said that he was worried about me and could not understand why I had not replied to his correspondence. He had sent me a poem in each one. I wrote him immediately, telling him almost everything that had occurred and that I was moving to New Orleans. My sons and their families returned that night, after I had retired for the evening. They asked to speak with Charles and me early the following morning. When we met them in the library, gone were their swaggers and condescending attitudes. They were now contrite and spoke softly. They asked me whether they could move with me to New Orleans, as there was no possibility of going back to Georgia and South Carolina.

"What would you do in New Orleans?"

"Perhaps we could search for positions in banking."

"I will think about this and speak with your uncle before I make a decision. I will be guided by what is best for your children, as they, like Clarissa's son, are innocents."

They thanked me and left in order that Charles and I could discuss the matter. I then called my sons back to the room.

"This is my proposal: Your uncle will assist you in extricating your money from the banks. In the meantime, you will both begin to learn how to manage a plantation. Your uncle will stay here through the beginning of harvest, and you will be responsible for its completion until the last cotton shipment is sent. You will send your wives to pack and move to your uncle's plantation. I will pay to build you homes there. I will invest $100,000 in Charles's plantation, and you will invest whatever money you recover. Do you accept these terms?"

They agreed to my offer and began working with Charles in the fields. Their wives departed the following day, leaving their children with Martha and me. Later that week, Charles found buyers for most of the estate, which had to be divided into small parts to be sold. I carved out a section of the land that had the burial plots and retained its ownership. An agent bought Allen Hall on behalf of an anonymous buyer. One of the planters who knew Charles well revealed that the house had been purchased at a low price by Mr. Tutwiler for his son, who was about to be married.

I left Alabama a week before the beginning of harvest, after almost all my belongings had been shipped. Martha and Charles promised to visit me often, and they and my grandchildren took me to our landing, where I boarded a boat to Mobile. From there, I took a ship to New Orleans. I had rented a house outside the city while my homes were being built in the French Quarter and St. Tammany Parish.

Three days after I arrived in Louisiana, I went to New Orleans to see my grandson. Cornelius had sent him to the orphanage at the convent of the Sisters of Ursula on Chartres Street. He had agreed to send them $700 annually until the child was seventeen years of age. When I had discovered the documents in the coffer at Allen Hall, I wrote the Mother Superior to confirm that Clarissa's son was there and to inform her that I was moving to New Orleans. Cornelius had named the child Francis Parker, in honor of Clarissa's middle and my maiden name. I told Mother Superior that I wanted his full name to be Theodore Francis Parker.

The nuns' lovely building was clean and tidy, and the children I saw wore crisp clothing. A nun brought Theodore to the office where I was meeting with Mother Superior and gave him to me. When they saw that he was content with me, they left us alone, and I was glad because they could not see my tears. He had Clarissa's eyes. I told him about his mother and how she loved him so much that she took him to safety before she died. After an hour, he began to cry, and I took him to a nun, who prepared a feeding utensil so that I could give him milk. They showed me the orderly nursery where the infants lived. When it was time to leave, I told Mother Superior that I would visit Theodore once a month for the time being, and then weekly when my house in New Orleans was built. She asked me whether I had any interest in helping them give the children lessons. I was delighted with her request.

When I moved into my home in the French Quarter, I knew that I had made the correct decision to go to Louisiana. I was not lonely because Charles had written letters of introduction to families who were distant relatives of the Allens. There was much to do, and when I was not writing in my journal, gardening, reading, or seeing my grandson and teaching the children at the orphanage, I attended concerts and the opera.

Kenneth and I wrote each other once a week. He tried to get me to move to New York, but I told him the reason I was living in New Orleans and asked him whether he would consider moving here. He declined, stating that he had become used to living in the North, where the "odious" institution of slavery had been formally abolished. I told him that all my servants were freedmen, but I admitted that I had invested in my brother-in-law's plantation. Kenneth visited me when the university was on holiday, but he stayed at a hotel. We went to the theater, and he read his poetry at literary salons. The second week he was in New Orleans, he asked if I would accompany him to a slave auction.

"Kenneth, is it that you want to teach me about the evils of bondage? I already know slavery is evil, but you should know that I invested in my brother-in-law's plantation because he is a kind master. Yes, he is strict when he needs to be, but have you given any thought to what would happen to slaves if they were all freed at once? Who would feed, clothe, and give them shelter?"

"Theodora, I will not preach to you, but I do want you to judge one aspect of keeping people in bondage for yourself. My motive for asking you to do this is partly selfish, to persuade you to return to the North with me. You could take your grandson with you, you know."

"I truthfully do not see a tremendous difference in how the North and South profit from slavery, Kenneth. It is simply that the South is willing to admit that we could not prosper without free labor. After all, it's our cotton that supplies the great Northern and European businesses that manufacture fabrics. You and I and everyone we know use cotton bedsheets and wear cotton clothing."

I agreed to go with him to the auction, but I asked him not to speak about the subject anymore after his lesson. He agreed.

The people at the slave market were kept in pens in a large warehouse, separated into groups by age, gender, and whether they were skilled or unskilled. All slaves were clean and attired in new clothing and shoes; the men had smart jackets and pants and hats and the women wore calico dresses. They looked well fed. The master of the auction gestured to the slaves, and they took turns parading so that all buyers could observe them. The young people danced for us while a Negro boy played the fiddle. Customers pointed at particular slaves in whom they were interested. The master ordered those slaves to the front, where the potential buyers inspected their teeth and sometimes told them to remove their upper clothing to show their backs to see whether they had scars, the mark of the recalcitrant slave. I was uncomfortable seeing them half naked and turned my head.

Several times, when sales of children were made, one heard their mothers wail and plead to be sold together with their sons and daughters. A boy told his mother not to cry because he was going to be brave and good. I thought of Emmeline and how she must have felt when Cornelius sold Belle and when Sarah ran away. After an hour, I told Kenneth that I had seen enough, and we departed. Kenneth honored my wishes, and we did not speak about what we saw that day.

During his stay, we spent our nights together at my home, but he left each time before dawn. We believed that we were discreet when we were alone in my house, but an Allen cousin warned me that the neighbors had commented on my conduct. It did not matter to me what they said, however, because no one could have forced me to stop, and I knew that widowhood shielded me from societal censure.

SARAH CAMPBELL

N athaniel, Mr. Ebanks, James, and Anthony met me on the main deck. They were going to be on home leave for two weeks. Everyone else was continuing to the mainland, Tierra Firma, or, as they called it, Spanish Honduras, and then on to British Honduras. The night before, the captain had given me a rucksack for my belongings, including ten books from the officers' library. I carried Mariner in a box that James made for me. I was wearing a dress and women's shoes that the pastor in Mobile had given the captain to take on the ship for me. James pointed to the horizon.

"That's it. That's where we live, and that's where you're going to live, Roatán."

They were correct, it truly was beautiful. I looked at the water surrounding the island and saw schools of brilliantly colored fish. We docked at Coxen Hole, which I learned was named after one of the pirates who settled in the strategic outpost to prey upon the battling Spanish and British ships. Mr. Ebanks's father and Nathaniel's brother met us at the wharf in coaches and took us to Flowers Bay, where eighty families of freedmen from Grand Cayman had established a village when slavery was completely abolished in the British West Indies in 1838.

Our first stop was where I met the four generations of the Ebanks clan, all but the youngest of whom had been born in the Cayman Islands. Grandfather Ebanks and his three brothers, using skills that they acquired in their homeland, founded a boat building and repair business in Port Royal, on the east side of Roatán. The men in the family were either merchant marines or worked in the company. James and Anthony were sons of Ebanks daughters. The Ebanks women were seamstresses, except for two, who were midwives. The day we arrived, the extended family was at the elder grandparents' home for a feast in my honor. Everyone had questions for me about my life in Alabama. I gave them an abbreviated version of my journey from Benton County. I was interested to learn that all the former slaves had similar memories of living in bondage. This revelation made me less homesick. After the meal, a little girl sat on my lap.

"Miss Campbell, you're our new schoolmistress, right?"

"Yes, I certainly am, but I look forward to learning from you and my other students about my new home."

Two girls held my hands as Grandmother Ebanks and other women escorted me to my house across the road, which previously had been occupied by a schoolteacher from Grand Cayman and his family. The teacher and his family missed their island and left after one school term. The pastor of the church at Flowers Bay had been teaching the children, but it was not an ideal situation because he also was the preacher at two other Bay Islands, Guanaja and Utila, and thus he was quite busy. The captain had suggested to the pastor on a prior leave at Roatán that I assume the position as schoolteacher. Not having any other option, he agreed.

My house, which was next to the church and adjoining schoolroom, had furnishings, cooking wares, and linens that Grandmother Ebanks had sewn for me. I gave a prayer of thanks for my home, which was a short walk to the beach. I put Mariner in the yard and watched him walk to the sand. The villagers had contributed funds and paid me, in advance, fifty pounds for my first month's salary. Mr. Ebanks, before he left on his next voyage, took me to the bank in Port Royal, where I opened an account and deposited my savings, the currency that my mother and Mr. Adams gave me, and the money that I earned on the steamboat and the British ship and from my schoolteacher's salary. I did not have to purchase groceries, as my kitchen was fully stocked, and the parents of my students were generous. They gave me a hen for eggs, and every morning one of the children put a fresh bottle of milk on my doorstep. I could not believe my blessings: in a matter of months I had gone from a bonds-woman to a schoolmistress with her own home.

There were teaching supplies for the school, which the captain had purchased when we stopped in Kingston. I met the rest of the village and my students, thirty in all, ranging in age from seven to sixteen, at Sunday service, where I joined the church and became a candidate for baptism. Lessons began the next day. The students, even the young ones, were well versed in reading and writing, but the pastor had not spent much time on mathematics and other top-ics. The captain told me, before we arrived in Roatán, to write him to request books and other materials after I had determined the abilities of the children.

"The British government has made funds available for Negro education in the Crown Colonies of the West Indies. Your salary will be paid from a parliamentary grant. Because the schoolroom on Roatán is small, I have requested funds to build a freestanding schoolhouse from representatives of the London Missionary Soci-ety. Also, when school is in recess, Parliament will pay for your education. Once a year, along with other schoolmasters and mis-tresses from the British Crown Colonies, you will travel to London for instruction."

James's mother, Marva, and Mrs. Winthrop were the midwives of the village, and when I told them that my mother and the mid-wife on the plantation had taught me how to care for pregnant women, they asked me about the remedies we used. They were pleased to learn that many were the same as those they knew. Speaking about my mother and Miss Mary made me think about them and Belle, and how much I missed my family. I silently prayed that one day the pain I felt whenever I thought of them would not be so sharp. The midwives took me to the woods, where we spent hours in search of herbs that we plucked and replanted in our yards. I had much to do. When I was not teaching or preparing lessons, Gran-Gran Ebanks, as everyone called her, was teaching me how to sew and cook their food.

Nathaniel, Mr. Ebanks, James, and Anthony returned after two months. They had bought school supplies and books for me in Boston, Philadelphia, and New York. After church, the first Sunday that he was back, Nathaniel asked if he could walk with me.

"The captain asked me to tell you that, unfortunately, he was unable to speak to the pastor in Mobile to ask about news of your family. When we docked there, and at New Orleans and Charleston, the customs officers warned the captain that the Negroes on the ship should not disembark. There is unrest in the country because Northern abolitionists have become more vocal in Washington. The Southerners, of course, have become more contentious and have enacted even more stringent Negro laws in their states. In Mobile and New Orleans, Negro preachers have been arrested for speaking against slavery from the pulpit. Some churches had to close. A customs officer told the captain that a visit to the church in Mobile would have endangered the pastor and the congregation. I'm sorry, Sarah, that I have nothing to report about your family. The captain said that, should matters improve, he will attempt to see the pastor the next time he is there.

"I thought you'd be interested in reading what the Northern newspapers are reporting on the slavery issue, and I brought you copies of the *New-York Daily Times,* the *Pennsylvania Inquirer,* and the *Boston Herald.* There's still a national controversy over the repeal of the Missouri Compromise. Congressmen make speeches against slavery, and a lawyer from Illinois named Abraham Lincoln, who served a term in Washington, has reentered the public arena to oppose the extension of slavery into free territories. At least I can tell you that the Northern abolitionists have had some impact on public opinion."

"Thank you for the newspapers. And please tell the captain that I appreciate his efforts. I'm not optimistic, though, that anything will change there. Speeches in the Congress won't make the South abolish slavery. As we learned in the Bible, the Israelites were in bondage for four hundred thirty years, and they had only one pharaoh at a time. There are many pharaohs in America, and each one is more evil than the next. I fear it will be a thousand years before the Negroes there will be free."

"We'll pray that you're wrong. Sarah, there's something else I want to discuss with you, and I hope that I'm not being too forward. Sarah . . . I . . . I thought of you, day and night, while I was traveling, and . . . may I have your permission to court you?"

Nathaniel had two young daughters, Angelina and Ann, who were my students, and a small son, Jonathan. His wife had died after a long illness when the boy was a year old. Nathaniel's parents were raising them, as he traveled most of the time.

"Sarah, this hasn't been a shock to you, has it?"

"No, Nathaniel, not at all. I want us to be together, but you know very little about me. You know that I was married. Well, he wasn't my husband, as we weren't permitted to marry, but there was someone in my life."

"Sarah, I don't care about that. I understand it all. Remember, I, too, was born in slavery."

"But there are things about my life that I can't speak about, things that I did."

"Sarah, what matters is that you are free now. You don't have to live in the past, and you can try to forget about the horrors you suffered."

"It's difficult to forget, especially since it just happened. But, yes, Nathaniel, you have permission to court me."

Nathaniel's proposal was unexpected and made me realize that I was "grown," as my mother used to say when I was being an inquisitive child, and no longer the jolly girl who liked to tickle her mama under the chin. No; now a serious matron, incapable of showing joy when a man proposed to her, had replaced that frolicsome youth.

"I'll do my best to make you happy, Sarah, and you are happy, aren't you?" Nathaniel asked.

"Of course, I am, Nathaniel, yes, yes, I'm happy, but I'll always miss my family, you know, and I never thought I'd say this, because I'm happy that I escaped, and, I even miss Alabama, and the familiar faces and food. But I'm thankful that everyone here has been so good and welcoming to me, especially you."

"Sarah, even though you'll always miss your family I'm sure that you'll get used to being here."

There are some matters that I tell no one. The truth is, there is a ball made of steel lodged within my heart and nothing will ever melt that ball of steel. The ball of steel has expanded in bulk throughout the years, but it has been there as long as my earliest memories, from when I was about six years old and those foul and rank men, armed with weapons, ransacked our home to search for evidence that we were planning to escape that abyss. The ball of steel is made of hurt, and it is always there, even when I am happy or even jubilant. If the ball of steel were not embedded within my breast, I surely would see life differently than I now do. Without the ball of steel, I would be merry and laugh often; yet, paradoxically, without the ball of steel, I would not have learned to appreciate the grandeur of the state of being free.

"Sarah? Sarah? What are you thinking about?"

"I'm sorry, I was thinking about back home, I'm sorry, what were you saying?"

"There's something else I want to tell you, and I want you to be the first person at home to know, other than Bradley, James, and Anthony. After five years as a first officer, the British West Indies Trading Company has promoted me to captain."

"Nathaniel, that's wonderful. Congratulations. I'm so happy for you. When did this happen?"

"The captain told me on the ship. I'll get my official commission when I report to London next month. Will you come to dinner this evening? I'll announce the news to everyone there."

When we arrived at the Trusty home, some of the Ebanks clan was there, including James and Anthony. It was apparent that everyone knew about Nathaniel's plans to court me before I did. I permitted myself not to worry about my family in Alabama, at least for that day. Everyone was solicitous and made me feel as if I had known them for years. James and Anthony reminded me that I needed a swimming costume so that they could give me lessons. The youngsters could not believe that I did not know how to swim and thought it funny that, in my entire life, I had only had my feet in the sea.

Nathaniel and the others had home leave for a month, every day of which he and I spent together. I had supper with his parents and children almost every day of the week, when we were not dining with the Ebankses, to whom I had become attached. One evening, as he was walking me home, Nathaniel had another matter to discuss.

"Sarah, we haven't spoken about my children and how you would feel about helping me raise them. As a captain, I'll have even less home leave. My parents are happy to continue to raise them, so if you don't want to do so, I'll understand."

"Nathaniel, I've come to love your children, and I'd love to be a mother to them, as long as your parents continue to help. There's something I've been thinking about, and perhaps this is an appropriate time to raise it. I haven't had the courage to tell you because I'm afraid that you may change your mind about me."

"Sarah, I doubt there's anything you could tell me that would change my mind about marrying you."

"I ask that you maintain this in confidence. I can't really describe the circumstance in detail; it's much too painful. It happened when I was still at Allen Estates, and I was expecting a child. There was a lot of bleeding and I had a fever. . . . That's not the entire truth. The truth is I didn't want to have the child because I knew that, if I did, I wouldn't be able to escape. I know that what I did was a sin. But . . . the midwife took . . . everything out, and she said that I may never be able to have children."

"Sarah, my darling, I'm so sorry that you had to go through that. It must have been devastating. But as I said, there's nothing you could tell me that would make me stop loving you. What do you say? Shall we set a wedding date?"

Nathaniel brought a smile to my face. "Yes, let's do that. Do you know when your next home leave will be?"

The following day, he asked me to walk with him to a bluff overlooking the bay.

"Sarah, I bought this plot of land to build our house."

"Really? We're to have our own home?"

"Of course. What did you think? The schoolmistress and the captain must have their own home. And, Sarah, this is the perfect place. It never gets too hot because of the trade winds, and when you wake in the morning, the first thing you'll see will be the water. There's enough room for your flower and vegetable gardens. And, Sarah, you'll be in charge of telling the carpenters what you want in the house."

"I want a room with shelves for my books and a desk for writing and grading papers."

"Whatever you want, you can have."

Nathaniel sailed again, and I missed him, but there was much to do at home. He wrote me letters from every port where he landed. I was glad he was not alone, because Mr. Ebanks, James, and Anthony sailed under his command. When they returned two months later for a week of home leave, Nathaniel and I decided that we could not wait for the house to be completed to marry. We were wed at our church in Flowers Bay. I wore a dress that Gran-Gran Ebanks and I had made from fabric that I bought in Port Royal. Mr. Ebanks honored me by walking me down the aisle. Late that evening, when the festivities had ended and everyone had gone home, Nathaniel took my favorite quilt, and we spent our wedding night at a small cove near our house.

I am happy with Nathaniel, and thankful that the Lord aided my escape from bondage, but my happiness will always be marred by thoughts of my mother and Belle. I pray that they found a measure of my own happiness. I also pray for my new family and ask the Lord to pardon me for not telling Nathaniel everything about my past.

Often, I recall that, when I was Clarissa's chaperone and Isaac and I traveled with her, Isaac claimed every night to be in the stable caring for the horses, but when he returned to me at dawn, I could smell the scent of Clarissa on him. I hid my pain and anger as best I could and said nothing because I did not want to admit he had betrayed me with my owner and sister. When I first saw Clarissa's baby, he had Isaac's nose, lips, and golden curly hair. It was then I began to plot my revenge against Isaac.

I encouraged Isaac to flee and wrote him a paper that he thought was a traveling pass. That pass instead instructed anyone who read it to take Isaac to Allen Estates for a reward of $200. My heinous acts did not end there. To prevent him from finalizing a document that revoked the promised freedom for my mother, Belle, Bessie, Dottie, and Eddie, and to avenge his sale of Belle to the Reynolds plantation, I killed Cornelius Allen, by mixing small poisonous amounts of bloodroot in his drinks.

Reader, I ask that you do not judge me harshly and that you view my deeds not through the prism of your time but through that of mine. It is true that what I did was evil, but I can see that only now. Then, I was a child who did not know the fortitude that I possessed. Now that I am no longer chattel, I know that a slave does not have to be like his master, and that retribution does not belong to any of us, but to the Lord.

Each day, from that first night that I spent in the woods after I escaped, when He humbled me by showing me fear unlike any I had ever, or since, experienced, I have prayed to God to forgive me for my sins. He has absolved me, I believe, but the torment in my mind that keeps me awake until dawn or causes me pain when I dream is an immutable reminder that He will never let me forget the evil that I committed when I returned my first husband to slavery and murdered the man who was my master, and my father.